Avarice Deception

The Lost Queen

ANGELIKA JASMINE

Quantum Discovery

A LITERARY AGENCY

Avarice Deception: The Lost Queen
Copyright © 2024 by Angelika Jasmine

ISBN
978-1-963254-62-4 (Paperback)
978-1-963254-63-1 (eBook)
978-1-963254-61-7 (Hardcover)

Table of Contents

Prologue:

Resistance

Serena

Roarick turns his attention back to me, and I cry out. "Open your mind, Serena."

"No!" I respond, fighting the agony that comes with defiance.

"Let me into where I belong!" he demands.

"No!" I scream. My entire body buckles in severe pain. My eyes are open, but I cannot see anything. It is difficult to even breathe.

"Serena!" Peyton panics, holding me close to him. "Stop this!" He demands of Roarick. "You are killing her!"

"She is killing herself. She will submit to me, or she will die. The choice is hers," Roarick answers coldly. "Let me in your head, Serena. You know I belong there."

I can feel the black dress part of my mind cowering in fear, ready to comply, but the other part of me wants to fight.

"Peyton," I whisper, trying desperately to hold on. I scream out, fighting Roarick's control, but he is winning. Against everything I have, I find myself crawling to Roarick. My head lays itself on his feet without my permission. I hear him draw his sword, and I know he is pointing it at Peyton. I scream out when his boot lands on my face. I cry out, feeling cord-like lashes tearing at my mind, and my memories flash in front of me… all of them, all at once. My mind lands on Peyton, then Keon, my aunt, Dex, Alexis, and lastly, my Prytore Roarick.

"She is mine!" my Prytore declares.

"The only way to prove that is with a mirror," Keon replies too calmly.

Keon's words seem strange. I work desperately to understand why he said that. Yes, I have been torn in two. One side is loyal to Keon, the other to Roarick. Once I have accepted Keon, that side is broken, and my reflection stabilized. The resistance is scared. She wants to come accept Keon, but she is afraid of Roarick. I am terrified right now. I have just lost. I know, because of it, I will be living in fear the rest of my life. Roarick is too strong; he has just forced me to choose him. It saddens me knowing Peyton and Keon are stronger, but they are not fighting for it. Wait… my mind starts to race with the conversations I had with my family today. Roarick can feel me resisting and presses his foot harder into me, causing my thoughts to scatter in a scream. I work to piece them together again. Then it hits me, I promised to willfully choose until my last breath, and I am still breathing.

With extreme effort and unpleasant pain, I jerk Roarick's foot from my face and work to get to my knees. "I. Am. A. Queen!" I reply, every word cutting into me. I can feel my flesh literally tearing and feel my warm blood rise to the surface.

"You are conquered. It is over! You serve me now!"

"No!" I scream, refusing to yield.

"You are killing yourself. Stop fighting me!"

"I would rather die than submit to you!"

One

Gemelli

Serena

Our suns, Eshnaine and Akatite, are purple. Or at least that is what the scientists claim. This is their explanation as to why our plants are purple. But if you ask me, all I see are two bright white balls that orbit the sky. Scientists go on to say that if we were closer to either one of our suns, life would be impossible. They claim this to be true based on the fact that our third moon, Zarla, which is closest to the two fireballs, is nothing but molting rock. They say it is so hot nothing can ever survive. Somehow, this has given this moon such a bad reputation; most of us use it to curse. The other two are supposed to be much more intriguing. Our second moon, Furgan, could be habitable if it had more water. But since it does not, long-term habitation is impossible. And our closest? The closest moon is actually my home world. Well, it used to be, before the war between Trorain and its planet, Artthemis, pretty much wiped out any possibility of anyone surviving there for the next half a millennium or so. Which makes this red planet, in the stellar system of Gemelli, with its purple plants, the only habitable place in the entire universe. Or so they say. If you ask me, the night skies are filled with so much light it is improbable to be the only habitable planet, surely. To think otherwise, one must have a much-closed mind.

It is not my place to worry about these things. I am a fiorriee. I am only ever to worry about my Prytore. Their needs and desires come before anything, especially my curiosity about the universe. I am being selfish. Well, I would be if I had a Prytore family. I am of age to be selected for the honor. I just have to prove myself worthy. Not everyone can; some, like my sister, are never chosen to serve. Without that honor, we are not fulfilled as a species; our lives are not over per se, but they may as well be. We end up in homes where we are simply maids or worse, we get sentenced to hard labor. Both scenarios doom us to never knowing the pleasure of the pain we thrive on.

Pain, something I should only experience myself through accident, though any other means except from a Prytore or Prytoree is strictly forbidden. Prytore's biology does not work like ours; pain does not reward them the way it rewards us. With the exception of poor mindset pain that hurts like zarla.

The home I have grown up in has both Prytore and fiorriee children. We fiorriees are considered freaks. I never understood the difference. We look so much alike; had it not been for a few small things like skin color, shapes of our ears, and fiorriees' second eyelids, strangers could never tell us apart. But when a Prytore child slips and falls, causing them to bleed, they do nothing but scream like a baby. For fiorriee, it is different. A scrape on the knee causes us to giggle, but the sensation does not last long. Soon enough, it goes numb, and we do not notice it. Unlike Prytore children, we do not need to wrap our wounds; they heal quickly enough, though they do tend to cause our skin to darken. This symptom lasts longer, reminding us, but in time, it too fades. Prytore's skin is not like ours. If they do not treat their wounds properly, their skin will be marked with a scar that will never fade.

"Serena!" a voice calls for me. It is my caretaker, Madam Takira. I quickly gather the water I have been sent to fetch and carefully yet swiftly return to her.

"The water, Madam Takira."

"My goodness, Serena, daydreaming again?" Prytoree Sine, complains. "Such a dangerous pastime. How ever are you to snag a good Prytore family when your head is always up in the clouds?"

"I am sorry, Prytoree." I frown, hating that her words ring of truth.

"Never mind, dear." Madam Takira dismisses her. "Eshnaine is starting to set in the sky. We need to get you ready. Oh, I do hope you find a suitor tonight. It is always best to snag interest early, my dear. You only have four nights to find your perfect fit, or you must wait another year. And that would be downright tragic!" She hands the water to Prytoree Sine so that she can use it to cook tonight's meal for everyone. "Come child, upstairs with you."

I follow her up the stairs and to her room. I am nervous to come in here; it is usually forbidden, but she is too involved in her task that sends her into her closet to notice my caution.

I notice hers and my bags are packed on the bed, we have been planning this trip for months now but to think it starts tonight makes me anxious. I am distracted from my thoughts as she emerges from her closet, as I am certain she has made some kind of mistake.

She hands me a slender silk dress that compliments my light-blue shivering skin. My eyes widen in shock! "Madam Takira!" I gasp. "Are you sure this dress is meant for me?"

She gives me a kind smile. "I am sure, Serena."

"But, madam, it is yellow," I protest softly.

"So it is," she confirms, spinning me around and stripping me of my day clothes quickly. Then without pomp and circumstance, she slips the beautiful silk off the hanger. "Arms," she demands, and obediently, I raise mine. She slips the dress on and proceeds to fasten the many elegant buttons in the back. When she is finished, she walks me to a mirror, though the image is not very helpful as it is blurry.

Looking down at myself, I cannot help but be nervous when I realize exactly how high the slit goes. I have never worn a dress that cuts just above the knee before. I do say I will find it useful and I will be able to walk normally. I take a moment to stare at myself in the mirror, wishing I could see myself clearly. My eyes start to tear up.

"Come now, child, why the tears?" She frowns, playing with my long white hair. "You look so elegant. Well, you will, once we tame your hair into submission."

"It is yellow," I state again. I take a deep breath as I try to compose myself while searching for a way to ask the question that seems just out of reach. She responds with a kind smile, which causes me to sob harder, but I try to hide it with a smile of my own.

In courting ceremonies, fiorriee are to wear black, grey, purple, red, or yellow. Each color has its own meaning. Black is the most common; it states to the eligible Prytores that we are available to any type of service they deem fit. Grey marks a fiorriee for services of care, which ranges widely from childcaring to the medical profession. Purple indicates hard labor service, which usually is reserved for the males. Red is similar to black, but it is a near devastation to the one unfortunate enough to wear it. It is supposed to signify age and that it is the fiorriee's last year to be eligible for service. But it somehow also gets twisted into shame and disgrace. Resulting in any unfortunate fiorriee finding themselves in red, at any of the courtings, if they show any signs of rebellion to their extensive training. Red has gotten such an awful reputation that there have been instances where caregivers lie and place older fiorriees in black, in the hope to pass them off without the scarlet shame. Then there is yellow. Yellow is held by so few fiorriees it seems magical. It is a sign of great honor, as it is the color of Prytores themselves. It indicates that the fiorriee wearing it has shown exceptional signs to training. Which means they are strong enough to handle the most important Prytore families. Those who wear yellow are taken to a court where they will compete only with other yellow fiorriee. It is rumored everyone gets picked every year because there are usually more Prytore families than fiorriees.

"You need to pull yourself together, dear," Madam Takira scolds, yanking on my hair with a hairbrush I did not see her pick up.

"My whole life you called me a dreamer. Told me that I would be lucky if I found a Prytore." I accuse.

"You are young, dear. There are things that I cannot teach you." She smiles, twisting my hair over a hot iron.

"You are avoiding my question." I complain, crossing my arms over my chest.

"You asked a question?" she challenges.

"How is it possible that I am wearing yellow when my sister Dex wore…black?"

"Your 'sister' Dextra and you do not have the same parents, Serena, you know that."

"I am an orphan. I do not have parents at all!" I shoot back, feeling angry every time anyone reminds me that technically I am an only child. I was never raised as such in this orphanage. I have been told both my parents died when I was very young, but I doubt that. Most likely I was abandoned like most the others, including my sister.

"Your parents were well respected for our kind, Serena, and therefore, you carry the burden of that legacy." She frowns.

"Burden?" I question, looking down at myself in the beautiful yellow silk. "How can yellow be a burden?"

Her stable reflection frowns at my blurry one as she yanks my hot hair from the iron. "As I said, child, you are young, and there are things I cannot teach you."

Two

Offering

Serena

I am nervous to leave my home in yellow. Those who live here seem as shocked as I am, that I am wearing the most honored color of our kind to my courting ceremony. It feels amazing to show up the Prytore children, who have shown such cruelty to me, that despite my species, I have been destined to live a better life than them for some time. Maybe one day they too will become powerful, but with such a long road ahead of them and the fact they hate learning academics, I doubt it.

We walk to the transport, show the staff our tickets, and wait in line. I expect to be transported to another station similar to the one we have just left, but instead, I find myself in a very small room with my caretaker. Speaking aloud in public places without directing that speech to a Prytore is highly frowned upon, which leaves me in an uncomfortable situation. Madam Takira has not prepared me for what is to happen after we arrive. By the looks of it, she too seems a bit overwhelmed with our destination. She takes my arm and leads me around the room. There is no exit other than the transport we have just arrived in. There are a few chairs, and after a moment, she intentionally sits down and pats the chair next to her. Timidly, I obey her silent direction, and we wait.

It does not take long before I find myself mindlessly bored. I want so desperately to ask what we are waiting for, but the look Madam Takira gives me makes me think better of it. In the past, I have not taken her nonverbal warnings seriously and have learned she is not one to tolerate insolence, especially in important moments like this. Annoyed, I puff my over-hair-sprayed hairdo out of my face, rest my elbows on my knees, and place my chin in my hands. I hear her click her tongue at me, causing me to roll my eyes and sit up straight, waiting in a proper, ladylike position, puffing again in protest.

After a hundred lifetimes pass, the transport lights up, requesting us by name. Elated that the waiting is over, I hop up with a smile, all but dragging my caretaker behind me. This time, the transport drops us off in a larger room where there are other fiorriees and their caretakers waiting.

We are greeted almost instantly by a Prytore. "Good evening, ladies. I am Butler Whilf. I trust your journey was… memorable, Serena."

I giggle at that. "Yes, Butler Whilf, that is a fabulous way to state it."

He smiles back at me with a raised eyebrow before he turns his attention to the room. "The courting will begin in about an hour. In the meantime, feel free to mingle amongst the others. This is Prytore Charles' private residence. You do not need to worry about public social etiquette here. Good luck."

"Serena, Prytores have a very stiff personality. There are cameras here, giggling is not encouraged," Madam Takira scolds me quietly.

"Sorry," I apologize. "I am nervous."

"Do not be, dear. I am sure you will find a suitable match." She smiles, though she looks just as nervous as I do.

"Hi, I am Bethany," I hear a voice say, bringing my attention to another fiorriee dressed in yellow. She looks similar to me. We share the same hairstyle, though hers appears slightly shorter; her face is a little thinner.

"Serena. It is lovely to meet you." I smile at her, but she does not smile back. Instead, she looks me up and down with her judging eyes. Realizing she is sizing up the competition, I drop my smile and cross my arms over my chest, becoming instantly guarded.

"What family do you come from?" She asks but does not wait for an answer. "I am a Leemeair. You know, the most powerful family of our time. Seeing as we are so valuable, we are sought after. I mean, can my poor mother give birth to any more girls? So, it makes sense that I get to choose first when the Prytores come to call on us. After I make my choice, my friends will be making theirs. Followed by the others. So, you understand, you will be the last one to make a choice and will either have the Prytore that no one wants, or you will go back to whatever nonelite educational family you came from. Got it."

"I was under the impression that Prytores picked us."

"Please, that was so last decade," she responds, rolling her purple eyes before walking away from me.

My eyes trail after her for a moment before I turn to my caretaker. "You need not worry about anything, Serena," Madam Takira assures me, "trust me." Her eyes have a strange shine that makes me believe her.

Not wanting any more unpleasant encounters with my fellow competition, I choose to hide out in the back of the room with my caretaker, waiting. Yes, I am being anti-social, but I honestly do not care. I am not here to make friends with fellow female fiorriee. I am here to find a good Prytore home. My caretaker says nothing more as we silently wait for this evening's events to begin. It takes several more lifetimes before the doors finally open.

When they do, I am expecting to see Prytores walk through, or are we expected to walk to them? I scan the room to see how the others react. No one makes their way to the doors, so I remain where I am. When males do filter through, I am disappointed to find it is male fiorriees, not Prytores. They first approach Bethany and her friends who are so happy to see them you can almost see drool coming out of their mouths. Or is that my wishful thinking? Either way, I am bored again. I hate waiting. When are the Prytores coming? I stare at the door, waiting, ignoring the male fiorriees.

"I must say, I have saved the most beautiful of all for last." a breathtakingly attractive male fiorriee states, smiling at me, distracting me from my impatience.

"Last?" I ask, studying his silver eyes. My heart skips a beat, and I blush, looking away, as I am most definitely staring.

"To introduce myself," he clarifies, offering his hand, "I am Peyton."

"Serena." I smile, taking his hand with confidence. "It is nice to meet you Peyton."

"Is it?" he questions, closing his fingers tightly around my hand, "Or would you prefer one of my friends to introduce themselves to you?"

The question catches me off guard. "Why, sir, I do not know what you mean." I admit, letting him keep my hand.

He studies me for a moment then looks at my caretaker for the first time. Something strange seems to cross his features but he corrects them so quickly, I cannot describe it. Was it relief? Recognition? Both? Before I could dwell on it, he turns his attention back to me. He holds my stare for such a long time, and in such a distracting way, I do not realize I have stopped breathing until he releases my hand.

"Surely, you have been informed as to how a yellow courting works? Or at least, the significance of offering one's hand!"

"Do not fault her for her ignorance," Madam Takira chimes in. "I do so apologize, I am Serena's caretaker, Madam Takira, and yellow court is above my station. Which means, I, nor anyone I know, was completely informed as to the yellow customs. As far as the hand offering, she was never taught, as I believe it to be sacred, and if it were to happen to her, it would be genuine."

"Happen to me?" I ask her, but she gives me a look that tells me now is not the time for questions.

Peyton turns his attention to me. "Serena, your caretaker is correct. A genuine hand offering for our kind is not only sacred, it is rare. Very rare, just as you are." He smiles at me, causing me to blush. He holds my gaze for a moment then turns to Madam Takira, "If you are so ill informed about yellow courting, how are you here?"

"My kind, sir, the hand that you just reluctantly gave back belongs to none other than Serena Gelsomino herself."

Peyton's eyes widen. His eyes shoot from hers to mine to hers again.

I study him silently, is he really as surprised as he is betraying? He seemed to recognize Madam Takira, or did I imagine that? Does

Gelsomino hold some sort of meaning I do not know about? Why is this the first time I have ever heard the name? Up until this moment, I honestly thought my name *was* Serena Rosa. I am startled from my thoughts when my caretaker starts to toss her bags at me, while she sifts through others.

"I have all the documentation to prove it." She looks up at Peyton who is patiently waiting. I, however, am glaring at her for causing such a scene. "I realize she is registered as Serena Rosa, but I am under strict orders to use a pseudonym up until I deem it necessary at her courting." She hands Peyton documents, and he studies them for a moment.

"What makes you deem it necessary so early in her courting?" Peyton challenges.

"Have you ever known a fiorriee to willfully give her hand without thinking?" my caretaker answers with a question of her own, embarrassing me further.

"I only know of one, before today that is." He answers, looking at the paperwork he was handed. "You understand I must show these to my Prytore."

"You understand that I am not letting them leave my sight," she replies so matter-of-factly you would think she was talking to a small child.

"Of course, madam, if you would come with me then." Peyton smiles, indicating a direction.

Madam Takira grabs my arm and starts to follow him. Peyton pauses when he realizes she is taking me with her. "Without Serena."

"You, sir, have a very poor sense of humor," Madam Takira responds, keeping a tight grip on me.

He glares at her before he reluctantly leads the way for us.

I am so confused as to what is happening, but I choose silence over questions. I do know this. Gelsomino is a very important name, though it is the first time I have ever heard it in my life. And by the looks of Bethany's face, as I pass her and the others, Gelsomino trumps Leemeair. That in and of itself makes all the headache I am bound to go through for having such a last name worth it.

We follow Peyton down several long hallways. Eventually, we enter a room full of what I can only assume to be eligible Prytores. Feeling insecure, I step as close to my caretaker as she will allow.

"Peyton, I am sure you have an explanation," a very handsome Prytore demands, ignoring me completely, while other Prytores look me up and down in disapproval.

"Prytore Keon, please pardon the intrusion. I realize this is highly unusual, but the circumstances are as well." Peyton rushes, handing Prytore Keon the paperwork my caretaker has given him. "She claims to be Serena Gelsomino, and this is her caretaker, Takira."

Suddenly, the disapproving looks vanish from these men's faces and are replaced by looks of awe and wonder. Many gather around the paperwork, studying them for their authenticity.

"How do we know this is not a trick? Some sort of glamour?" A Prytore asks.

Someone answers him, "Our computers would have detected that kind of deception, Prytore Tokala."

"She will need to submit to a blood sample," another Prytore says.

I turn to my caretaker, questions burning in my eyes. She squeezes my arm in reassurance.

"That is a bit much Prytore Umang," another dismisses. "This can be resolved tonight if they can prove the branding."

"Branding?" My mind quickly registers the only scar my skin has ever shown. It is on the inside of my right thigh. I have always been curious about it because fiorriees do not scar easily, and it does not seem to be a birthmark, as it does not seem natural to me. I have questioned it over the years, but Madam Takira has told me it is a birthmark and not to let it spoil my thoughts.

"I am sorry, did you just speak without being spoken to in a room full of Prytores?" one asks in disgust, snapping me out of my rushing thoughts.

"Do not be so hard on her, Prytore Charles," Prytore Keon responds, approaching me. "She seems more confused than we are surprised."

I swallow loudly. Nodding he continues, "Seeing as I am the designer of the mark, I am the most qualified to verify its authenticity. Agree."

"Makes sense." several Prytores agree.

Prytore Keon turns to me. "Do you know the brand in which we speak?"

"I do."

"May we see it?" he asks.

I bite my lower lip and turn to my caretaker; she gives me a reassuring nod. Suddenly, I realize the long slit in my silk dress is not meant for walking. Carefully, I inch my leg forward enough to reveal my lower inner thigh. Prytore Keon kneels down to see the brand just above my knee. He glides his fingers over the raised edges of it, and then he pinches it so hard it hurts, giving me a pleasant sensation. Surprised, I pull back and bite hard on my lower lip, hoping no one has seen that.

He rises quickly and breathes in my ear. "Good girl, keep that up, and I will keep you."

The whole thing has happened so fast I am half curious if I dreamed it.

"It is genuine, my fellow friends. This indeed is Serena Gelsomino."

Three

Open Doors

Serena

"I do not understand," I admit, talking out of turn but not caring. "Obviously, you are not only ignorant to who you are but how you should act as well!" Prytore Charles criticizes, not looking very pleased, whether to my behavior or my name, I cannot tell. He turns to Peyton. "Tell me, boy, did she choose you?"

Peyton's eyes land on me then to my caretaker. I can swear she jerks her head approvingly, but I cannot be confident as it is subtle, and I am to the side of her. Peyton looks to Prytore Charles. "She offered me her hand." The commotion that erupts in the room makes me uncomfortable. I turn to Madam Takira for help, but her gaze is locked with Prytore Keon's. I swallow nervously. I do not like all this attention.

Prytore Charles turns his glare to my caretaker. "Did you teach her to do this?"

"You should be careful with the way you speak to me," Madam Takira warns, making me even more confused. What does that mean? Why is she not afraid to stand up to them? "Never accuse me of deception."

Prytore Charles glares at her but says nothing. He turns his attention back to Peyton. "You seem hesitant, boy," he accuses. "Are you the first one she talked to this evening?" Peyton looks to Prytore Keon, his reluctance to answer has me curious. "Well, were you the first one she talked to this evening or not?"

Peyton frowns at the room. "The ceremony had only just begun. She did not have a chance to choose another."

With that response, Prytore Charles stares at me eagerly and in such a way that I am beginning to get scared. He is not the only one. I suddenly feel I am standing among a pack of wolves. The only Prytore who is not doing this is Keon. I give him a pleading look.

He smiles at me and raises his hand, commanding attention of the room. "Did you verify her choice, Peyton?"

I meet Peyton's gaze and give him a reassuring nod. He seems to relax and answers with a smile. "I did. She has confirmed."

The wolves-starving looks are replaced with disappointment. "Well, all is not lost." Prytore Tokala smiles. "There is always a chance she changes her mind. Gentlemen, shall we go meet our eager ladies?"

The Prytores start to clear out, giving Prytore Keon glares or handshakes while giving me one last, lingering stare before they go.

The room suddenly feels too large and way too quiet. Prytore Keon breaks the awkwardness. "To say you did well, Peyton, is an understatement." He walks over to the fireplace and puts a metal poker into the flames. After a short while, he withdraws it, bringing the hot end to Peyton. "You may grip it." Peyton happily does so. It is interesting to watch. I have never seen a fiorriee rewarded before. "Very good." Keon praises as Peyton lets go.

"Thank you, Prytore." Peyton smiles. "Prytore, there is something you need to know." I watch his hands fall to his side. They are healing so quickly that within moments, there is no evidence he has ever been injured. Prytore Keon's face falls into a frown. I decide instantly I do not like that look on him. "It is Serena. She did not confirm until we were in this room." Peyton turns to me. "She has admitted that she is naive to yellow customs and her caretaker has taken the guilt."

"You waited until we were alone to tell me, why?" Prytore Keon asks, but his tone does not give away his emotions to this news.

"She did confirm. We are not breaking any courtship rules," Peyton answers confidently.

"And?" Prytore Keon presses.

Peyton meets my eyes with what I can only categorize as bashfulness, but it is mixed with confidence. "I know she is what we are searching for."

Prytore Keon turns his attention to me. "Serena. Does it please you to be here with us, or would you prefer others for your company tonight? Rest assured, you can make another choice tomorrow."

"You and Peyton have shown me much kindness, Prytore. I am happy with my choice." I look to Madam Takira, who seems indifferent, which I take as a good sign. I have a feeling I will know if she is unhappy with a choice that affects the rest of my life.

"Well." Prytore Keon smiles, returning the poker to its stand. "Now that it is all settled, and binding, by all means, ladies, follow me. I take Madam Takira's arm and follow Prytore Keon down a long hallway. Peyton is behind us, almost as if on guard. We walk by several rooms with open doors, and eventually, he stops in front of the very last door on the left and enters it.

"Please, ladies, sit," Prytore Keon orders kindly, adjusting the handkerchief in his pocket. "Seeing as you are unfamiliar with yellow customs, I will explain it to you. Forgive me for not trusting the other yellow contenders to guide you in this task, as you must understand, they may be fiorriee, but they are ruthless and should not be trusted. Especially since they, no doubt by now, know who you are." He studies me. "You honestly do not understand the significance of your own name, do you Serena Gelsomino?" His eyes turn disapproving to my caretaker.

"I trust that someone will tell me eventually," I answer with annoyance in my tone. I want so desperately to ask, but the setting does not seem right for what must be a taboo topic, seeing as it has been hidden from me for the first twenty-three years of my life.

"You were raised with patience." He smiles, causing a light to come to his eyes. "I must admit, that makes me even more intrigued." He reaches for a glass, fills it with water, then hands it to me. "Tell me, what is your understanding of yellow court, limited as it may be?"

I study the glass for a moment before I answer, "I was simply told I had four days to impress a Prytore family. But when I got here, one of the girls told me that we would be choosing, not the Prytore family."

"Anything else?" he asks, tucking a stray white hair behind my ear. I look up at him, alarmed, and shake my head no. "Serena, please, give me enough respect not to lie to me."

"I am being honest, Prytore Keon. I do not know anything else about the yellow ceremony. Just that Peyton introduced himself. I gave him my hand and told him it was a pleasure to meet him. We spoke for a short moment, then he quickly figured out I have no idea what I am doing! He challenged Madam Takira, and she randomly drops a last name I never knew I had. Next thing I know, I am taken into a room of Prytores that scared me so much with the way they looked at me. You and Peyton seemed to treat me like the fiorriee I am, and well, you know the rest."

Prytore Keon gives a small chuckle. "I was referring to what the others told you about the choosing, but I can understand how you would mix that up. Your recount of events seems truthful. I am just curious if the girls were cruel to you in some way?"

"Not really." I frown, avoiding eye contact. "Just that they were important and not only was I not. It seems I have outdated ideas about the ceremony."

Madam Takira scuffs, causing Prytore Keon to look at her pointedly. "Forgive me, Prytore. Serena is putting that conversation into such proper form it takes the cruelty out of it."

I give her a pointed look.

"I see," Prytore Keon states, dropping his fingertips to my wrist. "Care to be a little less polite, Serena?"

I find myself trembling. "No, Prytore, I do not." He pinches my wrist hard, and I gasp.

"Very good." He praises, taking my wrist to his lips.

I can see Madam Takira is about to protest, but the glare Prytore Keon gives her stops her cold. He opens his mouth, and his tongue touches the spot he had delivered pleasant pain to just a moment before. My eyes widen when I realize I can taste him in my mouth. He smiles to see the surprise on my face. He keeps my wrist in his light grip and offers it to Peyton. Peyton quickly leans forward, and with a nod from his Prytore, he drops his mouth to the same spot, but the taste he leaves is much different. Peyton quickly moves back to his chair as though nothing has just happened.

Prytore Keon releases his hold. "Now that you have been properly marked, let me explain exactly what you are in for, because of that yellow dress."

I place my almost forgotten water glass down with the others on the table. When I sit back, I find his fingers lacing into mine. "As I hope you are aware, yellow is the highest honor for a fiorriee. Which means you can and will only serve the elite Prytore. But even we have daunting and mundane tasks. And most Prytore are here to find someone to meet these needs. Others, like myself, have different opportunities, but that is neither here nor there. You are not meant to worry about what we want. You are meant to worry about who it is you want to serve. The pitfall in all this, my beautiful Serena, is that we must agree to have you in our service. If you choose me and I do not choose you, then you will be going home with your caretaker."

"I see," I answer, guarded. "May I ask what pleases you, Prytore Keon?"

"Such a wonderful response. You are quick. I like that. I will answer your question, Serena, but we do have four days. Let us see how things progress."

I do my best to hide my disappointment. He distracts me by bringing my wrist to his lips, causing his taste to fill my mouth once more. I am curious as to how and why this is happening, but I am not against it.

"You are tested from the moment you step onto the transport. I must say, your impatience can be quite humorous, though it did put off some Prytore families. None of which you should concern yourself with. When you are left with the other girls, actions are not recorded. They used to be, but we found that it is simply too much pressure to be under a Prytore's watchful eye when one is trying to win our approval. So instead, we send other fiorriees to find those they feel will meet their Prytore family's needs. Which is why Peyton approached you. You are on a very short list of awaiting fiorriees that sparked our interest. Not to mention, he too has shown interest in you."

I look to Peyton and back to Prytore Keon, confused.

"Peyton and you are physically compatible for children, Serena, assuming you two would choose to embrace parenthood. Then of course, there is the aspect of meeting the demands I, as your Prytore, place upon you."

"Oh." I register, surprised again. Why my future of having kids never dawned on me, I do not know. I guess I simply was not raised that way. Thinking of making a family for myself is, after all, quite selfish.

"Does motherhood not become you?" Prytore Keon asks.

I meet his eyes, trying to find the words. "I must admit, Prytore Keon, I am unsure. I have never been asked to think that selfishly before. I have been raised to please my Prytore family, and it never dawned on me that having children would please them."

"Motherhood requires so much more than pleasing a Prytore, Serena. It requires having the ability to love and be loved."

"Must I give an answer tonight, or may I have some time with my thoughts before I give you a response?"

"To have a quick response after admitting that you never considered the possibility would be highly inappropriate. I am very much in approval of you having time with your thoughts." Prytore Keon praises.

"Another step in this process is for a Prytore, who is head of household, and their fiorriee to get to know one another in a formal setting, such as this. This is why we do not have doors here. We want and encourage conversations to determine if a match is possible. Both parties are welcome to leave at any time, and no one will stop you. Regrettably, the lack of privacy serves another purpose as well. In the past, there has been some inappropriate behavior, which is highly frowned upon."

I blush three shades of blue, trying to pull my wrist away, but he is not having it.

"Your response tells me that you have not had such experiences."

"You are correct, Prytore Keon," I whisper, avoiding his eyes.

"You are so very pleasing, Serena." I can hear the others at this point. But Prytore Keon ignores them. "You will be asked to report to meals on time. Throughout your time here, you are to perform tasks. You must remember every moment of these, you will be judged. And I caution you again, Serena, please, do not trust those around you to be anything but hindersome." He turns his gaze to Peyton then back to me. "During the day, Prytores can and will stop you from whatever task you are doing. They may change it, add to it, or lessen it. But you must follow their order until another Prytore or Prytoree comes around. You are only to follow the last order given to you. Upon the setting of Akatite, you will write up to three Prytore families you request company with. If they too request your company, then it shall be granted. If none of them request your company, then you are put into a pool of others, and the Prytore family chooses who they spend their evening with. You can repeat a request unless the Prytore family forbids it." He takes a drink of water. "How are you doing? Can you remember all of this?"

"I am fine, Prytore Keon. You need not worry about me." I smile, rubbing my thumb on his hand. He responds by doing the same thing.

"Are you the head of your household?"

"I am." He smiles.

"And the Prytoree in your family? I am sorry, I do not even know your last name." I blush.

"You will meet my Prytoree in the coming days, I assure you." He smiles. "As for my last name, you will either earn that from us or find out with your own curiosity."

I glare at him, but correct my features quickly, he is testing me. "I do have another question, if I may?"

"You may," Prytore Keon grants, moving our hands to his lap.

"Is all of this necessary?" I ask.

Peyton is so surprised by the question he chokes on his water.

"Come again?" Prytore Keon asks.

"Serena!" Madam Takira scolds.

I glare at her before bringing my attention back to Prytore Keon. "What I mean to say is, there seems to be a draw here. Or is it just me?

Did I make the right choice today? Or do you make all the girls feel so… welcome?"

It is time for Prytore Keon to be shocked. Peyton too seems taken back, but Madam Takira seems as though she has half expected my forwardness and is embarrassed by it.

"You are a very unusual fiorriee, Serena," Prytore Keon finally responds. "You are not wrong in believing in the draw. But I do think it fair that everyone involved gets a chance to be sure."

"Please, Prytore Keon, I ask that you too be honest with me," I retort.

"Serena!" Madam Takira gasps in shock, but I continue to ignore her.

"You both marked me, did you not? Now I am, by far, the last fiorriee on Artthemis to know exactly what that means, but I do know that I can taste you both from a simple touch of your tongue on my skin. And by my caretaker's reaction, doing so is very taboo, unless it has a purpose. Considering the circumstances and the stakes, I have a strong feeling you want me in your service. So, I ask again, why drag this out? Surely, you can train me into exactly what you want after the courting."

"There are two reasons, Serena," he answers with hard eyes, though he does not necessarily look unhappy. "You yourself asked for time to think about the possibility of motherhood, did you not?" I look away in embarrassment. Obviously, I have gotten ahead of myself. But the truth is, I am worried. I really feel comfortable, and to know that the others may have a chance to take them away is not something I want to even think about. The simple fact is, I have made my choice already, and motherhood is something I will have to adjust to. "The second is simply because of who you are, Serena Gelsomino. To be chosen by you means something to us Prytores. Because of that, I cannot have one conversation and declare you mine. It simply does not work that way. Every Prytore here must have the same fair chance as I." I raise an eyebrow at him. "Granted, Peyton's quick thinking may have tilted the scales in our favor, but you have not had a fair chance to meet the others. While I am sure you will not choose Prytore Charles, there are others who are just as nice as Peyton and myself. This is not as easy as it sounds, Serena."

"The mark?" I press.

"Our selfish way to have you dream of us tonight. Without a full breaking, it will not have lasting effects. But it is interesting that you are so forthcoming with your hand. I do wonder if you will be like that in all Prytores' company or just my own."

My eyes flash with understanding. He is admitting he has taken advantage of the situation at hand while warning me how not to make that mistake again. From now and until the end of this courting, marking will be something I alone have control of. He loosens his grip on my fingers, but I stubbornly do not move my hand away. He squeezes my fingers with a smile but mentions nothing of it. Before I can ask more questions, a bell rings.

"I am afraid our time is up for this evening. I have given you a lot to ponder." He drops my hand and starts to stand up. "I hope you have a good night and pleasant dreams."

"Wait," I protest softly, reaching for his wrist. "Please, Prytore, I really would like to dream of you tonight."

He smiles, sitting back down. "And Peyton?"

"I believe I have already embarrassingly declared how I feel about him." I blush, standing up and happily offering my free wrist to Peyton.

"Good, now remember, there are no doors here and it is no one's business but our own," Prytore Keon warns.

I nod. Neither him nor Peyton hesitate as they drop their lips to my vulnerable skin. My body quivers as a combination of their taste fills my mouth, but this time, they linger longer. I gasp quietly as all my senses seem to fill with this mixture. It is overwhelming. My entire body falls into a tremor, and the next thing I know, I am in Prytore Keon's arms with Peyton covering my mouth while Madam Takira stares at the empty doorway.

"Good girl," Prytore Keon praises. "I was certain you were going to scream. Not that I would have minded, but it is not the setting for such things. I do want to keep your innocence attached to you until you are in service." He nods at Peyton, who drops his hand from my mouth. "You asked me earlier how you can please me. You are doing such a great job at it today already, but I do have a request, if you are serious about choosing me for your lifetime of service."

"Anything," I respond, still struggling to gather full strength in my legs as I try to stand on my own two feet, but he shows no sign of letting that happen.

"You do not willfully allow anyone else, fiorriee or Prytore, to mark you. Only Peyton and I shall have that honor, and we shall do so anytime we see fit, but no one outside of this room shall ever know it." He lets me put weight on my feet, but he does not let me go. "Serena, I warn you, we know your taste now. If you taste differently from today, it is because you were marked by another."

"I understand."

"If you are forced," he continues, causing his eyes to darken at the thought, "do not be submissive to it. If you truly do not want someone's taste to penetrate your senses, it will not. Personally, I would want you to cry out, fight for your arm, cause a scene. While marking is acceptable here, it is meant to be private and never forced, though some Prytores think they have more power than they do."

"You lost me," I admit.

"We can only truly be your Prytore family if you want to be our fiorriee, Serena. Some have lost sight of this and think it is just because we are different, we are superior, but that is not the case. Having a true symbiotic relation means that both parties surrender to the other willfully and completely. It takes time and trust. And the more of those a match has, the stronger the connection is."

That annoying bell rings for a second time. "May I, Prytore?" Peyton asks.

"Of course, Peyton, please walk Serena to her chambers." Prytore Keon smiles. "Good night, Serena. I do hope we have more of these conversations." He kisses my wrist one last time, sending a jolt through me, and walks toward my caretaker. "Now, let me give you a brief explanation as to what is expected of caring for a lady in yellow during her courting."

"Shall we?" Peyton asks, sneaking in his own kiss on the wrist as he takes my hand. He pulls me close to him as we walk back down the now familiar hall. "You have a lot to think about, though it seems you have done a lot of thinking already. You have taken to my Prytore?" I smile at him, careful as to what to say with such ears around us. We were not the only ones walking back to the sleeping chambers. "I wonder, what thoughts do you have of me? After all, we will be spending a lot of time together, if you have what you seem to want, Serena."

"I must admit, Peyton, I was not expecting a situation like this." I pull him closer. "But I do not find it concerning."

"Some Prytore families do not make it this complex. They simply do not allow their fiorriee to raise families. Others are like us. You must keep in mind, you are taking on the whole package, Serena. Not just one of us. You must like all of us."

"Will we have time to spend alone together?" I ask.

"During the courting, moments like these are rare," he admits. "After, there will be plenty."

"I see."

"I hope you do, Serena. I would hate for you to be unhappy. Yet I cannot find it in me to apologize for not giving you much of a chance to meet the others tonight. You are so beautiful and unique. I acted selfishly, rushing through the other contestants to get to you, eager to be the first to speak to you. My selfishness comes at your expense. You seem to fear the other Prytores now."

"Did you see the way they looked at me? Like I was some prized possession they were drooling to get their hands on," I respond in disgust.

"Because you are." He frowns. "But very few had interest in you before they knew your real name."

I start to walk slower. "You two both seem keen on me making a well thought-out, educated choice, right? Despite me perfectly content on finishing this here and now and going home with you tonight?"

"Hush now, Serena, be careful, not all ears are as forgiving as ours," he warns, walking stiffer and with more speed.

"You just said that you knew those who seemed interested before they realized who I was," I add in a softer voice. He shrugs. "So have them say hello to me, but make sure they tell me that you sent them. That way I know the difference between the genuine and the fakes."

"Technically, I cannot do that." He frowns. "But if someone asks you if your favorite flower is a lily, know they came from me. At least that will be the code for tomorrow before lunch. I will probably need to change it by the rising of Akatite. We do like to gossip for the right things to say to everyone."

"I appreciate it, Peyton." I lean into his left ear. "When I choose you and your Prytore family, you can sleep with good conscience that I did it willfully." I kiss his cheek quickly, hoping no one can see it.

He pulls away with a smile. "Good night, Serena. I do hope you have sweet dreams."

Four

Disgrace

Serena

"Who do you think you are?" Bethany screams at me the moment Peyton departs, and I enter my sleeping chambers. "Prytore Keon is mine!"

I look at her, astonished. Prytore Keon did not even attend her portion of the courting. How does she know about him? "I was simply doing as I was told. Peyton told me to follow him, so I did." I shrug, realizing every girl in this room hates me.

"You stay away from them! I told you that we are making our choices and then you are getting the leftovers. What part of that did you not understand?" I glare at her, causing her purple eyes to harden. "How were you even separated from the rest of us? Your caretaker starts making a fuss about zarla knows what, and then Peyton, the one I have offered my hand to, takes both of you away! Whatever you are up to, I will not stand for it. Am I clear?"

I honestly wonder if she does not know my last name, though that is doubtful with my caretaker's embarrassing commotion about it. Still, the look she gave me when I left with Peyton may have simply been anger and jealousy. Unsure which one of these possibilities it could be, I decide to play coy. "I do not know why I was separated. I do know, it is what Peyton wanted. You would have to ask him, I suppose," I suggest, attempting to walk away but she blocks me.

"Oh, I shall, and then he will take me to his Prytore, and you can forget about ever spending time with either one of them again. They are mine! Do not get in my way again!" She and the rest of the girls break away, leaving me standing next to the door.

I take a few calming breaths to then start to walk the room looking for an empty bed. I find one, only to be stopped. "Taken." Nodding, I move to the next, only to be told the same. I reach the end of the chamber and turn back, seeing Bethany smile.

"I guess you will be sleeping like an animal tonight. It suits her, girls, do you agree?" They all break out in giggles.

Crossing my arms, I simply lean against the wall and stand. They will not have the satisfaction of seeing me lying down on the floor. Doing so is an extreme insult to fiorriee. I refuse to give any of them the gratification. Little do they realize that this is not the first time I have slept pridefully on my feet. But sleep is not something I find easy. I am scared to close my eyes. Therefore, I simply stare off and listen to the others as they gaggle and chatter about their experience. Some are happy with the blind selection of tonight as their choice in fiorriee has brought them a pleasing Prytore. I can relate to that. Others were not as fortunate. They either have selected a very pleasing fiorriee but the Prytore turns out to be disappointing or they are not happy with the fiorriee and the Prytore is either pleasing or they are not.

Bethany grabs the room's attention telling everyone how her Prytore tried to mark her. The entire room gasps. "He sure did." She continues smiting everyone's disbelief. "As if I would ever let a Prytore mark me! What would my future husband think?"

"He would think he could never trust you." A random girl speaks.

Bethany agrees with her and continues on with her recount of tonight's events, but I get bored listening to her. I did believe her though, and it made me curious how Peyton felt about my willingness to allow Keon to mark me.

After Bethany's story, the girls' conversation turns to motherhood and if they will or will not choose someone who wants them to raise a family. That strikes a nerve. I have never considered it until today, and I am on the fence about the idea of it. Not because I do not want children of my own but because raising them will take time away from my Prytore family. After all, many of my siblings are living at the orphanage because their Prytore families felt their fiorriee young were too distracting. I do not want that to be the fate of my children. But how do I express that to Peyton? How do I admit to him and Prytore Keon that I grew up on the wrong side of that, believing I was a castaway like the others when, it seems, I am in fact a true orphan.

Eventually, the lights are turned off and the chattering turns to whispers in the dark, which seems to last forever before silence finally comes. I do not plan on sleeping, but I doubt leaving this room is a good idea. I so want to dream of Prytore Keon and Peyton, but given the circumstance, that is impossible now. I consider going to find my caretaker, but I have not seen her since I have parted ways, and I do not know where to go. Wandering the halls in the middle of the night looking for my caretaker seems ill advised. What if I accidentally come upon the Prytores' sleeping chambers? That would be a humiliating nightmare. So instead, I turn my thoughts back to motherhood as I am sure my consideration will please Prytore Keon, though admittedly, I am unsure if I will ever see him again. If these girls have their way, it is unlikely. He is right to warn me not to trust them. I am going to have to keep my guard up. But how? I cannot go three nights without sleeping. Annoyed that the petty girls are keeping me from my goal of considering the things Prytore Keon has asked, I think back to him and Peyton marking me, and I realize I can still taste them. That makes me smile. I let my thoughts drift to places where they should, causing happiness to engulf me.

Prytore Keon and Peyton are in the garden with me, we are laughing and enjoying a very nice meal, but then there is a sound of a bell. I look toward it and realize they are gone. The bell sounds again, and immediately, I open my eyes, realizing I have been dreaming. I start to move, but I find my wrist is stuck. Frowning, I turn to figure out why, and I find my left arm chained to the wall.

"Problem?" Bethany asks with a wicked smile as she notices the shock on my face from the sight of my now tattered yellow dress. I turn to her with a glare while I tuck pieces of my dress into my surprisingly undamaged slip. "Oh, Serena, I do hope you make it in time for breakfast. Being late in the middle of courting is blasphemy." She laughs as she and her friends walk through the door, fully dressed and ready for the day, leaving me chained to the wall, with no hope of escape.

I struggle with the chain, but it is no use. I am truly trapped. Desperate, I look around for something to pick the stupid lock, but nothing is within reach. I am so angry my eyes fill with tears. How could I be so reckless as to fall asleep? Why did I let my guard down? How did I let my guard down? Never once have I made this mistake among my enemies, and I have had plenty of them throughout the years. Now, amid the most important time of my life, I mess up! Seriously? I cry out, but I doubt I am heard. Something tells me it is going to take a while for me to be discovered. I doubt my caretaker even knows where I was to sleep, much less how to ask for help without drawing negative attention to me. She is probably searching room by room, thinking I have messed this up. Which I have. Helpless, I look out a window as best I can. I see the girls greeting the male fiorriees from the night before. But they are so far down, and the window is closed. There is no hope in being discovered.

The minutes tick by, and the girls start to pair off. I watch as Bethany speaks to Peyton, and he seems reluctant about taking her to Prytore Keon. But someone seems to be hurrying everyone along, and she takes his arm. As they are walking away, she flashes a triumphant smile toward my window, and we both know I have officially lost my chance. Heartbroken, I sink down the wall as best I can, crying in anger.

I lose track of hope and time. When I hear my name being called out, it bewilders me. Surprised, but not lost enough to think I am hearing things, I call back, begging for help. I am shocked to find Peyton come through the door.

"Serena?" he questions, taking in my predicament.

"How? I thought you were with Bethany?" I reply, bitterly, struggling against my prison. He gives me a curious look. "I could see the greeting through the window." I explain, causing understanding to cross his features.

"I was, but Prytore Keon wanted answers as to why you were not there this morning. He sent me to find you." He explains, tugging at the chain with a frown. "Who did this?"

"I think you and I have a good guess, but seeing as I was asleep, I cannot prove it," I reply bitterly. "I cannot believe I fell asleep. It is not like I have not stayed up all night before." Peyton stops tugging the chain and looks at me. I realize he is waiting for more information as to why I would do such a thing in the first place. "It is complicated." I deflect, "Can you free me?"

"Not without help, I am afraid," he admits, dropping his arm. He grabs my free wrist gently. "It was us."

"What was you?" I ask, confused. Though at this point that is not much of an emotion, considering I have felt it since I got here.

"When we marked you, we wanted you to dream of us. If you wanted it too, you would do exactly that. You would not be able to fight off sleep if you tried," he explains.

"Well, I guess this predicament gives me away then." I reply, embarrassed and blushing deep blue.

"It makes me pleased that you wanted it." He smiles, letting go of my wrist and placing a finger under my chin, causing me to look at him.

"Does it? The way the others were talking, marking is something personal between fiorriees and should not be shared with Prytore's."

His thumb glides up and down my cheekbone. I find myself holding my breath, but I cannot stop staring into his beautiful silver irises. "Most fiorriees cannot hold a candle to the relation I share with my Prytores. You did not offend me Serena, on the contrary, you pleased me."

"That is a relief. I do not like the thought of displeasing you." I admit, staring in his eyes.

He leans forward and bites my shoulder so hard, I need to bury my face into him, to keep from screaming out from the pleasure of the pain.

"You have no idea the restraint it is taking not to reward you further." He confesses. "I must go and get help. I promise, I will not be long."

"Do not go, please," I protest, grabbing him with my free arm.

"There is no reason to be scared, Serena. I will keep you safe."

"I am not scared. I trust you will return quickly." I reassure him, then bite my lip with his curious gaze. "You stated that being alone with you is rare, and with those brats, I fear that it will be impossible."

"You want to be alone with me?" he asks, raising an eyebrow.

"Only if you want to be alone with me," I answer timidly, suddenly shy.

His lips are on mine before I could register his movement. My entire body ignites in fire, and I find myself opening my mouth to his probing tongue. His taste is so much stronger. My freehand gets tangled into his wild white hair, and he wraps both arms around me, bringing our bodies so close together there is no air between us. The kiss is slow but hungry. I could do this for hours and am very disappointed when he breaks it.

"Would you have come with me this morning?" he questions, slowly putting distance between our bodies.

"I am saddened you have to ask me that, Peyton." I frown. "What makes you think I would want to choose another?"

"Because this is your chance to, Serena. You should see what is out there. Making a choice so early is not advised." He warns, but I can tell by the tone of it, he is not liking the idea of me with another. "Once you are free from this chain, you will not be with us for a while. The morning choosing has come and gone. You will be with another."

"Then I shall be miserable." I pout, angry again at my predicament.

"I hope this stolen moment gets you through," he whispers, pulling me close again, kissing me breathless before he lets me go. "I must go now. They will all be wondering what has happened to us." He does not give me a chance to protest; he vanishes quicker than I can blink. I hate that, but I cannot complain; I have been known to run like the wind a time or two myself.

I take the short time to gather myself before I am greeted by my caretaker, a Prytoree I do not know, and Peyton. "And what were you doing exactly to find her here?" the Prytoree challenges.

"I was calling her name in the halls, Prytoree Alexis. Serena had shouted back, which is why I came here," Peyton explains.

"Why were you looking for her?" Madam Takira asks.

"Prytore Keon asked me to," Peyton answers.

"Interesting." Prytoree Alexis states. "You have done well, Peyton. You should return to Prytore Keon and your morning choice."

"As you wish, Prytoree," Peyton replies, stealing one last look at me before he leaves.

"So, you are Marcello and Aurora's daughter. We all thought you were dead, and here you are, raised in an orphanage, of all forsaken places." I look to Madam Takira, then back at Prytoree Alexis. It is not the first time I have heard my parents' first names, but I am surprised that a complete stranger, especially one who is not a fiorriee, would say them with such admiration. "Tell me, Serena, who did this to you?"

"I am unsure, Prytoree." I turn away from her. "I seem to have a lot of enemies here."

"And how did you acquire that in such a short amount of time? It is my understanding you did not exactly spend a lot of time with these girls?" she challenges, going across the room and looking through the girls' things.

"If I had to guess, it has something to do with having favor with Prytore Keon, Prytoree. Apparently, he was spoken for, and I was unaware of it," I answer, annoyed.

"Spoken for?" the Prytoree challenges, causing Madam Takira's eyes harden. She understands exactly who did this to me. "Why, girl, how could that even be possible so early into courting?" Prytoree Alexis asks. "Not to mention, you seem to have taken Prytore Keon out of the running before he had the chance to meet the others."

"Your guess is as good as mine, Prytoree." I frown as she comes up with a key.

She walks up to me. "It seems Prytore Keon is not upset with the idea that his company was monopolized by you last night." She smiles at me then reaches for the lock that is holding me captive to put in the key. "You are not the first fiorriee to face sabotage on her yellow courting, my dear. But it is very rare that a Prytore sends a fiorriee looking to help a victim of one. You must truly have impressed my husband, and I doubt your last name has anything to do with it." She unlocks my wrist, allowing my arm to drop.

I grab it with a hiss at the sudden unpleasant rush of blood circulation. I collect myself quickly, processing her words. She is the Prytoree that completes Peyton's and Keon's family. "Thank you." I smile, truly grateful. "Peyton and Prytore Keon are very kind to me. I appreciate all the assistance your family has given."

"Why were you not in your bed last night?" she asks, studying me.

"I do not have one." I shrug.

"Of course you do." Madam Takira snaps, looking around. "Where are your things?" She starts to roam around the room looking for them. When she finds my luggage, she opens it for confirmation, only to squeal in shock. Every last bit of yellow fabric that I brought, has been torn to shreds.

"Funny," I mutter, trying to keep my temper, "they acted as though I was invisible and would be lucky to be chosen at all, but obviously, they are intimidated by me nonetheless."

"This is uncalled for," Prytoree Alexis seethes. "I want a name, Serena." I stare at her in stubborn silence. She glares at me. "You realize it will not take much for me to figure out who did this. I am sure she is with my husband right now. I will get her name, one way or the other."

"Forgive me, Prytoree, but we cannot prove who it was. All I can say is what I am sure of." I point out. She waits. "As I told Prytore Keon, I seem to have outdated ideas in thinking that Prytores chose the fiorriees in waiting. But it seems the fiorriee get to choose the Prytore." Prytoree Alexis' eyes harden at that comment, but I continue on, "this was pointed out to me by the same girl who was very displeased that I had Prytore Keon's attention last night. She even went so far as to warn me to stay away from him and Peyton. She had already laid claim to Peyton by offering her hand before I did. Still, it is unclear to me if Peyton accepted her gesture, as he did with me."

"She offered her hand?" Prytoree Alexis asks. "Funny, Peyton only told us about yours."

I blush. "I am still a little embarrassed by that. Now that I am grasping its meaning."

"You should not be." She replies. "This fiorriee, whose name you withhold from me, sees you as a threat." Prytoree Alexis studies me but I stay silent. "So as punishment, they took your bed?"

"They wanted me to sleep on the floor, but I refused. I did not plan on sleeping at all, to be honest." I frown, still annoyed that I did.

"But your choice of last night's company made that impossible, did it not?" I look at the floor, unwilling to answer what she seems to already know. "Tell me, Serena, did they mark you?" My eyes shoot to hers, but I refuse to answer. She waits a while longer before she gives up. "I see that your time in the orphanage taught you when to keep your mouth shut. I must admit, I like that, though it means I must hunt down Peyton and Prytore Keon to get my answers."

"What happens now?" I ask, turning my attention back to my ruined outfits.

"Normally, this high amount of sabotage means that you disrespected the others, and that type of disrespect sends the violator back home with their caretaker. But seeing as you have barely had a chance to offend anyone, except by breathing. I sincerely doubt this is the case." She closes my luggage and takes it from Madam Takira. "Besides, despite direct questioning by your superiors, you refuse to damage anyone's reputation and their hopes for a Prytore in this choosing. Therefore, I will not be sending you home."

"Thank you, Prytoree."

"Tell me, Serena, are you interested in meeting other Prytores and their fiorriee? Know that your answer will not offend me either way, and it is between the three of us. However, I am asking for your complete honesty."

"The only interest I have in meeting the others is for the singular effect of clearing Peyton's conscience when I choose him." She raises an eyebrow at me. "He feels he did not give me a fair chance to choose and confirm last night. And my liking to him is only because he is showing interest in me," I explain.

"If I understand you correctly, Serena, you are personally not interested in others. Your needs could be met with Peyton, Prytore Keon and myself, but because you want to be sure that a male fiorriee is confident in your choice, you are willing to continue on?"

"I have a desire to please the entire family." I blush deeply. "Prytore Keon has expressed a quick decision on my end will not reflect well on his."

"Well, you are a rare find." She notes. "Come with me." She walks away from what was once my possessions and out of the room. I follow her, and Madam Takira follows me. We walk the halls for a long while before we climb an elegant staircase and enter into a grand hall. Once there, we enter a door. The room is beautiful. The paintings on the ceilings are stories of Prytores' religious beliefs and their god, Qatmjir. I wish I had more time to examine them, but I am led into another room full of dresses. I watch as she sifts through them and gasp when she pulls out a beautiful white one.

"It is lovely, Prytoree." I admire, confused it is not yellow, but not saying anything.

"You may call me Prytoree Alexis." She smiles, studying me and then Madam Takira. She drops the dress onto a nearby chair carefully then turns to me. "I can see that you were raised not to use our names unless given, as you clearly heard Peyton use it, and you have given me the respect not to until I granted permission."

I nod, remembering that test all too well in my education.

"I am curious if you are aware of what it means for a fiorriee in courting to call a potential Prytore's wife by her name, and as to why you truly seem confused about a white dress."

"I am only as informed as Prytore Keon seemed fit to tell me last night," I confirm.

Prytoree Alexis turns to Madam Takira, obviously annoyed.

Madam Takira defends herself, "Part of keeping Serena hidden meant that I could not seek answers above my own station, Prytoree."

"You have served the Gelsomino's well." Prytoree Alexis praises her, then turns to me. "As for a fiorriee wearing white in an elite courting, it signifies that she has a claim to her. Normally, this is reserved for the third morning, but considering the circumstances, I am offering you the honor early. Understand Serena, should you choose to wear this dress, everyone here will understand the Silviu family's claim to you. Usually, you have more than one white dress to choose from, but this is not a usual circumstance. Also, as you can see, I brought more than one, as more than one girl can have this choice. Though if Peyton has expressed such powerful interest in you, I doubt Keon would ask that I use it on another, risky as that is for us."

"Forgive me, but I am lost," I admit. "I understand that this is an honor, but how is this not choosing?"

She smiles at me. "It is, in a way, but it is not final." Her answer does not help me at all. "The way this is working for the rest of the fiorriees in yellow is simple. Last night everyone had fair odds, and the choosing was left to the male fiorriees. But the females must not only accept but confirm which is why everyone is meant to speak to everyone else. Peyton's guilt in forgoing this process with you is genuine. You have only met him, and if you chose to serve our family, he will always carry the burden that he took your choice away. Add to it your sabotage and most Prytore's unwillingness to look past it, and it boils down to Peyton's burden or you going home with your caretaker unchosen."

My eyes water with tears. "I do not want to give Peyton a burden. I would rather go unchosen."

"That is a decision you can make, my dear, but Peyton is leaving with a mate. Do you not want it to be you?" she asks kindly. "This white dress can save your union, burden free. I promise."

"How?" I ask, embarrassed I cannot keep the tears in my eyes. The idea of Peyton going with another upsets me so much it is taking extreme effort not to shake.

"On the third morning, you were to wake to a bed of white dresses. Some will have more than others. Some will not have any at all. Those without are eliminated. Those who can choose have a choice to make. The conversations you have had along the way help you determine which dress to put on that morning. It shows that you and a Prytore do agree and unless something changes, which to be truthful it often does, you will be selected and select that family by the end of the day."

"It often does?" I ask surprised.

"Those who dresses you choose not to wear tend to get competitive and sway a fiorriee to their liking. Not to mention, most only want one fiorriee, and we are allotted four dresses. And that can get… complex." She shrugs. "So, as you can see, this dress is not a death sentence to Peyton's burden. Others will approach you and try to persuade you. Most likely, more aggressively since you will be wearing it so much earlier than the rest and your last name is what it is."

"And if you are not instructed by your husband to offer another girl a white dress, you run the risk of Peyton leaving without a mate." I conclude, understanding at last. "You are not just being generous in allowing me to continue, you are risking Peyton's happiness that I will in fact choose him."

"It is what he wants, Serena." Prytoree Alexis answers. "I have a hard time denying him this just as much as you seem to."

"You love him," I conclude.

"Just as Prytore Keon will love you," she answers. "Different than mine and Keon's love but love just the same."

"Please, Prytoree Alexis, he must offer a second dress, what if I disappoint?"

"Do you plan on disappointing us?"

"No, but I did not plan on being chained to a wall either," I argue. "Please, I do not want him unhappy."

"I think the only way Peyton will be happy is if he takes you home with us, Serena." She smiles kindly. "But Peyton is not the only consideration here. Prytore Keon is as well."

"And you, it seems," I add, studying her reaction to this. "Would you be happy if you brought me home?"

"You are very pleasing, Serena. I find you to be very rare, and I believe you would fit with our family nicely." I smile at her. "Does this mean you will wear our dress?"

"I would be honored," I accept.

Five

Lady in White

Serena

Prytoree Alexis waits until the second meal before she allows me to join the others. During that time, she asks to do my hair. Madam Takira was very encouraging to that and insisted that I do not look in a mirror until after Prytoree Alexis was finished. When my hair is set, Madam Takira sends me off to a mirror alone, though this is pointless as the image is always blurry. Madam Takira knows that, though, so I figure she just wants time to ask Prytoree Alexis more questions about the courting. I must admit, I enjoy my time with Prytoree Alexis, and we share broad but pleasant conversation. The white dress she has honored me with is much fuller than the yellow dress I have been wearing. It has a corset to it that she has bound quite tightly, a wide waste that has layers and layers of silk, decorated with blue beads. It accents, yet hides, desirable parts of my body from view. My favorite part is the corset itself. It has a design of beads that starts out as lines but ends in a large circle around my ribs and in that circle is the shimmering silver beads that bear the Silviu family crest.

I must admit, I am not looking forward to making such a grand entrance, but there is not much of a choice in the matter. I am doing this for Peyton, and I know there will be consequences. Prytoree Alexis does not make it easy; she waits until right after prayers to have me enter, which means every eye in the court is on me. I hear the gasps from some of the fiorriee as they obviously have assumed I have been sent home. Ignoring them and their instant gossip, I follow Prytoree Alexis to the end of the open court, in which the meal is being served, straight to her husband.

"My dearest husband, may I present to you, Lady Serena of the Gelsomino house, as you requested."

Embarrassed by all the attention and formalness, I blush as I take a bow.

"Tell me, husband, does my choice please you?" I hear more extreme gasps and murmurs erupting throughout the courtyard. I do not completely understand what her last sentence means, but I am not lost in the words of it. She is telling him she chooses me. Bethany, who is sitting in between Prytore Keon and Peyton, is glaring at me, extremely unamused with these events.

"That depends, my dearest wife. Are you the reason for Serena's tardiness?" Keon asks, looking very displeased.

"Not completely," she answers truthfully, "but when I discovered she had been sabotaged, I got the unique chance to have time alone with her. My desire to get to know her kept her more delayed than the simple sabotage would have. I would apologize, but I am not sorry, for I enjoyed her company."

"Is this true, Serena? Were you in fact sabotaged?" he asks me, his displeased expression even more defined.

"Regretfully so, Prytore Keon." I confirm.

"And do you know who did this to you?" he asks pointedly, obviously expecting a name.

"As I was asleep Prytore Keon, I do not," I answer truthfully, avoiding Bethany's eyes, refusing to accuse anyone of something someone else may have done, though highly doubtful.

He studies me for a long moment then turns to Prytoree Alexis. "I am pleased, my dearest wife. Please, as Serena has had the advantage of spending time with you, feel free to spend time with Bethany, and let me know if she too deserves one of our white dresses."

"As you wish, my dearest husband." Prytoree Alexis smiles, offering her hand to Bethany, who is hesitant to take it. Peyton and Prytore Keon wait. Reluctantly, Bethany stands. Prytoree Alexis takes her arm and leads her away from her seat. I do my best to keep the smile off of my face.

"Lady Serena, would you be as so kind to join us? Peyton, please dispose of this and get Serena a nice wholesome plate." Prytore Keon instructs him as I work to sit down. Peyton nods, takes Bethany's plate, and goes to the buffet, following orders.

"I warned you the others would be hindersome." Prytore Keon hisses, helping me with my chair before settling back into his own, right beside me.

"To be fair, I was not planning on sleeping." I hiss back, giving him an accusing look. His response annoys me when he takes my wrist and brings it to his lips for all to see. I gasp, as best I can in this restrictive dress, from his taste filling my mouth. He smirks and brings my hand to the table.

"I thought that was no one's business but our own." I whisper, looking around and confirming everyone who was watching clearly seen it.

"Circumstances have changed," he replies, taking a bite of his meal. "Does it bother you that they know?"

"Not at all." I shrug.

"Why not? It is after all, taboo for a Prytore to mark a fiorriee." He asks, studying me. His eyes tell me he already knows this answer, but I speak it out loud anyway.

"I am not embarrassed by anything that pleases Peyton." I answer proudly.

"Very nice. That pleases me as well Serena." He boasts, causing me to blush. "Peyton told me about your predicament. I must to say, I am surprised Alexis reacted this way. It is such a bold move," he whispers, moving my freshly styled white hair off my ear. "She even did your hair for you, did she not?"

"I fear there was not much of a choice Prytore Keon as all my clothes were shredded," I answer softly enough not to be overheard. His eyes harden into a glare. "My offense was having your company," I answer his unspoken question on how I could be so highly disgraced. He pulls me closer to his seat. Peyton returns with the food then. My stomach turns. I truly do not want this, but it would be very impolite not to eat it. Madam Takira had warned me that I will have to eat too much. I just hope with all that is going on, I do not get sick from it. Both of them notice my hesitation and encourage me to eat. With reluctant silence, I nibble in compliance. Slightly grateful, Prytoree Alexis made me wait long enough that I was forced to miss breakfast.

"Tell me, Peyton, did you like Bethany?" Prytore Keon asks, causing both Peyton and myself to stiffen.

"She has a positive upbringing and desirable looks," he finally answers, staring at his food.

"Would you want to mate with her?" Prytore Keon asks, more directly.

"No," Peyton answers firmly, still staring at his plate.

"She is the one behind your sabotage, is she not Serena?" Prytore Keon guesses.

"She is the only one who has bothered to speak with me, Prytore Keon. She was the fiorriee who kindly informed me of how things are and made my station very identifiable. The rest of my competition seems to follow her lead. Which is why I cannot say who sabotaged me, for I fear it could honestly be any or all of them, to keep one from being guilty."

"Do they know who you are?" Prytore Keon asks.

"If they did, they did not show it." I stab my food. "I cannot hide that any longer, can I? Not with the introductions Prytoree Alexis just made." I take a drink of water, knowing that it was not Prytoree Alexis who revealed my identity, but my caretaker. However, I must choose my words carefully in this political landmine. Putting the glass down, I turn to him. "To be fair, I think my caretaker was not overheard last night, and it did come as a surprise to my fellow female fiorriee. Otherwise, Bethany would have never told me that my only choice was to sleep like an animal." Prytore Keon's eyes widen in disbelief. Peyton looks at me, obviously angered. "Which is how I managed to get chained to a wall. I was leaning against it, refusing to sleep at all, but…" I stop myself from finishing that sentence, putting food in my mouth as a distraction.

"We hindered you, leaving you victim," Prytore Keon finishes in a soft, disbelieving whisper. "You can be sure, Serena, Bethany will be dealt with. You have my word."

"And you have mine," Peyton adds, his voice angrier than when he first discovered me.

"I appreciate all the kindness and protectiveness all three of you have given me." I smile, filling my fork with food. "I am truly honored."

Before they can respond to that, a male fiorriee that I have never met sits at our table. "Please forgive the intrusion, Lady Serena. I am Jonas, fiorriee to Prytore Theo. We were hoping to spend some time with you, after your meal, of course. Assuming it is okay with your preferred Prytore?"

The idea of Jonas' offer makes the food in my stomach sit a little too heavy. I turn to Peyton to be sure this is what he wants. He raises an eyebrow at me for a moment before he gives a small nod. Not liking that, I turn my attention to Prytore Keon, who seems to give me no help at all. Finally, I give Jonas my attention. My eyes give him a quick study. He is nothing like Peyton. His hair is buzzed short; his arms and shoulders are disproportionate and too thin. Even his eyes are too simple and dark blue like most of us. Unhappy, I give him a nod. Jonas lights up with a smile and turns to Prytore Keon, who sets his fork down with purpose.

"The lady has expressed her willingness. But I warn you, Jonas, the moment she decides otherwise, she shall be returned directly to me, in no different of a state than she left." To prove his point, he takes my arm again and kisses my wrist.

Jonas sits up a little straighter, understanding that I am not just Prytoree Alexis' choice, but his as well. "I understand," he replies dryly, excusing himself and leaving me to my meal.

"Considering you two are the ones wanting me to mingle, you are quite possessive of me." I mutter into my plate. "Not that I am complaining."

Prytore Keon chuckles and continues eating.

Peyton stops and looks at me. "Why did you say yes, if you do not want to?" he asks, studying me.

"Because, I promised you a clear conscience. Remember?" I smile, stabbing my food. "Besides, I am sure, if either of you did not trust them, I would not have been given a choice, as this dress seems to imply Prytore Keon has the final say over me."

"A dress you look amazing in, I might add." Prytore Keon answers as confirmation.

I blush. "Thank you."

I eat my meal as slowly as I can, but soon, they both lose patience with me and encourage me not to leave Prytore Theo waiting much longer. When the time for me to depart comes, Peyton is the first to speak upon my farewell. "I so want to give you my taste, Serena, but I do not find it fair to Jonas or any other. But know, I do want to." I give a small nod and turn to Prytore Keon.

"Remember our arrangement, Serena, we know your taste." I nod in acknowledgment. With reluctance, I turn to go, but I find Prytore Keon has gotten up from the table. He wraps his arms around me. "I do hope you take my warning to heart this time, Serena. I warned you about the girls and we almost lost you because you did not go to your caretaker when you felt threatened!"

I twist in his arms, glaring. "To be fair, I did not know where she was!" I explain, hurt that he would believe I did not take him seriously.

"What do you mean? She was right behind you and Peyton. Did you not see her pass you into her chambers?" I shake my head no.

"That is not right." He frowns, letting me go. He turns to Peyton. "Accompany her while I find her caretaker."

"Prytore?" Peyton asks in surprise.

"Forgive me, Peyton. I am trying my best to release your burden, but I am in fear of Serena's safety," he explains.

"My safety?" I question, confused all over again.

"Just stay with Peyton. I will return when I can."

"And who will look out for you?" I demand.

He raises his eyebrow at that question, but he does not answer. Instead, he makes his way past the tables, and I find Peyton's breath in my ear. "Do not make a scene, Serena. If he fears for your safety, causing drama will only make it worse."

"If anything were to happen to me, it would have happened when I was alone in that tower for who knows how long." I mutter, walking away in annoyance. I know Peyton is behind me, but he seems to think better than to finish this conversation with all the eyes on us.

It does not take me long to find Jonas and who I assume must be Prytore Theo. "I was under the impression you were coming alone, Lady Serena," the Prytore complains, watching Peyton.

"Forgive us, Prytore Theo, but something has come up that has Prytore Keon questioning Lady Serena's safety. And since our family has boldly laid claim this early in the courting, I have been asked to be her personal guard. I assure you, I will not stand in the way of normal proceedings, and if she proves to favor you more and you agree, Jonas will be welcome to take my place."

"Her safety?" Prytore Theo questions.

"She is a Gelsomino, Prytore Theo, one who has been in hiding for twenty-three years." Peyton replies patiently.

Prytore Theo considers this. "Of course, this is in fact an unusual situation. It makes sense that rules are bent to accommodate. Please, Lady Serena, have a seat." Feeling uncomfortable I do so. Peyton makes no move to do the same. "Tell me, how is your courting going so far?" he asks, trying to break the ice, but it feels like the wrong question.

"It has not been dull," I answer truthfully. "I have come to adore the Silviu family. But they are insistent that I make an informed decision."

Jonas eyes tighten. "And what did they tell you your service would be?"

I glare back at him, deciding to quote Prytore Keon and his wisdom. "It is not about what I am asked to do. It is about my willingness to do whatever is asked of me."

"Do you know you are signing up to be a mother, with children you will actually be expected to raise for the rest of your life?" Jonas challenges. I say nothing. "The Silviu's may be the best known Prytore family here, Serena, but their intentions are not one for an intelligent mind. We, on the other hand, offer a much more dignifying service."

"I am sorry, are you trying to sell yourself on what services you expect of me?" I ask, taken aback.

"Of course, that is what you are choosing, Lady Serena." Prytore Theo informs me. "This is the rest of your life we are talking about. My family is searching for a fiorriee interested in pleasing their Prytore family with assisting in research. While there will be time for mating practices, we see you more for your brain, not your body."

"And if these mating practices happen to produce a child?" I ask cautiously.

They frown. "I fear there is not room in our home to keep a fiorriee child, Lady Serena."

"Then I fear you are wasting your time speaking with me, Prytore Theo," I answer coldly, standing up. "Thank you for your interest, but please, do not waste a white dress on me." I take Peyton's hand and start to walk away in anger.

He takes control of our direction and heads back to the table we were at earlier. It offers the most privacy for the setting, but it is not much.

"That was an intense reaction," Peyton observes, helping me into a chair. "Does this mean you are willing to have and raise children?"

"If I have a child, I expect no less than to raise it. I will not allow my offspring to live in an orphanage as a castaway." Anger overtakes me, and I force myself to breathe in order to stop the shaking. Peyton takes my arm and brings my wrist to his lips. His taste immediately calms me. I turn to him. "I hesitated last night because I witnessed it over and over again, growing up. Fiorriee children are cast away all the time because motherhood takes the fiorriee away from being able to service their Prytore family's needs. I swore I would never be a mother, because I could never do that to a child. Especially, since before I arrived here, I thought I was a castaway. I never believed my caretaker when she tried to tell me I was not."

"So, you forced yourself not to want something because you did not think it was possible. And we have offered you the impossible, which is one of the reasons why you want to say yes." He concludes.

"No." I counter, thinking out loud. "Motherhood was not something that made me want to rush the decision. That, I honestly, did need time for. Not sleeping some of the night did help. I was able to remind myself that I was not against motherhood, just the possible bad outcomes of it. Thinking I was a castaway nearly destroyed me. I could not imagine being able to survive if I had to cast away my own flesh and blood."

"You love your unborn so much that you would rather not have them, if you knew you could not care for them?" he asks, looking at me with such amazement, that I look away.

"When you put it that way." I shrug.

"Lady Serena, it would break my heart if I could not marry thee," he whispers aloud. "For I love you more now than I ever dreamed I could love another."

"Including Alexis?" I ask, causing him to frown. "That is different." He dismisses.

"Yet the same." I add. He does not respond. "Is motherhood the only term of the service being offered by this family, or were Jonas and Prytore Theo just trying to make theirs seem more appealing?"

"Our family expects complete and irrefutable surrender." He answers seriously. "Most, like Prytore Theo are offering partial service. Which means, you work as an assistant or whatnot and usually they have selected their male assistants before their female. That is why you see male fiorriee here. They are looking for someone that can serve the Prytore family's needs, but also entertain the fiorriee to keep from boredom. As you must be aware, our species does not do well with mundane work without extreme adrenaline release. Now that does not always include mating rituals, yet it does not always exclude them."

"But Prytore Keon is not most Prytores." I answer with a flash in my eyes.

"Prytore Keon wants complete surrender from his fiorriee, Serena. Something that is not easy for any of us. While both choices involve breaking, part-time service only breaks the fiorriee to the Prytore's desired tasks. Full-time service breaks the fiorriee's mind, body, and the soul so you can be molded into what your Prytore desires of you. Your past twenty-three years of desire will fall away, and you will be taught what is desirable to you from then on. The full-time breaking process is horrific. You will hate him and, I fear, me, before you love us. But when you love us, you will serve deeper than any fiorriee here dares to dream they could. We make no secret that this involves motherhood from the beginning of life to the end. But it is not the only service you will be asked to do. Nothing would be off limits. If asked, would you die for your Prytore family?" I look at him in shock as he continues. "That is something most fiorriee have a limit to. Most of the fiorriee on Artthemis surrendered or are of descendants who surrendered in the war. The idea of dying for their enemy does not sit well." He studies me. "You understand now why the Silviu are sought after by our kind? The idea of complete surrender is a challenge to our nature. But most are not cut out for what is required."

"And you want me to consider others why?" I ask. "Is it because you do not think me capable of the challenge or worthy of being your children's mother?"

"On the contrary, Serena, I know you are very capable, and I would be highly honored to share parenthood with you. But you need to understand that for yourself. Plus, the added bonus of us asking you to do things you have expressed disinterest in is a test." He takes my hand. "You will need this knowledge to survive the breaking, Serena. Please know, I am not just trying to relieve a burden. I am looking out for your sanity."

"Are there any other families here who are looking for full surrender?" I ask. "Because I am not interested in what Prytore Theo or anyone like him is offering."

"Are you sure?" he asks, his silver eyes meeting mine with such intensity that I almost forget to breathe.

"I grew up doing mundane tasks, and it left me unsatisfied. I am considering the rest of my life here. Until now I only ever believed existence was about mundane tasks, followed by a few hours of release then sleep, only to start all over. You are telling me that I can have more than that. Something I have been craving for as long as I can remember, yes, Peyton, I am sure."

"Sure, about what, Lady Serena?" Prytore Keon asks, sitting down beside me.

"She has expressed interest in full service and wishes not to be bothered by Prytores offering less." Peyton answers for me.

"Good girl." Prytore Keon approves, though he does not seem relaxed in the slightest.

"What is it?" I ask, alarmed.

"Your caretaker, she has been threatened." Prytore Keon informs me. My eyes widen in disbelief.

"It is all right, Serena, I have taken care of everything. You both shall be guarded at all times. No one will harm either of you."

"I do not understand, why is this happening?" I ask, fighting the shakes. Peyton wraps his arms around me. "Please, Prytore Keon, enlighten me." I beg.

"I will, Serena, I promise, but not here. It is not wise to cause a scene or to speak of such things," he whispers, rubbing his fingers on my wrists. "For now, let us talk of more pleasant things. You are now aware of full service and part-time service, and you choose full?" I nod. "Good." Prytore Keon smiles at Peyton. "Have you explained the two types of full service?"

"Not yet. She does have the understanding that not all Prytores are the same... some are much more selfish than others," Peyton answers.

"Well, let us make sure you understand the contrast completely, my dear. Peyton, I would like you to please escort Lady Serena to Prytore Charles and introduce them properly."

"Must I?" I ask in protest. "I do not get a good vibe from him."

This causes Prytore Keon to smile, but his words do not match the expression. "If you want to serve me, Lady Serena, you shall follow every command without question."

"Apologies, Prytore Keon," I mutter.

He quickly scans the courtyard before turning his attention back to Peyton. "Also, Prytore Oba and Prytore Fulton."

"As you wish, Prytore," Peyton replies, taking my hand. I frown when I see Bethany and Prytoree Alexis joining Prytore Keon's table upon our departure.

Peyton feels the tension. "You need not worry, Serena. He is not keeping company with her for reasons you might think."

I do not respond. I still do not like it. Reluctantly, and with a heavy heart, I am brought to Prytore Charles' presence. "May I help you?" he sneers, looking disgusted.

"I have been asked to properly introduce myself." I smile, with a small bow.

"No need to waste your time. You obviously are flaunting your choice around like the whore you want to be. I have no interest in you. Be gone from my sight at once."

"That is no way to speak to a lady!" Peyton replies, stepping in between me and the Prytore.

"She is no lady," Prytore Charles replies. His fiorriee stands up and faces off with Peyton.

"Peyton, no, he is not worth it. Please." I beg, tugging on his arm. Peyton ignores me.

"Listen to your mindless babymaker and go," the fiorriee adds.

"Peyton, please." I beg, keeping my weight on his arm. "What would Prytore Keon and Prytoree Alexis want?"

Peyton turns to me with hard eyes. "I am not in the wrong to defend your honor, Lady Serena."

"I do not want you to," I respond, causing hurt to cross his eyes. I wrap both my hands around his arm and face off with both of these dagets who have done nothing but try to humiliate me. "I can defend my own honor. For I have done nothing wrong."

"Nothing wrong? You have not followed a single rule since you stepped foot off that transport!" Prytore Charles argues.

"I have followed every rule," I counter. "It is not my fault that I happen to be the first girl to be chosen to wear a white dress. It was offered to me, just as every girl here will be offered. And from my understanding of the rules, nowhere does it say it must wait until the third day."

"It is customary." Prytore Charles challenges.

"It was a gift to me. Was I to deny it and offend the one offering it because it was not the customary day? If you have an issue, Prytore Charles, it is not with me."

"The only reason the Silviu would put on such a show is if you have already chosen!" Prytore Charles seethes, turning darker yellow than I have ever seen a Prytore turn. "They want a full-service baby- making mother raising slave, and you are the first in line for a reason. They want your bloodline, Serena, 'Queen of the fiorriee'. They want your males!"

Queen of the fiorriee? I am about to question him, but I am interrupted by a shout from behind me.

"That is enough!" Prytore Keon bellows, stopping me from saying more from my temper. "What is the meaning of this?"

"He disrespected her," Peyton answers, not breaking his glare from Prytore Charles' fiorriee. "She chose to defend herself."

"Prytore Charles, are you honestly suggesting I broke the rules and am having a lady lie about her sacred choice?" Prytore Keon asks in disgust.

"How else would you explain that dress?" Prytore Charles challenges.

"My wife offered it to her without my knowledge, though I am happily surprised," Prytore Keon answers honestly. "And you, above all, Prytore Charles, know how difficult wives can be, especially when they want something." Prytore Charles stutters a few times, but Prytore Keon cuts him off. "Lady Serena is right. Prytoree Alexis did not break any rules. And I daresay you have managed to offend not only me but my wife, my fiorriee, and a lady in waiting because, why? She introduced herself to you?" He shakes his head. "I daresay, Prytore Charles, you have forgotten your place." Prytore Keon's words strike a nerve not only with Prytore Charles but others watching the scene. I find it curious; Prytore Keon must be more influential than I first realized, though Jonas did mention, I was wearing the best-known family crest here.

Prytore Charles takes a moment before he huffs. "I am sorry, Prytore Keon, I did not mean any disrespect to you or your family."

"And the lady?"

"Lady Gelsomino has my apologies as well. But I do hope, the lady reconsiders her choice, as her fate with this one will be nothing but disrespect to her born name." He walks off with that, leaving me flustered and feeling alone.

"Anyone else have an issue that I am here to find a mate for my fiorriee? As I am sure some of you are doing the exact same thing for yours." Prytore Keon calls out to the embarrassing crowd. No one speaks up. "Well, go on with your lives then. There is nothing more to see here." They all scatter slowly away. "Are you all right?" Prytore Keon asks. I shake my head no, causing him to frown. "Peyton, take her to her caretaker. I think she has had enough socializing for now. The others can wait."

"Will she be attending this evening's events?" Peyton asks, concern in his tone.

"That, Peyton, is up to her," Prytore Keon responds. "I hope to see you soon, Lady Serena." He walks away without another word.

"Come on, this way," Peyton offers.

"How do you know where to go?" I ask.

"Because I know where my Prytore guards those he cares about." Peyton answers, walking us out of the courtyard. We do not speak again until we are alone in the hallway. "Why did you not let me fight them?"

"I did not like the idea of you getting into trouble and disqualifying yourself," I answer. "Selfish, I know."

"You care, even after all these warnings of what you are getting yourself into? You are clear, we are not denying them, right? That you will be in service mostly as a mate but also for whatever Prytore Keon asks of you. Not that parenthood will be your only life. Once earned, you do get to do other things, but your primary purpose is exactly as they say."

"Do you hate your service?" I ask, looking at him and causing him to stop walking.

"I did, at first, until I was broken," he admits. "Finding a mate that I could love is my reward for great service. As you can see, they trust me. But I am the family's servant. I am aware of being owned much more than most fiorriee. Not that it is a bad thing. It is not. But it does hold a stigma." He brushes the loose white hair from my face. "This is not an easy decision, Serena. We want you to choose us because you are beyond sure. Please, talk it over with your caretaker. Think about it.

You will be called upon tonight, but considering what just happened, I doubt it will be by us. Go, enjoy yourself."

"How can I do that when I have fallen in love with you?" I ask honestly.

"It is not just about me, Serena," he reminds me, starting to lead me down the hall again. When he stops in front of the room, I pull myself into him. "It is all right, these guards, Draskin and Riywok, are here to protect you, not harm you. You are not a prisoner to this room, but you must express your permission to them for anyone to enter it. If you leave, they will follow you. They are yours until the end of courting."

"I was liking *you* as my bodyguard," I complain.

"It hinders your freedom of choice," he retorts. My pouting causes him to lift my chin. "I will miss you." He kisses me lightly and vanishes before I can register his taste. Annoyed, I walk into my new room.

Six

Dear, You Are Our Queen

Serena

The moment my door closes, I turn to my caretaker. "They said you were threatened, and I need not to worry, but I am worrying anyway."

Madam Takira looks up from her knitting. "I am fine, dear child. They swore no harm would come to either one of us, and they kept their word."

"They as in the ones who threatened you?" I asked, annoyed. "You trusted them?"

"I had reason to." She frowns, putting down her needles. "Come now, I am sure you have much more interesting questions than what happened to me."

"You realize that by following their orders, you got me sabotaged, and I was almost disqualified!" I hiss, angry. "You should have said something!"

"I was waiting for Prytoree Alexis' move before I revealed my hand. Good thing I did too. She saved the day without a lot of upheaval," she answers dismissively.

"Yeah, except for the part where Prytore Charles called me a whore and accused me of already officially choosing Prytore Keon and Peyton. Were you aware the service they are offering was full-time?"

"Come, Serena, do not tell me you are that naive. You allowed them to mark you, more than once. They stressed you would be mating with Peyton. What did you expect?"

"I expected you to stop me from making bad decisions," I snap at her.

"What makes you think this is a bad decision?" she challenges, causing me to look at her in a new light. "Serena, you feel safe with them. You and Peyton had a connection the moment you laid eyes on him. You think it natural for a fiorriee to offer their hand? When have you ever had the instinct in your entire life to offer your hand?"

I stare at her, thinking back, she was not wrong, it is not a natural thing for us to do.

"So, what if your service means that you get to have lots of children with someone you feel safe with. And to boot, you seem to like his Prytore too. Do you have any idea how lucky you are? Most fiorriee on Artthemis see mating as a burden, much less being able to raise their offspring and care to their Prytore's needs. Most do not like one another much less agreeing on how to raise children. The Silviu want a fiorriee that brings happiness to Peyton and his mate. This is an ideal situation, I promise."

"Great, I can be a mom," I reply a little too sarcastically. I understand all too well how amazing that is for our kind to have such a rare opportunity. "But full-time service to Prytore Keon?"

"This will not make sense to you Serena, but Prytore Keon is offering you more freedom by demanding more of you than any other Prytore here. His offer carries a stigma because others simply do not understand it."

"Prytore Charles remarked that the Silviu family only wants me for my bloodline. He said they had plans for my sons."

"Do you feel they are only interested in you for your name?" I raise an eyebrow at her.

"I am serious, Serena. You need to consider long and hard what is being offered to you. This is a life sentence. You need to be sure they have the true intentions you seem to want to give them credit for."

I ponder that in silence for a long moment. "Peyton feels I need to talk to others, just to be sure."

"And you do not?" I shake my head no. "Then you do it for Peyton," she encourages.

"Why have you kept my identity from me?" I ask, tucking her advice aside to consider later.

"Because your father wanted it that way," she answers.

"How did you know my father?" I ask.

She stares at me for a very long time before she answers that. "He was my brother." I look at her, very confused. She stares at me for a long moment. "You used to know that, but the knowledge was lost with time." The comment surprises me, but I do not respond. "This is not an easy story to tell, nor will it be easy for you to hear." I sit down on the bed and wait. She picks up her sewing needles only to put them down again and looks at me. "I do not speak much about the war. Mostly because it is painful to me. You see, your father and I were born to the most honorable family on Trorain. Our parents were the King and Queen of the fiorriee, your father the Prince, I the Princess. In our kingdom, the bloodlines follow the male heirs, which meant when my father was killed, my younger brother became King. But by then, the war had destroyed most of our world. It was very difficult, though not impossible, to survive there. Prytores consider it uninhabitable, but I know a few fiorriee who stayed behind, and though their survival is grim, they do survive."

She shakes her head. "Your father met your mother when a Prytore was trying to steal her from Trorain. While Marcello was rescuing her, Aurora offered her hand. They married quickly after that and then they had you. But the war was so intense that they feared for your safety. Your father brought you to me and asked that I hide you away on the planet. You were not to reveal who you were until you had made the choice in a yellow ceremony. He made me promise that I would keep my silence on your identity until after you made your choice. Which is why I spoke up when I did. I knew the moment you instinctively gave your hand to Peyton, you had. And I was most confident when he had a hard time returning it to you."

"So why are you encouraging me to look at other options?" I demand.

"Because you need a real understanding of Prytore and fiorriee relationships. Besides, I am your aunt, and I have the right to make sure you choose happiness."

"Are my parents really dead?"

"The Prytores say they are. The kingdom fell years ago, and Trorain has been theirs for the taking ever since. They mine the moon for its uranium and coal now," she answers. "I have not been able to confirm. I could not risk giving away who we were."

"Princesses?"

"Not princesses, Serena. I am a princess. You are the Queen of the fiorriee."

"You are joking, right?"

"Afraid not." She frowns. "Your father did not have a son. Thus, the responsibility falls to you."

"Why was I never taught this? I never even heard of my last name in my studies."

"You were taught the history of Trorain royalty by a fiorriee for a reason. We never had a use for last names. They were assigned to us by Prytores." she answers patiently.

"My parent's names were not in those teaching, nor were ours."

"We were in hiding." She dismisses me unapologetically.

"What does all this mean?"

"Had the war turned out differently, it would mean a lot more," she answers honestly. "But since we lost, well, mostly it means a very strong bloodline. And that is something most any Prytore wants their hands on. You see, Serena, your father knew that if we tried to hide your identity forever or after your courting, then it could all be illegal, and you would be sold to the highest bidder. Announcing it during courting gives you the chance to choose, as a courting is Prytore law."

"If this is true, then why am I being shamed?" I ask. "Much less sabotaged?"

"That dress stands out, my dear. Most have realized they do not have a chance at winning your hand, so they are choosing very poor tactics to get you to change your mind, or at least feel guilty about it. As far as the sabotage, would you want to compete against a Queen?"

"They did not know that at first," I challenge. "I did not know."

"They knew you were beautiful. You are the most beautiful fiorriee here." She smiles, "It is intimidating, and the walls have ears here. Before you went to bed last night, everyone knew who you were, no question."

"Do you support my choice?" I ask, not wanting to think about those petty girls.

"Did you miss it, Serena? The moment your mother met your father, she offered her hand. As I said, doing that is not a natural instinct for us. Honestly, Serena, it usually only occurs naturally once, if at all. Which is why I was asked if you had practiced it."

"But I had not."

"I know." She smiles. "Think back to it for a moment. Why did you give him your hand?"

"Because he offered his and I did not think anything of it, I simply offered mine."

"Exactly." She smiles widely. "Males are known to offer Serena, but females rarely accept without thinking." I look at her, still not grasping it. "Come child, let me show you." She offers her hand to me, "take my hand." I hesitate before I appease her. "No, no, not like that." She corrects me, letting go.

"Like what? What did I do wrong?"

"You grabbed the top of my hand, not my palm."

"I did?"

"Try again." She encourages, offering her hand once more. I go to grab it, but I have to stop myself and think before I grab her palm. "See, it is not natural. Never in your life had you ever grabbed a fiorriee or a Prytore's hand on the inside, always the out. And never has a fiorriee, even your sister, appreciated having their hand held for very long. Think Serena, did you allow your sister to hold your hand for more than a few moments?"

"No, it is uncomfortable." I admit, thinking about it.

"Yet when you grabbed Peyton's, you simply put your hand into his palm, surrendering to his grasp until he decided to let go, and you were at complete ease."

"I would not say complete ease. His eyes are so silver, when he looks into mine, I forget to breathe." I admit.

"All the more evidence that you are meant for each other." She smiles.

"Then why is Peyton so hesitant?" I asked, frustrated.

"Hesitant?" she questions. "He did not exactly give your hand back to you, now did he." She reminds me. I glare at her. She rolls her eyes at me. "He is protecting you, dear child. There is more to the equation than just him. He wants you to be sure."

"You sound like him." I complain.

"Then I like him all the more," she replies with a smile.

"You said it mostly means a very strong bloodline," I clarify, turning to her as my mind digests all this information. "What more does it mean?"

"Serena, it is not important."

"It is important to me," I reply, annoyed.

"You have claim to all things fiorriee, and whoever owns you has the same claim."

"You mean the land, the minerals, and the jewels." I frown. "Everyone becomes very rich from my dowry."

"Which is why you had to choose without this knowledge, Serena." She sighs. "I am telling you now because you have done that. You need to be careful not to lose it, especially since their request is that you have company other than their own. I doubt it is to make sure everyone is sure. It is simply their way of being able to stake the claim fairly, stating you had the choice of others and declined."

"Thank you for letting me know all of this, I appreciate finally being able to step out of the dark." I walk over to the window and stare out of it, processing all the information I have been given in such a short amount of time. The day fades into night before I am disrupted from my thoughts.

"Forgive the intrusion my lady, but it is time for this evening's events." Guard Draskin informs me. I look to my caretaker who nods at me, and I exit the room with both Draskin and Riywok following me. When I get to the main hall, I place myself in the back of the group. The room itself is empty except for two open doors, one with the answer yes, the other with the answer no, above it.

"Good evening, ladies." Butler Whilf calls out to the audience. "Tonight, is meant to help you with your daunting choice. You will be given a handful of questions and, depending on your answer, will depend on which door to choose. Once all three answers have been selected, you will find yourself in the room of Prytores who are looking for the same qualities as you. Feel free to mingle among them. At the end of the night, you will be offered a flower. It is your choice to accept or decline one if not all of the flowers. Do not take the acceptance lightly, you are promising your time to these Prytores for tomorrow morning. However, deciding not to accept any will be considered a voluntary exclusion and you shall return home. I caution you, there is a limited number of flowers, and a limited number of opportunities to stay."

All the girls in front of me look amongst themselves. They all appear just as nervous as I do. "First question is: Do you want to embrace parenthood?" Some of the girls immediately head to the no door and I confidently approach the yes, leaving behind those who hesitate. I am grateful to Peyton and Prytore Keon for making me think that one through. "Second question is: Do you want part-time service?" The large group of girls that followed me in, did not follow me to the no door. Only a few did, Bethany being one of them. "The third and final question of the night is: Do you have limits in how far you will serve your Prytore?"

My thoughts flash to a conversation with Peyton, he obviously knew these questions before hand and prepared me well. Not even wanting to contemplate yes, I walk to the no door. And there, just as promised, is a group of Prytores. Prytore Keon is not among them.

"Impossible," Bethany hisses. "I was told he would be here. My caretaker went to great lengths to get the questions and answers. Where is he?" She scans the room frantically then turns to me. "You! You did this!"

"Is there a problem?" one of the Prytores speaks up.

I shrug. "Not for me, but Bethany seems very upset believing I did something, but my guards as my witness, I have not left my room since entering it until now."

"Prytore Booneya you must help! Serena is keeping Prytore Keon away from us," Bethany accuses.

"Do not be absurd!" Prytore Booneya bellows. "If you do not see Prytore Keon here, it is because you did not fall into his criteria. I assure you, he is in a room down the hall, where different answers led to him." Bethany looks astonished. "If you are not pleased with any of us, you are welcome to leave. But you are not allowed to change your answers."

I try to hide my smile, wondering which question Prytore Keon is hiding behind. I am sure it is a technicality; one he will reveal to me later. I was warned I would not see him tonight, so I am not worried that he is not here.

"I am happy to stay, thank you." I smile, walking away from Bethany, who tears up and works to compose herself by wishing to stay as well.

"So, you are Lady Serena. There has been much talk about you," a Prytore from my left notes, catching up with me, ignoring Bethany's drama. "I am Prytore Fulton."

I bow politely. "I have heard of you, Prytore Fulton."

"Oh?" he questions.

"Just as a suggestion as to someone I should want to meet."

"Are there any others you were suggested to do so?"

"Yes, Prytore Oba."

He smiles at me. "And do you trust this source?"

"I do."

"Then by all means, Lady Serena, join us." He walks me over to a table with three individuals. "May I have the pleasure of introducing Lady Serena."

"Lady Serena, this is my fiorriee, Roald, and this is Prytore Oba and his fiorriee, Zane."

"Good evening, gentlemen." I bow before I take the seat Prytore Fulton offers and helps me into.

"I must say we have been eager to meet you since you were first brought into our holding room. Such a disappointment to hear you confirmed your choice so early that evening. You did not give the rest of us a sporting chance," Prytore Fulton comments.

"Well, we do have the evening. The final decisions are not for two days' time." I smile, feeling nervous.

"Yet you wear Prytore Keon's dress, and he obviously does not share the same interest as you. Does this make you reconsider? Will we find you in yellow tomorrow?" Prytore Oba asks.

"Well, that depends on this evening, does it not, gentlemen?" I answer curtly.

"Indeed, it does," Prytore Oba agrees.

We have general conversations after that. Prytore Fulton spends his time bragging about his fiorriee, Roald, and what a great warrior he was. Apparently, he had served in the great war at one point in his life, but once he was released from prison, he became a prizefighter, which among our culture is a very noble profession. Prytore Fulton was looking for only the best to mate with his champion, and they are to raise the kids and tend to all of Roald's needs.

"So, you see, Lady Serena," he concludes the long, proud sell, "your motherhood would be much less demanding than those of Prytore Keon's, as we will acquire a fiorriee maid and you can spend more time with Roald and his career."

I smile at him. "That gives me a lot to consider. Thank you." It does not escape my notice; Roald has not said a word. I am curious if it is because he is not interested or because his Prytore does not give him a chance to speak.

"Before we discuss Zane, I would enjoy hearing about you, Lady Serena." Prytore Oba smiles. Zane shifts nervously in his chair. "You are a mystery to us all. Some of us thought you were long dead."

"My father wanted it that way," I reply dryly. "He was a strong believer of choice. He and my caretaker, or should I say, my aunt, went to great lengths to ensure that I have the opportunity to become my definition of happy."

"Is it true, you were in an orphanage this entire time?" he asks with sincere curiosity.

"It is. One place where you are never lonely, that is for sure. I had lots of brothers and sisters growing up. Always had someone to play with. We were all educated in Prytore and fiorriee ways. Personally, I had a private tutor on how to please a Prytore when in service. I was never told why, but it all makes sense now," I answer, wishing I had more water in my glass for a distraction. I am painting over a lot of ugly parts. I do not want them to see the pain that my childhood memories left me.

"You were never in service before this?" Prytore Oba asks.

The question takes me off guard, causing me to make direct eye contact. "How could that even be possible?"

There is sudden tension at the table until Prytore Oba waves his hand dismissively, looking away. "Forgive the question, Lady Serena. You just handle yourself with such poise. It is sometimes hard to believe you are new at this. I give compliments to your personal tutor."

"You are well trained then," Prytore Fulton notes. "Excellent. That is simply excellent." He nudges Roald, who smiles awkwardly in my direction.

"When did you discover your true identity?" Prytore Oba asks. "Are you aware of what it means?"

"I discovered my identity and subsequent dowry the first day of the courting ceremony," I answer truthfully, leaving out that it dragged out for two days.

"I see," he answers. "Has your caretaker been doing her homework? Has she informed you the Silviu family is in financial trouble? They need a lady of importance to save them."

"Oba." Prytore Fulton scuffs at him.

"What? The lady deserves to have all the facts. She is, after all, making a lifelong decision. And I think it is fair she knows what all the other ladies surely know already." He turns his attention back to me. "Not to say the Silviu name is mud. It is not. It is highly prized in our society. But it is in trouble."

"I appreciate the information," I reply, finishing what was left of my water in one quick gulp.

"May I?" Zane asks, grabbing my glass with a smile. I meet his eyes for the first time and realize he seems hopeful, completely opposite of Roald, who seems bored and will not stop staring off in the distance.

"Of course," I agree politely. Surprised at the pull I feel for him.

"Thank you." He smiles back, jumping up to refill my glass.

Boldly, I turn to Prytore Fulton. "While I appreciate your company this evening, I have a very strong impression that Roald is just not that into me."

"Nonsense. You like her, yes?" Prytore Fulton turns to Roald, hoping to calm my doubts. Roald simply shrugs. Prytore Fulton turns to me with a frown.

"I am sorry, you seem very nice, but if you want to keep your fiorriee a champion, you are going to need to find someone who is going to make him happy."

Prytore Fulton stares at me then at Roald. "Is she right? Do you have a preference you have not told me about?" Roald leans into him. "I see. Well, Arabell is from a good family. We will determine her interest." Prytore Fulton turns back to me. "You are very special, Lady Serena. Whoever you choose is a very lucky family." He excuses himself and Roald in search for a better suited fit.

"I admire you not allowing them to waste their time." Prytore Oba compliments me. I give a nod, and Zane returns with my water, surprised to find less company at our table, but he does not seem disappointed. "If you will excuse me," Prytore Oba continues, "I believe the two of you need to be more acquainted, and my presence would only hinder your ability to actually get to know one another. That is, if I am understanding your interest correctly, Zane."

"You are, Prytore." Zane smiles, keeping his eyes on me.

"Lady Serena, dare I say, you would like to satisfy your curiosity?" I give a bashful smile, causing Prytore Oba to excuse himself.

Zane leans back in his seat. "You know, even if you were not a true Queen, I would treat you like one."

I raise my eyebrow to that, but I do not reply. "I was raised to believe that a true relationship allows for two individuals to stay individual but also to be a pair. Now I know that sounds complicated, but it basically means, I am not going to suffocate you, or change who you are. You get to be you, I get to be me, and we get to enjoy each other's company." I nod encouragingly. "I am in royal service, as you would be if you joined me. We would have our task for the family, which means we would have plenty of fiorriee friends to speak with, but we would go home to each other every night. We would raise our kids in Prytore teachings, and when they came of age, they will attend a courting like this and make our Prytore family stronger."

My eyebrow raises; he is definitely seeing me as some sort of prize to win, as it would most definitely please a noble family. Not that any of that matters to us fiorriee. We are meant to please our Prytores with their instructions and then meant to celebrate each other. I am unsure what to say. I had just told my aunt that this is the exact life I do not want. The silence is awkward between us.

"You are beautiful," he mutters. I smile, unable to deny the pull between us, but I honestly do not believe it would be enough to satisfy me. I simply cannot see myself happy in his Prytore's service. "Tell me, Lady Serena, what can I do to make you happy today?" I look at him with curiosity, realizing he is simply trying to please me. And he is trying too hard.

"Tell me the truth, Zane, what do you mean by royal service? Is Prytore Oba really a nobleman, or are you keeping his station broad for another reason?"

"He is not a nobleman, my fiorriee Queen." He leans forward, speaking so only I can hear him. "He is in fact Prytore Maleko, the King of Artthemis."

"I am…I, umm…. Seriously?"

"Yes." He frowns, studying my reaction. "I have lost your interest."

"I am sorry, Zane." I frown, grateful he understands what I am thinking. "I find you interesting." He raises an eyebrow. "Okay, more than interesting." He smiles at that. "And I adore your honesty with me. But this is not an arrangement I am looking for."

"Is it because you have eyes for Peyton and Peyton only?"

"No." I assure him. "Believe me your red eyes are difficult not to get lost in. Not to mention the rest of you is rather appealing." I blush when his smile broadens. I force myself to look away. Wow, when did it get so stuffy in here? "But despite this, I simply do not see myself working for the royal family that destroyed mine. It is insulting and would be a humiliation to all our kind. You understand?" I ask kindly.

"So, it is not me. It is my Prytore." He frowns.

"If you were me, could you?"

"No, I could not." He admits.

"So, you were chosen by your Prytore?" I ask.

"Yes." He answers, his red eyes suddenly guarded.

"Are you in his full service?"

"Yes."

I lean forward and whisper lowely. "Zane, be honest with me. Do you need help? I will find a way to save you I swear."

He gives me a genuine smile. "You just made me even more pleased to call you my Queen." He replies, but his eyes are clearly guarded. "I am fine, Serena. I assure you. All I ask is that you please, I allow me keep my Prytore's secret. It will be announced, just not yet."

"Why am I special?"

"Because of who you are. I could never mislead my Queen, no matter the personal price to myself. I understand your opposition. Thank you for your honesty, Serena." He exits the table quickly. I have obviously wounded his ego.

"Something you said?" a fiorriee laughs, taking a seat without my permission. "Wow, this is proving infuriating."

"How so?" I ask, stabbing my straw into my ice.

"Have you not looked around? All these Prytores care only about the status they will gain from marrying us off. When in fact it is meant to be our choice. Well, at least, that is what the treaty said it was. Us fiorriees were meant to have free choice of who me marry and the dowries go to the Prytores. And look at it. They have mocked it down to the core dividing us down by class with colors, and even then, the politics of it all. I simply want to find a girl that I enjoy spending my time with. It should not be this tedious." He turns his attention to me. "Apologies, where are my manners? I am Erland." He offers his hand, but I know better than to take it. Instead, I rest my chin on my hands and smile at him. He drops his hand with a laugh. "Cannot blame me for trying. I guess your offer to Peyton might be genuine after all." His purple eyes penetrate mine.

"It was."

"Yet you are here, talking to me." He notes seriously as I look him over. He has long white hair, but I cannot tell the exact length as it is combed into a beautiful braid with silver beads. I realize I am staring, and I look away with a blush. "Do you mind my company, Lady Serena?"

"Not at all," I reply.

"Interesting. You do seem to be making the rounds of all the different types of options available to you. But none of them will compare to me."

"Oh?" I ask, in a bored tone. This guy is really into himself.

"You see, I plan on winning you over with my dashing good looks and charming personality," he answers, showing his beautiful teeth. Well, he is not wrong about his good looks. I realize I am staring again and look to my drink for a distraction. "Rumor has it you are very cultured. But have you been outside of the city?"

"I cannot say that I have," I answer truthfully.

"There is a lot to do there. More than the city can offer, really. We can explore all the possibilities together."

"Sounds interesting. What does your Prytore have you doing in his service?"

"Almost anything I want, so long as the crops grow. He does not much care how I spend my time. During harvest and planting season, I am rather busy and could use a hand, but my day-to-day chores are much relaxed and done by noon. My Prytore is a rich landowner, so he brought me here to find a wife. He should not have bothered. All these girls seem to have ever done is stare at themselves in the mirror. I have nothing in common with any of them."

"And you are hoping to find common ground with me?"

"Not with you wearing that white dress." He frowns. He studies me for a moment, "Unless that is why you are here, talking to others. You are confident in your choice, but you are not sure of Peyton's. After all, did he give you that dress or was it his Prytore?" I find myself narrowing my eyes at him. "You did not give him much of a chance, you know. Peyton barely greeted these ladies before you gave him your hand. Next thing he knows, he is staring at papers, revealing you are our long-lost Queen. He would have lost his head had he not taken you to his Prytore and tried to court you. How I would have loved to have been in that room, seeing how they persuaded you so quickly, making sure the rest of us do not have much of a chance."

"You are a very confident speaker, Erland, but I assure you, your theories bare no fact," I reply coldly.

"Do they not?" he asks. "You know your version of the story, Serena. I am sure they keep asking you how you feel about your choice. After all, this mockery is designed to make it all about the female fiorriee. But can you honestly tell me, my Queen, that you bothered to verify Peyton's choice?" I drop my gaze to the table. "Is tonight not proof enough that he is hoping you might find another? Look at the predicament he left you in. If you do not earn a flower, how will you proceed?" My gaze shoots to his purple eyes. "You seem to have shooed off those you spent most your evening with. I doubt they will be giving you yellow flowers." He pulls his from his pocket, taunting me.

"You want something," I conclude.

"You are quick." He smiles.

"Well, go on then, out with it," I reply, unamused.

"I want you to sit here and give me a fair chance." He smiles. "Truly forget about Peyton for the rest of the evening and allow yourself to enjoy my company. Not as an obligation to clear any political doubt that is surely to follow with your boldness but as a true gift to yourself, to take the time to get to know another."

"I have gotten to know others."

"Okay, but they are all friends of Peyton's." He shrugs. "He and I have never formally met. You are our Queen, Lady Serena. Are you setting the best example to all of us?" I adjust uncomfortably in my chair. "Is it true, you really did not know who you were?"

"Not for most my life, but I am quickly adjusting," I reply, seriously.

"Are you feeling the burden of it yet?" he asks.

"I am sure it has only just started," I answer, leaning back in my chair and stabbing my ice some more.

"Lady Serena, would you be as so kind as to accept this dessert as a good will gesture?" Prytore Tokala asks, placing a plate of pie and two forks on the table between Erland and me. "I am not sure if you remember me from last night. Allow me to reintroduce myself, I am Prytore Tokala." He smiles hopefully. "We are honored that you are spending time with us, possibly allowing yourself to consider a more leisurely life."

"If I were not open to possibilities, I would not have come," I reply. "Thank you for the pie. May I ask the flavor?" It looks like an orange pie, but the smell is all wrong.

"Oh, it is a rare fruit for a rare lady." He answers evasively. "If you will excuse me, this is about Erland and you, not me." He walks off, smiling proudly.

"That was cryptic," I complain.

Erland looks around and then leans forward to whisper. "Because it is smuggled." Shock crosses my features. "It is from Trorain," he adds, leaning backward.

"Erland, it is not polite to lie." I frown.

"As if I would ever insult my Queen in such a way." He picks up his fork. "But if you do not want to try it, more for me." Hesitantly, I take up my fork and try it. I am not expecting the jolt of electricity that greets me. He holds back a laugh. "Sorry, I should have warned you about the flavor. It tends to tickle purebloods like us."

"You seem too young to be a pureblood," I challenge. The Prytores have gone to great lengths to nearly eliminate purebloods from existence. Most those my parents' age have been forced to mate hybrids. Almost every fiorriee in this court, male or female, is a hybrid.

"I am nearly the same age as you." He shrugs.

"I was in hiding."

"I was left to starve." He frowns at his memories. "But I am stubborn, refused to die. Lived on my own for a bit before I was discovered. Got a purple shirt and a one-way ticket to the dreadful planet, for punishment of being captured." He takes another bite and chews slowly. "Guess I got lucky. My Prytore has seen me as a good agriculture fit. He really only cares for the crops. I was not kidding when I said we would be left alone for adventure. You ask me, it is as close to freedom as either of us will ever get on Artthemis."

"You mean to say you were left to starve on Trorain?" I ask, astounded.

"It is not something I share with just anyone," he answers, meeting my gaze.

"I do hope you respect the privacy of this knowledge."

"I am a true lady, Erland. I know how to be discreet and respectful."

"Spend the day with me tomorrow," he pleads. "There are two left, one for me, one for Peyton. What is asking your potential family for a day in the grand scheme of all this?" I hesitate, unsure how to respond. "Think about it, Serena," he warns with a coldness that causes chills. "Accept my offer or face elimination." I glare at him. "Forgive my bluntness, but those really are your options. Choose wisely." He winks at me as he excuses himself, not giving me a chance to respond.

Zane crosses the room and looks at me. "Serena, are you all right?"

"Fine," I answer, studying the tablecloth.

"Liar," he says, sitting down next to me. "He upset you, it is obvious."

"He was just taking advantage of my vulnerability," I answer truthfully, swallowing my tears and trying not to shake.

"Vulnerability?" Zane questions, wrapping an arm around me. I am shocked at how comfortable that feels. "What do you mean?"

"The flowers, Zane, if I do not receive flowers tonight, I am disqualified, and the one Prytore I could count on is not here."

"And what did he want for his flower?" Zane asks in disgust.

"My open mind and willingness to commit tomorrow with him," I answer.

Zane's features etch themselves into anger, and he waves his hand at his Prytore. "I do not advise that, Lady Serena."

"Zane, what is it?" Prytore Maleko asks, causing me to look up and stare at his ridiculous Oba glamour.

"I have decided who I want to give my flower to," he responds. "It goes to Lady Serena."

"The fiorriee who has shown interest in you but not me?" Prytore Maleko questions, looking at Zane in disbelief.

"Prytore, please, she has been nothing but honest with us all evening. We each get a flower. I am asking that she not be disqualified for spending time with us to make the informed choice her father went to great lengths for her to make. Even if we do not agree with those choices."

"There are others here, Zane. She just spoke to another," Prytore Maleko persists.

"One who offered her a flower in exchange for an entire day with him? Do you not see she is wearing white? Accepting would insult and shame the family whose crest she is wearing," Zane replies bitterly. "Please, Prytore, if nothing else, I would be honored to have Lady Serena as my friend."

"You forget, Zane, I am not exactly friends with Prytore Keon, much less Serena's entire family," Prytore Maleko replies dryly.

"Then think of this as an olive leaf for peace and acceptance between our two species. She is my Queen, Prytore. To have her eliminated in such a humiliating way is unbearable to me. Especially since I can stop it. I am sure it would not go well if it were discovered that you had an opportunity to maintain peace and you chose not to."

"I do not take kindly to threats, Zane. I am your Prytore. That trumps your once Queen," Prytore Maleko answers coldly.

"It is okay, Zane. I appreciate all you have done, especially being so bold as to stand up to your Prytore in public like this. It is not necessary. I promise, I will be all right," I answer, trying to pull away, but Zane grips me tighter.

"I will marry your favorite, just please, do this for me, Prytore."

"Zane, no," I protest, "do not. He knows not his own mind." I snap at Maleko.

"Your choice will be granted, Zane." Prytore Maleko smiles, walking away from us.

"Why did you do that? Do you even like her?"

"Not really, no. But it would not matter. I am very particular when it comes to caring for females. I tend to lean more toward males, though my Prytore need not know I told you that."

"Oh." I frown. "Who is your Prytore's favorite?"

"Bethany." He sighs. "

"Zane, I cannot let you marry her! No matter how disinterested you are."

"Are you kidding?" He leans in close, speaking so softly I must strain to hear him. "After what she did to you, it is the perfect revenge. Plus, she does not realize she is not only being a lifelong mother, but her extra duties are also to include royal laundry and cooking the rest of her days. She will be miserable. All her mail will be censored and rewritten of happiness. Meanwhile, the Prytore and I will have our own happiness. It works out. Do not fret, Lady Serena, even this was a bit of a show. I was asked by my good friend Peyton to make sure you advanced. He told me you should compare these flowers to your favorite, lilies, is it not? So please, do not take Erland's offer, okay?"

"Peyton asked you to advance me?" I ask in just as low of a voice, feeling grateful yet offended. "This whole thing was a charade?"

"Oh no, Prytore Maleko and Fulton, not to mention Erland, are quite real. I was not lying. I would treat you like the Queen you are, but I could never love you the way Peyton does. The others in this room are self-interested Prytores who treat their property poorly. Peyton could not stand the idea of you spending a second with them, but he wants you to make an informed choice. Forgive us for interfering, but we are simply trying to protect you from ill intention Prytores."

"What do you mean by treating property poorly?"

"It varies… limited food, embarrassment, neglect." He shrugs.

"Are not your plans for Bethany neglectful?" I ask cautiously.

"Ha, no, she can have whoever she wants in the castle. She will be satisfied. She will get pregnant through medical means. She need not worry. She wants to be a mother. Her time will be spent raising hybrids and teaching them how to cook." He turns to me. "Do you seriously have an issue with her fate after she had all your clothes shredded?

Especially after she knew you were her Queen and wanted you to lay down on the ground. She needs to be taught a lesson in humility."

"How do you plan on getting her to say yes to you?" I ask, avoiding a real answer.

He smiles. "Leave that to us."

A bell rings, and we are told it is time. Zane lets me go, and I feel the loss of his touch. Shaking it off, I walk over to the stage and stand with my competition awaiting flowers. The Prytores and their male fiorriees each line up with one flower a piece. Zane ends up at the end of the line which makes me uneasy. All I can do is trust him now. The line moves slowly as each male walks in front of each female, stopping and starting as flowers are given. Bethany is three fiorriee down from me and is starting to look nervous as her hands are as empty as mine. Near the end of the line, Roald steps in front of me, whispers thank you in my ear as he continues to avoid my eyes, and hands his flower to the girl standing beside me. She must be Arabell. I smile at him, happy that he got the freedom to choose. Directly afterward, I find myself surprised when Prytore Fulton hands me his flower.

"For your honesty, Lady Serena." He smiles.

I smile back in relief, and whisper thank you to him. Erland is right next to him, meeting my eyes. I shake my head no, and he gives his flower to the other girl standing next to me. Avoiding Erland's furious expression, I watch as Prytore Maleko gives his flower to Bethany. Before the line shifts, I feel my arm being grabbed. I cry out in shock and panic when I feel lips touching my wrist.

"No!" I scream, trying to pull away, terrified I was going to be flooded by an unwanted taste.

Seven

Humiliation

Serena

Roald is the quickest to react and punches the offender out cold. "Are you all right, Lady Serena?"

I am shaking all over, fighting tears and trying not to vomit. "I do not taste him. I did not want that. He had no right!" I cry out, staring at Erland's unconscious form. I hate the attention I am drawing. I feel violated, ashamed, and just want to run away to the nearest shower, but Keon had made it clear that I make a scene if someone tried something I did not want.

"It is okay," Zane says, cutting the line and giving me his flower. "You are okay. You did not let him in. You are going to be all right." Zane turns to my guards. "Are you going to do something?" he demands.

This annoyance seems to dethaw both Guard Draskin and Guard Riywok from their confusion and together they come over, pick up Erland and take him away.

"My Lady Serena, I am so sorry. Please know Erland will be punished greatly for this," Prytore Tokala apologizes, looking embarrassed. I am too stunned to notice he is placing his flower in my hand. Before I or Zane could react, a guard that is dressed differently than the others, grabs Prytore Tokala with a scarred hand and escorts him away. I say nothing as Prytore Tokala pleads for me to help him while he passes Prytore Charles in the doorway. Thankfully, Tokala's drama ends quickly. I am about to look away when Prytore Charles catches my gaze, gives a small bow with his chin, then follows behind Prytore Tokala and the guard. When he is gone, I realize I have not stopped shaking.

"Come, let me take you to Prytore Keon," Zane offers.

"No!" I cry. "I want my Aunt. I feel so…" I cannot speak the words; instead, I fall into sobs.

"I know we are not friends," Bethany starts, standing next to Prytore Maleko. "But I am proud of you for denying him. It is not an easy thing to do." I nod, not sure what to say to her. "I did not believe that you were our Queen. It seems I was sorely mistaken." Prytore Maleko glares at her but says nothing as he is still pretending to be someone he is not. "I am truly sorry for the disrespect you have experienced the past few days. I know Peyton and you have taken interest. If I somehow managed to interfere with your choice in any way… Oh my Queen, you were rushed into white. If it pleases you, I have a spare yellow dress that will give you more freedom to choose."

"Selfish," Zane whispers in my ear. He was not wrong. I just received one of the top three biggest insults of our kind, and she makes a subtle move for Peyton. "Do not worry, Roald is getting Peyton. He will be here soon."

"Please, no. I do not want them. I want my Aunt," I beg Zane. "I want to wash this off, can I please wash this off?" I reach for the nearest water glass, but Zane moves it away.

"I know, my friend. I know. But you do not understand, you must wait." He sighs, guiding my hand away. As I fall to pieces, I find comfort in Zane's embrace while I soak his shirt.

"Where is she?" Peyton cries out before he even enters the room. He does not take but a moment to find me. He dashes at fiorriee speed to me, kneeling in front of me in the blink of an eye. "Serena?"

I cannot look at him. I am too ashamed. Instead, I sob and shake harder in Zane's chest. Peyton takes my arm, and I cannot help but look. It is not blue; it is bright pink, and it is on fire.

"Who did this!" Peyton demands, jumping to his feet.

"It has been taken care of," Zane answers him.

"I assure you, it has not!" Peyton responds coldly. "Who did this!"

"Peyton?" I cry. "Please, I just want out of here. This hurts badly," I bury my face back into Zane's chest, embarrassed by the crowd. "I need to be clean. Please."

Peyton's anger seems to melt. "I know, Lady Serena. Do not worry. I will help you. I promise." He assures me as he takes me out of Zane's arms and into his own while standing up. "Zane, this is not taken care of until I say it is. Understood?"

"Understood." Zane acknowledges, turning his attention to Roald. I do not get to see what happens with that because Peyton carries me out of the room and into another one.

"I apologize for the intrusion, Prytore Keon, but your presence is needed immediately," Peyton calls out.

Prytore Keon turns his attention from the girls in line to Peyton. I feel my burning arm being pulled away from my stomach and outstretched for viewing. I cry out in excruciating unpleasant pain, and I see the flowers that must be his and Peyton's being handed off to another Prytore in line as he rushes over to me.

"Who dared?" Prytore Keon demands.

"Trust me, I am on it," Peyton answers turning and taking us out of this room.

"It hurts!" I whimper when I feel my arm being examined again. I look away, feeling a fresh wave of shame washing over me.

"It is okay, Serena. We will help you. Peyton, take her to her room. I will meet you there as swiftly as I can."

Peyton does not need to be told twice to go to warp speed. He stops at the door, knocks once, and enters in a hurry. "What the zarla is going on? Who dares to break down the door?" Aunt Takira demands then sees my arm.

"Oh dear, oh my precious Serena," she says, looking at my wound. "My bag, Peyton, give me my bag." Peyton places me on the bed then rushes to give my aunt her bag. "Serena, it is me, Aunt Takira, I need you to calm down for me. If you do not calm down, this is not going to work. Can you do that?"

I look at her but she is out of focus. "Just wash it off." I cry, feeling a cool sensation on my arm, but it quickly starts to burn. I cry out in true pain.

"It will not work, not until she calms down."

I feel myself being lifted, and suddenly Peyton is under me, his arms wrapped around me.

"That is not going to help much." Aunt Takira scolds. "Your anger is matching her agony."

I hear him give a loud huff as he takes my uninjured arm and tilts my head to the side. His warm breath is in my ear. "Serena, my beautiful love, I need you to breathe for me," he whispers calmly, rubbing his finger on my blue palm. "What is that for?" he asks as a flash goes off.

"Evidence," Aunt Takira replies. "If you can get her to calm down soon, it will not scar, and we will need it."

"Scar? This can scar me?" I ask, shocked, causing the tears to fall harder.

"It is all right, Serena. It will not come to that. I am so proud of you for not letting him in. You are going to be all right," Peyton attempts to soothe me, but I can detect a hint of tension in his tone. "Calm for me, please." His lips gently press against my neck as he tries to get me to relax.

Prytore Keon enters the room. "How is she?"

"In agony and scarring!" I cry out, still shaking violently.

"Shush, Serena, you are going to be just fine. You need to breathe," my aunt counters.

I can feel Prytore Keon's gentle fingers on my arm. "I do not understand," he tells my aunt, "I have never known a fiorriee to react this way from denying a mark."

"Because you have never seen it happen to a pureblood," Aunt Takira answers. "Now you understand the concern I had the first day, though I could have treated it faster had she rejected you."

"Takira, it burns!" I scream, unable to control myself, and fall into more screams.

"What do we do?" Prytore Keon asks Aunt Takira.

My aunt studies my arm for a long moment before she speaks. "You two, help me with her dress, quickly now," Aunt Takira orders. I feel hands all over me stripping me down to my slip. "Now the two of you, stay here. I might need you yet," she barks, picking me up and taking me into the shower. Closing the door, she strips me down, and I cry out when I feel water hit my sore skin. "I know, Serena, I know. It is all right. It is almost gone. See, cleaning you off. Making it go away," she encourages. I feel her scrub at it the way I want to, and then I feel her leave it alone and work shampoo and conditioner through my hair, scrubbing my scalp with her nails. "That is it, calm down for me, sweet child. You are going to be all right. You did it, my child. You found those whom you love and who love you in return. I am so proud of you," she whispers, rinsing the soap from my hair.

She scrubs my arm for me one last time before she takes me out and helps me dry off. She puts me in a clean robe and takes me back to the room. There she puts me behind a dressing shield and places me into a white nightgown. I am surprised there are clothes at all until I see the Silviu crest on the gown. Alexis must have given me more than just one white dress. Takira carries me to the bed and places me back into Peyton's awaiting arms. "Now, let us try this again, shall we?" She smiles, encouraging Peyton. "Here, let me show you what needs to be done." I hear her tell Prytore Keon. She applies the medicine in stages, and soon, the burning stops altogether.

"Why did it work now and not before?" he asks.

"Because she was hysterical. She needed to be calm, which is not an easy thing for a pureblood to be after denying a mark. You need to be careful, Prytore Keon. Purebloods are more delicate than hybrids like Peyton." She pats Peyton's hand. "No offense, love."

I cannot see his response, so I have no idea if he is offended or not. "Serena, have you come back to us?" Peyton asks in my ear, kissing my neck. I nod. "Good, you had me really worried there."

"I did not encourage that. I did not even realize he grabbed my arm until it was too late," I whisper.

"We know. You resisted, just as you should have," Prytore Keon answers taking my healing arm.

"I feel strange," I reply, my stomach is all twisted in knots.

"You will." My aunt explains, "Your body is designed to accept markings, Serena. If your mind chooses to deny someone who got that close to you, your body reacts violently. This will pass, once your mind settles. Your skin will heal in time." Her kind tone vanishes when she turns her attention to Prytore Keon. "I hate having to stay away. This is how things happen."

"She was with friends and guards," Prytore Keon defends.

"What good it did her. Explain to us again why you deem it necessary to stay away from her when you clearly want her and she wants you?" Aunt Takira continues. "Enough is enough."

Prytore Keon turns to me. "Are you all right?"

"Getting there." I smile. "My mouth tastes like acid."

"Side effect of the medicine, my dear," Aunt Takira answers.

"Does this help?" Peyton asks, taking my good wrist and kissing it lightly, filling my mouth with his taste. I smile, feeling a little better. He offers my wrist to Prytore Keon, who gingerly accepts and hesitantly kisses me. I smile.

"You taste good. Did you eat something with pepper?" He laughs, placing my arm at my side.

"See, when she wants it, it is a very pleasing thing," Aunt Takira reassures him.

"Would she react like this if ever she decided she did not want it from us?" Prytore Keon asks her.

"Not this severely, no. She has let you in. Resistance would definitely give her away, but it would not harm her like this," she answers.

"Good, I do not ever want to hurt her like this," he replies to her. I feel a cool rag on my skin. "She is healing and likely will not scar. She is fine. You should not stay much longer. It is not good for her reputation as a lady in waiting."

"I am reluctant to let her out of our sight," Prytore Keon admits.

"My niece is in good hands with me. Has been for the past twenty-three years," Aunt Takira reminds him.

"Would it be improper for us to be alone with her, for just a few moments?" Prytore Keon asks.

"Yes," she answers, "but you need not worry. I know how to mind my own business." She walks away from us with her back turned, and I know her well enough to know she will not move until they are gone.

"Come, Serena," Prytore Keon calls. I lift myself off Peyton and fall into Prytore Keon's arms. "I am so sorry. We should have been there. Had we not been hiding behind a technicality we would have been."

"It is all right. I got to meet a champion fighter in person." I smile, pulling him close.

"And what did you think of him?"

"Could he be more boring?" I ask, rolling my eyes. "Zane was… nice. We started a friendship. But that is all." I pause, and I can feel Keon holding his breath. "His Prytore is my father's worst enemy."

"Picked up on that, did you?" Peyton frowns.

"You call him a friend." I note, causing Peyton to study me. "How are you friends with a fiorriee who is so close to our enemy?"

"Careful, Serena." Prytore Keon warns. "That is my King you are referring to."

"I apologize Prytore, I mean no disrespect." I frown. "Forgive me, I am still processing the fact my parents are actually dead, much less the circumstances."

"Adjust to the past quickly, Serena." Prytore Keon warns. "It has no place in our home."

I nod, surprised at how difficult that command is. I am about to pull away from Prytore Keon all together when Peyton places his hand in mine.

"How are you friends with Zane?" Peyton asks, causing me to bite my lower lip.

"I cannot explain it." I admit in a small voice. "I just trust him."

"So do I." Peyton replies, moving my hair off my face. "I do not fault him for his choice of lovers, Serena. Fiorriee have benefited greatly with Zane at Maleko's side."

"Was that intentional?" I ask, causing him to raise an eyebrow at me. "Do not underestimate my intelligence, was it not you who asked Zane to marry Bethany?"

"He may have volunteered." Peyton replies, looking away. "Even Roald was willing."

"That is strange to me." I admit. "Roald will not even bother to look at me." This causes Peyton to give both Prytore Keon and my aunt a strange look before he brings his attention back to me. "Well, now that you know who Zane's Prytore is, how were you treated? Fairly, I hope."

"Prytore Maleko was cordial enough." I shrug. "Though he seemed a little threatened by my title. But perhaps that is my oversensitivity to everything going on." I shake my head. "He allowed Zane to give me a flower."

"Your only flower?" Prytore Keon asks, curious. Looking around the room.

"No, Prytore Fulton gave me one for honesty," I explain. "I refused to waste their time when I realized the champion fighter was pining over another."

"And the third flower?" Prytore Keon asks.

I lift up from his arms. "There should only be two."

"But, Serena, there are three." He points out, looking at me and at the table where Peyton had left them. "My room had a different kind. These came from yours."

"It could not have been Erland. He had given his away after my refusal," I mutter, my mind thinking back. "It was his Prytore."

"Erland offered you a flower and you refused?" Prytore Keon questions.

"Of course, I did. He wanted a day with me. I never agreed, but he upset me with the fear of being disqualified, until Zane reassured me, I would not be." I swallow hard. "Then Erland…" I hide my face as the memory repeats in my head. "Roald knocked him out in one punch, and I sat down. I was so upset, but Zane was with me. Prytore Tokala apologized to me then begged for my mercy when a guard with a scarred hand took him away."

"Ershprek." Peyton states in a flat tone. "I thought you had reassurances he would stay clear of her."

"I did." Prytore Keon replies. "I cannot explain his presence."

"I screamed." I state. "Prytore Charles was in the doorway. He nodded at me." I reply pulling my eyebrows together. "Then he followed Prytore Tokala and the guard down the hall."

"Well, that explains Ershprek. He was with Prytore Charles." Prytore Keon sighs. "Do not get upset about either of them, Peyton. They helped her."

"This time." Peyton states. "But you are just as protective of her as I am. And we both know how Ershprek got that scar."

"How?" I ask curiously.

"That is a story for another day, Serena." Prytore Keon dismisses my question, causing me to bite my tongue in annoyance.

"Do you have any other details of this gruesome story?" Peyton asks me. "Or can we lay it to rest?"

I give him a smile. "No, you know everything." I assure him. "Even Bethany was surprisingly nice. Well, what she and her friends pass for as nice, anyway." I look away from both of them. "I hate this place." I decide. "I want to leave now."

"I will see what can be arranged," Prytore Keon responds without hesitation, kissing the top of my head. "Serena, are you a thousand percent sure you want to leave with us?"

"Yes." I answer, sick of this question already. "What must I do to convince you two that I am sure?"

Prytore Keon hooks his finger under my chin and kisses my forehead. "Be good for us, your fate is almost sealed." He kisses my sore arms wrist softly, his eyes examining the skin to be sure I am in fact healing. He finds that the mark is not completely gone yet, and with a tight voice, he gently returns it to me, "Come, Peyton, it is time Serena comfortably dreams about her new life."

"Prytore Keon," I call as they climb off the bed and walk to the door.

"My Serena," he replies, looking at me over his shoulder.

"Could my aunt come with me?" I ask, hopeful.

He raises an eyebrow to that. "Not at first, but if you earn it. I will not deny you. Assuming she would want to." He smiles at her before he and Peyton leave us in our secure room, guarded by those Prytore Keon seems to trust.

Eight

Be Mine

Serena

When I wake the next morning, I feel restless. I do not want to go through these ceremonies anymore. I have chosen, and they have chosen me. My caretaker, who has been my aunt this entire time, seems to support my decision. Admittedly, it is something I would have never dreamed of selecting as a young girl, but I am a young woman now, and after peeling away the thin layer of fear, I see the beauty in my choice. It saddens me that others cannot. What is so wrong about motherhood? My arm still hurts. I look down and frown, realizing it still has a pink tint to it. "Do not worry, Serena, it will fade. It is just a reminder," Aunt Takira reassures me when she catches me staring at it.

"Will I forget this feeling too?" I ask softly.

"I am afraid that will stick with you, dear." She sighs, running her fingers through my hair. "Let me curl this for you?" she offers.

I follow her to the bathroom but before I sit for her, I do my morning hygienic routine, dreading today. After she curls a few strands of my white hair, she touches my face gently. "Aunt Takira, what do you know of Zane?"

"Are you having doubts, Serena?" She worries as she rolls a hot iron in my hair.

"No, I just… why do I feel so safe when he holds me? How has he even gotten that close to me? You have known me all my life, Aunt Takira. I have never allowed anything like this, much less within a day."

"It is not uncommon for fiorriee to bond with friendships just as quickly as we do relationships. This just shows Peyton is good for you. Your heart is blossoming." She smiles at me. "I am proud of you, Serena. Your parents would be too."

"Tell me about them," I plead, knowing this is my last chance for a long while to ask.

Before she can answer, there is a knock on my door. I frown, but we go to it. There we find Prytoree Alexis. "Good morning, my dearest Serena." She smiles, holding a bag as long as her. "May I come in?"

"Of course, Prytoree Alexis." I nod. "I was just getting ready for the morning gathering."

"Yes, about that." She smiles. "Prytore Keon has made some arrangements. You need not worry too much about them. Just know that you will be at Peyton's and his side most the day."

"That is comforting news," I reply in relief, relaxing for the first time since I woke.

She places the bag on the bed. "Come, Serena, I have a surprise for you."

"Another?" I ask. "Prytoree Alexis, you have been so generous already! I have not even gotten a chance to wear half the clothes you brought here."

"You should not, for you are no longer a lady of white, Serena." She smiles, unzipping the bag.

I cannot help the gasp that leaves my throat when I see the most elegant dress. "I take it you like it?"

"It is stunning. What does silver stand for?" I ask, unable to stop staring at it.

"It means you have made your choice, Serena, and that we accept your decision," she answers.

I turn to her. "So, this too is an early gift?"

"Yes, it is. Prytore Keon is quite insistent that the process be rushed in order to honor your request," she informs me. "Something about you hating it here?"

"After last night, who can blame her?" Aunt Takira replies.

"Yes, everyone has heard." Prytoree Alexis frowns. "May I?" Turning away from her gaze, I allow her to examine my arm. She lightly glides her fingers over the angry pink skin. "From my understanding this was worse last night. It is healing then?"

"Yes Prytoree," I answer, feeling vulnerable and pulling away from her, covering my arm.

"My dear, if you are having a hard time showing me, the onlookers." She worries. "Look at your hair. It is only half finished. I shall be back in a Prytore flash." We watch her go. When we are alone my aunt turns to me.

"Serena, you realize the moment you are seen in silver with their family crest, there is no turning back, right?" Aunt Takira asks.

"I am okay with that," I assure her, causing her to give me a strange look. "Honest, Aunt Takira, it is Peyton, not Zane."

She studies me for a moment before she speaks. "I worried so much about you finding your mate. I forgot to worry about it being in proper form."

"My dearest aunt." I laugh. "When have you ever known me to do things the way they are supposed to be done?"

"Oh, you." She laughs with me, walking us back to the bathroom. She turns the ends of my long hair into large cascades of curls and pulls the sides into a fancy braid then twists them into a bun. While she is doing this, I try to ask about my parents again, but she tells me it is too long of a story for such a short amount of time. When she is finished, Prytoree Alexis is waiting.

"I could not get you gloves." She informs me, clearly frustrated. "Prytore Keon is being selfish about it," she explains, "but I got you this." She holds up a silver silk shawl. "You can cover your arms in this to avoid prying eyes."

"Thank you," I smile, truly grateful.

"Oh, that is not all." She beams. "Sit down here. You are going to love this." She reaches into her bag and pulls out nearly invisible strands of tiny silver flowers. "I am not sure if you are aware of this, but Peyton's favorite color is silver." She works the flowers into my hair, braiding them together to create a beautiful crown. She adds some smaller ones to drape from it that mix in my hair "From a distance they are almost invisible, but if someone is fortunate enough to be close to you, like Peyton is, they are noticeable." She smiles, studying me "Come, let me help you into your dress."

The dress is more sophisticated than any I have worn so far. It is pure silk and slender but wide enough for me to run in like the wind, if I so desired. The beading is dark navy, and while the designs are different, the emblem of the family crest is the same. She works the shawl around my arms, showing me how to cover the ugliness. Then she opens a box, revealing the most beautiful royal-blue strappy heels I have ever seen. Together we twist them around my legs then she helps me to my feet.

"Stunning." She compliments me. "Absolutely stunning."

"As are you, Prytoree Alexis." I blush, for she is expertly dressed herself. "This is almost too much."

"No, it is not enough," she disagrees. "There is something missing."

"Oh?" I ask.

She walks me to the door and opens it, revealing Peyton and Prytore Keon standing in slim silver suits. I look at my aunt, who just smiles with a shrug, and I turn to Prytore Keon. "Good morning, Prytore Keon. Good morning, Peyton," I offer my hand.

Prytore Keon is the first to take it but quickly hands it off to Peyton.

"Shall we?" Prytore Keon offers his arm, but Prytoree Alexis takes it before I can. I look to her apologetically. "Ah, I see my wife has left you completely in the dark. Good, I do enjoy pleasant surprises." Prytore Keon notes. "This morning, our beautiful Serena, is meant for you and Peyton."

I look at him and then at Peyton. Peyton clears his throat, a bit nervous, and nods. Content, with my hand in his, I pull us a little closer, feeling happy and secure.

Peyton leads us down the hallway. Prytore Keon and Alexis are behind us but not in Prytore earshot, and behind them are two guards I have never seen before. The ones I am familiar with stay at the door, protecting Aunt Takira. I absolutely hate that they are necessary, but I know they are.

"Where are we going?" I ask, my curiosity getting the better of me.

"Somewhere special."

"I am already in your arms, Peyton."

He laughs. "Thank you."

"You seem nervous."

"I am."

"Why?"

"You will see," he answers, giving nothing away.

He takes us down the stairs where the rest of the court seems to be amid their morning rituals. I look at him strangely when we walk past the sea of white dresses and into the courtyard. I do not miss the stares of astonishment and annoyance as we do so. Nor do I miss that one of Bethany's friends is wearing red, a color she did not start out in or that Zane is standing a little too close to her for my liking. Nor does Bethany seem all that amused. Feeling disturbed, I shake a little as I try to push past these strange feelings. When the doors close behind our party, Peyton turns to me. "You seem disappointed not to join them. We could go back," he offers.

"Never." I glare, hoping he is teasing me. "Where are we going?" I ask again when he leads us out of the beautiful courtyard.

"I am not going to spoil it now," he answers, pulling me tighter to him.

"We could run like the wind," I offer.

"We could, but we will not." He shrugs. "Zarla, you are absolutely stunning. And I love your hair."

"Please, I am ordinary standing next to you. Look at how handsome you are. Have I ever told you how much I love the way you style but do not style your hair?"

He laughs. "No, I cannot say I have heard that before." He turns me to him. "Close your eyes, Serena." I do not even hesitate at the request. I feel my body being lifted from the ground and then gently placed back down. It only takes a moment. "Open them." I do so and find that he and I are alone next to the most beautiful waterfall I have ever seen.

"Peyton, it is wonderful." I smile.

"We only have a moment alone, Serena. The others will catch up to us." He cautions. I turn my attention to him with the intention of kissing him, but he stops me. "Serena, please, this has been so unusual. I need to hear it one more time. Are you sure it is *me* that you desire for the rest of your life?"

Annoyed with this insecurity, I resist the urge to roll my eyes at the question. "How much time do we have?"

He seems taken aback by the question, but he answers. "Two minutes, tops."

I look around and realize we really are alone. "I will answer this for you, Peyton, but you must promise it will be the last time you ask." He raises an eyebrow at me. I delicately and purposely drop my body to the ground, expecting the gasp that comes from him. Fiorriee are very proud species, and to intentionally lie on the ground in front of another is a sign of truest respect. But I take it further and grab his ankle.

"Serena," he whispers, his voice unsure. But I tug on his foot and place it on my cheek.

"This is my answer, my Peyton."

He quickly removes his foot and jerks me to a standing position. I am surprised at his sudden movements, but I cannot ask because his lips are attacking mine.

"Aw, here they are!" I hear Prytore Keon holler from a distance. I turn my attention to him and realize he and Prytoree Alexis are with more than just guards. My eyes widen in terror.

"Do not worry," Peyton whispers. "I swear, they did not see."

"Thank you," I whisper back on his lips.

"No, Serena, thank you," he replies, kissing my forehead and putting too much distance between us, little as it may be.

"Could not resist getting her alone, I see." Prytoree Alexis smiles when they get closer.

"Do you like the waterfall?" Prytore Keon asks as he and the others get into conversation distance. I blush. "I cannot say I noticed it much."

Everyone laughs. "You have not spoiled the surprise?" he asks Peyton.

"No," he answers as Alexis picks up my shawl and hands it to me. I blush deeper and work to wrap it around me quickly.

"Good." Prytore Keon praises. "Peyton." He nods encouragingly.

Peyton's nerves come back to him, and he drops his lips to my ear for just a second. "Please, behave." I look at him, confused, but he is smiling. "Serena Gelsomino, from the moment I met you, I knew my days would not contain happiness without you. Getting to know you in this short time has been a wonderful experience. You are a breath of fresh air. Serena," he says, dropping down to both his knees, presenting a large black box. "Would you do me the highest honor of becoming my wife, acknowledging that you feel the same, that I am your other half?"

I do not bother to even open the box. I set it aside and take his hands. "The honor, Peyton Silviu, is all mine," I smile with tears in my eyes.

Prytore Keon applauds and turns to the two men that I recognize as Prytore Umang and Prytore Booneya. "Prytores, you are witnesses to this beautiful event. Lady Serena has willfully accepted Peyton's proposal, and they shall be wed by the setting of Akatite tonight."

"We agree she has not been pressured," Prytore Umang states.

"Well, assuming one cannot pressure a lady in a few moments time." Prytore Booneya retorts.

Prytoree Alexis frowns and turns to Prytore Keon, looking worried. "Excuse me, Prytore," I chime in, dropping my shawl from my injured arm. "Forgive me for talking out of turn, but I am assuming you are aware of last night's events?"

"It is not secret," Prytore Booneya replies, looking to my arm, the pink standing out from my blue shimmering skin.

"So, it is known that I can resist a mark if I so choose to." I continue. "And I can accept one if I choose that as well."

"Your point, Lady Serena?"

"If you are questioning if I am being pressured, then let me be tested."

"Fine, but not with that arm," Prytore Booneya agrees as Prytore Umang nods in approval.

I turn to Peyton, and without hesitation, I offer my good arm. He takes it in his grasp and makes a show of marking me, one I am not truly prepared for, and I find myself needing to brace my weight on his shoulder to avoid my knees buckling beneath me. When he finally releases me, I am flushed and blushing.

Prytore Keon approaches me. He makes his actions very clear, but his influence is very mild. When he is done, he shows my arm to the Prytores. "As it is known, Serena's skin had an immediate reaction when she resisted. There is no reaction here, for she is not resisting."

The Prytores look at one another. "We shall witness freely." Prytore Booneya states. "They shall be married by the setting of Akatite." Without another word, they head down the path in which they came, leaving us alone.

"Come, Serena," Prytoree Alexis calls as she picks up the black box and the shawl. She hugs me tight, pinching and twisting the skin on my shoulder, rewarding me with desirable pain. "Good girl, very quick thinking." She pulls away and helps place the shawl back. "I am only sorry you had to endure further embarrassment to prove your point."

"It is all right." I frown, feeling better that it is covered. "Guess it proved useful."

"My Peyton," Prytoree Alexis calls. Peyton is at her side instantly. "I believe your future wife needs this for your wedding." He nods. She touches his face lightly, and they share a stare so intimate I look away.

Prytore Keon notices and takes my hand. I look up at him, not too uncomfortable with the gesture, though it does feel strange. "I do hope one day you and I can share moments like that."

"We will," I reply confidently.

Prytoree Alexis breaks away and opens the box. It is customary for a married fiorriee to wear a collar. Aunt Takira always has. But I am astonished to see this one. It was delicate and much smaller than most. The silver is laced with purple and navy blue.

"It holds secrets, but time will reveal them," Peyton teases me.

"There are no words," I shake in awe.

He places it around my neck. "My beautiful, Serena, when the Trorain moon is at its crescent tonight, this lock will seal forevermore."

"It is too long of a wait," I reply turning to him. He responds by kissing me.

Nine

Prytore's King Revealed

Serena

I was not expecting this when I woke up this morning. Living it does not make it any more real. I feel as if I am dreaming and the last thing in the world I want to do is wake up. The Silviu's had planned a semi-private picnic for us near the waterfall but in a distant view of the courtyard.

"This food is amazing." I compliment, hungrier than I thought I would be today.

"It is nice to see you have a healthy appetite considering how much you have gone through these past few days." Prytore Keon notes. He takes my injured arm in his. "I do hope, it helps this heal faster." My eyes lock in on his knuckles, and I grab Peyton's hands and stare at them as well. Keon's are scabbed over and Peyton's show marks of recent healing.

"Is there a problem?" Prytore Keon asks when he sees me glaring.

"That depends. Is Erland alive?" I ask coldly.

"Does it matter?" he retorts.

"Very much so," I reply, causing even Prytoree Alexis to hesitate. I understand it; this is her fear. Her family has laid themselves out onto a branch, and depending on how I feel about this answer, everything can fall apart before their eyes.

"We prefer him not to be, but we had a feeling you would object," Prytore Keon answers, bitterly.

"You harmed him?"

"If you are expecting an apology, do not look to me for one." Prytore Keon sneers. "Look at what he has done to you. You are a Queen of his own kind, for zarla's sake!" His eyes turn hard, and he turns away, hiding the anger in them.

"Serena," Peyton interjects, "you understand that we will defend your honor. It is part of what you are agreeing to."

"I am not an advocate for violence." I frown.

"Nor are we," Prytoree Alexis reassures me, "but you are our family, and there are things that must be done to protect that. Serena, I know all this is new to you, but do you understand the risk it is to accept a fiorriee Queen into our care? We are painting targets on our back. But we do not mind because we know it is worth it. However, small threats like this cannot be tolerated. If they are, worse things are surely to come."

Alexis always has a way of showing me the whole picture; it is one thing I truly like about her. "To be honest, I do not understand all the risks you are taking, Prytoree Alexis, but I am aware there must be some. Otherwise, why would my aunt have kept me hidden until now." She gives me an appreciative smile but does not speak the rest of her thoughts. I turn to Peyton. "Promise me, it is done."

"Serena." He frowns.

"No, you made your peace and carried out what you consider justice, with these hands. Promise me it is done. I do not want the reminder of this. Once my skin heals, I never want to think of it again."

"You are asking him to promise something only I can give you," Prytore Keon replies dryly. I turn to him. I can tell he is not happy. "You are asking me to promise something I do not want to give you." It is my turn to show frustration, and I do so by stabbing my food. "Serena, he harmed you." The memory is so vivid my body starts to shake. "I am sorry, Serena," he decides, "but I will only promise to end the physical violence."

"It is the best offer you are going to get, love," Peyton whispers, wrapping me in a hug. I cannot look at Prytore Keon, but I nod my acceptance.

"Good, now I believe that Eshnaine is setting. We would love to prolong this meal, but you have expressed that you will miss your aunt, and I find it fair that you spend the rest of your limited time as a free woman with her."

They all start to pack up, refusing my help, though I offer it several times. Once everything is packed away, we walk back down the path and into the courtyard. The ladies in white are paired with possible suitors at this point. And sadly, the girl in red is nowhere to be found. As the crowd begins to notice us, some look at us with envy, some with respect, and others with disgust. I am surprised when Zane makes his way over and stops in our path, halting us in the middle of the courtyard. "Fine choice, Lady Serena. Peyton is envy to us all." He is smiling but I can see the hurt in his red eyes.

"Thank you, Zane." I smile. "Peyton truly does make me happy."

"Do you hear that, fellow fiorriee? Our Queen has found true happiness." He bellows out, grabbing a glass from a nearby table. "To Peyton and Serena, may your years be blessed."

I am shocked to see how many fiorriee take up their drinks, especially since most of them had a hand in sabotaging me. He turns his glass to his Prytore. "And to you, Prytore Maleko. Long reign the King of Artthemis!" Suddenly the glamour of Prytore Oba flashes away revealing Prytore Maleko's true face.

"Hail to our King!" The crowd chants before another drink.

Zane sips his glass then steps aside. We clear the courtyard without any other disturbance, and when the doors are shut behind us, I turn to Peyton. "Surely, there was intent behind that."

"Whatever do you mean?" he asks, studying me.

"Please, Bethany may be a snob and may know a lot of things, but I doubt she knew exactly who Prytore Maleko was until Zane's little display." I shake my head. "All part of their act, I suppose. The King was not introducing himself properly, and Zane blatantly told me the truth. He probably told her too."

"You are not wrong, Serena." Prytore Keon smiles. "He did that so publicly just now because she was not believing him. Especially since you turned him down."

"Selfish fiorriee if she believes her Queen would do anything less." I hiss, causing Prytore Keon to raise an eyebrow at me. I shake my head. "To be clear, that is not the title of royalty going to my head. That is my pride, defending my parents' sacrifice. The idea of serving their enemy for life sickens me. And the idea any fiorriee wanting to, knowing what happened to their ancestors…it is insulting, is all."

"Except for Zane?" Peyton questions, studying me.

"He has earned my friendship. Though, I do not, by any means, support all his choices in lovers. Besides, I get the impression I am missing facts." Peyton gives me a half smile that confirms my assumption.

"You were taught of the war by a fiorriee?" Prytore Keon asks, changing the direction of the conversation.

"My personal tutors included both Prytore's and fiorriee." I shrug. "The topic of the Trorain War was very interesting to me, as none of my tutors ever seem to agree with each other. I found it fascinating, considering the results ended native life on the moon."

"They never told you who you were during those teachings, not even a hint?" he ponders.

"I am sure my aunt forbade it," I reply, thinking back on it. "But anything with science and life on other planets has always fascinated me. I find it a shame. Both our species had the opportunity to explore it, but avarice destroyed the scientific wonder."

"Did they speak of your royal family?" Peyton asks, climbing the stairs toward my chambers.

"Of course, I can name them all, up until my parents and aunt. Guess they were left out for a reason. Ugh, I found those tests so dreadful. I never understood the reason for stuffing all that knowledge in my head, and to think, I was learning my family tree." I shake my head. "My entire life has a new perspective on it. I guess it will take a while to see it all with the knowledge of this filter."

"That will take some time," Prytore Keon agrees, shooing away the guards to my chambers.

"Which is why I want my aunt to come with me. Her husband died years ago. I hate knowing her fate is to return to that wretched orphanage." I frown, pleading with my eyes.

"Who says she is returning to the orphanage?" Prytore Keon asks. "You think I would bring you into my family and not protect those you love? My sweet Serena, you have a lot to learn about me." I do not respond to that. I just keep his gaze, waiting for him to elaborate. "Your aunt has the freedom to settle where she chooses, within limits of course. Once you have been broken, you can and will be rewarded with visitation. This is not a permanent goodbye, Serena, simply a temporary one."

"How short is temporary?" I ask, trying to hide my nerves.

"That ultimately is up to you, Serena," he answers. "But expect it to be a while. You have much pride to you, and that will not make the task easy." I swallow hard, nodding. He kisses my forehead. "We shall see you soon." He steps away and takes Prytoree Alexis' hand leaving a distance between them and Peyton and me.

"You have honored, pleased and surprised me so much today I fear I am in a dream," he confesses.

"Funny, I have the same feeling." I smile.

"If it is not real, I never want to wake up." He pleads. He kisses me softly on top of my hand. "Soon, we will not have to part like this." He lets go and moves to join our Prytores. I smile at them while I open the door.

When I close it, I fall to the ground in tears.

Ten
Overwhelmed

Serena

"Serena, dear, what is it?" Aunt Takira asks, worry etched all over her features. She picks me up. "Not the floor, dear, never the floor." She scolds, bringing me to the bed and sitting me down onto it. "Did they upset you? Have you changed your mind?"

"No, nothing like that," I mumble into her shoulder.

"Then what is it, dear?"

"Everything!" I scream out, crying harder. She falls into soothing tones and holds me close, doing her best to calm me, though she surely has no idea what 'everything' really is. I pull her closer, crying until my body is exhausted from it. I pull away and see the purple stain on her clothes. "I ruined your outfit!" I realize, causing a fresh wave of hysteria.

"Come now, Serena, they are just clothes," she mutters, holding me. We hear a knock on our door. She pulls away from me. "I will not be long. Grab some tissue by the nightstand. The last thing you want is to ruin that dress." She walks so swiftly to the door she is a blur. "Prytoree Alexis," she answers, "I am afraid you have come at a poor time."

"Serena? Is she all right?" Prytoree Alexis worries.

"She is fine, dear, just a little overwhelmed, is all. She has had a lot thrown at her these past few days. It was bound to catch up with her sooner or later. Judging by the collar, I am sure it is best this happened with me and not with her future husband on what I am assuming is their wedding night." Her words cause me to cry harder.

"Perhaps you are right. Peyton is a bundle of nerves himself. Having his wife fall apart would make both the men feel she regrets her choice."

"I assure you, that is not what is happening," Aunt Takira replies. "I have known Serena her whole life. She is very passionate yet very controlled. Sometimes, her control slips, and she feels everything all at once. You need not be concerned about it. She is very good at hiding this from everyone. The only reason I am witness to it now is because she has nowhere else to hide."

"I see," Prytoree Alexis replies. "Please, give this to her when she has gathered herself. It has been in my family for generations, and I would be honored if they too were represented in their union this evening."

"I promise, I will." Aunt Takira takes the small package. "If you will excuse me, I do believe I need to help my niece gather herself rather quickly."

"Two hours," Prytoree Alexis, replies.

"I have no doubt I can meet the deadline. See you at the wedding, Prytoree Alexis." She gently closes the door and rushes back to me. "Are you able to speak yet?" she asks, taking my arm gently. It takes effort to focus, much less focus on my breathing to calm myself. She waits me out, studying me. "So, what is 'everything' exactly?"

"I do not know how to explain it." I frown. "I never knew you as my aunt, but now that I do, I feel so much closer to you, and the idea of us parting ways, even for a short time, has me really upset. Not to mention the minefields exploding in my brain. I am the Queen of an entire species, one who are suppressed aliens on this planet. I am hunted. I have been all my life, not just by those who want to kill me but by those who want to liberate our kind. And here I am, accepting suppression, leading an example that I am okay with what the Prytores have done to us."

"Are you?" she asks.

"How could I be? How could I insult our ancestors that way? Doing so feels as if I am personally betraying each and every one. Yet when I am with the Silviu's, I do not want to be anywhere else."

"It is natural to feel conflicted, Serena. Our species is submissive by nature, but you are not wrong. The Prytores have taken advantage of our submission and turned it into suppression. Though it does not seem to be the case with Prytore Keon and Alexis. They seem genuine in wanting true submission."

"Perhaps. But it could simply be a deception like the Prytore King is doing with Zane."

"Do you think Peyton is acting?"

"If he is, he is good at it," I mutter.

"Would you rather we leave? Not choosing is an option, Serena." She points out.

"Doing so would cause a war." I frown. "Do not bother denying it. Others would see it as me not accepting this way of life, and a revolution would start, whether I wanted it or not."

"Your education has paid off, I see. I always wondered. You never seemed to want to listen." She teases.

"They hurt Erland, the one who hurt me."

"Good."

"I am not pleased." I frown. "And they refuse to stop, though they promised no more physical contact."

"He insulted his Queen. Marcello would have had his head on a pike for it," Aunt Takira defends them.

"My father and his willingness for war caused my kind to lose our home," I remind her of the sad truth.

"There is more to it, Serena. Surely you know that." She defends her brother.

"I do." I frown. "I want to change things, Aunt Takira. But I do not know if it is even possible. There are girls out there trying to win the Prytores' King favor, to be in service of our greatest foe, to be the truest example of suppression, and they are throwing themselves at them. It is disgraceful! I have no respect for them, none." Tears fill my angry eyes. "What happened to the fiorriee in red?"

"You noticed her, did you?" Takira frowns. "You need not worry, Serena. Like you, Geela stood up for her right to choose. And she too went on a difficult journey because of her refusal to conform." I frown at that. "The ancestors noticed her courage and took pity on her. She is now under their protection and could not be in better hands."

"The ancestors?" I ask, stunned. "Zarla, does that mean there is a god here?"

"Even if there were Serena. I could not tell you. The walls have ears here." She reminds me, looking around.

"Zarla this zarla suppression!" I seethe. "I have the mind to walk up to Maleko and slap him in the face!" I cross my arms over my chest. "I hate this suffering. Yet as it had been pointed out to me, I consider Zane my friend."

"Not everyone who serves under the King is doing so because they believe in this version of peace."

I study her for a moment before I speak, "Zane is playing a risky game if that is the case for him, considering what the King expects of him." She raises an eyebrow at me, but I shake my head.

"What do I do, Aunt Takira? Should I marry Peyton? Should we run?"

"I cannot answer that for you, Serena."

"Do you know what breaking is?" I ask, curious.

"It is a stripping of identity, of self, and above all, pride. It brings the submissive into a very pliable state. Once there, they are molded into whatever their superior desires of them." She shakes her head. "It is not a pleasant process, Serena. I hope they at least warned you of that."

"You know then."

"Of course, I know," she snaps, insulted that she would not have gathered every bit of intel that she could. "But it is not something for a true submissive to fear. It creates a bond like no other, one that is not easily dissolved. The fact that they expect this of you, Serena, tells us both that you are truly going to submit, not allow yourself to be suppressed."

"Is it true, is my dowry something they need?"

"Not financially, but yes, it is important." She takes my hands in hers. You must remember, Serena, you and Peyton chose each other before he knew who you were."

"What is Peyton's bloodline?" She raises an eyebrow at me. "Do not look at me like you would not know!" I snap, impatiently. "We are running out of time."

"His family is important, just as you, Zane, and Roald are."

"Zane, Zane serves the King of Artthemis!"

"Despite that, Zane can be trusted." She shrugs. "You have good instincts. You should follow them."

"You are telling me you trust three hybrids, two of whom you have never met?"

"Who said I never met them?" she asks. I glare at her; she looks at me, defeated. "Serena, there is not time to explain. But I trust those three with our lives."

"Wow." I whisper, knowing she is serious.

"Their parents also died in the war, Serena." I stare at her in disbelief. "But they are older than you, they remember them. And they are sworn to look after each other and you."

"Did they grow up in orphanages?" I ask, curious.

"Each one of you has had a unique experience on Artthemis." She answers. "And all but you have been forced to drink the life elixir." My eyes widen in terror. "It is not my place to tell their stories, Serena. But of the four of you, the ancestors have chosen to shield you the most." Tears fill my eyes to that statement.

"Why them?" I ask.

"They served in your father's army." Takira answers, causing my jaw to flex.

"Roald was a warrior before he was a wrestling champion." I recall, staring at her. "Which means Peyton and Zane." I swallow loudly. "Why have you kept this from me?"

"Because our home was not safe to speak of these things. Nor is this place." She answers. "I will not apologize. At least you had a childhood before you had the burden of this zarla crown." I stare at her. "The same crown that your father wore. And in the end, the weight of it took his life."

"Zarla." I frown, suddenly feeling the true weight on my shoulders.

"I am telling you this because you need to be careful, Serena. One wrong move and you will start a war. And you truly are not prepared for that." She warns. "Not yet. But after your breaking, I promise to tell you all that I know."

"Which leaves me with today's problem." I moan. "I am still unsure how Peyton truly feels about me. I know my feelings for him, but his…can hybrids ever give themselves away like purebloods, from an unwanted mark?"

"You think a mark from you would be unwelcome by Peyton?"

"If I am to do this, I do not want any doubts."

"No, not that I am aware of." She shakes her head. "You should go to him. You need to know his intentions are what they say they are." I nod. "Did you mean it? That by choosing the life that I am about to is the freest I can be?" I ask. Her eyes sparkle as an answer. "So once I am broken, there is hope in saving us all from crude suppression."

"Making a stand so young and naive to your heritage is risky, Serena. Lying low for a while is not a bad strategy for the end game. Besides, they take so well to you. I am sure you can persuade them to your views if you are subtle enough."

"You are truly your brother's sister."

"And you are your father's daughter, who possesses your mother's wit, innocence, and beauty."

"I shall marry tonight, Aunt Takira, if his intentions are true," I reply. "Do you remember how my favorite sister and I used to communicate?"

"Of course, but I never could figure out the source of your cipher."

"Do you find it ironic that we chose the *History of Royal Blood on Trorain?*" I ask. "We figured it was the one book you would never think that we would read."

"Clever."

A knock comes at the door. This time when Aunt Takira answers it, Prytoree Alexis lets herself in. "Are you well, Serena?"

"I am, Prytoree Alexis, thank you." I reach for the box she had left earlier. It contains a silver bracelet that I slip on my good arm.

"Are you ready to officially become a part of my family?" Prytoree Alexis asks, smiling.

"I will be, in just a moments time," I reply, flashing over to the bathroom so I can wipe my face with a towel to make sure no trace of my tears remain. I then flash to my aunt. "Promise you will be there."

"I would not miss it," she answers happily.

"I thought you might request that." Prytoree Alexis smiles, stepping through the open door and thanking a guard. She comes back inside with a dress. "But you must understand, we are leaving directly after the celebration. I am afraid this is your best chance at a goodbye."

I turn to my aunt once more. "You have taught me so much, how to be humble, wise, and most of all, how to follow my heart. I love you so much. I am going to miss you dearly."

"Thank you, Serena. Do not cry on me now. You just pulled yourself together."

"I will not." I laugh, blushing on purpose. "Thank you." I stand and walk to Prytoree Alexis. "I understand that she cannot come with us, but surely, we can write to each other?"

"Once the privilege is earned, I am sure my husband will show no objections."

I look over my shoulder and meet my aunt's gaze. "I do look forward to the books and letters you send, Aunt Takira."

She replies with a smile and a nod, and I know she understands. "Twenty-three years I have spent with you, know I treasure them. Farewell, Serena. May you be blessed with happiness."

I smile and exit the room with Prytoree Alexis.

Eleven

Elixirs and Blood Vows

Serena

"Are you sure you are all right? All that crying was simply from an overload of information, not because you have made the wrong choice?" Prytoree Alexis asks as she walks me down the hall.

"I have made my choice clear since the moment I have gotten here. Though I am beginning to think Peyton is the one who is uncertain," I reply, causing her to study me with disapproving eyes.

We walk in silence for a while. "Peyton is not unsure, Serena." She can tell I am not convinced. "I expected this. Erland has not exactly been shy with his theories. I figured he might have gotten into your head. Which is why I came earlier." She takes my hand and places a bottle of elixir in it. "A few drops of this, will temporarily cause Peyton's Prytore DNA to fall dormant. If you mark him in that state and he does not want you, you will know."

My eyes look at her skeptically while I shake my head, "I am sorry, I do not want to hurt him, the way Erland did me."

"Even if he did not want you, you do not run that risk. He is a male. He can only accept females that he truly desires, and doing so will cause such an intense reaction, it is unmistakable. But if he denies you, nothing will happen. This will allow you proof of his word. I warn you though Serena, it will be excruciating for him, not only physically but mentally. He might refuse to participate, as this will insult him. You ask at your own risk, for he may simply turn you away for not trusting his word."

"Thank you." I accept, watching her tuck the bottle in my dress. She picks up our pace. "You must make it appear to be your idea, but I will support you if you fall into trouble." I look at her, concerned. "Keon need not know the full extent of my involvement in helping Peyton be with his soul mate."

"Have I mentioned I really like you?" I smile as we walk into a wing that I am completely unfamiliar with. "We have a potentially beautiful relation ahead of us. Though I warn you, if he does not really love me, I love him enough to walk away from it all." She nods, looking blatantly nervous when she stops at a door and knocks. Whether from her own doubts of Peyton's feelings or if he is going to be insulted beyond forgiveness, I do not know.

"Alexis?" Prytore Keon answers surprised, he pushes the door open wider. "Serena? I thought you were headed down to the courtyard. Is everything all right?"

"Forgive the intrusion husband, but I think Serena and Peyton need a few more moments together before the ceremony." Prytoree Alexis answers, leading me into their chambers.

"Are you having doubts?" Prytore Keon asks, worry crossing over his features after he closes the door.

"She is experiencing nerves. Quite similar to the ones I had when I married you," Prytoree Alexis answers, causing understanding and a smile to blossom on Prytore Keon's features.

"You need not worry about your wedding night Serena, though being as pure as you are the nerves are natural."

I blush three shades of blue. "Prytore Keon, my dearest husband. Serena needs her future husband, not her future Prytore." Prytoree Alexis presses.

"Of course, she may enter his room, which will stay open at all times." Prytore Keon agrees, walking deeper into his chambers and opening the doors that lead to Peyton. I smile and walk through them when Prytore Keon politely steps aside.

"Serena?" Peyton asks, surprised, rushing from the window to my side instantly. "Is everything all right?"

"What were you looking at?" I ask, walking to the window to get as much privacy as possible.

"Nothing really, just thinking. I do not understand. I was not expecting to see you until the ceremony."

"That was before I realized I was being selfish." I answer, looking out the window myself. "All this time, you keep asking me if I am sure, and it has me wondering if in fact, you are the one who is unsure." He stares at me with cross features. "You took my hand Peyton, but from then on, you knew exactly who I was before even I understood any of it. Even now it is as clear as mud to me." He continues to be silent. "Are you being pressured to be with me because of who I am?" His features become more pronounced with disgust. I can tell I have indeed insulted him. "Please," I whisper reaching for his hands, but he crosses them over his chest, keeping them out of my reach.

"If you have changed your mind, Serena, do not try to turn it on me."

"I am not. I have not. I swear." I press on. "This is not about me, Peyton. It is about you. You, the one that had a prearrangement with Bethany before you happened to step away from her and introduce yourself to me." His eyes widen. "So, I am right."

"You think I want Bethany? You know her fate. You even called me out on having a hand in her punishment. She insulted you! You, the Queen of our kind, over petty jealousy. The denial of a bed possibly could have been forgiven, but to sabotage you and go as so far as to try to disqualify you. She needed to know her place." I glare at him. "I will defend your honor, Serena. I have made no secret of that."

"Is that all it is? Defending my honor, or is it a convenient way to tie up a loose end for breaking your arrangement? What made you speak to me after you met her? According to her, you were hers. She even told me she offered her hand the moment the ceremony started." He gives a harsh growl and turns away from me. "Peyton, we are about to wed for life. I deserve the truth."

"The truth?" he snarls, through clenched teeth, avoiding my gaze. "The truth was I introduced myself in hopes that I could possibly find a way out of that dreadful prearrangement. Bethany is out for herself and wants Prytore Keon, not me. And she can lie about wanting children all she wants. It is exactly that. A lie." He meets my eyes. "Most of us fiorriee studied together, Serena. We all know each other. You are the one who is a mystery to us."

"You were hoping for a hand, any hand at all." I accuse.

"Not any hand. The hand of the one I was drawn to. But this courting was my last chance to find it. Speaking to every female fiorriee was my last-ditch effort, and I thought what I wanted was impossible to find," he replies, not denying it. "Her friends knew her choice, but even they would not be able to resist an instinct if it happened. But I was kidding myself, to have a fiorriee instinctively give her hand? It is things you read in books, at least these days on Artthemis." He walks over to the window, checking his temper. "She did offer her hand. It was so practiced it made my stomach knot. I distracted her by placing a flower in it and told her that it was too soon, revealing affection within moments of the opening of court would cause unwanted questions. She agreed, told me to roam and come back to her. So I did, and then I met you and bent every rule in the book to keep you. If you recall, Serena, I did not want to let you go. I was terrified you were not going to confirm your choice. The papers presented to me meant nothing."

"I was an escape?" I ask, putting my hand over my mouth, trying not to cry.

"No, Serena, you are an answered prayer. I would not have been happy with her. I will be with you," he replies. "You are the one."

I shake my head, not wanting to hear any more. I do not trust that I am some miracle. I was just convenient. I turn to leave.

"Do not go, please," he begs, calling out to my retreating form while he stays next to the window.

"There is no reason to stay," I reply as tears fall down my cheeks. I remove the collar he gave me and place it on the table, heartbroken.

Not wanting him to see me cry, I dash to the doors of the adjoining chamber only to find it blocked by Prytore Keon and Prytoree Alexis, causing me to stop abruptly to avoid a collision. "Please, excuse me."

"Not happening," Prytore Keon replies with a shrug.

"You cannot keep me against my will. And you cannot force me to marry someone who does not really want to marry me," I hiss. "He simply just does not want to marry her."

"You are wrong." Prytore Keon frowns. "Not that we would ever force this on you. It is not our way."

"Then step aside."

"No," Prytore Keon responds again.

I look around for another exit, but there is not one. My eyes fall to Prytoree Alexis. "You always seem to know the right thing to say. Obviously, you want me to hear something."

"You have all the information you need, Serena. I simply wonder if you just do not understand the importance of it," Prytoree Alexis answers. "Your education is lacking in the most intimate rituals of your kind, which is astonishing to me, as you seem well educated in everything else."

"She is speaking of you offering your hand to me." Peyton clarifies from across the room. "A natural occurrence is extremely rare. So rare, it was believed to be myth before your mother presented hers to your father." He walks slowly toward us. "I understand why your aunt chose to leave it out of your teachings, Serena. The moment fiorriee girls hear of it, they tend to practice what looks natural, and it puts the entire thing to shame. Over half the claims out there of a natural hand are false, just so the girl can feel better about making a forced choice. I could not be more grateful that you were oblivious to it."

"My choice is not the one in question. Yours is." I remind him, refusing to turn and face him.

"You yourself have seen the façade a yellow ceremony is, Serena. Choosing Bethany was what we believed to be the best fit for me and our family needs."

"Her dowry, you mean."

"I will not deny I was shocked at the papers your aunt presented. Nor will I deny the relief because it meant that my family would be much more accepting to my choice. Did you not feel how formal our first meeting was? We barely spoke! You were being scrutinized down to the way your skin shimmers." He grinds his teeth. "Do you think I would put you through all that if I did not want you? That I would willfully mark you the moment I had a chance! And above all, challenge my family's prearrangements without speaking to them first! Do you have any idea what they could have done to me? That I could have been disowned and disgraced where I stood! You think I would do that for just any other girl, to avoid my Prytore's choice for me? I love my Prytores, Serena. I am very cautious not to put our family in any unfriendly light."

"Maybe but I was not just any other girl, I happened to have a larger dowry. You did not have much risk!"

"That is uncalled for." Prytore Keon hisses at me. "You think a lot of your dowry and a title, which means nothing to Prytores. It is irrelevant and had no consideration as to why Prytoree Alexis and I broke our word to some very powerful Prytores! We did it because we are in love with Peyton, and we value his happiness above all else."

I stare at Prytore Keon; he has just satisfied half my doubts. His glare, however, tells me he does not understand that though. "Thank you," I reply firmly. "Please understand I meant no disrespect, but I am also more aware than I let on. I never lied about knowing who I was. I honestly knew nothing of it until my aunt told Peyton. But I know my family history, and I know I am important, at least to my kind, and that concerns Prytores. You said so yourself, there are some here who would want me just because of my relatives and dowry, not giving a thought about my personality and happiness. I am aware of your family strains. I needed to be sure that you were rushing this because I asked you to, not because your need to obtain something I possess."

"You are protecting your family. Prytore Keon and I can understand and respect that. There is no harm done. I assure you," Prytoree Alexis says, giving her husband a pointed look.

He glares at her before he turns his attention back to me. "You are a very unique fiorriee, Serena. If Peyton did not love you the way he does, you would be dismissed from my sight indefinitely for pulling a stunt like this."

"So, I am not forgiven?" I ask, touching his hands. He raises his eyebrow at me. "Even after you have asked me over and over again if I was sure, and this is the first time I asked questions. I realize the questions are not pleasing to you, Prytore Keon, but are not you at least pleased that I asked? It was a green whale. It needed to be slain."

"Peyton, your future wife is almost as persuasive as my own," Prytore Keon responds, taking my hands in his. "I will forgive you for this, seeing as I did encourage you to be a hundred percent sure. I trust that you are satisfied, and we will not endure insulting questions or accusations like this ever again?" he replies in a very cold voice.

"One condition."

"There are conditions now?" he asks, astonished.

"It is a request for Peyton, assuming you will allow it." Prytore Keon's features remain hard, but there is no stopping now. I take the elixir out of my dress and present it to him and Peyton. "This temporarily blocks Peyton's DNA from interfering with a true reaction to a mark."

"You want to mark me and see if I react poorly?" Peyton asks in disbelief.

"No, I want you to take a sip of this and see your truest reaction to me," I answer truthfully. "Rumor has it, males' acceptance is legendary."

"What a lovely idea." Prytoree Alexis intercedes taking the elixir, not giving away the fact she was the source of it. "Peyton will drink it, and if he has the reaction you are hoping for, then it substantiates everything he has been claiming to all three of us since our arrival. But if he has a poor reaction, as is a possibility, he shall march himself downstairs and beg Bethany to forgive him. If she offers her hand, he will be punished but forgiven. If she does not, he will be disowned in disgrace." She turns to me. "Do you still want him to drink this, Serena? I know you love him. Do you want to risk him being disgraced?"

Before I could answer that, Peyton swipes the bottle from her and downs the entire contents in one hard swallow. My eyes widen in shock. He starts to choke immediately, gasping for air. "Water! Get him water. Now!" I cry, rushing to his side as he screams. "You fool! You were not supposed to take the lot of it. What part of a sip did you not understand?" He grunts as his eyes squint in pain. Prytoree Alexis hands me a full glass of water. "Drink." He shakes his head no. "I said drink," I demand, causing him to focus on me for a moments time. He takes the water and drinks it as fast as he did the elixir. He breathes with a grunt for several more moments before he manages to compose himself. "That tastes awful," he complains.

"Prytoree Alexis, maybe you can help him out?" She looks at me, puzzled. "Forgive the assumption, but I carry little doubt that you two have kissed before. Maybe you can help as he is unfamiliar with the way his body was originally designed, before all the meddling."

Understanding, she approaches Peyton and calls his name softly. She touches his wrist. "Shh, it is okay, love. May I mark you?"

"You have marked my soul, Alexis, you need not ask," he answers, squeezing his eyes open and shut, still fighting the effects. She smiles and brings his wrist to her lips. He gasps in surprise, and a smile crosses his face. When she stops, he looks at her. "It was worth it, that was amazing." She laughs but stops when he coughs. "It is all right. It is getting easier," he assures her. "Well Serena, must you keep us waiting?" he asks a little too sharply, but I brush it off because he is obviously in uncomfortable pain.

Gingerly I approach him. "Forgive me, for this test, Peyton, as I have forgiven you and Prytore Keon for testing my aunt's claim of my pureblood status the first night we met." He shakes his head. "I was the real thing, Peyton. Not a hybrid in a glamour."

He smiles. "You really are observant, my beautiful Serena." He climbs from his knees and stands before me. "Of course, the moment we realized you were in fact a pureblood and you had such beautiful reactions to our markings, we could not get enough."

My eyes click as the final piece of the puzzle falls into place. He does not notice as he is still randomly squinting. He offers his wrist. "Thank you for this, Peyton. It is an honor to have the possibility of marking you the way you have me."

Nervous, I delicately take his arm. Timidly, I kiss his wrist and press my tongue to his skin. His reaction surprises me so much I give a tiny squeal and step back. He gasps for air then looks at me. "I am sorry. I did not mean to frighten you. Please, do not stop," he whispers, offering his wrist again. This time I take it more firmly and bring more of my tongue to his skin. His entire body shakes, leaving no doubt in my mind. I am about to stop what I am doing when I realize he has grabbed my wrist and started to mark me. I gasp on his skin; the electricity that flows through our connection causes such intensity we are both shaking. The lights flicker around us. We hear a throat clear, and Peyton breaks away. He puts his back to me as we both gather ourselves from embarrassment of forgetting our surroundings. When we have both stopped blushing, he turns to me. "I hope this lays to rest any silly doubts you have of me and my choice."

"It does, thank you." I smile.

"No, Serena, thank you. You have satisfied more than just *your* curiosity." Prytoree Alexis praises. "I daresay we are cutting it close." She taps her watch for emphasis.

"You realize you used your only chance to ever take this off?" Peyton asks, picking up our collar. This time, it is for eternity.

"I could not be more pleased for that fate," I reply happily, lifting my hair so he can set it just right.

"You should prepare yourself; this collar is very unique." When he finishes securing it, he puts his hand around my waist. "Despite my prideful responses, I am grateful you came here, verifying this is what I wanted too. You are many things Serena, selfish is not one of them." He kisses my neck and releases me. "Prytoree Alexis, if you will."

"Wait."

"Serena," Prytore Keon replies to the new delay with caution in his tone.

"Erland."

"We have been through this, Serena," Prytore Keon snaps, his patience at its end.

"Do you not see? He did what he did to test me. What better way to prove to everyone that I am a pureblood and not a hybrid in a glamour, than to have me resist a marking? My arm still is not healed. He hurt me because he was testing to be sure I was who I claimed to be. Just as you and Peyton did."

"That is an interesting theory," Prytore Keon states. "You seem overly alarmed by this, Serena, why? Your identity is no longer a secret."

"My confirmed identity is not now either. My aunt kept me hidden for a reason, Prytore Keon. There are many sides to this dormant war, if any faction gets ahold of me."

"You think Erland was a part of a faction?"

"I do not have enough information to answer that. I just know his Prytore is a rich landowner who is not one to care much for law, or so I got a strong impression." I look at the window. "How much do you trust the wedding guests?"

Prytore Keon's irritation turns to concern; he looks to his family, who are looking at him for guidance. "We are going together." He decides. "Peyton, she is not to leave your side. Not for any reason. I do not care if she needs to empty her bladder. She is next to you; do you understand me?"

"Perfectly."

"Do not worry, Serena, we will keep you safe." Prytore Keon assures me.

The four of us walk through the chambers and out the door together. We make our way swiftly to the hall. "It is all right to look like a nervous bride, Serena, but you need to also look happy. You are safe," Peyton whispers in my ear. We walk down the stairs, and to my surprise, the courtyard is transformed with the courting guests all in attendance of our wedding. I look to Peyton with complete shock. "Tell me that you are not surprised so many of our kind would want to attend a wedding like this?" I nod, fearing once more this sends the wrong message to every last one of them here, including my fiancé.

We walk to the altar together and three Prytores performing the ceremony begin the very long drawn out process of songs, rituals, and speeches about choice. The only noteworthy ritual that I experience is not when Alexis and Keon give permission to allow Peyton to marry me. Nor when my aunt gives her permission for not only me to marry

Peyton but to join the Silviu family. It is when the four of us are bound as a family and Peyton and I commit our lifetime of service to Prytore Keon and Prytoree Alexis. This involves a blood donation that is mixed together to make a true union. I feel different after it happens, but then the feeling passes, and well, I hate to admit, I am bored, but it is the truth. Peyton picks up on my mood, and we both find ourselves having to stifle giggles. The Prytores are not amused by this, and we work to be better participants, though it almost makes it harder. Finally, we get to the part where we can speak, and I realize that is something I have not prepared for, consciously aware that I am setting an example. I have no choice but to think on my feet, trying to cryptically state my cause.

"Peyton, you surprised me. I came here worried that I would go through four courtings over four years and end up a cast off as so many I have known. Yet when our eyes met those worries vanished. There was no one else in the room, no proper rules of etiquette to be followed, there was simply you and I. Two fiorriee who never crossed paths before our fateful day. You have done nothing but honor and cherish me since, and I plan to give you nothing less in return. I love you, my dearest. I always will."

I risk a quick glance to my aunt, who nods in approval of my words. Subtle as they may be, I am rebuking the system of backdoor bribes and courting laws. Peyton is more nervous than me when he speaks; his skin starts to flush in embarrassment. "I cannot believe I dreamed you into existence. I cherished you the moment I laid eyes on you. I cherish you today and I will cherish you always. You are mine now Serena, and I will never let you go."

The Prytores go back to perform another ritual that involves our blood, hair, and reciting words of commitment. At this point my mind has almost shut off from boredom. Not that I have anything against committing to Peyton, but I do not see the need to recite a thousand words each on the matter, not to mention the Prytores' thoughts and opinions.

"And now, it is time for Peyton to claim his bride."

I snap my head to the Prytore, surprised, unsure what he means. Peyton smiles reassuringly and touches his neck, indicating the Prytore is referring to our collar. I smile and nod.

Peyton's eyes move to the sky, watching Trorain's nightly rise; he tugs my hand gently. "It is okay, Serena," he whispers, placing me in front of our audience while he stands behind me with his arms wrapped around me. "Brace yourself, love; this is going to be intense." Before I could ask, I feel a burning sensation on the back of my neck, from my collar fusing itself in place, but it does not stop there. I cry out in shock from the intense pleasurable pain that silver and navy snakes are creating as they slowly creep their way all over my skin. My entire body is on fire, and the burning only stops when I feel it in my toes. I blush in embarrassment when it stops, highly aware of our guests. "This is why you had to be sure," he whispers. "I would have never requested a collar like this for just anyone, Serena. Only for the woman I truly loved and wanted as my wife." He lifts my hands to my field of vision, and I look down in surprise; the silver-and-navy collar seems to have melded with my body. It shines and seems to act like my skin, but it is not. "It is more beautiful on you than I dreamed."

"Peyton." I turn to him, my eyes showing bewilderment that I do not want the audience to see.

"I warned you this was permanent, that I was going to keep you," he reminds me.

Unsure what to do, I kiss him despite the Prytores telling us to hold off. I break the kiss upon their insistence, and we are then asked to stand in front of the audience and display the collar. I feel ridiculous doing so and avoid all eye contact. I do not miss the gasp when my back is turned to them and Peyton moves my hair, revealing the collars marks. I look up at Peyton nervously. He just smiles and kisses me lightly. Then we both wait impatiently through three speeches about claiming. When they are finally done, they finally give us permission to kiss. But Peyton chooses to surprise everyone. "You think it is still working? I did drink the lot of it after all." I shrug, this wedding lasts a century at least. He brings his wrist to my lips and takes my wrist to his. To both our surprise, the elixir is working just fine. He does not hold back, which encourages me not to either. But something unexpected happens; there is no electricity between us like last time. Instead, the wind seems to kick up and twirl around us until he reluctantly breaks the connection. I follow suit, blushing, leaning forward to kiss his lips quickly just to satisfy the Prytore who is screaming at us that he said kiss, not mark. The crowd lets out a light laugh.

"We present to you, Peyton and Serena Silviu," one of the Prytores announces. "And their Prytores Keon and Alexis Silviu."

Peyton walks us back down the aisle with Prytore Keon and Alexis directly behind us. I notice Zane and Roald in the front of our greeting guests. Both looking on edge. Before I could ask, Prytore Keon steps in front of us, the look on his face so alarming, I lose my ability to smile.

"I do apologize, but an urgent family matter has come up. I fear we are needed elsewhere at once. Please enjoy the drink and food, and above all, mingle and find the happiness that Serena and Peyton did." He takes my free arm in his, and Alexis does the same to Peyton.

Walking us directly into the house and through a transporter. When we walk off, it is not unlike the room I found myself bored in, just days before. After a short while, we travel through another and then another, sometimes waiting, sometimes not. Eventually we find ourselves in a room, and Prytore Keon heads for the door.

"Taking you directly to our home seems risky. I spoke with your aunt. There is a safehouse of your families here," he tells us as we step into the bright night.

I am shocked to find we are literally in the middle of nowhere. "What is wrong? Do not deny that I missed something important." I demand.

"Zane intercepted some poisonous wine you and Peyton were meant to drink." Prytore Keon answers me.

"How do you know that?" I ask.

"You are not the only one who finds weddings boring." Prytore Keon smiles. "The audience tends to whisper amongst themselves, though considering you had your back and attention away from the guests, I am not surprised you did not notice. Despite your obvious boredom."

"Sorry."

"Do not be." Prytoree Alexis dismisses. "You and your husband were not the only ones trying to stay in proper form."

"Peyton, Serena, I am afraid you are going to have to take our light luggage, your Prytores, and run. I will guide you, Peyton."

Prytoree Alexis looks at me nervously. "Have you ever traveled with cargo before?"

"Nothing as precious as this." I smile, picking her up. She seems uncomfortable. "Hang on, this usually is not fun for your kind."

"I assure you, I am not an exception to that," she replies, squeezing her eyes shut.

I follow Peyton a good twenty minutes at top speed before we come to an abandoned cabin in the middle of the woods.

"Creepy," I mutter aloud, causing Peyton to laugh as our Prytores find their footing.

"Do not worry, love, I will keep you safe. I am sure there are giant insects I can kill."

"You tease, but you have never seen how deathly afraid I am of bugs," I mutter, jabbing him in the side. He laughs a little harder and takes me in his arms. I hide my face in his shoulder, and he enters the cabin after our Prytores.

"How long must we stay here?" Prytoree Alexis asks, wiping who knows how many years of dust off a table with a finger, looking repulsed.

"Just until we can sneak them into our house safely." Prytore Keon reassures her, looking around the small place. "This seems to be our room dear." He notes. "The make do bridle suite is on the other side of this room."

"May we?" Peyton asks.

"By all means, Peyton, this is your time. Enjoy her." Prytore Keon encourages.

Peyton hollers a polite thank you as I squeal in excitement from being lifted off the ground. The door closes behind us and he places me down on my feet gently, revealing his beautiful grin. "Alone with you at long last."

Twelve

My Love

Serena

I stare at him, suddenly subconscious and nervous. I have never been alone with a male of any sort before. I knew that mating rituals happened, but I have never been informed as to how. Fear overcomes me, and I start to shake. What if I do it wrong? Nervous, I start to mess with my hair, my fingers accidentally get tangled in the small flowers I had forgotten were hiding in it. They snag and I pull most of them out.

"Serena?" he asks, cautiously coming to my side.

"I am sorry. I just…" I choke on the words. "I am unsure what to do. Well, not what, I mean, I know what, but I am unfamiliar more with how…" I am cut off by his kiss. I wrap my hands into his hair and kiss him back with vengeance.

He breaks our lips apart but keeps me close. "Do not be nervous. I am familiar with the how."

"You and Alexis?"

"That 'how' is slightly different." Peyton answers. I pull back a little, the question I dare not speak is all over my face. "She was a long time ago, a different life. I did not love her like I do you. When she died, I felt…relief." He frowns at the memory. "Prytoree Alexis swore to me then the next time I marry, it would be my truest love. Which is why I am happily standing in this room alone with you right now."

Unsure what to say, I step away from him, accidentally finding myself staring at my reflection. I hate my reflection, it is always wrong somehow, but it is different now. I do not even recognize the woman in a black dress staring back at me. I look down at myself just to verify; my dress is indeed silver. I find this strange, but at least, for once, it is not as blurry. My collar has spread what looks like veins down, what I presume to be my entire body. I touch them in surprise and twist this way and that, forgetting about the mirror, as I conduct a personal inspection of my skin. Gasping, when I see Peyton's name etched into my upper shoulders. But his name is not the only thing there. Both also bear the family crescent, though small, thankfully.

"Is there anything you do not like? Or would like to add?" he asks, studying me. "There are some things I will deny you to change, but others can be negotiated."

"I thought you said it was permanent," I challenge.

"Oh, it is, that collar is welded into your skin, Serena. Removing it will kill you," he warns. "But I would never do something this extreme without your permission if you could not change it. This collar is top in technology. And programmable. I simply input what I want, and it molds it."

"Can we make it a little less conspicuous? I mean, I like the vines, I think, but maybe just your initials on my shoulders?"

"Of course." He smiles, working with the collar to make the change.

"What is its energy source?" I ask, fascinated.

"Your heartbeat. Well, it lasts three weeks after your heart does." He shrugs.

"And only you have access to these codes?"

"Of course. While Prytore Keon may own us, this is a symbol of me and you." He cradles my head in his hands and points me back to my front reflection. I gasp when I see a beautiful silver emblem with the letter *P* with an *S* wrapped in it etched into my forehead. Truly, surprised, the reflection is showing me my true face, but the rest of my body is blurry. "This will never change, Serena. You are my wife.

You should carry pride and show off our initials. Due to it being so predominant, you will always have a design on your face, though you can choose one more fitting if you so wish. There are always updates, so you can feel free to play with it."

"Do you not mean your initials," I correct, studying it.

"No, I mean ours." He shrugs. "It is not my fault your first name starts the same as my last."

"Double meaning then."

"Always the clever one." He smiles, kissing my neck. "Do not worry about the strangeness of your reflection. It will be out of sorts for a little while."

I give a small smile, relieved he is not alarmed by it. "What else is non-negotiable?"

He gives a light chuckle. "I am not giving it all away. You will discover that soon enough. You will find that no matter how hard you try, some things simply will not change."

"Is it the family crest?"

"No, it is much more personal than that." He answers.

"Oh." I reply, studying my new skin.

"In the olden days, it was customary for a fiorriee to scar his wife," he explains. "I hoped you would appreciate the heritage."

"I do," I whisper, turning to him. "It is a lot to get used to."

"I can take away the vines."

"I do not want you to change anything else tonight, husband." It is the first time I have said the word out loud, and admittedly, that is going to take some getting used to as well.

He smiles. "I truly love the sound of you saying that."

"I love you," I whisper, touching both his cheeks with my palms as my fingers slide into his wild hair.

His eyes drop back down to my skin as his tongue traces a silver vine, causing me to gasp. Suddenly, I realize why he likes them.

"Serena, my beautiful wife," he whispers, happily. "Will you do me the honor of showing me your love, in the same way you affirmed your choice to me?" His silver eyes meet my stunned gaze. "We will not be interrupted. I assure you. I want to enjoy it, as I was unable to the first time."

I drop my arms and turn around. "Only if you check for bugs." He laughs happily and complies with my silly request.

"Bug free, though it is a bit dusty." He promises, kissing my lips then slips out of his socks and shoes. He then works to release me from my fabric. As my dress falls, I try not to think about what I am doing, and I remind myself I have done it before. But this time, we are not being rushed. This time we are married. This time I am as vulnerable as he wishes me to be. As gracefully as I can with my nerves, I bring myself down to my knees. I hesitate, he says nothing as he patiently waits me out. This is so much more intimidating than the first time. My body is fighting against my mind. This is not natural. I meet his eyes, pleading he understands, I want to, but I am frozen. He rubs his thumb on the side of the silver designs on my face, causing pleasant warmth to run down my body. "You are doing well," he encourages softly, "just a little bit more, let your body and your mind accept the place you have vowed to be in. You are my wife, Serena, bring yourself to the floor in my presence, show me your willingness to trust me."

Taking a deep breath, I lower myself, almost touching the floor but not quite. "Good girl, now relax, rest your face on my feet, and place your arms behind your back." I hesitate; he waits. My body starts to shake with nerves. "It is all right, Serena. I am your husband. I am fiorriee. It is natural for you to submit to me. Embrace our heritage." His words help me follow his directions. "So very nice." He praises, moving his feet from under my face and placing his right foot on top of it. The moment our skin contacts we both receive a surge of painful pleasure. I could swear I hear him call my name, but I am in doubt that he even spoke.

"I am yours, Peyton," I whisper, bringing on a stronger surge. I can feel the transfer of power that is causing my vulnerability to heighten, and I feel...owned. It is a feeling I heard we could have, but I never experienced it until this very moment. When I first heard it, I giggled, thinking it was peculiar. But here, now, in this moment I realize how amazing it is. How it helps complete who I am.

"Yes, Serena, you are," he whispers, moving his foot off of me. The surge between us stops, but the feeling lingers. He walks around me, studying every angle he can. "This is why it is disrespectful for our kind to be on the floor. It is meant for our mating rituals, nothing else. This is a position you shall only ever give to me, one you will learn not to hesitate with. One that Prytore Keon and Prytoree Alexis do not get the honor of. You will find there are a lot of things that will be asked of you, Serena, but you will never share this. We can only do this when we are confident that we are alone. Never, risk this display in public again." His words are filled with authority, and they feel like lashes in my brain.

I know I will never forget them as long as I live, though I do not understand how I could remember such a long speech, word for word so quickly, after hearing it only once. "I warn you my beautiful wife, breaking this command will cause you severe unpleasant pain, whether it is willful or not. If an enemy gets ahold of you in this manner, you will not be able to comply for long without naturally curling into protection. Understand this is not meant to harm you but protect you. Who do you belong to, Serena?"

"You, my handsome Peyton."

"Good girl," he whispers, in praise. "I will admit, I was expecting more resistance. I am honored you trust me so much my love." He gently lifts me up from the ground. "I will treasure you always." I blush, and his lips gently meet mine. Our eyes lock, and everything falls away; the only thing that matters is being with him in this moment, and I could not be happier.

Thirteen

Death Trap

Serena

I wake to such uncomfortable pain; I cannot help but cry out. I look at my arm and discover it is fiery red, worse than before it was treated. I jump from the bed and run to the bathroom, desperately trying to cool my skin with water.

"Serena, what is it?" Peyton asks at my side. "What the?" he asks, shocked, dashing away. "Keon, Alexis! Help!" I hear him cry out.

It is but a moment before he returns. "Is the water helping?" he asks, covering us both with sheets.

"No." I answer, giving up. "Just cut it off! Please!" I beg, shaking.

"Peyton, what is it?" Prytore Keon asks, coming into the bathroom.

In the back of my mind, I am aware that I am only being covered by a sheet, but I am in too much agony for modesty. "Please, Peyton," I beg again. "Cut it off!"

"No," he answers firmly, concern written all over his face, turning to our Prytores. "We need a doctor."

"That is not going to be easy." Alexis warns, "She is a pureblood."

"My aunt," I reply, forgoing all formal protocol. "She trusts someone, being a pureblood herself."

"It is dangerous to go back to any part of your old life, Serena." Prytore Keon worries.

I cry out in agony once more. I cannot resist the shakes any longer. My legs give out, causing me to fall into the protective position my instincts naturally provide. I hear Peyton gasp, pulling my body into him. It was no secret that if a fiorriee is stuck in this position for too long, death follows soon after.

"If we do not do something, she will die!" Peyton worries, trying his best to calm me by giving me a light touch. "Please!" I hear the pain in his plea.

"We cannot risk Prytore doctors. If we have no idea what is happening, I doubt they would be much better." Alexis frowns.

"Fine, I will take her to Takira. But we must stay on guard." Prytore Keon warns. "You are going to have to gag her, Peyton. We cannot have her drawing unnecessary attention."

Hot tears fill my eyes, and more talking hits my ears, but I stop listening. I feel a blanket being wrapped around me, as there is no way to properly dress me. I am doing my best to calm myself, but my body simply will not stop shaking. I hear a murmured apology and taste something metal. But it all feels so far away. All I can feel is the burning, and it is creeping up my arm. I just want it cut off. I do not think I can handle it if it passes any further.

I can smell Peyton. I try to concentrate on him, but it is very difficult. The more I do, the more intense the unpleasant pain becomes. I have a vague idea that we are moving, but I have no idea where or how we get there. Then it all stops and the little distractions I have fade away, leaving me nothing but agony.

"Serena," I hear a familiar voice and a familiar song. It snaps my attention into focus. I manage to see with my eyes, peering at my aunt in surprise.

"What is happening to me?" I ask her, unable to disguise the fear. She frowns, she obviously does not want to answer that. "Do I not get to know the reason behind my own death?"

She runs her fingers through my white hair. "I believe your body is in rejection."

"Rejection?" I ask, looking around with my eyes, the best I can, to see three very shocked and unhappy faces.

"What possibly could I be rejecting?"

"Peyton." She frowns.

"Why would she be rejecting me?"

"Serena, have you eaten any strange pie lately?" my aunt asks me. She looks at me and understands I did just that. "Oh, Serena, why did you not tell me?"

"I did not realize I did anything wrong, besides it was a couple of bites. Erland ate most of it." I defend.

"Are you telling me she shared a pie with Erland, and it altered her in some way?" Prytore Keon asks with disgust and worry.

"Not exactly," my aunt clarifies. "She rejected Erland. Which is an insult to our kind. Had we been on Trorain, I would have realized what she had eaten, but the atmosphere here does not give us the same colors as it did at home."

"I am being punished for denying him?" I ask, petrified.

"No, but you would have been secluded had you been on Trorain. Rejecting a second pureblood's fluids of any kind would have killed you.

Accepting him, however, binds them for life. Her straying, then going to Peyton has put her in rejection. Without forgiveness from Erland or this stranger, Serena will die." She shakes her head. "Had I known she ate that pie, I would have warned you to keep her from other purebloods. But it seems she has already been exposed." Tears fill her eyes. "All these years, I protected you, and when you needed me most, I failed you. I am so sorry, Serena, but whoever it was, you are his now."

"I have only been with Peyton!" I cry out, insulted and in agony.

"She is telling the truth," Peyton defends me. "I drank an elixir she gave me before our union. I marked her when I was in a pureblood state. Remember the wind? That was our pureblood energy."

"Well, it obviously wore off. Otherwise, this would not be happening," Prytore Keon mutters.

"I did not know," I cry, fighting this pain.

"None of us did, Serena." Peyton assures me, making it clear he does not blame me.

"Wait, if you are the second pureblood…?" my aunt starts, looking panicked.

"Why do you look haunted by that? Should you not be relieved?" he challenges her.

"Tell me Peyton, how much of that dangerous elixir did you take?" my aunt asks. He does not answer her.

"Will it kill him?" Prytoree Alexis asks.

"No, but if he took too much, a second dose, might." My aunt warns. "I fear taking that risk, is the only way to save Serena's life."

"How so?" Prytore Keon asks.

"Serena's body is in a state of confusion. She not only accepted the second pureblood mark, she made a blood vow with it. When Peyton's Prytore DNA became active again, her body turned on her, believing she has committed adultery. But it was mixed with his natural DNA, which is why she is in agony and not already dead. Neither of you can mark her." My aunt warns Prytore Keon and Prytoree Alexis, doing so will surely kill her."

"Takira, adultery is a death sentence for purebloods." Alexis worries.

"Only for those who eat the pie." Takira confirms. "Unless a miracle happens."

"You are telling me, I killed my wife?" Peyton asks in disbelief.

"Not if you take risks to your own."

"My life means nothing without her." Peyton responds, dismissing the risks to his own life.

"This is reversible, but there will be a price. If we are to do this, we must hurry." My aunt assures him, then turns to Prytore Keon. "I need to call on my friend, he will have what we need."

"Go." Prytore Keon orders her.

She squeezes my arm before she vanishes, leaving me alone with my new family.

"Did you know this could happen?" Prytore Keon asks Peyton. "My memory of Trorain is still very damaged. I do recall a fruit that can do this, if it is shared amongst purebloods, but I do not know its name, much less what it looks or tastes like. I am truly at a loss as how any could have survived my father's intentional extinction of the plant."

"It is called dysty. It survived because Hollis stopped all the living trees from producing the fruit, but some fruit was already harvested. The seeds that entered the ground all died, but those in pots, were not affected." Prytoree Alexis answers him.

"You know of this?" Prytore Keon looks to her astonished. "They do not grow here. The soil and air mixture do not allow it. You can only get dysty on Trorain and even then, growing them is difficult and they spoil easily. The only way to get them to Artthemis is through smuggling. But our atmosphere cuts their shelf life to mere days." Alexis explains. "I knew the plant still existed, but I had no idea Serena was at risk to it."

"Somebody did. Somebody, knew exactly what they were doing." Prytore Keon replies, angrily.

"Serena, my love, where did you get the elixir?" Peyton asks me. I close my eyes, refusing to answer. "Serena?"

"Serena, answer the question," Prytore Keon orders me.

My eyes flash to Prytoree Alexis, my head killing me from the conflicting desires of my new family.

"It was me." Prytoree Alexis answers. "It is all right, dear, you do not need to protect the secret anymore."

I open my eyes, grateful she gave me the relief of that burden, while my arm still burns. "I got it from Zane. He swore Peyton and Serena would not be harmed."

"We were not," I defend. "Zane is trustworthy. We are missing something," I whimper, struggling to get the words out. "Zane did not do this on purpose. He would not."

"I am inclined to agree with her." Peyton supports me.

Everyone falls silent for a moment before Prytore Keon speaks up. "You realize this means there is someone at Maleko's court that Zane should not be trusting."

"This is all my fault. Why did I eat that pie with him? I knew it was smuggled. Erland told me." I cry in shame. "And doubting my husband. If I did not let Erland seed my doubts, Peyton would have never taken that elixir." I turn away from Peyton. "Leave me to die. I deserve nothing less!"

I feel a strong hand on my good arm. "Do not ever believe such a thing is possible." My husband scolds me.

The burning is getting worse. It is taking effort not to give in to the pain. "I am aware of a lot of our traditions and customs. I have even participated in those that applied when I became of age." I take a deep breath. "I do not have any knowledge of this fruit. If I did, I would have never eaten it."

"We believe you, my beautiful wife. You did not do anything wrong." Peyton reassures me again, his fear weakly disguised in his voice. "Do not worry about anything but fighting to survive. Do not give into the pain, I beg of you."

"Is there anything you can do to help her fight it?" Prytore Keon asks, helplessly.

"If there was, I would do it." Peyton answers curtly, stroking my hair.

Prytoree Alexis takes Prytore Keon's hand and pulls him into her. They share a short moment before they embrace, all aware they are witnessing my death bed, all wanting to fight it and all helpless to do so.

Fourteen

Only Pureblood Will Do

Serena

"**S**erena, it is Doctor Currelt," I hear a familiar voice whisper. "I have been informed of your predicament. If you are strong enough, all hope is not lost."

"Do whatever needs to be done," Prytore Keon tells him.

"I hesitate to that request until you realize that you too must suffer," Doctor Currelt replies, looking at my arm. "She is rejecting the Prytore DNA in her husband's blood. Had you marked her after the elixir wore off, you would have killed her instantly. As it stands, there are things you must do, if you in fact want to touch her, after I save her life."

"Start with saving her life." Prytore Keon snaps, impatient. "She is fading quickly."

The doctor places my arm down and turns to Peyton. "She must first be forgiven by the pureblood she has committed herself to."

"She has done nothing wrong. There is nothing to forgive," Peyton replies sternly.

"Says your hybrid self. You need to become her pure blood again," Doctor Currelt clarifies.

"Give me the elixir then. I am happy to swallow it," he replies, catching a bottle the doctor tosses to him.

"Just a few drops Peyton, no more." Doctor Currelt warns.

He quickly opens it and takes a sip; suffering as he did the last time. Tears spill down my cheeks, as I watch him endure the agony because of me. When he is able to speak, he asks. "Now what?"

"Now, we leave you two alone," Doctor Currelt answers. "I warn you, this will not be easy. The more pureblood fluids and touch you offer her, the more her strength will return but at a cost. Forgiven as she may be, she will be punished."

"She does not deserve that." Peyton frowns.

"Her life will be saved?" Prytore Keon asks.

"Temporarily, yes. There is not much time." He turns to the others, leaving in expectance that they will follow him. Prytore Keon gives Peyton a stern look before leading Prytoree Alexis out of the room.

"Serena, I am so sorry, I do not want to hurt you like this. You do not deserve it. You have done nothing wrong," he whispers, running his fingers through my hair as he squeezes his eyes open and closed.

"I shared a smuggled pie with someone that was not you." I counter, accepting my role in this.

"I would have done the same. It came from home. I would not have believed it would be harmful to me," he rebuts, refusing to let me blame myself in any way. He presses his lips to mine, but I break away from him as I cry out in pain. "Okay, harder than I hoped." He frowns, taking my wrist again. The moment he touches me, I try to pull away from him, but his grip is strong. My mind is flooded in agony. I beg him to stop but he refuses, trailing his tongue up my arms and to my neck. When he realizes I stopped breathing, he pulls away. Purple tears are streaming down my face, but I am still unable to release myself from my protective position. He wipes them away. "I love you, please know I would not do this if I did not need to." His hand touches my face gently. "Breathe for me, Serena." He encourages while taking my other wrist to repeat his actions. My body burns worse than it ever has. I struggle for air, trying to get away but he tangles his body with mine. I try to block the pain, to bring my mind anywhere but where I was, but it is overwhelming. He pauses only enough for me to catch my breath before he does it again. After a long while, my body starts to uncurl, but not completely. "I do not ever want to force you to accept me, Serena. I know this hurts. I am so sorry."

"Just keep going," I whimper, needing this to be over.

He is shaking a little when he starts again, causing me to fall into screams. It cannot be over fast enough, but it takes time. When my body finally relaxes to a normal state, we are both struggling with tears. He leans forward and kisses me, holding me to him through my sobs. He does not break away until all the burning stops.

"Thank you," I whisper, pulling him into a strong hug. "I know that was painful for you as well."

"Anything for you, my Serena" he states in relief. "We will get through this together." He gets up and retrieves a bag, handing me a green dress. I slip into it quickly, and crawl into his lap.

A knock comes to the door. Prytore Keon walks in. "The screaming has stopped. Does that mean you are okay?"

"I feel like myself." I smile. "Thank you."

"Oh, Serena, it is wonderful to see you in full form." Prytoree Alexis smiles.

"I am sorry for the scare and my actions Prytore Keon and Prytoree Alexis."

"Just Keon and Alexis are fine in a family setting." My Prytore smiles, pulling me into a hug and then only slightly pulling me away, putting his hands in my hair.

"No more titles, Prytore?" I ask, smiling at him.

"No more titles, Keon." He smiles. "At least in a private setting. You are, after all, family, Serena. Now stop apologizing for things that are not your fault."

I see the doctor and my aunt enter the room. "You said this is only temporary. What must be done to make it permanent?"

"There are a couple of things." He answers, turning to Peyton, "But the most difficult will be for you, I am afraid. I can make your Prytore genes dormant, as they are not natural, but it is not a pleasant or short experience and there will be side effects."

"What kind of side effects?" Alexis asks.

"Does it matter if it saves Serena's life?" Keon questions her pointedly. "Unless of course you would banish her to a life of loneliness and fear."

"I only ask, dear husband, because I know Peyton will not. Should he not be informed of what is going to happen to him on a molecular level?" she replies coldly.

If the doctor picks up on the tension, he ignores it. "The side effects are mostly your senses. You will experience life as you were meant to as a fiorriee, not as a Prytore. Reactions to touch and sight being the most affected. The procedure itself will leave you weak for a long while, vomiting, sensitivity to light, changes in tastes, headaches, mood swings, and there is also the possibility that your skin tone may change, but that does not always happen."

"Could it kill him?" I ask.

"I will not lie, there have been cases, but those seem to be the result of not following the proper protocols." He answers.

I look to Peyton. "Alexis knows me well, my love. I could care less as long as I never hurt you again."

"What is the rest of it?" I ask the doctor.

"For Peyton, nothing. For your Prytore, it is more complicated. Peyton owns his wife completely now. To share her, even with a simple thing as a marking, means he must give his permission." Keon raises an eyebrow at that. "Peyton must mark his wife within minutes after she is marked by another, signifying his acceptance. But it only last for three days or so, any longer and it will kill her."

I do not dare look at Keon or Alexis, feeling slightly uncomfortable at the thought of them needing permission like that, after I have sworn my loyalty.

"Then of course, there is the inherent danger of this happening again." He worries. "My child, this ritual was designed to make the female dependent on her husband. Only Peyton can heal you from this, and that all depends on if he wants to." The doctor frowns. "I have lived a long while. I have spent way too many Trorain nights pleading with husbands to forgive their wives. It haunts me that I was not always successful." He closes his eyes to the memory.

"Can you give us the specifics of this ritual? We do not understand how she can eat a piece of pie and die for it." Keon asks the doctor, which I am grateful for, because I wanted to ask the same thing.

"On Trorain, before Hollis banished the practice, it was customary for a fiorriee to become engaged by sharing dysty in a pie form. This bounds the two, and usually engagements, lead to marriage. However, there were occasions where the engagement fell through. In those cases, the gods allowed each fiorriee to be able to commit again once more.

But only once. This warning even marked the fiorriee by skin color, until they marry, though it is difficult to detect on Artthemis. Not that it is needed here much. Hybrids are immune to its power. He frowns, adding, "If we were on Trorain, we could plead our case to Shrealm, the guardian of the nalet fruit, grown in the heart of Jynevt's garden.

"Jynevt's garden?" Alexis replies stunned. "That is in the depths of the Trorain Seas." I give her a strange look. "Or so I have heard." She adds, looking embarrassed.

"Indeed, it is." Doctor Currelt confirms. "But even if you managed to get there, you cannot pick it yourself. The cure only works if Shrealm were to pick it then present it with a blessing. To my knowledge, that has happened so seldom, you only need one hand to count its occurrence in the past five hundred years." He shakes his head. "In either case, Peyton becoming a pureblood has a much higher chance of success."

"I was engaged to Erland!" I cry, admittedly not registering much after that bombshell, feeling even more violated than ever before. Looking to my all too quiet aunt.

"Which you broke, when you denied his mark, leaving you free to submit to another." Doctor Currelt confirms. "You needed not to consume dysty pie twice, only willfully surrender to another pureblood. When you did this to Peyton's pureblood form, you became his for life. If ever you share any fluids with another, without his permission, it will kill you, unless he forgives you in time."

"But I submitted to Peyton before he took the elixir." I argue.

"Serena!" My aunt gasps, in shock. I glare at her, not caring that she knows I submitted before I married.

The doctor studies me. "Define submit."

"I laid before him and placed his foot on my face." I answer, unashamed.

"Were you clothed?"

"Yes."

"Was he wearing shoes?"

"Yes."

"Did you feel the electricity you surely felt when you were naked and his barefoot was on your face?" Doctor Currelt asks, knowingly.

"Oh." I reply, understanding.

"That is the difference, Serena." He clears his throat and looks at me. "You were set up, my Queen, while this assassination attempt failed, it did succeed at making you a very easy target. I would not recommend public places or being apart from Peyton too long. It truly could kill you." He turns his attention to Peyton. "And you need to be careful as well. The last thing we all need is for you to be taken away from her and unable to save her life."

"We understand. I will take precautions, but I absolutely refuse to live in fear," I reply stubbornly.

"I only ask that you be careful, my Queen." He smiles with a slight bow. He turns his attention to Peyton again. "We cannot start your change until that elixir is out of your system. I shall return after Akatite rises. Please, eat heartily tonight, you are going to need your strength." He takes his bag and exits the room.

"Engaged!" I snap at my aunt, unable to control my outrage. "How could you forget to mention that?"

"I did not know until you told me you ate that pie." My aunt defends herself. "Why add insult to injury? You were dying Serena. It was not the time." Peyton sits next to me and pulls me into him. "I am sorry child. I wish I could have protected you from all of this." She whispers, glaring at Keon while she fights her own emotions.

"I believe we all feel that way." Alexis replies, trying to alleviate the tension.

"Yes well, Peyton needs to eat, and Serena could use a meal herself." Aunt Takira replies, "I will just get started with dinner. I am happy for the help, if one finds themselves with idle hands."

I watch her leave. When I find myself alone with my new family, I work to calm down while I notice the others' emotions. Keon looks angry. Peyton is showing nothing but concern for me and Alexis is worried, very worried. After a moment, I smile up at them. "Peyton, Alexis, may I have permission to be marked by Keon? While I enjoy my husband's company, I would like to get to know Keon a little better tonight, and I do not want that hindered with the silly possibility of it killing me."

"Always perceptive." Peyton smiles, looking from me to Alexis. We both know, with Peyton's pending procedure, Alexis needs him right now. "I am not offended by your request my wife. Keon? Alexis?"

"You may have my husband's company, if he so desires it." Alexis smiles.

"I accept, and before you ask Peyton, I am fine with Alexis having yours. As Serena no doubt agrees, I am sure my wife is more worried than she is letting on. Having you in her company, may help relax her." I silently offer my wrist, and Keon hesitantly marks me.

I cringe in pain, feeling sick to my stomach, but Peyton is right there with a smile. "I am curious on what is going to happen this time."

"I just hope we do not crumble the walls around us." I giggle, offering my wrist to him and taking his.

Peyton's tongue feels amazing but not as amazing as the taste that fills my mouth, and the intensity adds when my tongue tastes his skin. We are not wrong to expect something to happen; the sudden wind blows open the window, startling us apart.

I feel better instantly, giving a reassuring nod to the room at large. Alexis takes Peyton's hand, and Keon captures mine, squeezing it.

"You two may go." Keon tells them. Peyton takes Alexis in his arms and dashes away, leaving me alone with Keon for the very first time.

Fifteen

Inadequate

“That bothers you more than you let on,” I tell him. “I can only hope to be a fun distraction to it.”

“Does it bother you?” he asks.

“It should, as fiorriee seem to be designed for jealousy.” I shrug. “But no, mostly because I accepted it after it already happened. Watching it happen must make it more difficult.”

“I have adjusted,” he replies, still holding my hand. He drags his fingers lightly on my healed skin. “You are meant to be much more than a fun distraction, Serena.” He brings my arm to his lips and kisses my wrist.

“I feel like a curse.” I frown, causing him to pause and study me. “Now you must always look over your shoulder. Peyton must suffer just to be with me. All because someone tried to kill me by means of using my own kind’s heritage against me.”

“Hush, Serena, it is all right,” he whispers, pulling me into him. “Peyton will be all right.”

“I need to believe that. I know I would never be able to talk him out of this risk if I tried.”

“Is that why you did not?”

I shrug. "Is it wrong of me to send him away in hopes that she can talk sense into him?"

"No, but you do not need to worry. Alexis will worry enough for both of you."

I graze my fingers over his hands, both of us comfortable with the others' company. "Did you talk to him before you hurt him?" I ask, running my finger over his healing scabs, indicating who I meant.

"Why would I waste my breath?" he asks, tensing and flexing his fingers.

"Because you must study your enemies if you ever want to conquer them." I answer. "I must admit, he was interesting."

"Interesting?"

"Do you believe Trorain is truly uninhabitable?"

"For normal day to day life yes. But there are some things that can be done for temporary amounts of time like research, mining, and historical preservation; assuming smugglers do not beat them to it. But the longer they stay, the shorter they cut their life. Trorain's atmosphere is toxic, and it will take longer than our lifetime for that to change. What makes you ask?"

"Just curious, sometimes I think about it. Is it strange to miss a place I am too young to remember?"

"Feelings are not always explainable." He answers. "You are avoiding my question. How was our foe interesting?"

"Lots of little things, I guess." I shrug, playing with his fingers again. "Before he did what he did, he was a pale contender to Peyton."

Keon turns in such a way that with a gentle tilt of my chin he meets my gaze. "You considered another?"

"It is what you wanted, is it not?"

"Do not mix want and necessity, Serena." He frowns. "Have you told Peyton?"

"I have not, not told him. We just have not talked about it, is all."

"Was Erland the only one?" He presses, causing me to bite my lower lip. "Zane." He states, knowingly, causing me to look down at my hands. "Well, I understand why you did not pursue Maleko's fiorriee, though it does make me leery to leave you two in the same room alone together until trust is earned between us. Not to mention Peyton's and Alexis' stipulations will be considered." I nod, not even wanting to argue with that. He squeezes my hand. "I am curious about the little things that held your interest with Erland. Will you be more specific?"

I concentrate on his yellow skin. "I liked his view and bold statements about how insulting courting was no matter what color we are placed in. That the Prytores' politics seem to dominate the fiorriees' choice." I can tell by the way his eyes harden he does not like that answer. "I got lucky, though. My aunt protected me from all of that." He forces a small smile, studying me. "He made the countryside sound interesting, that after morning duties, there were a lot of lazy days and time to spend with each other."

I fall silent for too long, thinking in my head. "There must be more than that, Serena. His incredibly handsome looks had to play some part," Keon states, curiously.

"He was a charmer. When I first arrived there, I was so confident about Peyton and me, but when I left, the things he said. Well, he was not wrong to say them to me." Again, Keon waits patiently for me to continue. "He pointed out the others I had spent time with were all of Peyton's friends. That everything seemed to push me toward Peyton and do not deny that Zane admitted I was being protected by those with poor intentions."

"Obviously, not guarded well enough," Keon replies in a hard tone.

"I do not fault anyone but myself. I should have stopped talking to him the moment he tried to shake my hand, but I could not seem to pull myself away. Mostly because he did it in a manner that did not appear offensive to me at the time. He wanted a day with me before I made my choice. I will not deny I was considering it, mostly to stay qualified, before Zane told me that would upset Peyton and informed me of your plan to advance me. Thankfully, I listened to Zane's advice, seeing what Erland's true intentions were." Keon's eyes are tight, but he keeps his silence. "He is the reason I doubted Peyton's feelings." I continue, "Erland twisted our story of events in a way that seemed to make it out that I pressured Peyton into my choice. That Peyton was not happy, only you were, because of who I was. That is why I tested Peyton the way I did. Why I had to be sure." I look away from Keon. "Look at all the trouble that caused, all because Erland had a point. I am my kind's Queen. I am setting an example whether I want to or not. I had to be sure it was something we both wanted. And I am angry at Erland for what he did, but mostly I am angry that it took a fiorriee with such eccentric claims about himself, to point out the way the others viewed me." I turn back to Keon. "Some Queen I am. I was tricked by my own customs and traditions."

"What do you believe to be his eccentric claims, Serena? Surely his offer of joining a neglectful Prytore does not deserve that description." I give him a confused look. "Serena, if your kind does not have a form of hierarchy with regular submissive acts, it leaves you... unsatisfied. The way your kind functions is to have a true balance where one is slightly more dominant than the other, or the dominant one submits to another. It is very complex. One slight altercation can mess up a lot of fiorriee. But in this case, Erland most likely wanted to submit to you, not the other way around. By having you eat dysty pie, without your knowledge..." Keon stops for a moment, controlling his temper, "he could have made you submissive to his demands. You would have been trapped in a true kind of zarla." He touches my face. "I am so glad you did not choose that fate." I think on that for a little while. I understood the submissive hierarchy he was talking about. I have studied it enough, but even I get boggled by it sometimes. He leaves me to my thoughts for a moment before he speaks again, "Share with me what bothered you the most, my Serena."

"He claimed he was abandoned on Trorain and only found later in life," I answer, causing Keon's features to harden. "What is it?"

"Thank you for sharing these things, Serena. You have helped enlighten me as to who we are up against." He answers, evasively.

"Please, tell me."

"You need not worry," he replies.

"Must I not? Without all the information, Peyton and I are vulnerable. Please, Keon, we need to understand."

"You give a compelling plea. All right, I will tell you at dinner, when we rejoin the others. For now, I would rather spend time, getting to know you better. What can I do that would be pleasing for you, Serena?"

"You want an honest answer?"

"I expect nothing less," he responds firmly. "Just sitting here with you is nice."

"It is very nice. Is there nothing else?"

"May we help my aunt cook?" I ask, hopeful. "I know it sounds strange to you, but it really is satisfying, and I could really use as much comfort as I can get after being so close to…"

He touches my face when I cut myself off, his eyes studying mine, discovering the fear I cannot put into words. "Yes, let us put some distance from this memory by making happier ones."

<h1 style="text-align:center">Sixteen</h1>

<h2 style="text-align:center">Giggles and Grain</h2>

Aunt Takira is surprised to see us, but she quickly accepts our offer with a smile. As we cleanse our hands, she sets up stations. Keon is placed at the vegetable station. His task is easy, he simply needs to cut up plants add flavor to our fake meat. I am settled at a baking station. Aunt Takira knows my favorite cake, and after this whole ordeal, she seems to want to treat me.

Keon seems immediately uncomfortable when he stands where he was told, staring at the items but not starting the task. I try to hide a smile but fail miserably when he picks up the cutters and starts to split the vegetables vertically, causing liquid to squirt all over him. He looks at himself in surprise and looks up to see if we noticed. The look on his face causes me to laugh out loud. My aunt turns from the stove to see the mess, but before she can clean it up, Keon flicks some of the juice at me. I gasp in surprise and react by tossing a mixture of flour and sugar at him. My hand immediately covers my mouth when I realize what I have done.

Keon holds my stare for a moment before he bursts out into laughter himself, leans over to my station, and tosses flour at me. I scream at him in shock of delight and start laughing, gathering more ingredients as ammo. "You two, you are supposed to be helping, not making a mess!" my aunt complains.

Keon responds by tossing flour at her. I burst into more laughter. Her face is covered in flour, and she is too stunned to react at first. But it does not take her too long to recover, and suddenly a warm paste is sent across the room, hitting Keon squarely in the chest. He looks down in surprise and quickly retaliates. I take advantage of his distraction, getting him with a cracked orstams egg.

"Ganging up on me?" he laughs, hitting me and my aunt while he dodges one of us but gets hit by the other. "This is not fair! I am outnumbered!"

"What is going on in here?" Alexis asks, staring in disbelief. She gets hit in the face by an egg Keon had managed to get ahold of. "What?" she asks, and I cannot help but giggle harder.

"Oh, is that how it is going to be?" Peyton asks, diving for some ingredients and joining in.

Soon all five of us are covered in raw food, laughing hysterically until we run out of ingredients.

"So much for a hearty meal." Alexis observes, causing the laughter to die away. Her face is etched in worry.

"Nonsense, I have more food in the cellar. But this one is banned from my kitchen; he simply has no talent for it," Aunt Takira says, causing me to giggle again. Keon tries to look offended but cannot seem to express it right. "What? I am not wrong." Takira laughs, "Cutting plants vertically, you have never cooked a day in your life!"

It is Alexis' turn to giggle, understanding now how all this started. "Oh, husband, how on Artthemis did you get persuaded into even trying?" She wipes tears from her eyes.

"It just happened." He smiles back. "Obviously, Takira needs help with a meal Peyton needs, but I will leave that to the ladies once they have washed up. Peyton, come help me retrieve fresh ingredients from the cellar."

I look around when they leave. "Sorry about your kitchen."

"Do not be, I did not exactly treat it kindly myself." Aunt Takira smiles, leading the way toward the bedrooms.

We break our separate ways. When I find myself alone for the first time since before my courting, I take a deep breath. Then I quickly take off my food-stained clothes and walk into the bathroom, wrapping myself in a towel while I wait for the water to warm. Bored, I try to stare at myself in the full-length mirror. For a moment, I feel as if a stranger is looking back at me, which helps me realize some of the braided flowers are still in my hair. However, the image does not move while I work to get them out, as they are ruined anyway. The task proves a bit difficult because my hair is in desperate need of washing. Realizing I have egg in it, I scrunch my nose, drop my towel and quickly jump in the shower, despite it not being really warm. Not caring I scrub my hair, desperate to get the food out. It takes about a quarter of bottle of shampoo before I am sure it is clean, then I work the rest of my body. My skin has returned to normal, no hint of pink whatsoever. The vines of the collar do not seem to be affected by the shower or my touch the way they are by Peyton's. I find I am grateful for that, how is a girl to concentrate if she is so easily distracted? That is when I notice my right ankle. I pull it closer to me and find Peyton's name scrolled in a beautiful anklet design. I smile, knowing this is what he was referring to when he said some things would not change. When I finish showering, I step out and dry off, wrapping a towel around me then wiping the mirror down so I can stare at myself again, trying to adjust to the stranger looking back at me. I was used to my image being blurry, but this is different. I lift my left hand in a wave, but my reflection does not wave back. I drop my hand, feeling silly. "Your conflict is expected, Serena," Peyton tells me, pulling my wet body into his arms. I look up at him, questioning him. "Your mind and body are not synced yet. They will not be until after your breaking." He explains.

"How did your appearance differ when you went through this?" I ask him.

"I do not remember." He answers. "I just know it did. And I know what you are feeling right now is all normal, I assure you." He pulls away. "Shame the flowers had to go. I liked them."

"You could make some with the collar, I am sure." I shrug.

"True, but I think they should be reserved for special occasions."

He moves my wet hair to the side. I can feel his touch on the collar, and then I hiss in pain when I feel metal crawling onto my scalp. I watch in amazement as the metal grows to the length of my white strands and turns into a texture that mimics my wet hair."

"How does it do that?" I ask.

"I do not understand the technology. I just appreciate it." He shrugs. "It will harden and be flexible when it is dry. It is meant to be a part of your hair but also to stand out a little. I do hope the look pleases you."

"If it pleases you, then it will please me." I smile.

He grins. "If it causes your hair to be a nightmare to take care of and style, how could that please me? Let us find out how it reacts to the things you normally do to your beautiful white locks, my love." I lift my right leg a little. "By the way, I love my anklet."

"Oh, you found it, did you?" He smiles. "I am glad you like it. It is not ever going anywhere."

I turn to face him. "I am surprised to see you. I thought you would be with Alexis."

"Keon has generously given me a moments rest from her excessive worrying," he mutters, rolling his eyes. I raise an eyebrow at him. "Not to say you are not worried, love. Keon might have mentioned you seem to be having a very brave face about all this."

"I trust Doctor Currelt. He has saved my life more than once." I answer, walking away from him and start messing with my hair. "He would not be doing this if he thought you would not survive it. He has a very strong code about life in general, risking it is not something he would support."

"Were you not listening when he mentioned it could kill me?" he asks, turning to watch me drag a towel through my hair.

"Apparently, you missed him saying if the procedure is performed incorrectly it can lead to death." I point out, "I trust his confidence in his knowledge of the procedure. Otherwise, I would be a complete mess right now." I twist the towel I am using around my hair, hold it for a quick moment, then pull it away; my white strands fall softly to my shoulders nearly dry. The metal seems to match this mixture too. "Fascinating." I note, running my fingers through my new hair. I turn to him. "Besides, you have Alexis worrying enough for her and me. Not to mention, I know neither of us have a chance in zarla of talking you out of it, so yes, Keon is right, I have a brave face." I walk up to him and study his eyes. "How are you feeling about this? Truthfully."

"I am fine." I give him a knowing look that tells him I do not believe him. "Okay, fine, you got me. I will be much better when it is over, but I do not want to dwell on the anticipation of it. It is happening. It is going to hurt like zarla, I have come to terms with it."

"And the changes?" I ask.

"I already have a preview of them. My eyes seem to dry out faster, but I can see further and my hearing is amazing." He smiles. "I know you might not understand that this is a gift, Serena. I am going to experience the rest of my life the way nature intended. I am actually excited for it."

I kiss his cheek lightly and leave the bathroom, hunting in a luggage bag for something to wear. I dress quickly. "I am sure I am needed in the kitchen by now. Thank you for stealing a moment." I head to the door. "Peyton."

"My love?"

"I know you are going to be all right," I reply over my shoulder and dash away before he can see that I was nowhere near as confident as I sound.

"Serena," Keon calls, stopping my dashing form before I make it to the kitchen. I approach him at a normal speed. "Hmm, I like the change to your hair." He touches it and then brings his fingers under my chin. "Come with me for a moment." I nod and follow him out the back door into a small but private courtyard. "Fiorriee hearing may be superior to Prytores, but we raise a high bar ourselves."

"You heard us," I reply in understanding.

"More like overheard you." He shrugs. "Alexis and your aunt were too far away with noise from the kitchen to have the same effect. Do you mean what you said to him? That you are confident everything is going to be all right?" he asks. I turn away from his piercing stare. I have never seen his brown eyes so intense. "Why mislead him?"

"Alexis is in pieces." I answer in frustration. "He loves her, claims she holds a piece of his soul. I know I do not have anything near that with him yet, but I do have a small piece of his heart. If he has the knowledge of both of us worried on top of his own, when he undergoes this procedure, it increases the chances of a bad outcome."

"You are protecting him." Keon smiles, touching my chin lightly and bringing my eyes back to his smiling stare.

I cup the hand he is using that is holding my chin. "I am his wife. He can be as brave as he wants, all male-like and all that, but at the end of the day, he needs me to be strong for him. If that means I must carry the burden of hiding my true emotions, so be it. I will do my best to make sure he finds me a true companion and confidant. He needs to express how he feels, not be overwhelmed by what others feel for him."

I gasp when I feel Keon's lips on mine. He has never directly kissed me before. The feeling is strangely different from Peyton as Keon's tongue is shaped differently and his teeth are much sharper. He keeps the kiss gentle, sweet, and when he pulls away, he keeps my chin in his hand.

"You please me very much Serena." He stares at me for a while longer. "Even more since you have chosen to confide in me." He lightly brushes his lips to mine. "We should go inside. I am sure Alexis is hindering your aunt more than helping her. She is not herself."

Seventeen

Disconnected

Serena

I am awoken in the middle of the night by Keon shaking me. "Serena! Serena! Wake up! Serena!" I cannot understand why he is so upset, until I realize that I was projecting a fiorriee death scream.

"What is it?" Alexis asks, keeping Peyton behind her at the door.

"I do not know." Keon answers truthfully.

Peyton pushes past her and dashes to my side. "Serena?"

"Peyton?" I question, curling into him, touching his face. "You have forgiven me?"

"Forgiven you? What do you believe needs to be forgiven?" he asks, confused, turning to Keon for help. Keon shrugs, while Alexis wraps herself into his embrace.

"My breaking, you were displeased with me. You said your pleas and influence should have made me want to be broken. But I resisted for almost two years, and you…" I swallow hard. "You were so disappointed you left me to die in shame."

"It was a dream, Serena, only a dream. You have awakened now, there is no reason to fear." He assures me.

I drop my hand down to my collar, which is securely in place. I could have sworn it had burned itself off of me. "Just a dream, you swear you still love me, you still want me?"

"More like a night terror." He frowns, kissing the top of my hair, giving me a pleasant sensation running down my scalp from the collar. "I will never stop loving you, never stop wanting you. Even if you ever hear me speak such blasphemy, I would never mean it, not even in your dreams."

I let him hold me for a moment before I pull away. "Thank you." I look around and realize I am in my aunt's sitting room. I remember I was sitting next to Keon and we were talking. I must have fallen asleep.

"Peyton, you need more rest. Your procedure is soon." Alexis worries. "You need your strength."

"Of course," he replies, taking my arm and kissing my wrist. I am grateful for his taste. "Sweet dreams, my dearest Serena." He and Alexis leave the room, leaving me and Keon alone in the sitting room. I hear the others reassuring my aunt and look around a little dazed.

"Are you truly all right?" Keon asks, pulling me into him.

I shake my head no as tears crop into my eyes. "Of course." I answer, knowing it is too quiet and we risk being overheard. He understands and frowns, kissing my shoulder. "I need real sleep. I should join my husband in rest."

"Not tonight, Serena. There is a reason I let you sleep where you dropped after dinner." Keon states. "Peyton needs his rest, and Alexis thinks you would be more of a distraction."

"Oh." I frown.

"I made her go rest in our bed chambers about an hour after she forced Peyton to go to his. I did not want you to wake alone."

"Thank you. You should join her. I will be all right." I shrug.

"Not going to happen," he replies, keeping me in his embrace. "If you are having night terrors on top of all this chaos happening around you when you are awake. Peyton would not rest thinking you were alone. You should try more sleep. You will not be alone."

I close my eyes and let my tears fall silently. The combination of discovering the burden of being the leader to my kind, the worry for my new husband's life, the reality that I was almost murdered twice, the getting married, and having a breaking hanging over my head. It is almost too much. I know my aunt would tell me to find my inner strength, to persevere, but it is not always that easy. Keon lets me cry, gently stroking my hair while I do. He keeps his arms around me, and eventually I fall asleep in his embrace.

When I wake in the morning, I find myself struggling between dream state and reality. My eyes pop open instantly when I feel a strange sensation on my arm. I focus on it and find it is Keon, lightly tracing one of the veins from the collar. "Good morning." He smiles at me.

"Is this really morning or am I dreaming?"

"Eshnaine rose a while ago, actually. Akatite will soon."

"Peyton," I whisper.

"We will join him soon enough. Alexis is having a rough morning," Keon replies, drinking repulsively fresh pigats. "For now, I think it is time you understand what is expected of you from me and Alexis."

"I think I have a grasp of it. Nothing is off limits, including love."

Keon studies me. "Fiorriee have the strangest ability to fall deeply and genuinely in love with each other almost as an instinct, which is what happened with you and Peyton. I never questioned it because I have seen it before. Though admittedly, it has been a long while." He takes a drink from his morning cup. "Loving a Prytore well, Serena, if something happened like that with us, I would be truly honored."

"It happened with Peyton and Alexis."

"They are a rare example." He takes another drink. "Now that you are here, things could possibly change between them," Keon replies, setting down his cup. "I do not expect it from you. I only expect obedience and respect."

"Changing what they have is not necessary," I reply, looking away and out the window. "I knew what they had when I agreed to marry him, why would I ask him to change who he is? How is that fair?"

"I have no doubt you believe that Serena, and maybe it will not. But you two will naturally find and crave each other. Alexis and Peyton understood what they were searching for at that courting. True happiness for Peyton and we found it."

I study him for a very long moment before I ask my question, catching him when he is raising his cup to his lips. "You do not expect it for you and me, but would you want it?"

He pauses and meets my eyes. "Would you?" He takes a drink, studying me.

"I am not against the idea," I reply, causing him to set his cup down. "I feel safe with you. Is that not the first step in a series of things that Prytores experience before they realize it is love?"

"One of many, Serena," he replies. "And there are many kinds of love."

"Peyton asked me to choose both of you, Keon" I reply.

"I am sure he meant that you would be willing to serve me, Serena, and that cannot happen without trust. That is what you are feeling."

"Maybe." I frown, taking his hand and guiding it lightly over a collar vein. I smile at the sensation. "When I touch these, I can only feel the metal. When Peyton touches these, my whole body ignites in flame. When you touch these." I purposely glide his fingers up and down my arm. "There is a pleasant reaction."

He pulls his hand away. I look up at him wounded. "I need time, Serena." He responds. Hurt, I look away from him. I find myself surprised when he grabs my wrist and his taste floods my mouth. I try to pull away from him, but he keeps me in his grip. "It is easier for your kind to submit when your senses are overcome. Having this ability hindered is very annoying, but I am grateful it was not taken away completely."

"What does it matter, if you do not want me?" I ask, fighting tears, trying to break free again.

"Stop," he replies so sternly I can feel the weight of his word, causing me to cringe. "I am going to let go now but you are going to keep your wrist right here, next to my lips. Do you understand?"

My eyes narrow, but I find it impossible not to comply with his demand without unpleasant pain. Giving up my resistance quickly, I do as I am told. "Better, Serena." He praises. "But we have a long way to go." I turn my head away in frustration and feel his lips kissing my wrist. He stops and touches my chin gently. I meet his eyes reluctantly.

"Do not misunderstand, Serena. I am not rejecting the idea, but it is not what I want us to focus on now. Your full submission, even when you are hurt and angry, should never have any resistance to it." I raise an eyebrow at him. "Not a drop," he replies firmly. "Breaking you of your pride is not going to be an easy task. You should prepare yourself." He gently pushes my arms to my side. "Let me show you something."

He leads me to a full-length mirror in the bathroom down the hall from the sitting room. The room is not much bigger than the one Peyton and I were meant to share and it has a similar mirror. He places me in front of it and steps out of view of it. I stare at the stranger for a moment, I still cannot seem to shake the strange feeling of misconnection that is still there. "Look at her, Serena." He orders. "I know Peyton tried to explain this, but he missed something important. Your reflection cannot be faked. You can comply to every request I give you without me believing you are resisting, but if your mind and body are out of sync in any way, she will always give you away. Every time, even if you submit and your mind shifts. Your reflection can never lie. Just as you are resisting me now."

"I do not understand, how do you know I am resisting?" I ask, wanting to look away from the mirror but unable to.

"Last I looked, you are not wearing a black dress." He answers with a smile. I study the image and realize he is right. "It is not always that obvious. As you become more submissive, it will take me longer to see any difference."

"I did not notice." I frown.

"Because your body and mind are out of sync. From my understanding, this gives you a headache, and after a few moments, your reflection becomes distorted." I nod. "Breaking takes a while, Serena. But soon, she will not be a stranger to you, and she will simply be your true reflection." Keon smiles. "You may look away now."

"Thank you," I reply, relieved, turning away and fighting my headache.

"You should take this time for your morning routines. I am sure you want to be at Peyton's side today." He reaches around a door in the bathroom and presents me with a red dress. I take it smiling.

"I shall meet you for breakfast shortly." He leaves the room without another word.

I quickly take a shower and step into my new dress after I rush a towel over my skin. I find a hairbrush and work to try to style it, but my reflection is more stubborn than I am used to. So I toss it in a simple ponytail and forget it. I brush my teeth then quickly dash into the kitchen to find Peyton eating cooked eggs with warm pigats blood. "Good morning, husband." I smile, hugging him from behind. I feel him tense and then find myself on his lap, his eyes hard at first, but they soften.

"I am a trained warrior, Serena. I have an issue with being approached from behind. Not that you would know. I apologize for startling you."

"Seems I am the one needing to apologize," I reply, kissing his cheek. "Forgive me yet, husband?" I ask, kissing his other cheek.

He smiles at me. "Nope, not yet."

I kiss him lightly on the lips. "How about now?"

"Uh-huh." He smiles before taking me into a strong hold, tangling his hands in my freshly brushed hair, destroying the ponytail I attempted. He proceeds to kiss me so passionately. I find my fingers tangled in his unruly hair, encouraging him. Everything around us seems to disappear, and I find myself pouting when he breaks away from me. I am about to verbally protest, but I realize we were no longer alone. Alexis had joined us. I attempt to move off Peyton's lap, but he holds me firmly, keeping me there, causing me to blush and hide in his shoulder.

"You need not concern yourselves," Alexis states, breaking the awkwardness. "If I did not want or accept this, I would not have allowed it to happen. You are welcome to kiss each other in mine or Keon's presence." She pours herself some pigats that was warming on the stove, adding, "Most the time."

"We have said our good mornings," Peyton replies, picking up his cup to drink.

"Are you hungry, Serena?" Alexis asks, staring at Peyton's food with a look of disgust.

"Not really," I admit.

"Seriously?" Peyton asks, looking at me disapprovingly.

"Do not be too worried about her appetite. It comes and goes like the wind," Aunt Takira interrupts. "She will eat when she is hungry, no point in trying to force it. It simply will not stay down if you do."

"She is not wrong." I blush, watching Peyton's shocked reaction. "If I eat when I am not hungry, I get sick. I went almost a week before the courting to make sure I would not embarrass myself."

"That is not healthy." Peyton frowns.

"For you. But for her, not so much."

"You are full of surprises, Serena." Alexis notes, kissing Peyton's cheek. He grabs her arm when she pulls away and leans forward, inviting her for a much more intimate kiss. I try not to be uncomfortable as he continues to hold me tightly in his lap. When they break away, she smiles before moving to look out the window and drink her pigats.

"Will you at least drink something?" Keon asks, joining us. He walks over to the stove and pours a cup offering it to me.

I wrinkle my nose. He raises an eyebrow and drinks it himself. Aunt Takira makes a cup of water and hands it to me. I smile at her gratefully.

"Is it that you do not like it or is it because you are not hungry?" Keon asks, walking up to his wife and wrapping his arms around her.

"It is disgusting. Even when I am starving it makes me ill." I answer, shaking off the memory of the last time I was dared to try it by a kid Prytore.

"It does more than make her ill. It nearly kills her." Aunt Takira corrects me, causing Peyton to choke on his and set the cup far away from him. "I figured she would be bashful about her physical corks," she continues, "that is why I gave you that letter after the ceremony."

"I admit I have not had a chance to read it." Keon frowns. "But it appears I am going to need to put it on a priority list."

"It is all right, Peyton, you can drink it." I smile at him. "Your consumption will not affect me. I mean, after all, we did just share a wonderful kiss."

"It was a fresh cup. I had not had any." He frowns. "Are you sure, if I were to mark you right now, it will not harm you?" he questions with a glare, causing even Keon to pause.

I turn to my aunt for help. "I am not a doctor, Serena. I know as much as you do."

"I will not risk it," Peyton tells me.

"But you like it." I frown, feeling like I am taking something from him.

"True, but I love you most."

Before any further discussion could be had, a knock comes to the door; it is Doctor Currelt. It is time.

Eighteen

The Cleanse

Serena

I wish I could say I was strong enough not to show worry in my eyes as the doctor describes the lengthy procedure, preparing Peyton for the upcoming pain. I wish it did not make me uneasy when I heard it will take several treatments to be successful. I wish I could say that when the doctor was finished explaining the difficult road ahead, I continued to support my husband without hesitation as he shrugged it all off and said he was ready. I wish all of this, and yet I simply could not.

"No!" I cry out, surprisingly furious. Peyton turns his head. "You cannot do this. I will not let you."

"Serena, this decision is already made." Peyton answers calmly.

"To zarla it is. You are trying to change the very cells that make you, you!" I reply, fighting tears. "For what? A wife you barely know. This is absurd!"

"Serena, I understand you are scared for me."

"No!" I hiss angrily. "Do not try to make this okay, this is not okay. This is my fault for talking to a stranger. I should be punished for this. You should find another and leave me alone."

He crosses his arms over his chest, all amusement withdrawn from his expression. "You want to go down this road. You can blame your aunt for announcing your identity in a room full of strangers. Or further back still your parents who signed you up for the yellow courting at the time of your birth." I pull back, offended at his words, "Do you not see, Serena, there is no fault here. This is fate, not just yours but mine. I was destined to meet you, to love you, to be who I was born to be. Think of the Prytore unnatural molecules as a cancer, a curable cancer. Would you not want me to go through cancer treatment to save my life?"

"I hate your logic." I complain, realizing he has really thought this through.

"You and me both," Alexis chimes in.

Peyton smiles. "I love you both." He then turns his attention to the doctor. "I am ready."

"Okay, I just need to set up a few things." The doctor smiles. "There are things that will not change from this procedure. The damage is already done. Basically, you are stuck with the minute physical changes of your outer appearance, though you seem to only be affected with your ears. Their shape will not change. With the exception of your skin darkening to its natural blue over time, only the internal things will be noticeable. The hardest part seems to be adjustment on how you process thought. Some describe it as having to be rebroken, but it is not something anyone can do for you. It takes a variable amount of time, so Prytores, please do not be hard on him for things he cannot control. But do not worry, he will be able to get a handle on it. Never seen a case where someone has not."

"How many times have you done this?" Alexis asks, raising an eyebrow.

"I would rather not answer that," he replies, working on his machine.

She is about to protest but Keon shakes his head. "It is all right, Doctor, we do not expect you to," Keon replies. "We know you are taking enough risk trusting us not to turn you in for breaking Prytore law to start with."

I snap my head to Keon and then to my aunt. It never occurred to me that changing a hybrid back to a pureblood state would be illegal.

My aunt gives me a nod. "If that is the case, will it not be realized when others see him? His skin is going to change."

"We have thought of this. After the procedure is done, Peyton and Alexis are going to be very visible tonight. A very trusted set of my guards are going to fake a kidnapping, and we are going to be pleading publicly for their return. When they are returned safely, Peyton will start to show changes, and I will be furious that he was forced against his will. You see Serena, you can change the first few generations of hybrids back to a pureblood, but you cannot change him back to a hybrid."

"What would happen to newer generations, if someone tried to make them a pureblood?" I ask, watching a needle being put into Peyton's arm.

"It would kill them." Doctor Currelt answers.

Tears fill my eyes again. "Are you sure you are one of the first few generations of hybrid?"

"No doubt." He smiles at me from across the table. "Will they not trace the guards back to you?" I ask Keon.

"No, if they dig enough, they will find the trail ends, with me." Aunt Takira answers proudly.

"What!" I ask in protest.

"Come, Serena, you are not the only royalty of our kind. Need I remind you I am a princess? Do you think I want your children to be hybrids, if I could help it?" she asks. I raise an eyebrow at her. "No, I did not send Erland your way. What he did to you is repulsive. But I am not complaining about this particular side effect either. Forgive my pride, child, but I am happy for this silver lining."

"Are you all right, Peyton? You look white." Alexis worries, ignoring most of the talk around her.

"Just a bit nauseous." He answers, attempting to look reassuring but failing. "Nothing a warrior cannot handle."

"That is to be expected." The doctor reassures Alexis more than anyone else. "His blood stream must be saturated with this drug. It has to seep into his muscles, especially his brain, before I can start the second part of the treatment."

"How long will that take?" she asks concerned.

"Until the setting of Eshnaine." Doctor Currelt answers. "Maybe longer. Forgive me for the suggestion, Prytoree but I do have some antianxiety medication with me, if you feel it will help you endure this better." She glares at him for a moment. He shrugs. "Just an offer." "One she and Serena will take you up on." Keon answers firmly.

Both of us look to him unhappy. "Do not start, you two. It has been less than ten minutes. You are both so tense you will be useless to him when he needs you in a few hours."

"I will just throw it up." I shrug. "My stomach simply will not keep down water or food right now. Which is needed to take the medicine."

"Thought of that." Doctor Currelt smiles, pulling out a pressurized syringe. I glare at him; he knows how much I hate needles. He walks up to me. "I need your neck, Serena." I do not move. The doctor's blue eyes dart from mine to someone behind me and I feel my hair being moved without my permission, while Keon's arm wraps itself around my waist. I struggle against them, but it is pointless. The needle pierces my skin, and the medicine burns as it enters into my veins. I cry out in frustration. Getting even angrier when Keon does not let me go. I struggle against him to prove my anger, while Alexis simply complies with the doctor. Her acceptance irritates me more, I fight harder.

"Serena!" Keon growls. Peyton is watching but he seems too ill to do much about it. "Calm yourself at once, or I will take you away from him."

"Let me go!" I hiss, unsure where all this anger has come from, but unable to stop it.

"No." Keon answers firmly. He is not expecting my next move. I manage to maneuver and get my elbow directly into his gut. He releases me, curling up in shock from the instant pain. I dash behind my aunt's back, shaking in fear.

"Serena?" she questions, holding up her hand to keep Keon at bay. I am shaking from head to toe. My mind registers the room just for a moment before I am no longer there.

I am at the orphanage. I am staring at Jasha and Reeve, twin Prytore children who were especially cruel to me. Jasha has a knife in his hand, stained purple with my blood. Reeve is holding me down, "Stab her again. She likes it." I cry out when the knife digs into my stomach.

"Serena." I hear my name echo over and over again in a soothing tone. I hear a familiar song, and I struggle with my brain. The memory slowly fades into the past, and I find myself shaking in the kitchen, staring at my aunt. "Have you come back to us, sweet child?"

I nod cautiously, working to control my lungs properly. I fight the tears in my eyes, along with the urge to reach out and hug her. She may be my true family, but the things that happened to me growing up were because of the place she chose to hide us in; and some things, I am not sure I could ever forgive.

Keon is closer to us than before. "Explain yourself." He demands in a gentle tone.

"Bad memory." I answer truthfully. He waits patiently for a more descriptive explanation. "I do not carry my scars on my skin, Prytore; I carry them in my mind."

"What scars, what are you talking about?" he asks, upset. I turn to my aunt who also looks upset and walks away. She is obviously unwilling to be between Keon and me for this. Keon grabs her arm. "One of you better answer me."

Takira gives him a warning look and I notice he winces as he lets her go. She then shakes her head. "Serena speaks of things I hate myself for." My aunt answers weakly. "Things I did not know occurred, or they would have been dealt with. I cannot answer beyond that. She has never chosen to confide details with me."

Keon walks up to me with purpose, but his embrace is gentle. "I need you to surrender yourself to me, Serena," he whispers, "Even the ugly parts. That includes your memories."

"There are things I would rather not relive, even in memory." I answer, the anger replaced with fear. Keon continues to hold me. I watch Peyton turning paler, yet just as concerned. "Please do not make me speak of it, not now. Not while Peyton needs me."

"Condensed version then. I need to know where your mind went, Serena," he replies, undeterred. But he does allow me to pull away.

"Children can be cruel, especially when they are literal aliens to each other." I answer. I feel his fingers on my chin, and I reluctantly meet his concerned brown eyes. "I used to be held down and repeatedly stabbed." His eyes widen in shock. "It is not something I like to remember. But today's events seemed to trigger it."

He pulls me into him, snapping his head to my aunt. "Like I said, there are things I was not aware of, but I will carry the guilt for the remainder of my days."

"We need to know these things, Serena," Keon whispers. "We do not want to damage your mind during your breaking. I will let you keep the rest of these memories locked away while Peyton is enduring this procedure. But you will not keep them to yourself much longer. Prepare yourself for that." He pulls back and kisses my forehead, then he gently guides us back to where Peyton and Alexis are sitting. Placing me on the bench between him and Peyton.

Watching Peyton getting sicker does not help me accept what I have just been told. It takes forever for Eshnaine to set, when it finally does Peyton is laid on the table, and Doctor Currelt slowly and meticulously runs a machine, set to a specific frequency, over his body. The task is difficult for everyone because Peyton is struggling in agony the entire time. His cries have me in tears and shaking. But thanks to the medication, I am able to control myself and withstand it. I wish I could touch him, but we have been warned not to. It takes until the setting of Akatite for it to finally be done.

"Is that it? Is it over?" Alexis asks, reaching for Peyton's hand.

"I am sorry, but no. He will need to undergo another treatment in three days' time."

"But the changes, they will have started by then." She worries aloud.

"I know, which is why your kidnapping plan will have more truth than you think. Do not fret Prytoree, you will be with him."

"But, Serena," she protests.

"It is a sacrifice that must be made to keep the heat off of your family and to keep her healthy," the doctor replies dryly. The doctor turns to Keon, "I am sorry, I thought this would work with a few treatments, but the progress is slower than I anticipated."

"How many procedures will he need?" Keon asks.

"I cannot answer that," Doctor Currelt replies. "In the meantime, he needs a little rest before he can show himself in public. I recommend it being a short affair. After of which, he needs even more rest. It should not take more than a few weeks. It all depends on how resistant his immune system is to the chemical treatment. I must get it all, Keon, not just most, like I have in the past. The point of this is to protect her after all, not to just change Peyton for the zarla of it. As for you and your fiorriee, Peyton's blood is no good for you in this state. For now, you must not exchange fluids with Serena."

"I understand," Keon replies. "Serena and I will use the time to get to know each other better. It seems there are going to be unforeseen obstacles in her breaking that need to be brought to light anyway. Our time will be well spent." He turns to the room at large. "We should let Serena be with her husband, as it will be a while before she gets to be again. Alexis, Takira, Doctor." They all nod and leave the room, though Alexis lingers a bit longer than the rest.

When we are alone Peyton turns to me. "You were tortured?" he asks with sadness in his eyes.

"Hush, do not worry about me. I came out the other side. It is you we need to worry about. That was not easy to watch. It had to be worse to live."

He shakes his head, speaking weakly. "Was it just stabbings?" I glare at him. "I did not mean 'just' as in something to be taken lightly. I meant, is that the only form of torture?"

"Must we speak of this?" I ask, kissing his hand.

"Yes."

I look away from him. "No, it was not just stabbings." I reluctantly answer.

"You will tell me their names." He glares, his eyes full of anger.

"It was a long time ago, Peyton. There is no need for anything like your thoughts now."

He touches my face. "You are wrong," he replies in such as strong voice it surprises me.

"Save your strength, my love. You need rest."

I start to soothe him with a song, but he resists me. "Please, do not. I do not know the next time I will see you. I do not want to sleep before I must leave you."

"Those are not the doctor's orders." I argue.

"I am resting." He smiles, but he is serious. "Let me look at the love of my life. I need to make a beautiful memory to hold on to while I am away." He brushes my hair from my face and studies me. My eyes meet his. I find myself lost in him in a way I have never been lost in anyone before. I can feel what he is feeling, and I know he can feel what I am feeling.

I am shocked when I feel a foreign touch on my shoulder. I am forced to blink, surprised it is so dark in the room. "It is time Serena." Keon states.

Peyton sits up with surprising ease. "Until we meet again, my love." Peyton whispers, leaving me alone in the room with Keon. Hating every moment Peyton and I are forced apart.

Nineteen

Tunnels, Walls, and Trust

Serena

"It does not help when you look at me like that." I frown, turning away from him. We have left my aunt's house a while ago, traveling in the dark to get to Prytore Keon's home. When he felt it was safe to speak on our journey, he started pounding me with questions. I have barely finished explaining the stabbings. I have yet to touch on the rest. Furgan has already set, and I am exhausted from the memories. I did try to gloss over the details, but Keon is not one for overviews. He wanted to know each time it happened, where it happened, where the adults were, where the other children were, how old I was when it happened, and why I never told anyone. It is enfeebling. "All this happened a long time ago, I survived it. What more do you want?"

"I want to be able to trust you. But how am I to do that if you can hide this, and what I fear is much more, from the woman who swore her life to protect you?" He answers coldly, breaking his long stare and continuing forward in the field.

"That is different." I dismiss.

"How?"

"I did not know," I reply angrily. "All I knew is this madam cared about children. I was one of many who she took in. One of many she gave her all too. I was loved by her sure, but so was everyone else. Including the ones that hurt me. I had no idea I was her favorite. I believed my siblings when they told me I was worthless." I force myself to fight the shaking that seems to be all too familiar lately. "If I had spoken up, I could have lost my home. Do you realize what happens to homeless fiorriee? What was this taunting compared to that fate?"

"You did not trust that she would keep you?" he questions doubtfully.

"She never once let on that I was loved any different from the rest. I was not favored by her. Even going to the courting, she acted as if it were a chore. But I see it now, it killed her not because she was taking me to my courting, it was because she had to walk away from all the others she cares for," I reply, my heart aching for her. "I was so excited to leave her. Now with just a few short days and having the truth revealed to me, the idea of not having her saddens me."

He does not reply to that. Instead, he leads us into the dark woods, cautioning me not to get my dark cloak caught on the branches. It is harder to travel here. Zarla is not known for giving off a lot of light, and the other moons have set. It is the darkest time of night for Artthemis, though short-lived. Daylight is but three hours away. I keep close to Keon, who seems more hindered than I, by the lack of light. More than once, I have to stop him from walking into a tree.

Eventually he stops and seems to enter a tree trunk. Surprised, I followed him, finding stairs that wind down into the ground. At the bottom there is an electronic lock. He must have used it up top as well and I missed it. I immediately know we are on his land. Dim lighting on the tunnels barely lights the way and he leads us into the darkness. "You are safe here, Serena. No harm will come to you within these walls. Forgive me for my decision of keeping you in them for the far future. I do not have any desire to risk your life by bringing you among the masses unless it proves absolutely necessary. Even then, I will resist it."

"So I am a prisoner for my own safety," I rephrase, feeling uneasy.

"That is one way to view it, yes." He answers, keeping his back to me. "If it helps, there is much land within these walls."

"A prison is still a prison." I sigh.

He turns to me sharply, causing me to almost run into him. "You will view it differently once you are broken, but that is proving a challenge with what has happened to you both before and after I met you. Which is the only reason I am tolerating such rudeness from you right now! You have been through a lot, and I have encouraged you to be open with me. I am grateful you are comfortable in my presence, Serena, but never forget your place, or mine."

"I am sorry, Prytore." I frown.

He growls as he walks away. "I cannot punish you the way you deserve. It is maddening."

I pause and watch him walk away before I dash up to him. "What would you do? I mean if you could." He glares at me. "Please talk to me. I realize you cannot do it, but maybe it will help to at least inform me."

"You think talking about things that cannot happen will satisfy either of us somehow? I only see that leading us down a road of frustration."

"You can mark me. It has not been three days yet." I encourage, taking his arm and rubbing my thumb on his wrist. He stops walking and glares at me. "Prytore Keon, please, if I deserve correction, do not deny me."

"I will *not* risk it," he replies, twisting my arm, causing me to hiss. "You need to learn to love yourself more." He lets me go violently and keeps walking ahead, seeming not to care if I follow him or not.

The tunnel system is vast. It is so easy to get lost down here with all the options to take; I am surprised he never hesitates as he leads us onward. Eventually, the path starts to climb up hill and that turns into stairs. There is another door, and when opened, I find that we are walking into a beautiful room. The carpet is lush green, the walls look almost gold, and there is a fireplace complemented with black curtains and white chairs. He walks to the fireplace and turns on the electric fire then sits in a sitting chair, indicating I should sit opposite of him. Feeling uncomfortable, I comply; worried that not doing so would lead to a temper I have no desire to meet. I move the chair slightly closer to the fire, grateful for the warmth of it.

"I have upset you," I finally speak, breaking the silence between us at last.

"Yes, you have." He confirms. "But I am not sure if you understand all the ways you have managed it." I sit back in my chair, wishing I could disappear. "You think I want to treat you like a prisoner after your breaking? You think I want to feel frustration and leave you feeling unconnected with your own body and mind? Do you have any idea how much I hate that the slightest slip I make can kill you! Yet you do not seem to give a zarla. Not now, not back when you were at the orphanage. All the risks you took, all the ways you managed to escape from watchful eyes just to be alone, only to be surprised they hunted you down and hurt you. So much could have been avoided, had you simply had more confidence in yourself. You are a leader of an entire species, yet you severely lack the poise to lead them."

"Lead them?" I ask, very guarded. It is one thing to talk about long term goals with my aunt, a fellow royal member of the fiorriee, but to a Prytore... new family or not, it is treason. "I have fulfilled that obligation. They are to accept their fate as a conquered species, just as I have."

"Why do you choose to lie to me, Serena?" He retorts in annoyance. "Do you believe me naive enough to think you support this corrupt system that gives the illusion of satisfying fiorriee choices?"

I carefully keep my expression of insult etched onto my face. This can go one of two very different ways. I cannot be the first to show my hand. If he is testing my loyalty to him and his family and traditions, insult is the best reaction. If he is a traitor to his species and supports mine, he will forgive me for my caution and make the next move. "I was not aware it was an illusion. I made a genuine choice."

"The others? Geela perhaps. You were aware that Geela was shamed in red for refusing to choose the family her caretaker wanted? Are you saying she received a fair deal in her choosing?" Keon presses. I bite my tongue. I know the ancestors blessed her in some way for that. But I am not going to tell my Prytore that.

"It is not my place to judge the politics of the species that won." I answer, turning back to the fire, working desperately to keep myself from shaking again. He is testing me. Am I with him or my kind? Are they different? Or are they the same? "The advantage of being conquered, is that I do not have to run the world."

"True, you do not have to. You could allow your kind to live in suppression despite your parents dying to save your kind from that fate. Or you could make a stand and fight for all fiorree. But the latter will not happen, if you do not learn confidence."

"Then why teach it to me? Doing so could cause me to act in a treasonous manner if ever I get outside these prison walls. That will not only remove mine and Peyton's head from our shoulders, but yours and Alexis' as well."

He studies me for a long while before he speaks again. "You are aware of the stakes. The question is, what does that mean to you?"

"If you are implying my feelings for Peyton are not genuine." He puts his hand up to stop me from speaking, I hiss in annoyance, but I fall silent.

"I am pointing out that I am not naive to the fact that you carry a split loyalty. One for our family, one for your fiorriee. Up until our talk this evening, I believed your loyalty to your fiorriee was stronger, but your lack of confidence in yourself tells me I may be mistaken. Not to say it does not exist, it simply is not what I thought it was."

"I cannot tell if you are insulted or relieved." I admit.

"Which do you want me to be?" It is my turn not to answer him and simply stare. "Your aunt has proven careful not to raise you with strong beliefs one way or the other. She wants you to choose your own path."

"I already did. I chose this family." I answer carefully. "I am at its mercy for its beliefs and desires as I have committed to serve you loyally for the rest of my life."

"Yes, you have. And yet you never asked Peyton's friends or us what our political stance was. It bothered me, but after tonight, I have a better understanding as to why." He studies me. "You have such disregard for your own life, Serena. I am inclined to conclude that you will disregard Peyton's too and are willing to risk his life for choices that Alexis and I do not support."

"Does that translate into your support for current Artthemis politics then, the fiorriee are in their rightful place?" I ask, trying to feel him out.

"What answer are you hoping to hear, Serena?" he asks evasively.

"That is not for me to decide. I am in your service. They are what they are," I reply, believing the words I just spoke but unsure if I would be happy with them. I cry out in pain and grasp at my collar for a moment as it heats up. I expected it to be unpleasant, but I am surprised when it is not. It cools almost instantly. Shocked, I look to Keon for an explanation.

He has not moved from his chair, but he is smiling. "That may be the first, but it will not be the last time that happens." I do not speak my question. "Breaking is not just physical, Serena, it is mental. Your collar can detect when you truly believe the actions or words you speak, and it reveals to everyone when your mind or body have experienced a positive break. I am surprised it did not happen with you and Peyton. He seemed so pleased with you."

"You forget, I had surrendered to him before he put a collar on me." I answer, looking to the fire to avoid his eyes. "Apparently, I resist you more than I thought I would."

"I was not expecting this to be any different than it is." He shrugs it off. "Actually, that is not true. I was expecting it to be worse." He falls silent for a moment before he asks me another question. "Did you get a headache when Peyton showed you your reflection or did that come once you spent time with me?"

"Both times." I frown, unwilling to admit it was not unusual for me.

"You will need more of those mental acceptances before the headaches vanish entirely, but they will. I promise." He smiles, before studying the flames.

"So what are they?" I ask. He turns to me with a raised eyebrow. "Our political views."

"I will tell you eventually."

"You promised me a delayed answer before, and you did not follow through." I challenge, remembering his face when I told him Erland's secret.

"I did. That too involves politics," he replies. "It has been a long night, Serena, come to me." I try not to hesitate as I approach him. He stares at me. "Every part of your being will surrender, Serena. Your body, your mind, your soul. It is just a matter of time." His words cut like a knife.

I do not understand my resistance; a few days ago this is what I wanted. But now that he knows things I was trying to escape from, I do not like it.

"Look at me!" he orders.

I turn my head, but I keep my eyes on the ground.

"Eyes on me, Serena," he orders patiently, but so firmly, my eyes meet his without my personal permission. Tears are spilling down my cheeks, but he is not fazed by them. "Your loyalty is with me and my family. I realize you have only known who you were for such a very short time, but that too is in the past. Here you are not a Queen, not even to Peyton. You are owned by me and Alexis. You have surrendered yourself to Peyton, who is also loyal to me and Alexis. Your place is there, at the bottom of this family. You are owned, Serena. There is no going back, no changing, and no room for split loyalties. You will surrender every part of your existence to us."

His words feel like a whip lashing against my skin. It takes effort to stand and accept it, even more not to cry out. But I cannot stop the traitor tears from giving me away. He says nothing as he stands up, wiping them away.

Instinctively, I take a step back from him, causing him to frown. He breaks our eye contact as he walks to the fire and turns it off. I follow him through the vast house we are in, climbing more stairs than I bother to count. Eventually, he comes to a room and unlocks it with the same technology from the tunnel. He walks to the bed and indicates I should sit on it. I comply.

"I will come for you when I desire. There is a food and beverage machine in here; order whatever you like, but know I do expect you to try to eat. The bathroom is just through there. You will not self-harm in any physical way."

"Please, do not go, not like this," I whisper, not liking the idea of being alone, especially knowing I have disappointed him.

"I must, Serena. Otherwise, how will you learn?" My eyes widen in fear. "Think about your place. Learn to accept it. Try to eat and rest. When I feel you have opened your mind to your fate, I will return." He turns quickly to the exit, locking me in the room, shrinking my prison to four small walls.

Twenty

Isolation

Serena

The moment I am alone, I drop down the wall and cry my eyes out so much my eyelids swell shut, forcing my body into much-needed sleep. I am embarrassed upon wakening when I realize there is a camera here. Keon can watch me anytime he wants. I scream at it for a while, baiting him to come to me, but I am answered only by silence which makes everything so much worse. I feel so vulnerable; I find myself crying myself back to sleep on the wall once more, wishing none of this was my life.

When I wake again, I have no idea what time it is. There are no windows here. And after much examination, I realize there is no way to turn off the lights either. I have no clock and the stupid cooking machine refuses to tell me the time; it keeps asking for a stupid password. So I entertain myself with offering up random curse words to prove my annoyance, surprised it is not locking me out. I take a shower to pass the time, but even that can only last so long before the water runs cold. There are mirrors all around this room. I choose not to stay in them long; the headaches have worsened despite my collar acting in an approving manner, though my reflection is a little less wobbly. I do not understand it very much, and I do not want to dwell on it. But there is not much else to dwell on. There are no books here. No blankets for the bed. Nothing but four walls and my thoughts. I stare at the camera, knowing he could be watching, but I doubt he was. I am sure he has some sort of work to do, whatever that may be.

I want Peyton, but I try not to think of him. I have no idea where he is, how many treatments he has to endure, or when he will return to me. I frown; he could be here right now, and I do not know it. He could be kept away from me until Keon gets what he wants. I grimace at that. I know exactly what Keon wants; he wants me to admit I have the feeling of obligations to my fiorriee. Which is absurd. I have only known who I am for less than a week. How do I feel such a burden? Regardless, I do and I am annoyed he knows that. So why must I say it? Speaking it aloud is treasonous. What are his intentions in all of this? He knew who I was when he approved of Peyton's choice. Is he wanting me to fight for my fiorriee or does he want to break my spirit so much I forego my inherited duties? Is he afraid that he cannot break it out of me? That if he brings me in public, I would run away, taking Peyton with me? I did, after all, tell him I considered others, did he read into that? Is there something to read into?

I cry out with frustration. There are too many questions and not enough answers. Answers I am not going to get until I am honest with him. He wants truths that I am not very happy about parting with. I would rather talk about my days in the orphanage. But he is not giving me a choice. I doubt he will speak to me again until I give him what he wants. Am I this feeble to break so easily for what suddenly feels like a short amount of time in isolation? Should I give it more time before I call out for his attention? Or am I simply just this trapped? Suppressed is a better term. This is exactly the kind of thing my father was fighting against, and here his daughter is, insulting him by managing to fall directly into a Prytore trap. I glare directly at the camera.

"The twins were quite creative with piano wire." I start and begin recalling all the ways in which such a flexible metal can become a very torturous instrument. I give details of how my skin smelt when they chose to burn it. How my purple blood stained the floor when I chose to struggle against my bindings. The type of bruises it left for a short time when it was struck against my skin. After I finish, I start to explain how I was almost pushed off the roof of the orphanage, only to be relieved to be interrupted by the door to my prison opening.

Keon's face is conflicted, tears are streaming down mine from the memories I just shared. He walks into the room and closes the door. Obviously fighting with himself to embrace me. "You wanted to know," I whisper.

"I need you to stop for now. It is taking a lot of energy not to discover their full identity and kill them," he replies angrily.

"If I told you everything, your list would be longer than two names."

"Did any of them ever…" he swallows hard. "Touch you?"

"Erland is the one who has humiliated me the most against my will," I reply. He crosses his arms around his chest, stepping closer, slowly losing his internal struggle. "Others have tried, but I either managed to get away or perform a fiorriee death cry which alerted my aunt."

"That is not an easy call to make, even for a pureblood." He frowns, dropping his arms and approaching me. "Which worries me, seeing how you are able to perform a muted version of it from your night terrors."

"Crying out allowed me to keep my honor for Peyton. It was worth it."

"How long did you lose your voice for?"

"Three weeks."

"What happened to him?"

"I do not know."

"Did he stay at the orphanage?" I shake my head no. "Good. I hope she skinned him alive." We are silent for a long moment. "I apologize that I cannot handle all your memories at once, Serena. I truly wish you did not experience any of them. I will ask again, after I am much calmer, and you have had much more rest. For now, let us keep the past in the past." He turns to go.

"You will not stay until I tell you where my loyalty lies." I note, stopping him in his tracks. He turns to me, waiting. "If I tell them to you, you win through suppression. If I do not, my pride will leave me very lonely. Yet if I speak and you like what you hear, all this is a lesson in submission. If I speak and you hate what you hear, it requires breaking my spirit, not just my mind, body, and soul. And even you are not sure you can go to such lengths. Which means, as we stand, you do not know if you can trust me outside these walls and my safety is not the only reason I live in this prison." He stays silent. "I grew up being tortured by more than one Prytore, heck even a few fiorriee, but none of them, not one was able to break my spirit, Prytore Keon." He raises his eyebrow at me. "I do not fear you or the choices you will make once you hear my answer."

"Then why will you not tell me?" he asks.

"Because I do not have an answer to give, Prytore." I frown, causing my collar to burn. I look away from him, but he is right there, holding me close to him. I cling to the warmth of his body, wondering how long it has been since I felt it. Was it merely hours? Days? How long did I hold out before I found I cannot handle his disapproval of me? "When I discovered my identity, I was so confused. But after a couple of days, I understood the burden of it all. I even embraced it. But all the while it was mixed up with Peyton and your family. I want to be loyal to you. I feel this pull in both directions. I cannot figure out which is stronger, and I do not think either is. I am the Queen of the fiorriee, just as much as I am a part of your family. I am terrified that you are a Prytore political supporter. It would make sense that you are. It is not lost on me that you are friends with the Prytore King, for zarla's sake! But if you speak that out loud, if you tell me that my loyalties must be split into two opposite directions, it will tear me in two. If you are a supporter of the fiorriee however, then the only power struggle there is between you and my fiorriee, and I know you want to win that."

"I will win either way," he replies, kissing my cheek. "This is what breaking is all about, Serena. You will be loyal to me above all else, including your own blood."

"I am scared."

"I would be worried if you were not," he replies. "So I was right then. You are loyal to your kind."

"What would you do if you were in my place?"

"Why did you not ask us or ask others about our political stance?"

"It was too dangerous, even before I realized the King was there. Any signs of treason would have surely ended my life." I pull away, but I do not fight him when he keeps his arms around me. "I figured it was one of three ideals. You either had no view, which is the least likely. Or you were a Prytore supporter and accepted your responsibility, most likely given from the Prytore King himself, to break me and crush fiorriee's hope of ever rebelling from the suppression that came with defeat. Or you secretly support the fiorriee and could not believe your luck when Peyton handed you my papers."

"Of the last two options, which do you believe to be true?" he asks, kissing my shoulder.

"You were the only Prytore who did not look at me like I was some prize to win. I misunderstood it at first, thinking it was simply bounty they were after, but it is more than that. It is glory for their king. You are in financial trouble. Is it because you recently disappointed the King and there is a strain on your relationship? Is that why he did not stop the others from shaming me and made you defend your name and mine on your own without his support? Was there more meaning to Zane's little speech than I understood?" I shake my head from all the questions I am not giving him a chance to answer. "Or is it simply because you knew Peyton was serious. I have given my hand, and you had already won the glory they all wanted?" I meet his gaze, pushing back the annoyance of his silence and stare into his eyes. "I trusted you from the moment I met you, Keon, you have never given me a reason to believe I was mistaken. I do not think you would betray me for the glory of your King. I think you knew what my stance would be even before I did. I think you support it, but you dare not speak of such things in such a dangerous setting, and you were hoping I would not be careless enough to do the same. I doubt you would have been so forgiving about my ignorance to fiorriee traditions and Peyton having to reject his Prytore molecules if you supported my family's enemies." My eyes search his more, "but there is something more important than all of that." He raises an eyebrow at me. "At the joining, when our blood mixed, there was such a pleasant feeling. You could not have poor intentions of crushing my spirit if our joining gave me such a harmonious connection."

"I so desperately want to kiss you right now, my fiorriee Queen," he whispers. I close my eyes in relief. He pulls me back into him. "It is all right. Everything is going to be all right."

"Please do not lie, Prytore. Restarting this dormant war is far from being all right."

"True, but we will make things right, Serena, I promise."

"How? Even if I manage to break my kind from this suppression, where are we to go? The only habitable world is the planet."

"That is not true, and you know it, Serena. Trorain is still habitable, though it is very hostile. Alexis is working on healing the atmosphere in a few years' time."

My eyes harden. "That was not your response a few days ago."

"A few days ago, I did not trust you as much as I do today."

"Is that why you got upset when I told you Erland claimed to be growing up on Trorain? He is supposed to be an ally?"

"Not the way you are thinking. He supports Peyton being fiorriee's king, as Peyton's bloodline has its own rightful claim. Erland sees you as a threat, and what better way to handle you then through poison that demands Peyton to become the rightful pureblood that he should be. His plan is clear. He knew you we would be able to temporarily save you. But now, all it takes if for a stranger licking your arm and keeping you and Peyton separated long enough for that to kill you."

My eyes widen in horror. "Zarla."

"But Erland and his supporters are not the only threat. They have a sound plan. Which makes me doubt that they were the ones behind the poison at your wedding. That would have killed you both." I look at him nervously. "Do not fret, I am working the problem. There is always a solution, Serena, even if it means for now, you must be a prisoner for your own safety."

We are silent for a while before I ask another question. "Did you know I was going to be there? Was my choosing a set up to bring you into my family?"

"Your aunt reached out to the resistance a few days prior. She had been keeping track of certain bloodlines. She requested that three of them meet you. You see, before you were born a blood oath was made between four very strong bloodlines. The pack guaranteed their children to be susceptible amongst each other, which encouraged the hand offering ritual. But it is not a guarantee. You, Peyton, Roald, and Zane each come from one of those bloodlines. Yet you only felt a pull toward Peyton and possibly Zane." My eyes flash to his and he frowns.

"So, the pull between you and Zane is stronger than you have implied." I do not answer that. "Yet, you feel nothing for Roald?" I shrug, not trusting my words. "It is also peculiar that you showed curiosity toward Erland, but I doubt it was the same thing."

"My choice was limited?" I ask, suddenly understanding my connection with Zane the moment our eyes met and why Roald would not directly look at me. He knew. They all did.

"You are royalty, Serena. You were given the fairest chance possible." Keon explains. "As you must be aware by now, Zane is part of the resistance, and his loyalty is not with Prytore Maleko."

"How is that possible? Is he not broken?"

"He is." Keon clarifies. "But very few know that Maleko is not Zane's true Prytore."

My eyes widen in shock and betrayal. "He told me…" I stop speaking, turning away from Keon as I struggle not to shake. Why would Zane lie to me? Did he not feel it? No, he must have. Why did he reject me?

"Serena." Keon states, softly. "By the time you met Zane and Roald, you had already given your hand to Peyton." I shake my head, struggling for calm. "You are still very new at this. But you need to understand, Zane and Roald are very loyal to Peyton. Especially, Zane." I turn around and stare at Keon. "It was unclear how the spell would affect you. Peyton wanted to ensure your hand offering was not influenced by it. When you did not offer your hand to Zane, he chose to mislead you about his Prytore, because you had chosen Peyton. Roald refused to even test the blessing, despite Peyton ordering him to."

"Ordering?"

"You and Takira were lost to the fiorriee for a very long time, Serena. Many believed you were dead. Which defaulted the crown to Peyton."

"Zarla, you truly are a part of the resistance." I state, shocked.

"Yes." He answers confidently. "But you are not the queen we were expecting. Takira put your safety above your education, and apparently self-worth." My eyes fill with tears on that. "You may carry the fiorriee crown, Serena. But you are by no means ready for it." I swallow hard. "Do not worry, we will help you. And when you grow into your responsibilities, we will fight."

"Promise?"

"It requires patience, Serena." He warns, causing me to nod.

"Why Bethany?" I ask, having a strong impression there is way more to that fiorriee than anyone is willing to tell me.

"Peyton was not meant to go to another choosing. Alexis had agreed to the first two because it was expected. There he showed no interest in anyone. We only agreed to go to his third courting, because of your aunt's request, but we made a prearrangement with Bethany's family in case you chose Zane or Roald, as it was his final courting. Simply put, Alexis did not want Peyton to be completely alone. He has proven to be a better fiorriee when he is married to one." Keon pauses in hesitation before he continues. "Still, him and Alexis are so deeply connected. She is worried about you and what it will mean for her and Peyton, and her and me, though she hides it well."

"As I have said before, I have no intention of standing in the way of anything," I reply, insulted.

"Which is why Alexis was grateful we did not come home with someone like Bethany. It was a risk that you would choose someone else, and Bethany would be trying to steal me from her, though the young fiorriee seemed to have little interest in Peyton."

"You would not have let her."

"She would have been put in her place." Keon agrees. "We only chose her because it was expected that the Silviu's seek out a very high-status family like the Leemeair's. Not because we found the lady intriguing."

"Oh, I do not know, her shallowness is rather interesting." I note with an eye roll.

"At times Serena, so is yours." Keon retorts causing me to bite my tongue. "You are her Queen. Having such a petty distaste is unbecoming of you."

"I was not the one who ordered her fate." I retort, crossing my arms over my chest.

"I never said I personally approved." Keon replies. "But Peyton has earned limited defiance from time to time. Besides, Alexis supported him. We need the fiorriee to fall in line. Insulting the queen cannot be tolerated." I stare at him. "I would have been more inclined to favor their decision had you admitted she is the one who chained you to the wall."

"I do not know who did that." I sigh. "But she is the one who told me to sleep like an animal after everyone in that room denied me a bed."

"Thank you for finally being honest with me." Keon replies, causing my collar to warm. "Still, you do not like her, even after you learned she was to be punished. That punishment should have brought her back into your neutral favor." I stare at him, not trusting myself to speak. "But it has not. Is it because she married Zane?" I look away from him, unwilling to answer that. "As I said, Serena. You have a lot of growing to do."

"I love Peyton." I state firmly. "I chose Peyton. I stand by that choice."

"And if hypothetically speaking, I were Zane's and Roald's Prytore?" Keon challenges.

"Peyton." I reply without hesitation. "Though I am not all that confident in you at the moment." He raises an eyebrow to that. "I thought you understood my feelings, but all you have done is question them." I shake my head. "I should not be surprised. Your family was relentless on asking if I was sure. And why I have calmed Peyton's anxiety. I still must calm yours."

"Our family." He corrects me. "You are committed to us now. There is no undoing it." I stare at him. "You are right, we still have trust to build. Still, I am proud of you for trusting us before you could even put it into words or understand its depth. You are very much an amazing creation. I am proud to claim you. But that is where we must start, Serena. Plans to save your kind will happen but on my timeframe. You will not act without my express permission. You must prove to the Prytores that you are broken. That your loyalty lies only with me. And believe me Serena, they will test you. I will be given the glory by the Artthemis King, because he must believe that you are not a threat. But it is not my goal, my fiorriee Queen. My goal is to free you and Peyton so I can take you back to a habitable Trorain. I want our two species to live in peace, even if it means we break off all contact and exist on our own."

"I do not think that could be done." I frown. "Peace yes, ignoring each other… doubtful."

"I think you would be surprised." He disagrees.

"But I would have to exist without you and that bothers me." I admit. "You being gone the way you were just now, bothered me."

"Did it?" he asks, studying me again. I nod in embarrassment. "I was beginning to wonder. It was three days before you even attempted to speak to me. Though admittedly, you slept through two of them."

"I did?"

"I came in three times, concerned you were not breathing." He admits with a blush of his own. "I was going to wake you, but I did not have it in me. I figured you needed the rest. You have been through so much, despite it being completely normal for your kind to fall deeply in love in under a day."

"A week now." I frown.

"Two." He corrects. "You have much pride, Serena. It took you a while to sort your thoughts and accept your fate."

I let that sink in for a moment before I ask, "How is Peyton doing? Is he all right?"

"It is too dangerous to reach out Serena. I have pleaded for his return. You will do the same in a few days' time. After that, all we can do is wait."

"How shall we do that?" I ask.

"Well, I could take you on a tour. That will at least keep me from the temptation of accidentally hurting you." He answers, putting some distance between us.

He smiles then leads me out of this dreadful room that I hope to never see again.

Twenty-One
Family History

Serena

Touring the grounds proved to be an adventure we could not conquer in one day's time. There were simply too many rooms, too many beautiful gardens, too many books from both worlds to even imagine leaving to see something else. I did not understand how this could not be a palace. I was beginning to understand the respect the Silviu name seems to command. After Keon finally persuaded me from a tragic love novel from the fiorriee home world, I decided to ask him.

Taking his arm while we walk down the fourth wing of his mansion. I turn to him, "May I learn of my new family's history Keon?"

"What is it you would like to know, Serena?"

"Lots of things." I shrug. "Forgive me for sounding rude, but how is it possible to acquire all this wealth and not be a king? Much less claim to be in financial ruin?"

"If you understand Prytore religion at all, Serena, you are aware to not make a yearly profit is a sin." He frowns. "Though in my later years, I could care less as I have been enlightened." He shakes his head. "You have heard of Aeroonic Technologies?"

"Who has not? They seem to be the creator or co-creator of everything."

"Not everything, but I have made many technological discoveries." He shrugs, as my eyes widen.

My mind starts to fly through my history teachings, trying to remember something. "Keon S. Mortal," I recall.

"Keon Silviu-Mortal, though the Mortal has been dropped due to poor family history."

"His company began a long time ago," I reply, glaring at him. "Are you, his decedent with the same name?"

"No. Alexis and I conquered the art of aging long ago. Peyton experiences its benefits as well." He shrugs as if it is no big deal. But it is a huge deal. That elixir is one of the most valuable assets on the planet. "Do not fret, Serena, you will too, once we perfect the serum to avoid your impressive list of allergies."

"You are serious?" I ask, rushing through the history again. One of Aeroonic Technologies was the conquering of space travel. "Keon, did you know my parents?"

"We were friends." He confirms, gently guiding me forward when I misstep. "I tried to protect them, Serena. I swear to you, I did not want this fate for the fiorriee." My eyes fill with tears. "I am ashamed at how my planet reacted to the knowledge of your species. We were aware of Trorain's minerals long before we were aware of you. Old money and avarice somehow trumped life, because you were different than us. It sickens me. Conquering space travel is the biggest regret of my existence. I will not rest until I correct this error."

"How can you do that when those who destroyed Trorain are not dying from natural causes of aging?" I ask.

"You do have a sharp mind." He smiles at me approvingly. "We have thought of that. We are working to conquer that obstacle, though it is proving complicated." He does not elaborate as he walks me into an ordinary room. "It is almost time to rest, my fiorriee Queen. But there is something I waited to show you until Trorain was in its full brightness." He walks through the room and into a garden. I gasp, staring at colors of plants I have never seen before.

"They are blue?" I question, rushing to view the leaves. "How is this possible?"

"Something about Eshnaine and Akatite shining purple, but Trorain's atmosphere changes the spectrum and causes the rays to reflect blue. You would have to ask Alexis. She is fascinated by it as well."

"Did you say…?" I ask, unable to word the question.

"Yes, Serena, all the plants here are from your native land and taken great care of to bloom exactly how they would on your native soil."

"Keon," I cry, covering my mouth, more moved than I could explain.

"I knew you would love it." He smiles. "Which is why this room is yours along with this garden. And if you walk thru that door over there, you will find yourself back in that library with those books you seem to love so much." I dash over to him with a squeal, squeezing him tightly, almost taking him off his feet from my excitement. "Warn me next time, I am an old man." He laughs, hugging me tightly. I pull away in concern. He shakes his head. "I have been stuck as a thirty-three-year-old Prytore, for two hundred and ninety-four years, Serena. Does that put a perspective on how I can be the inventor of almost all modern technology?"

I give him a teasing glare. "I would not brag too much. You do not just have the destruction of my world to apologize to me for. You are the inventor of all those stupid math equations I had to learn in school! Not to mention, the anti-cheating brain-scanning test of knowledge. I have cursed you to zarla so many times in my life I am surprised all your parts are attached."

He laughs so loud he surprises me as he sits on a sofa in the room he said was mine. I join him, and he pulls me into him, as he looks down at me, smiling. "I am sorry I put you through so much torture when you were young, but it seems to have paid off. You were forced to learn the material whether you liked it or not." I laugh a little, but my smile fades as I catch a reflection of Trorain. "Where did you go?" he whispers, touching my cheek lightly.

"If you have lived as long as you have and you knew my parents, it is reasonable to conclude you knew my aunt as well. Which is why she trusted you so easily that first night." I accuse. He nods. "But that is not where I went just now."

"Oh?"

"I am not your first female fiorriee, am I? You shared another with Peyton." His eyes harden. "She either chose not to take the antiaging serum, or you did not offer it. Yet you do not hesitate with me, and you gave it to Peyton."

Keon sighs. "As I stated before, the four bloodlines are important. Remember, if you in fact did not exist, Peyton would be the King of your kind. Which is why King Maleko turned Peyton, Zane, and Roald into hybrids. It not only distorted their bloodline, it shortened their life."

"But I am a pureblood." I frown. "How?"

"At the time, Maleko was unable to obtain leverage over your family as he did the others. By the time that leverage existed, the practice of first-generation hybrids had been abandoned due to their defiance."

"Timing?"

"Timing." Keon confirms, causing me to shudder. "And the fact you were hidden until now." I nod, as I try to grasp the danger I have been in my entire existence.

"But all three of them have taken the elixir." I counter.

"Maleko has an arrogant side." Keon explains. "Zane's influence switched his view from early death to flaunting the fact that the fiorriee royal lines were conquered. Thus, ensuring Prytore control for all current and future generations."

Tears fill my eyes at that statement, and I suddenly understand why my fiorriee are probably devastated that I did not marry a pureblood. I did not think it mattered. But it clearly does. At least here on Artthemis, with our enemy in control. "Fiorriee are meant to be fiorriee. I never cared to differentiate between pureblood and hybrids."

"It is okay Serena." Keon assures me. "Even your father declared hybrids fiorriee." I nod, happy to know that.

"Still, Prytores view it differently than fiorriee." I close my eyes to that. "Not only that; he is under the mistaken impression that all of you submit to loyal Prytores, now. King Maleko believes he has won his last victory. Leaving no hope at all for a fiorriee uprising that he has been dreading for many years."

"He is wrong," I reply, angry, tangling my fingers with Keon's.

"We know this." He smiles. "But King Maleko is not going to be happy when he discovers Peyton is no longer a hybrid. It paints a target on Peyton's back. One we were planning on putting there, eventually, but not for another decade or so, though Alexis was not aware of that yet."

"Zarla, so many lives hang in the balance."

"Let me worry about that for now. We are at the beginning, remember. And right now, you need to concentrate on being broken." I nod in acceptance. "To answer your original question fully, you are correct, you are not my first female fiorriee. But I have not taken the honor of one in many years. I loved Karissa. I think she loved me, but she was so homesick. Being forced to live here because Trorain was destroyed, broke her in ways we could not fix. We could not bring ourselves to let her live longer than her natural life. It would have only caused her to suffer. So, we let her go and built this garden in her memory when plants started to reappear on Trorain's soil. Seeing your reaction to it today, I could not be more honored. She would have been so pleased to see her Queen enjoy it so much."

"You will have to teach me how to care for them."

"Of course." He smiles. "Sleep now, Serena. Tomorrow is going to be difficult for you as I have some tests in store."

"Do not leave me tonight," I plead. "Please."

"Since you asked so nicely." He smiles, kissing my forehead and walking over to a machine that looks similar to the food machine from the other room. He presses a few buttons and comes back with a few blankets and nightclothes. "Blue seemed so fitting." He smiles, tossing it on the bed. I take what I need and make my way to the bathroom to change. When I return, he is stretched out on the sofa. I smile, taking the bed, grateful I am not alone as I close my eyes to sleep.

Twenty-Two

Divided

Serena

The morning light is harsh when I wake. I find Keon staring at me, causing me to become instantly nervous. "It is time, Serena," he whispers, kissing my fingers.

"I am nervous." I admit.

"Do not be, this journey has great rewards. Soon your mind and body will become one. Oh, and you will need to wear pants."

He leaves me to my thoughts as I am allowed to eat and do hygienic things. I am unsure what to expect today. I know he has already started the breaking but today feels different. Details seem to be forbidden, which is annoying when one is trying to style their hair. Using a mirror is useless, as always. I find it strange that they claim my reflection might one day be useful to me. I have no memory of that ever being the case. I decide on a messy bun to keep most of my hair out of my face. Besides, I am in pants. I hate pants, so why spend the time to make my hair happy about it?

Keon re-enters the room looking refreshed himself; he offers his arm and leads me to a new room. "Today, I want you to stack these three books on your head while doing a headstand. You may not use your hands or feet for support of any kind, and you may not let the books touch the floor. Good luck."

"Luck?" I ask patronizingly. "What you are asking for cannot be done." He gives me a half smile, then turns and locks me in the room. "Perfect." I mutter to myself, staring at the floor. Curious, I examine it, but it is just a normal floor. The walls are bare of any machines, so altering the rooms gravity is out. The ceiling, of course, has a camera. I glare at it for a moment before I grab the uneven stack of books and try to balance them on my head. They immediately crash to the floor. Undeterred, I try again. Finding the perfect physics to this takes longer than I expect, but eventually, I get there. Satisfied in my confidence on that achievement, I work on standing on my head. I am embarrassed the first time I fall and annoyed the twentieth. Refusing to give up, I find myself surprised as I go to remove my hands from the floor as Keon enters. I crash down, and somehow roll to my knees, making it seem I have planned that, but I have not.

"I brought you food." He smiles.

"I appreciate the kindness, but I am not hungry."

"Will you at least drink something for me?" he asks with worry in his eyes.

"I will just get sick. I am sorry, I need to figure this out," I respond, moving my body back into a headstand.

He watches my fruitless effort for a while before he leaves in silence. Two hundred and seventy-nine attempts later, I finally figure out how to stand on my head. The victory is uplifting, until I remember I am supposed to be doing this while holding books on top of my head, with the added bonus that these said books cannot touch the floor. I lose my focus and roll into a sitting position. My aunt would be furious for my choice in posture, knowing someone is watching, but I do not care. I ponder the puzzle in my mind forever, trying a few failed attempts here and there. Despite my wishful thinking, I cannot float. Frustrated, I throw one of the books across the room, having an added sense of satisfaction when the pages snap together. The book lands open, almost taunting me for not having the knowledge I need. My eyes widen, could it really be that easy? I grab one of the books and open it. It is a dictionary for science; the other is a double translation for Prytore and fiorriee. I rush over to the book I just threw, reading the title, *Understanding Fiorriee Physical and Mental Being*. I quickly open the very densely written text and realize the choice for the other two books. I frown; this is not a simple task. Sighing, I slowly start to dig into it. After the first few chapters my eyes are sore and heavy. "Prytore Keon, may I have substance now? And possibly something to take notes with?" I close the text and lean against the wall, closing my eyes only for a moment.

I am alone in a dark space. I cry out, but my voice echoes in the blackness. I begin to walk, hearing my footsteps echo on the ground. Stopping short, when a door appears in front of me. Looking at it gives me the chills. I do not want to be here. I do not want to know what is on the other side of it. But my fear does not stop me from hearing the voices. They belong to me and another. My ears strain to listen. I cannot make out the words. I step closer, causing the voices to come clear.

"Good girl, Serena, you are mine now. No other shall have you."

I recognize the male speaker, but I cannot place his name. It is not Keon, it is not Peyton, yet it is familiar. Why?

"I am yours." I hear myself agree to it. "I will forever only be yours."

I gasp in horror, running away from the door as fast as I can, but I am getting nowhere. It is gaining on me. I hear a creaking sound, and then a burst of light comes through. I scream out, my lungs regretting the instinct. They are on fire.

My eyes flash open. I find myself standing in an attack position, staring at Keon.

"Serena?" he questions calmly.

"Stay back!" I shout, pulling away but unsure as to why. I look at him, dumbfounded. "I did not mean that." I try to relax, but I cannot. "Why can I not move? What is happening?"

"You were dreaming." Keon answers. "Do you remember it?" I nod. "Was it a memory or a night terror?"

"Night terror." I answer. "I think." Whatever it was it felt real, forbidden, forgotten, locked away. I release a deep chest growl. "I do not want any part of it. Why did this come to me? Keon, what if it is true?" I ask as fear overtakes me.

"What if what is true, Serena? What did you dream?" he asks, staying alert but obviously confused.

"I have done this before," I reply gathering the books and releasing my all but forgotten dormant ears. I put the books between them and hold them tight. Then I do a headstand and rest on my ears, effectively keeping the books from touching the floor while my hands stay at my waist.

I slowly come down. He takes a step backward, anger replacing his confusion. I stand up and stare at him, unsure what to say. "Serena, who do you serve?"

The question causes me to cry out in such intense agony that I find myself fighting to stay standing. "You!" I manage, but the answer comes with such intense unpleasant pain I can barely see. "Make it stop!" I beg, screaming at him. I feel his arms wrap around me, causing me to struggle against his touch.

"You can fight all you want, Serena. I am winning this!" He warns. "You will be mine, all of you. I expect nothing less than complete surrender."

"Keon, please, what is happening!" I cry out, hating that his scent is making me ill. "I care for you, why am I resisting you? I do not want this! I want you!" My words cause stabbing white pain in my skull. I can barely breathe.

"You have surrendered to another, Serena." He answers angrily. "Tell me his name."

"I have not! I swear!" I argue, but the pain will not stop.

"His name Serena."

"I do not know! Keon, please! I only surrender to you and Peyton." My knees give out from the attack my body is giving to itself; if not for Keon, I would be on the floor. "Why does this hurt? I have not betrayed you," I cry, hot tears spilling on my cheeks.

"You were dreaming. Who was in your dream?" he tries, keeping me locked in his arms.

"No, noo!" I cry out, my brain feels a stabbing pain so severely that I feel something snap and then I do not feel anything at all. Suddenly, I am staring *at* my limp body in Keon's arms. "Keon?" I question, but my voice is an echo, and he shows no signs of hearing it.

"Stay with me, Serena, do not let anything lead you astray." He calls out to the room as a whole. "I am coming. I will save you. You just need to let me." I am unsure what he means as he pulls my body on top of his lap. I watch as he works to calm himself. Then I take a step back in shock when I see him connect his visible second set of ears to mine. I feel a strange, uncomfortable feeling, and his body falls as limp as mine. "Serena," he whispers at me, causing me to jump in surprise.

"It does not hurt," I reply, keeping our distance.

"It will not unless your thoughts conflict. Your mind is no longer connected to your body."

"Why?"

"Because you are torn, Serena. You have sworn to serve another!" He is silent for a long moment while his jaw flexes. When he speaks again, he is calm, but his tone is something I have never heard before. "I am very displeased by this."

His disappointment weighs heavily on me. Tears are streaming down my face, the searing pain my body just experienced almost forgotten. Replaced by the strong feeling of failure. "I have not." I argue weakly. "I do not trust these thoughts. I have no memory of them." I work to regain my composure, but his words have me so weighed down it is nearly impossible. "Please, Prytore Keon. I serve you." I cry out in agony the moment the words pass my lips. Something is wrong. Something…I cry out as my form starts to struggle with itself. I can feel hands and feet inside of me clawing to get out. I do not understand it, then I feel a violent rip and suddenly there are two of me. But we are so different I barely recognize the other, only the fact that she is wearing a black dress gives me a slight context to familiarity. "Only you, Prytore Keon." I speak. But she does not. I turn to my Prytore, scared.

"You are divided," he says in such an acid tone, I feel ashamed. "I do not know her!" I argue. "She is not me!"

"You are right. I am not a traitor." The other of me replies.

"Prytore Keon," I reply, shaking hard.

He is silent for a long time before he speaks. "Judging by your fear, I am inclined to give you the benefit of the doubt. You have either lost this knowledge or you were forbidden to speak of it. How this happened, Serena, I do not know. What I do know is that you are of two minds, and you will not survive long like this. You must merge again."

"Gladly." I whisper.

"Not while she serves the wrong Prytore." The black dress me sneers. She turns her back to us and then vanishes into the darkness.

Scared, I turn to Keon. "Please, help me. If this is true…I do not want another. I want you." I beg. I reach for him but something in the dark grabs me with such force it causes the room to fall away. I hear Keon scream my name and try to follow after me but the darkness swallows me whole. When the tugging stops, I find myself alone. "Keon!" I call, but there is no answer. I look around into the nothingness. "Keon, help!" I scream as loud as I can but he does not appear. "What is happening? Where am I?" I cry, truly scared. But there is no reply by him, or anything, or anyone else; including the other one of me. The darkness feels heavy, it is hard to be here. I struggle to think about what he had just said. It is impossible that I serve another. I cannot serve anyone until my courting. How would this even happen? A crack of light reaches my toes. I look up, there is another door. I frown. I do not want to know what is behind this anymore than the last one. I turn my back to it, ignoring it. I try to run, but it is as if I am going nowhere.

With a loud slam, the door opens, surrounding me with a bright burst of light.

I can hear my own laughter. I am happy. I look over to find myself playfully running away from a young Prytore with dark brown hair. "You cannot catch me." I taunt.

"When I do, I am going to keep you," he calls back, laughing. He lunges for me. I squeal with delight as he causes us to fall, covering my yellow dress in red mud. He looks up at me, his eyes are piercingly red. "All mine, forever and ever." He laughs, kissing me deeply. I do not resist him. I am shocked to find I pull him close to me, kissing him with what appears to be familiar passion.

Why am I wearing yellow? Why am I lying on the ground, much less with a Prytore?

"I almost wish I did not find you." Keon growls as he watches a memory, I had no idea I owned. I turn to him; his voice and stature give away his anger. His eyes carry a pain that one could almost describe as jealousy.

"Am I on Zarla?" I ask him seriously.

"No, you are in your mind. Being disconnected like this allows you to relive every memory you have ever made. Including those you do not want to forget, and those you do."

"I do not remember this." I frown. "I mean, yes, that is me, but I do not know who he is. Much less any context around this memory."

"If that were any other Prytore, I would not believe you. But seeing as that is Roarick, Maleko's son; your amnesia seems plausible."

"He is the Prytore Prince?" I ask, shocked.

"Where are we?" I look at him strangely, he seems to know that better than I do. "The surroundings Serena. Where did this memory take place?"

"At the orphanage," I reply, causing the memory to vanish and doors after doors slam open. We are surrounded by mini scenes of my introduction to new children, over and over again until it stops. Then there is a single door.

"Open it."

"I do not want to." I frown. He raises an eyebrow at me and waits. My hand is shaking when I reach out and open the door. I look away from the memory that plays, introducing Roarick as a new child. Takira is telling me that he lost his parents in a transport accident, and he has nowhere else to go. I smile at him, but I refuse to be distracted, going on with my chores; used to kids coming and going.

The scene fades into darkness only to be replaced by another and then another and then another. All my time with Roarick. It took him ages for me to say three words to him, much less spend an afternoon with him. "Persistent." Prytore Keon notes, watching this movie of my life in disapproval. I do not reply, these memories cannot be mine. I do not have any familiarity with them.

I watch as Roarick gives Prytoree Sine a hard time, causing me to giggle. He looks at me, winks, and smiles the entire time he gets yelled at. Things skip forward and he offers me half his sandwich. I happily take it, and he sits next to me on the roof of the orphanage.

"Interesting hiding spot." He notes.

"Apparently not an effective one. What do you want Roarick?"

"You." He answers smiling. *"Or have you not figured that one out?"*

"When are you going to figure out, I am not into you?" I retort, tossing the sandwich to the ground below.

"You are, you just do not know it yet." He smiles, causing me to get up and climb back into the building.

The memory fades out, this time replaced by one I do recall. I try to look for an exit but there is not one. "No," I whisper watching myself read a book.

"It is okay, Serena, it is a memory, it cannot hurt you." Keon reassures me. His phantom form gets too rigid as he understands my resistance to it.

The twins grab me and pull out a knife. I want to look away but my vision is glued. My screams are muffled from their gags and laughter. Then something changes, something I do not remember, it is Roarick. He grabs Jasha and throws him across the room, punching Reeve out with one hit. "Serena, are you all right?" Roarick asks, pulling me from the floor. He turns to Jasha. "Touch her again and you answer to me. She is mine. Understand?"

Other memories start flashing through my mind so rapidly they are almost a blur but each and every one of them contain me with Roarick. "I do not understand, how could I not remember?"

"Go to your last memory of him Serena, I am out of patience." Keon replies, in a hard tone.

"Love to, care to guess what that is?" I snap.

"You are resisting, me or the memory, I do not know which, but stop."

Suddenly, we are surrounded by darkness again. I stare at Keon who stares back at me with a look of betrayal. I decide I hate this look on him the most. I can hear voices behind a door that is at my back. I shake my head no, but Keon does not respond. All of his reassurance and caring are gone. It takes strength to turn around and open the door. I recognize the scene immediately. The memory turns black and white, the sound goes out. But the picture will not stop. Roarick is forcing me to my knees, I am struggling. My aunt runs into the room with a frying pan in her hand and rips him away from me. The memory fades out. I am in a room with her and our doctor, curled into a ball. Blood is taken from my hidden ear; I drink something and everything goes black.

"I do not understand."

"His betrayal, nearly killed you." Keon explains, angrily. "They locked your memories away, but they could not erase the trauma itself. Just the person behind it."

"So, what unlocked them?"

"I do not know." He answers. "But it explains why you remember every traumatic event in your past so passionately. It had ended for you and after he was gone, I have a feeling it started again. Your mind did not register the gap, it just made it seem like one long torment for you." He flexes his jaw. "How long have you been unable to see your reflection clearly?"

I hesitate, I do not like that he figured this out. "Five, maybe six years." I answer softly, causing doors to rearrange themselves in front of us. "He came when I was fifteen, gone when I was eighteen." Keon refuses to look at me, keeping his eyes on the closed doors.

"What happens now?"

"That is up to you, Serena. Being abandoned or betrayed by a Prytore is usually a death sentence; one your aunt temporarily saved you from. When you wake, all these memories will come back to you. You have to choose. Him or me? If you choose me, I cannot make promises of saving you. I can just as easily kill you. You have not been given a chance to let him go. If you want to serve me, you must do that. Even then, his memory will make that difficult for you."

"So, this is some elaborate plan?" I ask. "If I ran from Prytore customs, Roarick would have hunted me down and forced me back into Prytore rule under my enemy's kingdom. But submitting to another ensures my death, thus eliminating the threat all together. No wonder Maleko did not seem threatened. He knew I was walking into a death trap."

"Death by Prytore or death by pureblood fiorriee." Keon agrees. "I understand now how Zane got his hands on that elixir. It was King Maleko's back up plan."

"So, the King does view me as a threat, not a relic of a conquered species."

"Evidence is favoring that theory, assuming Roarick is working with Maleko on this." Keon replies, flexing his jaw. "Roarick may be clever, but I will not let him win without a fight. Will you?" Keon asks me. I am about to answer him but he shakes his head, stopping me. "Think about your choice Serena. Ask, and you shall be returned to Roarick." Before I can respond, he is gone. I watch him open his eyes and lie my body down on the ground. He walks away from my sleeping form and locks the door behind him. Leaving me to decide for myself what I truly wanted and how much I was willing to fight for it.

Twenty-Three

Loyalty

Serena

Getting back into my body was not as easy as Keon made it look. My brain kept forcing me to relive all the memories I had locked away. Ones that admittedly, I am kind of pleased to own. Looking back, I find myself enjoying the sight of the twins ducking away in fear at the sight of me. And despite myself, I cannot deny there are a lot of happy memories of Roarick and me until that one moment changed everything. That memory keeps coming back in flashes… adding color, sound, details. But every time I feel it is going to overtake me, I flash to Peyton and sometimes Keon allowing everything to right itself again.

I have no clue how long it takes me to figure out how to get back into my body. I tried everything from lying down inside myself to screaming at my slumbering form, to meditation, but nothing seemed to work. Nothing kept me from reliving all those memories. It got to the point that they became so repetitive; I no longer studied them or even feared the bad ones. I simply got bored of them. That is when it happened. Without warning I get yanked back into my body, finally being able to open my eyes.

I fly to my feet, taking in the surroundings. The memories come painfully flashing at me. It feels like forever until it finally ends. When it does, I stand up straight and turn to the camera. "Prytore Keon?" I call out. I am surprised when he does not answer for a long while. Bored, I grab the books from the floor and start to read again. I make it through one chapter before my eyes cross from all the translating. "Prytore Keon?" I call to the camera again. This too goes unanswered. Annoyed, I lean against the wall and glare at the camera. "I am fine. I am not going to collapse on myself over Roarick being a daget. At least he kept the twins away for a while. I swear I am fine; my aunt did not give me enough credit to think I would let it kill me. You should know better; I know what he was trying to do, and I will not allow it. I am stronger than that." But even this is greeted by silence. "For the love of zarla! Keon, I serve you!" I cry out in unpleasant pain the moment I say the words, with effort I do not let it take me to the ground. Angry, I scream out in frustration. "I serve you, Keon." I repeat, fighting the pain. Suddenly, I understand his silence. Undeterred, I say it again and again, feeling like my skin is being licked by a fiery whip both on my body and in my brain. But I do not stop. Each time, it is slightly less painful. Time passes very slowly, but I do not give up. Eventually, I can say it and tolerate the pain without even wincing. Determined, I stand in the middle of the room and look at the camera. "I serve you Prytore Keon. My loyalty is with you and your family." I manage to stand firm, but my voice shakes. Knowing I am going to be greeted with silence, I lean against the wall, desperately needing sleep. I close my eyes and work to fight the memories; truly hating my heritage.

When I open my eyes, I find myself on a bed. It takes me a moment to realize I am in the room Keon had given me. I search the room and find him sitting on the sofa. "Prytore Keon." I smile, jumping from the bed and rushing to him, trying not to wince from the unpleasant pain caused by the action. I force myself to ignore it and keep my smile, as I really am happy to see him. His facial expression is stern which causes my smile to fade a little. "Keon?" I ask, suddenly unsure, reaching out for his arm but withdrawing from his coldness. "I see." I sigh, pulling as far away on the sofa as the furniture will let me. "You are angry."

"Eleven," he finally speaks, though I do not understand, so I stay quiet. "Eleven is the age that most fiorriee begin their training about Prytore laws, and preservation for courting." I drop my eyes to the floor. "You met him at fifteen. You knew you were to be twenty-three for your courting and you were to preserve yourself." He glares at me. "Did you not receive this education, Serena?"

"I did." I answer, tears spilling out of my eyes.

"You knew better and yet…" he does not finish his sentence.

"Yet I did whatever it took to stop what was happening to me. All because I did not trust those I should have. It is my burden to carry Prytore Keon, one I must overcome. One I am willing to, if you will let me."

"How am I supposed to trust you, Serena?" he asks, defeated.

"You are not. I cannot ask that of you." I answer truthfully.

"For the love of zarla, Serena." He curses, holding his head in his hands. He looks up at me. "Why, why did you not trust her?" I do not answer him. "There must be a reason."

"If there is, I do not remember it," I reply honestly. "I can search my memories again. Maybe that will help."

"You mean split from your body?" Keon asks alarmed. "Did you not read that book at all? Doing what you did, it is dangerous! Being able to come back from it takes a lot, much less not die the moment you do it."

"So why did you leave me there all alone?"

"I should have never gone in, in the first place. But I knew you needed guidance; I knew you had no idea what was happening to you. You still do not. You are of two minds now Serena, as I am sure only half of you returned to your body. There are two outcomes. She will either kill you for choosing me, or she will join you in your submission to me. The first is most likely, being split like this is unnatural. Without balance, you could die within a season." I study my toes, unsure what to say. "I could not stay within your mind to help you convince her. If I did not leave when I did, I had no guarantee that I could get out. It was hard to leave, as I was unsure if you would ever wake again." He swallows hard, "You are important to Peyton, Serena, but I am the ruler of this family. I need to be alive for my wife and fiorriee."

"Am I only loved by Peyton?" I ask, feeling hurt from more of his rejection.

"There is no potential but without trust. I refuse to feel anything more for you than the guardian I am." He answers truthfully.

"How am I to earn that if I have no answers as to why I did not trust my own blood?" I ask, feeling helpless. More tears spill from my cheeks. "I have trusted you since I met you. Was I wrong to do so, is my past not forgivable?"

"I do not know." He answers getting up from the couch only to look at me in surprise when I grab his wrist.

"Please." I cry.

"What Serena! What do you want from me?" he asks, upset.

My pride stirs up and I find myself sitting up taller, releasing his wrist from my grasp. "Nothing." I answer, looking away from him. "I do not want a zarla thing." I furiously wipe my tears away, angry that he has not left like he had intended moments before. Eventually, I look up at him in annoyance.

"That pride of yours tells me that you were not broken properly, whether it be because you were too young, or he did not know what he was doing. Either way, it leaves the idea that there is hope."

"Hope?"

"Hope that with time and a more rigorous breaking than I ever intended, you may be able to overcome this, this… insolent and nearly inexcusable choice."

"Thank you," I reply, swallowing hard, trying to avoid shaking. "For the hope. I will do whatever you ask of me."

"Then leave me be for a few days, Serena. I am too angry to even want to forgive you right now." He walks out of the room without another word.

Twenty-Four

Birds

Serena

Iknew this house was ridiculously grand in size but the extensive detail that went into almost every room is mind boggling. The Prytores' religion is based on wealth. Not just of money but knowledge and the more they have, the more blessed they feel. It is such a barbaric religion if you ask me. It forces everyone to become avarice and deceive their own family members if it means they get ahead. How anyone trusts anyone based on this concept is beyond me. But somehow, it works for them. Mostly because they have set up a cast system that keeps Prytores from reaching too far out of their own station. Though with the blessing of knowledge or pleasing good looks, there are oddities that seem to advance higher than their birthright. This house is seeping with that religion, complete with paintings and symbols. There is no doubt in my mind this family once thrived on it before Keon and Alexis chose a different path.

Walking around the house makes me feel suffocated. So, I find myself on the very large grounds. Here there are beautiful gardens, woods, hills, streams. Everything you could want on Artthemis. Yet when I find a spot to sit alone, I find myself lonely. Not because I want

Peyton or Keon's company. I think it best I steer clear of them both at the moment, though Peyton has yet to return.

Artthemis' nature has always left me feeling incomplete. Mostly because there is not much to it except purple plants and colorful streams. The animals that once thrived on this planet are all but extinct. Prytores live off of synthetic food generators to mimic what they once knew as meat, but the real thing no longer exists. Just as they have destroyed Trorain, they are self-destructing to their own planet. It is strange. I miss the sound of flying animals the most. I always thought I made them up in dreams and my aunt never told me that I had not. My educators could not confirm or deny any possibilities of what Trorain was like before the war. Still, sitting here amongst the purple grass I believe they must have been real, though I know not the name of them. From what I have gathered during my courting, I was born on Trorain and those memories must be buried, long forgotten with time, yet the flying animals remain.

I stay in the suns' daylight for as long as Akatite's rays arc in the sky, avoiding being in the house. I have not seen or spoken to Keon in over two weeks. I am sure he is keeping eyes on me with his technology, but he has not bothered to hunt me down. Honestly, I am not sure what would happen if we accidentally crossed paths. I thought about it some, but I would probably just stay frozen until he gave me directions one way or the other. He is the one who asked for space, so I am giving that to him. I am careful not to even speak my thoughts aloud, for fear my voice over the machines, might add to his anger. I am not sure what to make of it, he seemed very much against neglecting fiorriee at the courting, so I do not know if this is neglect, punishment or something else. All I know is it is what he wants, and I will do it because he asked me to.

When I first made that decision in my mind my collar burned in approval, almost mocking me for the predicament I have put us in. I struggle daily with the conflict that I had no idea existed until I rediscovered my extra set of ears. While I do not battle it out verbally, mentally I challenge myself to express my loyalty to Keon. The pain from those thoughts can be so exhausting. I am almost grateful for the time to work through this, for I do not want either Keon or Peyton to see the pain it causes me. Pain I thought, two weeks ago had lessened. But it seems it all restarts in the morning and I must fight it every single time until it eventually gives way. That is taking less and less time, though admittedly I am counting in seconds. I can only hope that one day, it will not waste any of my time at all. But that is a long personal journey, and I am only at the beginning.

When Trorain starts to rise in the sky I head inside. Despite lazily sitting out in the suns' all day, I am exhausted. I make a dash for my room when I hear Keon call my name, stopping me in my tracks. Cautiously, I slowly return to where his voice came from, then stand in the hall, as I look at him, unsure what to say or do.

"You need not hover in the doorway, Serena. When I summon you, I expect you to stand in my presence," Keon remarks, inviting me into the room.

"How may I serve you, Prytore Keon?" I ask, working hard not to show the displeasure the sentence causes me.

"I would like you to share a meal with me tonight." Keon smiles, holding out his hand from his chair, indicating I should sit at the table with him.

"Thank you." I smile timidly, sitting in the seat uncomfortably. He gets up and orders meals from the food transporter then sets my meal in front of me. I wait for him to sit and eat before I try to.

"When is the last time you ate?" He asks me, putting food on his fork.

"Three days I think." I shrug. "I do not keep count."

"You do now." he replies, chewing his food.

"As you desire, Prytore." I respond, shaking my head and closing my eyes, wishing this did not hurt.

"It is not healthy Serena." He worries, ignoring my suffering. "Despite your aunt's reassurance."

"How much do you know about fiorriee anatomy?" I ask.

"I have done much more than simply read books," he answers, taking a drink.

I put food on my fork and concentrate on chewing it, forcing myself to swallow. "Were you aware that our healing abilities, amazing as they are, are limited?" He stops eating and stares at me. "My aunt could not figure out my eating habits because she assumed I would tell her about the twin's little games. But I did not. So, she did not realize that my stomach is scarred and unless I am completely relaxed, my digestive system does not work the way it should."

"That sounds fixable with the proper medication." he notes.

I shrug. "Maybe, I have never tried." The silence that falls between us is deafening. I feel awful about the wedge my younger self put between us. I wish I could go back and stop her, reassure her that she would be fine, that she was loved. I put my fork down and turn my attention to Keon. "You experienced Trorain before all the damage?"

"Yes." He answers, looking surprised at my question.

"I have the strangest memory from my childhood. So strange, I think I might have dreamed it, but no one could ever tell me if I had." He eats while he waits for me to share it. "I know they had animals there, like sea creatures but on land." He nods in confirmation. "Did any of them fly? Did they make a lot of noise?"

He smiles at me. "They are called birds. They made all sorts of amazing sounds."

"Birds." I repeat, feeling the strange word on my tongue. "Is it strange to miss something I never knew the name of?" He looks at me. "I mean, it is peaceful here. The streams and things are nice, but it is so quiet. How could I miss the sound of home when I was only there for such a short while, at such a young age?"

He studies me. "What were you taught about your religion, Serena?"

"Not much. Even my fiorriee tutors were careful not to upset Prytore laws, though I did do some ceremonies in secret. Mostly I was raised like the rest on Artthemis. Wealth, either in knowledge or talent is everything. We are all measured by our successes. Striving to do anything mediocre like raising children, is frowned upon because it does not bring financial wealth, it drains it. Though if you ask me, investing time in children is worth it if you base a society on success."

"You were never taught about your aura?"

"No, the word is not even familiar to me," I reply, taking a drink of water.

His eyes harden. "Your aunt did you a grave injustice." I put my glass down and stare at him. He puts his fork down and explains, "Fiorriee auras are very sacred, very personal. It is usually guided by animals, and if you are missing birds, especially throughout your life experience, your aura guide must be one."

His words cause the strangest sensation to overwhelm my body. I do not understand it. I cannot describe it. I just feel different. I look at him with sincere sorrow in my eyes. "I am sorry Prytore Keon." I all but whisper, my eyes filling with tears. "I should have trusted the process; I should have never let myself get talked into…" I stop, working to keep the tears from falling. "I should have waited for you. You are so good to me, and I have disgraced you, and…"

He gets up from his seat and pulls me into him. "Hush now, Serena." He runs his fingers through my hair, and I pull myself into him. He lifts me up from the chair and sits me on the table, meeting my eyes. "I accept your apology. I am not angry anymore. You have chosen to fight for your claim to this family, I will not hinder that. I know it is not easy for you. I will not make it any harder. We are risking your death as is. Though your will to fight is shrinking that possibility, so long as you do not slip. Thank you for giving me the time I requested. Thank you for using it to break ties to your past and not wallow helplessly in your room or ask to leave to go to him. I am proud of you, Serena. I am proud to claim you as mine and while it will take a little longer, my goal has not changed. You will surrender completely to me."

"Thank you," I whisper, pulling him tighter into me. His arms wrap around me, and I feel happy despite an annoying discomfort I am working to ignore. "Please do not let go."

"Not ever." he assures me, holding tightly.

That night the tension between us broke. When I woke in the morning Keon had restarted my breaking sessions. At first, even the simplest tasks were exhausting, as I was always fighting an internal battle just to accomplish them. But as the days pass it gets more complex. Keon has me work my mind, challenge my body and press both to the limits. Each night I am so exhausted, I can barely keep my eyes open the moment he allows rest. Each day he starts me with something so challenging that it takes me to the setting of Eshnaine to accomplish even a novice approach of it, much less master it. Six very long days go by, and I am struggling to stay on my feet after he dismisses me goodnight.

"I know what you are doing, and it will not work any longer." I accuse, fighting horrific exhaustion.

"Please tell me you are not going to start another wave of pride in your breaking Serena, you are coming along so well."

"Where is Peyton?" I ask, undeterred.

He frowns at me. "They have not checked in Serena. It is too dangerous to reach out."

"It was not supposed to take this long," I worry aloud.

"If you recall, there was not a timeframe for this kind of thing. Eradicating Peyton's blood of his Prytore technology is going to take much more time than simply stunning it with an elixir. One that would not stay effective long, as it would have simply adapted. Which is most likely what is happening now. The doctor has to struggle with Peyton's tolerance to the Prytores' technology's speed of adapting and replicating." He takes my hand. "It is not time to worry yet Serena, I promise."

"When can I plead for his return?" I ask, causing him to frown again. "The fact I have not done so by now has to cause some questions."

"I just do not want everyone to know where I have taken you. I do not want to move you. Understand, I am putting your safety first."

"I do not have to leave; we can just record it or something." He does not answer.

"If Peyton is discovered, we are all dead. It looks bad if I do not plea for him."

"In the morning, when you have rested, I will have figured out how to not risk either of your lives. Until then Serena, you need sleep. Go."

"As you wish, my Prytore." I smile, trying to hide the surge of unpleasantness that I cannot seem to shake. I move toward the door but stop myself, walk up to him, and kiss his cheek lightly. "Thank you for caring for us all." I slip out of the room, not waiting for a reply.

Twenty-Five

Mind Over Deathly Matter

Serena

Before the commencement of my morning training, Keon leads me into a holographic room. There, I record my plea to those responsible of kidnapping my husband. I have no doubt that he will see this, so I stare into the camera begging him to hang in there and promising him a safe return. I express my feelings for Peyton for all Artthemis to see. When the camera is turned off, I turn away from it, crying from heartbreak.

"Serena, he will be with us soon." Keon whispers, pulling me into his embrace. Thankfully his scent no longer makes my stomach turn, which I consider a massive achievement. It takes me a moment to collect myself, grateful Keon is here to help me through all of this.

I pull away from him, while keeping my hands on his waist. "I know you do not trust me yet, but I want you to know, that despite all of this, I truly trust you."

He moves a stray hair from my face. "That is a powerful statement from a woman who has a hard time trusting anyone."

"You have earned it." I smile, letting him go. "So, what is on the agenda today? Leading me through volcanic pits?"

He laughs, "You are close." I give him a weary look, if the blind maze of thorny bushes was not enough, then the temporary deafness was far from a cake walk. He had me practicing in both these scenarios the last four days. "I am going to be running some medical procedures." I raise my eyebrow and bite my tongue, stopping myself from asking what kind. It is not like I have a say in any of it anyway, so why bother. He touches my cheek with a smile, "You might be trained well to keep from voicing your curiosity my fiorriee Queen, but your eyes give you away." I look at the floor in response. "I want to get films to see the extent of your stomach damage. And I would like to draw some blood to figure out if your allergies are physical."

"You mean, you want to see if Prytore Roarick was messing with my head because of my stupidity to allow him access." I mutter, unable to control myself from voicing my shame.

"I will cut every cord Serena; I just have to find them." He vows to me. My eyes snap to him glaring at him in defiance, but I nod in acceptance, crying out from the conflict. "The sooner the better. I hate seeing you like this. Not to mention, it really gets under my skin." He walks away from me, "Come Serena, there is much work to be done today."

He leads me through the house for what feels like forever before, he activates a lock to a set of doors. Once inside I am surprised to see all the equipment. "Wow," I mutter in awe.

"Science is Alexis and my passion. I prefer making things, solving problems but she enjoys studying how things work. Especially the body. Together we have invented a lot of modern technology. What you see here are active prototypes. This is by far her favorite part of this house. And access is severely restricted." He takes me into a room with many machines. I tense the moment I see them all, unable to move. He notices almost immediately. "This is where we are going to put action behind your words of trust, Serena." He glides his fingers down the veins of my collar on my arms. "Relax for me. These machines are only taking pictures to see what physical damage was done to you." It takes a moment or two before I am able to break my stare away from the equipment and look into his eyes. It takes a few more before I can move again. "Good girl." he smiles, pinching me painfully in reward before walking me over to a large machine. "We used to run this test while the patient is lying down. But fiorriee are so proud, it took direct orders of torture to place them in it. So, I made a machine that allows everyone to stand up. It has proven to be very effective in both cooperation and diagnosing our patients. Added bonus, we can now get a three-hundred-and-sixty-degree view." He places me in a certain spot on the floor. "It does not hurt. I promise. I just need you not to move."

"Okay," I agree, watching him close me into this machine. I realize quickly his last instruction is pointless because I would not be able to move if I tried. I see some colorful lights, hear a humming noise and before I could even think to panic, he is opening the door again. "See, that was easy." he smiles, offering his arm. I take it. "Would you like to see the images?"

I look at him strangely. "I do not know. Will they be distorted like the mirror is?"

"That is a very good question, I never thought about it. I was just making sure you were comfortable with viewing parts of your body you have never seen before."

"I think I will be okay with that." I smile. He walks me over to some screens and pulls up the images. A frown forms on his face. I look at the pictures and my stomach looks like one big glob to me, but it does not seem distorted. "All I see is a solid mass. Am I seeing it weird because I am not fully broken by you?"

"No," he answers, zooming in and out. "You are seeing what is actually there."

"You look upset."

"I was unaware of the extent of the damage, Serena." he states, studying the films, seeing way more things than I am.

"I am fine, Keon. Have been all these years. Just because you see the pictures of it, does not make me any less healthy."

"You needed surgery years ago." he frowns, ignoring my reassurance. "If you do not get it soon, this will severely cut your lifespan."

"Are you serious?" I ask. "Because I honestly feel just fine."

Keon turns to me. "Did Roarick ever ask you not to tell anyone about your stomach aches because you will heal with time?"

"I do not know." I admit.

"Tell me now, Serena, I want your complete honesty. Does your stomach hurt?"

I blink at him, I shake my head no, but I stop myself, thinking about it. Then I shrug. "No more than usual I guess." I answer, fighting a sudden intense migraine. "No!" I struggle. "Not again!" I cry out, fighting a white flash of pain, but I force myself not to break my mind from my body.

"Serena?"

"He said." I hiss, fighting the memory, shaking for dear life to hold on. "He said there was no need to tell anyone. It was over and I healed. That it was phantom pain!" I scream aloud, unable to hide this torture from Keon. "I am sorry. I am sorry, I know I deserve this suffering, but you do not my Prytore. Give me a moment."

"It is all right, Serena, not every cord of control is easily ignored. This is tied to the fundamental reason you defied your upbringing. It makes sense that it would be like this. Breaking you free from it is going to be tricky." He frowns. "Not impossible, but most likely, impossible for you to hide from me." I turn away from him in shame, hating myself for putting pain in his eyes. I feel his hand on my shoulder. "I appreciate your immensely strong effort to do so, Serena, though you are not as successful as you might think. However, the fact that you want to, it is why I have not released you of the burden and sent you to him." The idea of that happening causes me to shake even harder from head to toe. I turn to him, fear clearly all over my features and in my eyes. "It is okay. I am willing to fight for you, as you have shown that to be your choice. But if it is going to kill you, Serena, I will let go. If only to save your life."

"It would not be a life worth saving without you and Peyton in it." I answer seriously.

"I would release him too, Serena. In vain hope that you two could find happiness without Prytore interference." I am not sure what to say to that, so I do not say anything. I just shake my head no and tangle my fingers into his, ignoring the discomfort. He seems to understand but he does not use words to tell me that. Instead, he keeps our hands together while he moves a few stray hairs from my face and holds my stare for a moment or two longer than he normally does. "We need to break this cord, Serena. I fear it is going to be especially difficult and the end result is going to be very unpleasant for you. The physical pain you must experience, is going to add to your mental resistance."

"I will fight it, Keon; I swear." I assure you.

"You need to understand, Serena. Holding on to Roarick in any way does not preserve your life either physically or mentally. It shortens it. I can save you, my fiorriee Queen. I am your protector. I am your safety. I am your guardian. With me there is a long happy life ahead, with Roarick there is only death."

Tears spill down my eyes as I respond. "I am ready to surrender this to you, Prytore Keon."

He squeezes my fingers with his. "Concentrate on your body, Serena. Does your stomach hurt?"

I take a deep breath, trying to concentrate on my body. "No, I am fine." I answer.

"You are not fine, Serena. The films show you have a lot of scar tissue on your intestines." He squeezes my fingers. "Does your stomach hurt, Serena?"

"No."

"Who do you serve?"

"You, Prytore Keon," I reply, crying out in pain, refusing to let go of his hands, despite the agony.

"Good girl. I am your only Prytore. You are loyal only to me," he replies calmly. I try to shake off the pain, but his words do not help much. "Tell me, your Prytore, who you do not withhold any secrets from, tell me how your stomach feels."

"I said fine!" I scream at him, shocked at my own defiance. I try to let go of him, but he expects it, keeping my fingers locked in his.

"If you are fine. Why can you not eat properly?" He challenges, keeping a calm voice.

"It is just the way it has always been," I reply, pulling against him.

"Not always. Think back, Serena, think back before you met Roarick."

"I had no life before Roarick," I respond automatically, causing my eyes to widen in shock.

Keon snaps his head up, also surprised by my words. His grip remains strong. "Think back to the birds, Serena, Roarick was not there."

"The birds. Birds are just a myth."

"No, they are real, Serena, trust me, trust your mind."

I stare at him holding onto the words, my mind suddenly flashing to Trorain's bright-green sky, black birds filling it. I can hear myself giggling. This is new, I have never heard my memory before. I grip Keon tightly, staring into his brown eyes, silently pleading not to break whatever connection we have. "Look, Mommy, birds," I whisper, repeating the memory as tears streak down my cheeks. There she is, the most beautiful fiorriee I have ever seen. Her white hair is as long as mine, maybe longer. Her eyes are pure silver, her smile and laugh are contagious.

"Yes Serena, birds. Ravens to be exact. You called them with your aura." She laughs. *"They always come when you ask them to, sweet Serena. Why are you always surprised when they do?"*

Keon cries out, causing the memory to end. I look at him in surprise. "Keon?"

"I am good. I am sorry, you just surprised me," he replies, rubbing his hands with a frown.

"You are bleeding." I note, watching orange blood come up from his yellow skin.

"Your nails." He smiles, walking over to the wall and ordering some bandages.

I look down at my nails and sure enough, his skin is under them. "I am sorry, I did not realize."

"Where did you go just now?" he asks, taking care of his hands. "I know your mother and birds were there, so I am assuming it is a memory from Trorain. But you stopped sharing whatever it was you were seeing."

"I have never seen it that clearly, or that long before," I reply, thinking back on it. "I did not realize I had a memory of my mother." I close my eyes, trying to remember her features. "She said I called the ravens to me, but I am always surprised when they come."

"Ravens?" Keon asks, stopping what he is doing on his second hand and staring at me in shock. "Are you sure they were ravens?"

"Yes, why?"

"Those are the most prized birds on Trorain. To be able to call them, Serena, in your religion you are a…"

"She was so beautiful." I cut him off, honestly shaken, barely registering a word he said. Keon finishes what he is doing quickly as I bask in the memory. Then I feel him wrap his arms around me and I allow myself the comfort, while I repeat the memory over and over, clinging to it. "I miss her."

"Of course you do, Serena," he whispers, kissing the top of my head, "of course you do."

He pulls back and our eyes meet, and it dawns on me… "You are doing it, are you not?" I accuse. "You are looking in my mind."

"Not your mind, you have not let me into your memories, Serena. You have offered a window to your soul however, and yes, I am helping you recall the memories attached to it."

"How did I do that?"

"It does not matter, besides, if I told you, your mind might close it and neither of us want that." He glides his fingers through my hair, causing my collar to tingle. "Go back to Trorain, my fiorriee Queen," he whispers, our eyes connecting. I gasp when my thoughts are once again flooded with green skies. I hear myself laughing again. It is strange, I rarely remember laughing as a child, but all of these memories are happy. I am with what must be my father, he is teaching me how to use a weapon I recall seeing in my books. Mine is purple, green, and blue. I can hear myself giggle with delight when it returns to me after I let it go. A raven appears in the window, joining me in my glee. Memories start to flood me, they are a blur, and then it is dark. I am in my mother's arms. She had been crying.

"Do not be afraid, Serena, never be afraid," she whispers, kissing my cheek.

"I do not want to go with her. I want to stay with you." I cry, causing several ravens to squawk.

"You must, Serena, I cannot protect you anymore. I love you always." I hug her tightly, but I am yanked away by my aunt.

"No!" I cry out, causing the birds to attack my aunt. She is prepared for it and somehow deflects them; one is thrown across the room.

"Mama! No!" I yell out.

"Serena!" she calls after me in agony, but she does not come, the chain on her ankle does not let her follow.

"I hate you, Takira! I will always hate you!" I cry struggling against her arms. "I am sorry, child, I must."

I snap myself to the present, releasing Keon from my hold and my gaze "I…" but no words come.

"It is okay, Serena. I have seen it too," he whispers.

"How? What did I do differently?"

"Still not answering that," he replies, looking down at the fresh cuts my fingernails made. "Though that does answer, why you do not trust your aunt."

"My mother was in prison."

"Your aunt took great risk letting you two say goodbye." He confirms.

"And it backfired on her. I hate her for stealing me away. And the raven…."

"I am sorry, Serena."

"I want to tell you, you are not to blame but, but in a way, you are. If you had never figured out how to travel to Trorain." I stop myself from finishing the thought and change direction. "Someone else would have, Keon. You and I both know that."

"I still blame myself, Serena. Nothing you say will change that." He starts to tend to his fresh wounds.

"I forgive you." He looks up at me in surprise. "I do not believe your intention was to harm my kind. You cannot control Prytore's actions or avarice. You have done nothing but show me kindness and my trust in you remains."

"Thank you, Serena," he replies solemnly. He finishes his work and stretches out his hands. I take them without hesitation. "Tell me again what life was like before Roarick." My freshly awakened memories from my soul and those of my blocked mind instantly fall into conflict. I cry out, but Keon holds me firmly. "Look at me." He demands. It takes effort to comply, but I manage. "Answer my question, my beautiful fiorriee."

"Happy? Followed by misery. True despair." I answer. "Then Roarick came and I was content, but not happy. When he left, I was miserable, then I became numb; until I met you and Peyton."

"What happened when you met us?"

"I think I found happiness again, but the feeling is so foreign I am not sure I am right."

"Did you have meaningful life before and after Roarick?"

"Yes." I answer, with such little pain it was almost not noticed.

"Good girl." He praises, breaking eye contact, and rewarding me with a pleasantly painful pinch.

I close my eyes and shake my head. "Why did you stop? We are not done." I hiss at my own words.

"Because I have decided to do surgery before you admit you have a problem." He answers. "Did you hear yourself just now? You know your body is injured but you cannot admit it, though you want to."

"But if you fix it and make me healthy then how can we break this cord?"

"By eliminating the lie all together. You will in fact be fine." He shrugs.

"No, please, not like this."

"Serena, you have been through a lot already." He worries, touching my cheek and causing a pleasant sensation all around my collar. "I will not put you through unnecessary discomfort."

"I am still standing," I reply, frustrated. "We are doing this."

"You are forgetting your place." Keon warns, causing me to flinch. "I understand you want to be free of him, but you need to trust my methods. You are not becoming free of submission Serena; you are surrendering to me. Every single part of you will surrender to me." I growl out in annoyance and frustration, turning my back to him. "And that pride of yours is going to be tamed to where you never show it to me." He touches my shoulders and whispers in my ear. "You gave me your soul today, Serena. That is something that cannot be undone. It is a part of you Roarick did not touch, it is your strongest part. All mine. I can enter it anytime I please, you can never stop me. For it belongs to me." I swallow hard at his words; I can feel invisible bindings tethering me to him as he speaks what we both know is the truth. "You feel it, do you not; the creation of my cords that can never be broken." I nod. "Good girl. Now, I can be persuaded to share this access with Peyton, but only after you share your body and your mind. Not a moment before." I cry out as I feel him pull the cords tight causing my knees to weaken, but I remain standing. He growls in disapproval stepping away from me. "Your pride is very tedious. Why must you fight me so?"

"I do not understand. What are you wanting, my Prytore?" I ask, hissing at my words.

"It is very rare for a fiorriee body to resist surrender after the fiorriee surrenders their soul," he replies. "You should not be standing right now." I start to lower myself to the ground. "Do not." he demands, stopping me. "I am not looking for compliance. I am demanding surrender. You stand there as long as you are able to, Serena; even if we must wait for Zarla to set, you will not be standing by the time I am through." I shake my head. "Trust in me, Serena, surrendering your body and soul to me helps your mind."

I watch him walk around me. "Prytore Keon, I must stand." I protest, "Peyton has forbidden me from surrendering in that way. He said you understood this."

Keon smiles at me, happy to hear my defiance lies with Peyton and not Roarick. "I can understand your confusion." He moves my hair from my eyes. "Peyton owns a part of you, only he can touch. A part that is sacred between the both of you. I am not asking for that. I promise. I am asking for your body. You need not lie on the floor Serena, just willfully kneel."

"I am scared," I reply, trembling.

"That is your mind resisting me, it is to be expected." He dismisses. "Normally, your mind surrenders first but this is not normal." He stops in front of me and holds my face in his hands. His eyes meet mine. "Show me everything," he whispers. I gasp, unable to stop visions of my past from engulfing me. The truest memories I own, the ones who define who I am, are shown to the both of us. But I am not merely observing them like I did when my mind was connected from my body. I am living them, fully aware of Keon's presence in watching them but unable to acknowledge him. As each memory plays out, he seems more and more pleased. When he finally releases me from his gaze, I find myself unable to support my own weight. The reason I am not on the floor is because I am being held up by his caring hands. "Good girl, Serena. Now surrender." He lets go, and my body falls to my knees right in front of him, tears streaming out of my eyes. He lowers himself next to my exhausted, kneeling form. "I own this now too, my sweet Serena. There is no escaping me." I know he is right, I can feel even more cords, different cords, tether to us. I feel defeated and fatigued. "You may stand up now." I flash to my feet so quickly, that if he had blinked, he would have missed the movement all together. He stands himself. "Furgan is setting, as much as I would love to heal your body tonight, you need rest first. Then Serena, we shall work on your mind. Oh, and before you go, understand I will no longer tolerate your mind controlling your defiant facial expressions; it irritates me." I feel myself wanting to glare at him but my eyes refuse. I hiss from the conflict. "Better." He approves. "Go quickly now and rest." Without giving myself permission, I dash from the lab and through the house to my room. I find myself changed and prepared for bed without even thinking to do so. A short while after that, Keon walks in to find me under a blanket on my bed. "I will not apologize for you feeling disconnected, that is the result of your own actions. You are mine, Serena. Your mind's resistance will not win."

"How can we find and break his cords quickly?" I ask, cringing in agony at the thought.

"Leave that to me, and my timetable Serena," he whispers. "Sleep now, it has been a long night."

Twenty-Six

Dancing

Serena

The next day, Keon does not awaken me until after Akatite rises. Even then, he lets me have some time alone and I find myself in my Trorain garden, missing home now more than ever before. I so wish the ravens were here. It saddens me to think of it. I turn my head to the two beautiful suns in the sky. I will never understand the claim of them being purple, they look white to me. White against a sometimes red, sometimes pink sky, depending on the suns' position in them. My heart aches for it to be green.

Pushing the thoughts aside, I smell the flowers, still unsure how to care for them properly but appreciating them just the same. My mind tries to wrap its thoughts around yesterday's events, while I enjoy the garden. I glare at the nearest flower, happy I can do so, still annoyed I could not last night. But I am not sure if my annoyance stems from my pride, or if it stems from my mind not being connected to not only my body but my soul. This is all so confusing. But there is no denying I feel different. Different because I feel more complete than I have in many years, but also restricted in ways I have never felt. It is all new and feels like a dress that is too small. I cannot breathe properly, but I can get air. "Good morning, my fiorriee," Keon calls, breaking me from my thoughts. "Or is it? You seem sad."

"It is too quiet." I complain, causing understanding to ring over his features.

"If you are good for me today. I will bring you a new piece of Trorain, one with birds."

"You can do that?" I ask, surprised.

"I can come close. But you must be good for me." I zip over to him, causing him to step back in surprise. "I thought you were going to warn me when you do that."

"Sorry." I smile.

He smiles back. "Come, let us heal that body of ours." I find myself following him back to the lab, though my mind has made several hundred escape plots that all failed. By the time we arrive, I am angry. I do not want to be here. I do not see the point of poking around my insides when there is nothing wrong. "Lie on the table."

"I do not want to," I tell him, as my body does it anyway. Causing my anger to triple.

"Do not speak your negative thoughts, Serena. Not today." Keon responds. I open my mouth but no words come out. "Good girl." He pinches me painfully in praise. I want to glare, but I cannot. He shows me a pressurized syringe that was similar to the one used on me at my aunt's cabin. "I want you to inject yourself." My mind is screaming out loud as to why that is never going to happen, but my arm is not cooperating with my thoughts. I hate it. I hate him. But I cannot even express these thoughts as the medicine enters my blood stream without my permission. Reluctantly, I find myself unwillingly closing my eyes.

When I wake, we are no longer in the lab. We are in some place new. Not that I am at all surprised. I could live here for years and not experience every room in this place. I look around and find Keon reading a book. "What happened?" I ask.

"You injected yourself with a mixture of nanites and a sleeping elixir. You slept while the nanites worked to repair your intestines and remove the excessive scar tissue." I rub my neck, surprised it is not sore. "Well, the majority were programmed for your intestines. I had a small reserve programmed to heal any other physical damage that it encountered. Your bones took the longest to repair properly. You have been out for almost a week."

"Makes sense, I used to jump off the roof a lot." I shrug, moving my ankles, surprised they were not popping.

"You cannot fly on Artthemis, Serena. Remember that." He scowls, disapproving.

"Did it work?" I ask.

"You tell me, does your stomach hurt?" he asks in return.

"No." I answer, but this time it did not feel like a lie. I turn to him and smile, "No, it does not." He smiles back at me. "Thank you, Keon, for fixing what is ours."

"That is my duty to you Serena, one I do not take lightly. You are going to have to pay more attention to your food intake now, as you will be hungry much more often." I nod, slightly annoyed with the side effect, but I have a feeling even Peyton will be happy with the outcome.

"Peyton, Alexis?" His smile falls to a frown. "Is it time to start worrying?"

"I do not see the need for it. If something went wrong, we would know. No news is good news, until they arrive here safely."

I frown but his logic makes sense. "So now we work on my mind? The anger I bared before I was repaired was so unpleasant."

"Now we eat, then you get your reward." He smiles, taking my hand and pulling me off the bed. "My timetable Serena, not yours. Surrender to me." I do not say a word as he takes me out of the room.

"I am surprised it has only been the three of you in a place like this." I note, walking down the hall and observing the art.

He turns to me with a smile. "I have many self-cleaning room devices."

"Oh."

He takes me into what resembles a city café, and we sit and eat in silence. Food tastes the same. But for some reason, even with my mood of not wanting it, I am able to keep every bite in my stomach. After lunch, he takes me from the room and walks me down the hall again. "I am from old money and each new member traditionally adds their own wing to it. Seeing as Alexis and I did not have children, and my brother died at a young age, we occupy the entire thing. The labs being our contribution."

"Did you not want children?"

"We did. But then King Griffith… Alexis and I have accepted our sterile state many centuries ago."

"Griffith?"

"Maleko's father." Keon explains. "He was one of many kings before Artthemis' civil war."

"That is right, Griffith struggled against the last few families. And when he did achieve unity, he died soon after, leaving the kingdom to Maleko." I recall. "Mortal." I state, stopping in my tracks.

"Alexis was born a Mortal." Keon clarifies, "not me."

"Wait, Adriana is her sister?" I ask, stunned. "I thought the Queen had a twin."

"Not all twins look alike Serena." Keon sighs heavily.

"You said the Mortal name was tainted. How could that be if it is the Queen's name?"

"Like the rest of her family, Alexis has not always been in good standing with Maleko." Keon replies, causing understanding to cross my features as pain crosses his.

"Zarla, they were the last holdout." I recall. "Prytoree Sine would never speak of what happened to them. Just that Maleko married the eldest daughter, Adriana." I shake my head as tears fill my eyes. "You said sterile. Oh zarla, no."

"This is not my story to tell, Serena." Keon states patiently, wiping tears from my cheeks. "Do not cry my fiorriee. All of this was lifetimes ago. Alexis and I are happy. We have moved on, honest." His look turns guilty. "That was the technicality we hid behind at your courting. I do not want children, Peyton does."

"If it helps, I expected you to do it."

"You did?"

"Just had a feeling." I shrug.

"Clever girl." Keon praises, stopping in a new room. I look around the room we just entered. It is almost nearly nothing but blackness until he presses a few buttons. Then suddenly, I am surrounded by the familiar sight of the Trorain home world.

"Keon!" I gasp in delight, seeing a raven to my left! I go to it, and it lands on my hand. I smile widely, happy that I can feel it. "What is this place?"

"It is a 3-D simulator. You can experience something new with every visit. You can even touch and feel things the way they should be." He answers, pulling me into his arms. "But you will not find the full satisfaction of it." He pets the bird in my hand. "You will not be able to call them like you did on Trorain. The technology cannot simulate things it does not understand."

"Do you hear the sounds?" I ask, smiling up at him. "Are they not precious?"

"Just as you are Serena." He smiles. "You may spend the rest of your day here. You will report to your room just before dinner."

"Okay." I giggle, chasing birds from the ground, causing them to fly. I think he watches me for a while, before he leaves me alone in a place where my soul is truly happy, but I do not give him much attention, nor do I notice when he leaves.

I stay there until the simulation ends, causing instant disappointment. Reluctantly, I leave and make my way back to my room. When I am there, I find a beautiful pink dress laid out for me. I take a quick shower before I put it on. As I am attempting to deal with my hair, Keon walks in. "Allow me," he offers, picking up a brush. "It is okay to close your eyes, Serena." I do so happily, feeling him tugging on my stubborn strands. My head is never tender until others start to brush my hair for me. "Alexis had me learn the art of styling years ago. She always seems to like things she needs someone else to do for her. She has trained me and Peyton quite well."

"But her hair is so short." I point out.

"That has not always been the case. She used to defy Prytoree norms, but then her work became so involved. She, like so many others, prefer it short because it takes less time."

"But she styles it so well. It is long and short. That must take time."

"She styles it that way because she knows it pleases me. Though she does not know it sadden me when she cut off half her beautiful brown locks. I miss doing things like this." He smiles, working on a stubborn knot in my hair.

"Remind me to thank her for training you two. I always enjoy others wanting to style my hair." I smile, keeping my eyes closed. I can feel his fingers work my hair into loose braids and twist it into a bun. When I think he is finished, I feel him tug on a few strands causing them to fall across my face. "I do so enjoy the slightly messy look you always seem to present. Especially with your collar falling naturally into it." His fingers brush the loose strands and I get a familiar pleasant sensation that comes every time he touches them. "You look stunning as always."

"All dressed up, where shall we go?" I ask opening my eyes and staring up at him.

"You will see." He smiles, taking my hand.

I follow him out of my room and down the hall. He takes me into another simulated room but this time it is full of Prytores and fiorriee. We interact with some of them. Each time Keon introduces me as his, I find myself struggling to greet them the way I should. Most of the time it all comes out as a stutter and I am frustrated with myself by the third or fourth introduction. "Please make it stop." I beg him. He pauses the simulation. "That is not what I meant. Please, will you reconsider going back into my mind?"

"You have already been told of my reasons for not doing just that, Serena."

"I can handle it." I argue, causing him to give me a disapproving look.

"This is going to take ages, Keon. And every time we accomplish something, we are only going to find something else. Can we not just cut it off at its hold and be done with it?"

"You think I want to drag this on?" he asks, offended. "That I like you divided into two different mindsets? Do you think I am satisfied with only owning part of you? I am trying to protect you, you impatient little child! Do you not realize the danger you are in? That if I cannot fix this, it is a guaranteed death sentence!" He takes a moment to calm himself. "The fact that we have managed to accomplish what we have, is unprecedented."

"You are scared." I realize, causing him to look at me.

"We should eat." He walks away from me and makes two meals, sitting them down at a table, watching to be sure that I eat every bite. After a lot of awkward silence, he continues our conversation. "If we move swiftly and without caution, the consequences could be irreversible. I am not sure why you are so impatient for it. It is either because you are happy with what happened to you yesterday. Or your mind is resisting, and that resistance would rather have you dead, than allow you to commit to another. Either way, it is making me very cautious." I am not sure what to say to him. I honestly do not know the source of my own impatience.

"Let us dance, Serena." He decides, taking me out onto the beautiful dance floor. I protest that I am not very good at it, but he simply tells me to follow his lead. Sure enough, my body surrenders to him so willingly it is hard not to enjoy the sensation from slow music, to fast paced beats and everything in between. We meld together, making such happy memories, I realize it touches my soul. When we stop for water, my mind catches up with his intentions, and I refuse to drink. "I was trying so desperately to keep you from your head." He frowns, recognizing my resistance immediately. "Drink the water Serena. Swallow it all." Annoyed, I do just that. He takes the glass from me and tells the computer to change the scenery. We are in Trorain's night sky, sitting on a bench, unfamiliar yet comforting sounds all around us. "I enjoyed tonight. It is amazing to see you smile."

I look away, keeping my thoughts for a moment before I speak. "I would rather risk death, then live like this much longer."

"Even if I were to give into that Serena, I would not do it without Peyton's permission."

"I miss him."

"I know." He answers, taking my hand.

"I miss them both."

"I am tired, my Prytore Keon," I whisper, accepting the pain I knew that would come.

"You should rest then." He cancels the simulation and walks me to my room. "You will find yourself locked out of all Trorain simulations; in case you try without me." I turn to him, hurt and confused. "You have your garden whenever you like, but the rest are rewards for good behavior. Resisting me in any way will not get you what you want."

"I do not want to," I whisper, wincing.

"I know, but you need to learn to let the parts of you that have surrendered to me, overcome the parts that are refusing. I cannot slay this dragon for you Serena. Only you can. I must leave tomorrow. I will not return for a few days. I am afraid you will not have access to the outdoors while I am gone. But this house is yours as much as it is Peyton's. Most rooms you are welcome to enjoy freely. In my absence, you will eat three full meals a day, no exceptions and because I do not know your mind right now, there will be no loopholes to any self-harm or anything like it."

"Prytore."

"Serena."

"I have never been alone before."

"Considering everything, that does not surprise me. You will be just fine and this house will keep you safe."

"What if something goes wrong?" I ask, nervous.

"Like what?"

"I do not know, anything."

He approaches me, places his hands on my face, his gaze locking into mine. But instead of being rushed by my past experiences we are in the ballroom and he and I are dancing. "You need not be afraid, my beautiful Serena."

"I am not, not really. I am just used to back up plans, safe rooms and safe words." I answer honestly.

"You are not hiding anymore, there is no need for such things."

"Please?"

"All right, if it makes you feel better. Our safe word is 'Hummingbird.' If you ever hear me use it in any context keep your guard up. Serena, you must trust me, you are safe. I would never put you in harm's way. I would never hurt you."

"Is this the same but different love Peyton and Alexis were referring to?"

He smiles at me. "Maybe the beginning."

"You are in denial," I accuse, pulling him close to me.

"Maybe I am." He laughs, twirling me around the dance floor. "You should rest now Serena." He breaks the gaze, and I am back at my doorway. I shake my head, trying to adjust to the sudden change. "It is just a few days." He promises, touches my face gently then walks away. Leaving me wondering how often I will find myself alone in this new life.

Twenty-Seven

Confronting the Past

Serena

One would think with a house as massive as this, being bored would not be possible. Yet here I am, bored. I was killing time by having a simulator act out a tragic play, but I upset the characters with my comments and made a poor decision to throw food at their performance. The computer has refused to act out any more books. It will not even accept my apology. I had no idea I could offend the stupid thing in the first place and now I do not know how to fix it. This did not help my mood. Nor does it help me comply with Prytore Keon's orders as the computer refuses to make anything I order. I have never used so many fiorriee curse words in such a short amount of time in my entire existence. I cannot even take a calming shower, as I am only granted access to cold water. The house officially hates me. I want Keon home. I wanted it for days and still his absence remains. I miss him almost as much as I miss Peyton. Though I think of Peyton more. Not just because he is my husband, but because it does not hurt to do so. There are moments when I want to kill Roarick where he stands but the idea of him dying leaves me feeling despair, so I shut the idea out of my mind.

After the second day, before the house turned against me, I realized I did not like being alone. I have tried so many things since then to occupy my time, but very little of it has proven successful. I do not have access to the outside world or to anything outside this house. The machines will randomly clean a room I am in every time I get into a book. I cannot open the doors to my garden, which upsets me greatly. There is not a kitchen to be found in this house. It is all machines, and I find that irritating and depressing. I found a few rooms designed for games but the simulator will not set up the players so I cannot do that. Literally leaving me with nothing to do but sleep, eat disgusting food and count the time. I tried walking around the place, but I am getting locked out of more than just the laboratory wing at this point. I hate this house more and more.

Trying to do something productive, I decide to stand on my ears again while holding books. I am hoping this separates my body and my mind like it did last time, especially when I call out that Prytore Keon is who I serve. But it only gives me headaches and I lose my balance easily. I have a feeling this falls under the category of self-harm, but it does not stop me from trying. Though it might explain why my body refuses to let my mind leave it. Stupid orders. It is during one of these attempts that I find Keon glaring at me with his arms crossed over his chest, as I stare up at him from his feet. I drop quickly and kneel in front of him. "Forgive me Prytore, I was just trying to force my brain into submission."

"And it did nothing because your body resisted your mind's wants," he replies knowingly. "How many times did you fight against that?"

"I have lost count." I admit.

"There is so much to do here, Serena, and yet you choose resistance."

"To be fair, this house hates me."

"The house does not hate you."

"Oh yes it does!" I reply defensively. "Cold showers, locking me out of the garden, horrific meals! Not to mention refusal of simulations, cleaning rooms I am in, locking me out of everywhere and everything!"

"Fakhir!" he calls in a very authoritative and annoyed tone. "Show yourself."

"Prytore Keon, it is lovely to see you." A simulated Prytore smiles, bowing in front of Keon. My eyes widen as I take in this plump butler. He is wearing an over exaggerated tuxedo with an ascot. "Did you have a good trip?"

"You need not concern yourself with me Fakhir, my fiorriee is telling me that you have been giving her a hard time."

"She is not yours yet, Prytore Keon, and she has a lot of manners to learn between now and then!" the computer snaps, looking down on me from its nose.

"You think you found a loophole in your code?" Keon challenges the computer.

"There is no thinking about it." Fakhir snubs.

"You will apologize and give Serena the respect she deserves."

"I am giving her the respect she deserves." The computer argues with Keon.

"Then you will give her the same respect you do for Peyton, Alexis, and myself," Keon replies, heated. "Now apologize to the lady, or you will get reset."

The computer looks from Keon to me. He snubs at me one last time. "Fine. I will accept her unworthy apology, but the moment she hurts you, I am going rogue." With that the computer vanishes from view.

"Like I said, the house hates me."

"What did you do to upset it in the first place?" he asks curious, reaching out his hand to pull me to my feet.

"Disliked its acting."

"Ah yes, well, Fakhir can be quite sensitive. Though that was probably just an excuse to treat you poorly. He is most likely upset that you have not surrendered completely to me yet."

"Not from lack of effort."

"It is a computer, Serena. It does not see effort as a reason." He defends his creation.

"Just do not leave me alone with it again, okay? I did not like it."

"I will try not to. But I do have an empire to run. Plus, I was trying to find information on our mates."

"And?"

"Nothing." He sighs. "I am reaching out to your aunt. Maybe she has some more information than we do."

"You trust her?"

"I do." He smiles. "She did save your life, Serena. Those memories had to be erased."

"I accept that." I note. "But there are… things." He raises his head up, clearly not happy with my vagueness. "When you get my full mind, you will understand."

"This resistance is tedious." Keon complains. "You claim to trust me, Serena. Are you standing here telling me you are intentionally withholding?"

"She had to know about the twins, Keon. You were there when she denied the knowledge of many things! But if I was important to her at all… how did she not know? I almost died at our enemy's hand, under her watch! What was so important she never bothered to truly care for me?" I start to shake, and I turn from his gaze.

"I understand that you are angry with her, Serena, but you trust her too. Otherwise, why go out of your way to help her write cryptic letters to you?"

"How did you…?" I ask then turn my attention to a camera. "Let me guess, Fakhir."

"He might have decided to show me some files that he felt I needed to see. Though I did not spy on you during the courting." I glare at the camera causing Keon to shake his head. "There are no secrets between us, Serena. And I hope in the future, I do not discover some from Fakhir being concerned about your intentions."

"To be fair, I did not know you then." I defend myself. "And after I did, I did not find it relevant."

"I would have discovered it without Fakhir's help, once I owned your mind. None of your thoughts will allow for things like that."

"Yet she let me believe they could. I should trust her, why?"

"Because she did not know. She has never submitted to my kind, only her own, which is different."

"So, you are telling me you are more evasive than my own husband?"

"In some ways, yes, I am," he replies seriously. "But your husband naturally trusts you. It is part of loving you. Just as you do him, it leaves you a little naturally blind, which is not a bad thing."

"She can only hide behind ignorance for so long. She has been on this planet for years." I snap in irritation. "Just be careful Keon, she disappoints a lot."

"I expect you to be on your best behavior when she arrives." He answers, annoyed.

"Arrives, she is coming here?"

"Something I believe you requested not that long ago."

"That was before I got my memories back."

"Your best behavior, Serena." He repeats, walking out of the room, leaving me glaring at the camera; hating it even more now that it has a name.

Thankfully, I find myself able to get into my garden again. I sit there for a while, wondering if I could honestly ever forgive my aunt for everything she has done. Had she not kept me blinded to who I was for so long, had she not taken in so many other children that I felt like she did not care, had she not stolen me from my mother's arms, this would be easy. But she did every last bit of that, which makes the idea of forgiving her, unsettling. Unhappy that I cannot seem to get past these thoughts, I decide on a shower. This time, I actually get to relax as the warm water is back. I ignore the mirror all together, throwing a spare towel over it so I do not have to deal with it. Then I dry my hair, style it in a bun, and find some comfortable clothes. I do not want her here. But if she must come, this better be a short visit. I go back to my garden and think of all the questions I want to ask, no demand, from her. I also, think of the things I want to say, but never will. Fakhir distracts me from this after a while, announcing my aunt has arrived and directs me where to meet her. I glare at the camera, take a deep breath, and dash out of my room, wanting this over already.

Aunt Takira makes her arrival in such a grand fashion I swallow vomit from all the formality she gives Keon. I so badly want to scream at her, but my vocal cords simply will not let me. Instead, I find myself taking her coat, getting her a warm cup of pigats and smiling at her. I turn my attention to Keon, letting him know I am in pure zarla. He just gives me a warning look and suggests we all sit in the room in which he and I did the first night I moved in here. "Now that the formalities are out of the way, Takira, do you have news of Alexis and Peyton?"

"Nothing that is going to please you." She frowns. "Peyton's body is resisting the change, and it is challenging Alexis' control over his entire being. The technology is simply able to replicate faster than they can exterminate it. At least that was the news ten days ago. But they made it sound like they were close to a breakthrough."

"It is as I thought then. They are not in any harm of being discovered, just dealing with this issue." Keon smiles, causing me to breathe a little better. "Still, I will only feel better when the four of us are under one roof."

"Peyton cannot be the only reason you summoned me to your home, Prytore Keon. Tell me there is a silver lining and my niece has come to accept her role as your fiorriee." Her voice sounds smooth and calm, but her eyes show her nerves. I snap mine to Keon, glaring at him before I correct my expression and politely give her a smile.

"Actually, I have come across a complication in that venture. One, I am hoping you can help me shed some light on."

"Oh," she replies, drinking her pigats, almost too properly as a distraction. "I can try, I guess. Serena has always proven to be a very stubborn child."

"Yes, I can see that. So stubborn she never shared with you her experiences with Jasha and Reeve."

"Experiences? She hated those twins, avoided them at all costs." Takira shrugs. "Never could figure out what they did to her."

"So, you claim no knowledge in them repeatedly torturing her with knives?" he challenges, almost too calmly.

"Jasha and Reeve? No, that was the menacing little Ofelia, who did it exactly once. He was disowned by the orphanage because of it." She states, appearing genuinely upset and spilling her drink all over herself. She sets it down. "Serena, what lies are you telling this Prytore!" I want to be defensive and smart off, but my mouth will not open. Keon gives me time to calm myself and find a better way to phrase my words.

"He is been in my mind, Takira. It is very difficult to lie to someone who can literally see my thoughts and experiences."

"Truth as it may be, that is no reason for you to disrespect me without a title." She snaps, causing me to raise an eyebrow and keep my silence. She turns to Keon. "I only knew of Ofelia, and I took care of it. She never said a word! Are you sure these memories are not planted somehow?"

"Interesting that you would suggest such a thing, Takira. Considering doing something like that would mean you neglected to care for her properly and allowed another into her mind." She stares at him in a way that terrifies me. "I have films to prove the physical damage to her body." He continues unphased. "And I am sure she lied to you as to why she was jumping from your roof as well, though I have not gotten specifics to it. I am sure it has something to do with the twins though."

"Serena?" she asks, visibly upset.

"Save it," I reply, coldly, hissing in unpleasant pain for not following orders, but deciding instantly it is worth it.

"Has another been in her mind, Takira?" Keon presses.

"You know zarla well there has. Otherwise, you would not be asking me about it!" Takira snaps.

"Your omission could have killed her!" Keon snaps back.

"My omission got her where she is. No one would have touched her had they known she was tainted."

"Tainted!" I reply in insult with a grimace, the pain has kicked up a notch.

"They were locked away deep. You should not have been able to find them." Takira adds, ignoring my outburst.

"Full surrender means just that Takira. You should have made her go to part-time service if you cared at all about her life."

"Are you accusing me of not caring for my own flesh and blood!"

"She is not yours; she is your brother's." Keon states and I can tell by the looks of it that hits my aunt below the belt.

"You are right, Keon. *She* is not mine. *Mine* is the one who is lost!"

"What?" I ask stunned. "What are you talking about?"

"You have a cousin." Takira says, looking down at her dress. "The Prytores stole her from Trorain while I was sleeping. I went to search for her, but the gods gave me a mission." She shakes her head. "I was to take you to Artthemis and protect you with my life."

"And my cousin?"

"Xylia is still lost to this day." Takira states, causing my stomach to drop. "I was ordered not to look for her. I could not do so and protect you."

"So, you surrounded yourself in children, in hopes to fill an unfillable void." I state, suddenly understanding. "That explains why you loved them more."

"That is not fair!" She stammers clearly upset. "I loved you most!"

"Really?" I reply accepting undesirable pain while standing up and stepping between them. "How could you not know about the twins? How could you love them more than you love me? How could you let someone into my mind? Where were you!"

"Oh, Serena, how soon you forget." She seethes. "I was there. I was always there. It was you who shut me out. Each and every time, you closed the doors to me."

"I was a child; you should have forced your love on me."

"I could not."

"No, you would not!"

"I killed a part of who you are!" she snaps, causing me to take a step back. She drops her voice. "You never forgave me. I doubt you ever will." She starts to cry.

"You do not mean that you killed..." Keon interjects in astonishment.

"What was I supposed to do? Let them take her at three years old? She was a child! I could not. She was not ready." Takira defends. "I made the choice, even if that meant she hated me the rest of her days."

I turn to Keon, who is still shocked from what he is hearing. "Still, I never dreamed you would hate me so much you would allow someone to harm you."

"Hate you for what?" I ask, my mind going to the worst. "My mother, my father? Takira what did you do?"

"Not your parents, Serena." Keon answers me. "But something just as precious."

"What the zarla are you two talking about!" I ask, frustrated with both of them, receiving unpleasant pain from my rudeness.

"Serena, how many orphans did you let harm you?" she asks, obviously distraught.

"There are some questions you really do not want to know the answers to Takira." I reply coldly, causing her to cry harder.

"I thought…I thought it was only Ofelia and Roarick. She stopped Roarick. She called for her ravens, but we were on Artthemis. They could not come. So I did. I saved her from…" She fights off her tears, trying to finish her words. "I had it buried, deep, practically erased. I do not understand how you found it, full service or not."

Keon's eyes narrow at her, "She trusts me."

"I do not trust you, Takira." I confess. "Which you know, because you have been learning exactly how much I was willing to endure, because I did not believe you would stop any of it."

"I did not know, Serena. I thought you would at least tell me if you were being harmed."

"But I did not. I even submitted to a Prytore before I was of age!" I hiss, annoyed with the unpleasant pain, raising my voice to her causes.

"And I saved you! I will always save you!" she shouts back.

"While I believe you believe that your efforts did not work." Keon informs her.

Takira snaps her head up, looking wounded. She studies me for a moment before she speaks again. "She seems fine. I am assuming you were able to overcome the obstacle."

"She is not fine." Keon answers coldly. "I own her body and soul, but I do not have her complete mind. Which is why, you are here."

"What can I do?" Takira asks, suddenly as confused as I am.

"You have done enough." Keon answers sharply. "Serena believes she hates you because you stole her from her mother. She does not realize it is because of your sacrilege."

"Sacrilege?" I repeat, feeling Keon's shock. "Seriously, what am I missing? Who died?" I ask both of them. The room falls silent, while Takira and Keon stare one another down.

"Well, are you going to fill her in, or am I?" Takira asks, annoyed.

"I am beginning to remember which side of the family Serena's pride comes from." Keon responds, working to keep his calm. He turns his head to me. "Before I answer you, I would like to know what have you gathered from all of this."

I shake my head, "I am unsure Prytore, but I am beginning to believe my aunt betrayed me somehow."

"That she did." Keon confirms.

He is about to explain but my aunt beats him to it. "Your aura shares a strong connection to ravens. When the birds realized that you were being taken to a world where they could not go, they wanted your aura to leave your body. I stopped your transformation from happening too soon, but in doing so, I had to kill several ravens. And that, Serena, is where your hate and distrust for me stems from."

"I hate you for killing birds?" I ask, dismissing the absurdity.

"Not just any birds, Serena, ravens." She clarifies.

"Okay?" I question, not really understanding the difference.

"On our world, ravens are very powerful, very sacred creatures." Takira continues. "It is a very rare gift to be able to call them."

"And?" Keon presses.

"She is young, Keon," Takira replies, with caution, "I do not see how knowing her fate is going to help her surrender to you."

"Because her and I do not keep secrets from one another." Keon answers patiently. "No matter how terrifying it is."

"Terrifying?" I ask, watching them stare each other down.

Eventually Keon raises his head just a little higher and turns his attention to me. "Serena, you are not only a part of a rare bloodline that makes you a Queen, but also a goddess."

"Goddess?" I question, looking at him as if he lost his mind.

"Not just any goddess." He replies. "You are a very special goddess, you are *the* Raven goddess."

"Blood, titles… they mean nothing on Artthemis. Here, we are just fiorriee." Takira snaps her head to Keon, "This knowledge will only damage her. It took her years to accept the loneliness of not having her birds, and here you are dredging it up all over again."

"She has the right to know. And I have the right to know if I am going to discover any more landmines before I continue my journey. I am trying to save her from the damage Roarick did to her."

"She called for her birds in a deep time of need, and they did not come." Takira repeats to him. "Do you have any idea the type of damage that can do to her soul?"

"You should have taken her to Trorain straight away."

"I could not." she defends. "So, I did the next best thing. I buried the memory."

"Wait, back up, you said we are just fiorriee." I glare at her. "You are a goddess?"

She looks at me dismissively. "Did you hear me, Serena? It means nothing on Artthemis."

"But on Trorain…" I push.

"On Trorain, we can control the wind." She answers seriously. "And you my dear, can control ravens."

"But I got hurt, my soul was damaged, and the only way to fix that is to go to Trorain?"

"It is too late for that. The damage is done." Keon answers me. "From what I can tell, your soul healed. But at the price of your aunt. You seem to have focused all of that hate on her."

"Why would I do that? She saved me from… from…" but I can manage the words just as easily as Takira.

"She did. But she is the one who took you from your ravens to start with. The one who killed them to save you from accepting your fate too early. The one who prevented them from coming in your time of need, and the one you blame for putting you in a situation where you needed them to start with."

"If you are looking for an apology, you are not getting one. I was on a god's mission. I did what was best for her. If I had to do it again, I would not hesitate," Takira replies proudly.

"What is my fate?" Neither of them answers me. "What is my fate!" I scream at them, fighting the pain for disrespect and wishing Keon would make it stop.

"The moment you could call ravens as a small child we knew you were special. But the war, you could not fulfill your destiny at three years old. So you were hidden, and you will stay hidden from those malicious birds until you are of age to go with them." Takira finally answers.

"What age is that?"

"Never, if I can help it," she replies "It is done, most the birds are dead from the toxins anyway. What is the point now?

"What is the age?" I ask Keon.

"It is not the age that is concerning, Serena, it is the fact that accepting your aura in its purest form will kill your body."

"The only reason you would do that is to protect Trorain. But the toxins were not natural. The ravens did not understand this, they called you. Had you come, you would be all alone with no ravens or fiorriee to look after. Your parents and I recognized that the moment we knew we were going to lose. They did not want that fate for you. They knew taking you from ravens would cause you to be restless, but they wanted you to have a chance at life, at love."

"Could I have saved them? Could I have won the war?"

"No." Keon answers firmly. "Your parents are right; it would have been a waste, and my species would have figured out how to kill you to get the minerals we wanted. You were too young Serena, and you would have been alone."

"And now? Today?"

"What would you be saving?" Takira asks. "Everything you could have fought for is gone."

I turn to Keon. "As far as my kind can tell, living on Trorain for any substantial length of time is a death sentence, no matter what species you are." He confirms. "Unless we can fix it."

"I appreciate all the information. May I be excused?"

"No, Serena, you may not." Keon answers firmly. "We are not done."

"We are not?" Takira asks in surprise. "Oh, this should be good. What? You want her to be honest with me and tell me how much she hates me for everything I put her through? How I did not save her life, I condemned it?"

"If you are looking for my empathy, you are not going to get it." Keon snaps, causing her to silence herself. "She was a child! You were the adult! You could have been honest with her, told her the truth every night, fought for her love! But you let a three-year-old shut you out! A three-year-old! And you let the rift get wider and wider! So wide that you did not notice when the children you were hiding her amongst, started to hurt her! You were oblivious to the knowledge of two Prytores stabbing her stomach on a daily basis for nearly a decade! With the exception of three or so years where Roarick was messing with her mind and forcing her into a death trap that was to be sprung the moment she surrendered to a different Prytore or chose to take a stand and not surrender to my kind at all. If she was not the goddess she is, she would be dead right now! Because of you! She was three! Why did you not fight for her? What could have possibly happened to you that caused you to let a child cut you out of her life!"

"Ilka!" she cries, falling to pieces right before our eyes.

"Who?" I ask confused, but she is inconsolable. I turn to Keon.

"Lapidos' other wife." He can tell that explanation still leaves me in the dark. He turns his attention to Takira.

"You never spoke of them?" Takira takes a moment to become coherent. "If I admitted Lapidos was my husband, how was I to hide her on Artthemis!" Takira snaps at him. "I had to hide behind Borak."

I stare at her for a moment. "So, Borak was not my uncle?"

"It is a story for another time, Serena." Keon frowns, turning back to Takira. "What does this have to do with Ilka?"

Takira's eyes fall on mine. "Her ravens killed Ilka, right before my eyes!" she cries out, causing alarm for both myself and Keon.

"I would never do such a thing!"

"Not you, you did not order it, Serena." She clarifies, working to pull herself together. "You were three. You did not have control over those birds! You were not there long enough to do anything but make friends with them. They knew I was stealing you from them. They were killing her, leaving me with the choice between saving her or taking Serena to Artthemis. Ilka told me to go. Accepting her death to protect Serena's life. It took everything I had to do it. Losing my child, my wife. It broke me, and to have Serena hate me for all of it. I am a flawed fiorriee, I can only do so much." She cries, unable to control her tears and leans against a wall.

Keon approaches me and holds my head in his hands, our eyes meet, and suddenly we are dancing again. "You need to forgive her, Serena."

"What?" I ask astonished.

"That is why she is here. It is what I want for you and me. What we need for your soul. You need to forgive Takira."

"I would rather walk through perpetual fire."

"That can be arranged," he replies seriously. "She lost just as much, if not more, to protect you. She does not deserve your hatred and distrust."

"Keon." I protest, but we are no longer dancing. Instead, he is holding me in place, making sure I see the tears she is shedding after speaking her secrets.

"Forgive her, Serena." I do not respond. I just stand there. "If you cannot forgive her, then you are not worth fighting for."

"Do you realize what you are asking of me?" I demand.

"I am asking the world from a future goddess. But today you are merely a broken fiorriee who will not survive her transition into her fate as a fiorriee on Artthemis. Much less as a goddess on Trorain, if you continue this hatred in your heart and soul. Do you not see, Serena, I am trying to save you."

"My mind does not want to. I was told I would never have to forgive her for anything she is done."

"Your soul?" he asks. "Look at her. Look what protecting you from a fate much worse than the twins cost her."

I take a moment before taking a deep breath and walk over to my aunt, embracing her in my arms, crying out the moment it happens. "Serena?" My aunt pulls back in concern, but I bring her back into me, accepting the pain. "What is happening?" Aunt Takira demands.

"Her mind and soul are starting to align." Keon smiles. "Roarick is losing his grip."

"She is in agony. This can kill her!" My aunt worries, causing me to want to hold her ever the more.

"Just let it happen, Takira. It is the only way." Keon instructs. "She is stronger than you give her credit for."

When I finally let her go, I pull her into me again. "I am so sorry. I did not understand, I did not know. I love you." She cries in my arms until she is so exhausted, she can barely stand.

"Keon, my aunt needs sleep."

"Of course." He smiles, he helps me take her to my room and she all but screams with joy when she sees the garden, running to the plants with more enthusiasm then I could dream anyone could muster, after an emotional drain like that.

"They are, they are… real!" she gasps. "How is this possible?"

"Alexis can work miracles." Keon answers. "The sky can be simulated and the garden climate controlled, if you would like to sleep here tonight, I could design a makeshift bed.

"I would be honored," she replies, causing Keon to step out of the garden to retrieve a few essentials, leaving us alone. "I do not want you to misunderstand child. I do not blame you for Ilka's death. I know that you value those birds amongst all else. I do not want you to hate them for it. They were doing what they believed was right."

"Now that your mission is ended. I swear to you Takira, I will help you find Xylia." I state firmly.

"I fear it is not that easy." She frowns. "From my understanding, Zane has been looking for her for years. And you know his resources, Serena."

"Then there is only one thing to do." I state, undeterred. "We need to return to Trorain. We will find her there."

"Maybe." Takira sighs. "Please know I do not resent you for the mission I was assigned."

"I am sure that is reserved for whomever assigned it to you." I note, causing her to frown. "All these good intentions led to so much heartbreak. Makes you wonder if it was all worth it."

"Oh, Serena, of course, it was. You are alive, happy, married. Your parents could not have asked for a better fate if you lived on Trorain itself."

"Thank you." I nod, grateful Keon came back quickly. There are too many ways to view all this new information and I do not really care to do that with company. She lays down with a large smile and I exit the garden, then the room.

"Will you not be staying in your room tonight?" Keon asks.

"She is not the company I crave," I reply, closing the door.

"I know I am not Peyton, but I would happily keep you company. It is either me or Fakhir, take your pick."

I give a small smile. "Thank you, I do believe joining you tonight is the best alternative to my husband."

He leads me to his room which is not far from my own. When we walk in, I go straight to the bathroom and stare into the mirror. "What do you see my beautiful fiorriee?" He asks, studying the image himself. "There are two of me, but we are not blurry anymore," I reply. "This does not give me a headache, it is just weird."

He smiles as he kisses my shoulder. "That is very, very good. Soon there will only be one and she will be all mine."

One of my reflections smiles at this, the other glares and makes an obscene gesture. "Okay that is messed up." I mutter.

"Two different reactions to my words." he notes unhappy. I nod. "Not unexpected, Serena. The negative is going to lose, do not pay her much mind."

My happy reflection sticks its tongue out at the evil one, and I turn away, unable to take all the contrast as I have not made any of these gestures. "Hold me tonight?"

He touches my face, giving me a pleasant sensation. "We can do that, but we must be careful. I do not want to risk any dreams causing accidents. It is so very difficult not to mark you, especially when you please me so. And my Serena, you have pleased me greatly." He steps away and goes to his supply machine. He comes back with a long sleeve top and long pants. I frown, taking the clothes while pushing him out of the bathroom. When I wear the excessive clothing, I lay down on the bed next to him. "Peyton would be pleased that you trust me with your sleeping form in the same bed," he whispers.

"I am sure he would, but I am not doing this for Peyton, nor am I concerned that this could upset him. I know it would not, as I am certain he holds Alexis from time to time." Keon does not respond. "That sounds crass, I just mean, this is not about Peyton, it is about you and I. I asked for this because I trust you and I really want to be held."

He pulls me into him. "You need to stop talking now my Serena. If you make me any prouder, I am going to need you to leave, for I will not risk hurting you."

I smile, pushing myself closer and letting sleep overtake me, hoping to the stars I never remember watching Ilka die.

Twenty-Eight

Reflections

Serena

My aunt stays for three days. I wish I could tell you I was sad to see her go, but that is a lie. I was so relieved to see her leave I almost cried. Not because I resent her for the past but because the past was simply too close with her presence. I am enjoying my new life, my mostly guilt-free new life. Her being here reminds me of all the bad mistakes I have made and the consequences to them, including the fact she and I are simply not that close.

After all the awkwardness had passed, she talked to me some about her life on Trorain before the Prytores' came, but it all seemed forced. Thankfully, after the first night, it was easier to comply with Keon's orders and my behavior did not receive many unpleasant corrections. She told me a little more about my parents and explained Ilka to me. She also admitted she was married to Borak before Lapidos but my father dissolved the marriage; she did not explain why. Nor did she go into detail as to why they chose her to take me to Artthemis and not do it themselves.

We did not have much to say about the orphanage. She asked me a lot of questions about her favorites and seemed relieved to discover that most of them did not hurt me, with a few exceptions. She explained the need to hide me. She chose an orphanage because it was the perfect cover to keep my identity from common knowledge. Because Prytores consider orphanages a necessary evil in their society, but when not needed, they are not thought about. She assured me it was not meant to compete for her affections. But it did make her happy after she thought she would never be happy again.

Thankfully, she did not bring up Ilka's death more than once or twice after the first night. It bothers me more than I want to admit to her, especially the part where I understand what the ravens were trying to accomplish, way more than I should. It is weird. I should hate them like she does, but I cannot bring it in myself to do so. I do not tell her this of course. I simply do not talk about ravens to her at all.

After we bid her farewell, Keon takes me to my room to help clean up her temporary sleeping arrangements from the garden. When the task is done, I find myself staring in the mirror. The images are still very stable, so stable in fact in one of them I can actually do my hair. As long as I can tolerate the other's mockery of it. I am in the process of doing just that, when Keon enters the image and causes my eyes to cross while I ignore the angry one's reactions. "Do not get too used to doing that yourself, now that you can see clearly. I rather enjoy styling your hair." I smile at him while I pull out a few strands near my face, giving him the messy look, he likes so much. "I want to try something different today."

"Anything to make her go away," I mutter, glaring at the image that is going ballistic.

"It is similar to a mind-body separation, but safer. Now that your reflection has shown signs of stabilizing. I think it is safe enough to try."

"Okay, do we need to connect ears or something?" I ask, setting my hairbrush down.

"No, nothing that dangerous." He smiles. "We need to go to a room full of mirrors."

"What will that do?"

"With the proper focus it will allow my reflection to talk to both of yours."

"You can do that?" I ask surprised.

"It takes practice, but I have achieved this feat in the past with Peyton. He too was particularly stubborn when it came to aligning his three parts, though his mind was not the challenge."

"His soul." I smile.

"His body, actually." Keon corrects my assumption. "He is a true warrior. Having anything hinder him is very disturbing for him. It took us almost five years to get him to surrender."

"That seems excessive, considering you are worried that my disconnect could kill me, if not corrected soon."

"Your disconnect is with your mind splitting itself in half. If it does not kill you, it will drive you mad." Keon worries aloud. "This cannot go on much longer Serena, we are pushing limits on a daily basis."

"Which is why you brought my aunt here."

"She served her purpose." He kisses my shoulder. "Come, let us get some food and then we shall start."

During breakfast, I was picking at my food more than I was eating it. The longer I sit, the more bitter my mood becomes. My mind literally a million miles away. "Please tell me this is just your pondering, and not you being deliberately defiant." Keon notes, taking a drink.

"It is Ilka." I answer, pushing scrambled eggs around the plate. "I just do not see the ravens killing her like that."

"Serena, you were three, you most likely blocked the memory, if you saw it at all."

"Still." I argue, staring at the plate.

"You still do not trust Takira?"

"I trust she believes that is what she saw," I reply carefully, "but I do not believe it to be the full truth."

"I see."

"Do you?"

"You are trying to justify the ravens' actions, because your aura is unsettled with what you have heard."

"There just has to be more to it, is all," I mutter, not looking at him and forcing food in my mouth.

"What if there is not?" Keon asks, causing my eyes to snap to him.

"Then I guess I have more to forgive than just her." I answer, taking a drink of water.

"You would forgive them for murder?"

"They are birds, Keon. They were trying to protect me." I frown. "They do not know right from wrong like we do."

"Or do they?"

I look back at my plate, forcing a few more bites of food. "There is more to this truth, there has to be."

"I am sure she told you what she knows," Keon replies carefully. "Maybe she is not fully informed."

"Well, being stuck on Artthemis, I cannot exactly find out, now can I?" I snap a little too harshly.

"Careful, Serena." He warns, studying me while I eat. Checking my temper, I look at him. "Is it dangerous? I mean, I know I was hidden because I am a fiorriee Queen, but to have favor with ravens."

"King Maleko will not like it, but there are no ravens on Artthemis, so he will not fear it."

"I do not plan on telling your King."

"It is best I do not hide information that he could have already obtained, Serena. Roarick might have seen more than you, remember."

"And we have come full circle," I mutter, stabbing the last bit of food I planned on trying to eat. I drag it between my teeth and chew in annoyance. He catches my mood, but he does not comment on it.

"Come, let us try to repair that mind of yours." Keon smiles, holding out his hand. I stand abruptly from my chair, taking his hand. I am not looking forward to this experiment of his. We walk in silence, and it takes effort not to be mean for no reason at all. My mind slips back to my aunt's story, and I am still at a loss as to how it can be true. We stop at a new room and he leads me inside. The entire place… floor, ceiling, and walls are covered in mirrors. There is no escaping our reflection. The moment I see mine, I take a step back. "Serena?"

"It is backward," I reply staring directly at the mean girl. The one I have grown to like much better is slightly behind the mean one on the right.

"Yes, I see that. It is not surprising, it explains your attitude at breakfast," Keon responds, unconcerned. He all but tugs me inside because I do not want to enter. When the door closes, I see a light and suddenly the door is gone. "Only I can open it, Serena. There is no need for you to dwell on things you cannot change." I look at him in annoyance, he lets go of my hand and moves to the center of the room. I watch as he sits with his feet pressed together and he places his hands on them. Then he closes his eyes, and his head drops. "I am here, Serena."

I look into the mirrors and realize he is standing next to my reflections. "How did you do that?"

He smiles, "I concentrated. Please, join me." I look at him funny, but my body does not have a will of its own, so I find myself mimicking his actions. But when I close my eyes, nothing happens. I open them annoyed, only to find myself standing up. "See, it is easy when you are in a room such as this."

"What?" I ask, looking down at myself and realizing there are two of me: one wearing a bright yellow dress and the other wearing black. I grab my head in pain, both of me reacting.

"It is going to take a minute to get used to. Your mind is split but your body does not allow it to have its own spaces. Give it time, you will feel like your normal self soon enough."

"I do not like this," my yellow dress self complains.

"Neither do I," Keon mutters, waiting. "Come, Serena, take my hand." The yellow dress Serena happily goes to Keon and takes his hand, very content on being with him. The black dress Serena stares at his other open hand but does not move.

"Who do you serve?"

"You, Prytore Keon." The yellow dress Serena answers while simultaneously the black dress Serena answers, "Prytore Roarick." The yellow dress Serena, squeezes Keon's hand, who squeezes back. This movement does not go unnoticed by the black dress Serena, who rolls her eyes.

"I would like to talk to Roarick's Serena. My Serena pleases me very much, but I need you still for the moment." Keon explains, causing the yellow dress Serena to nod.

"You are wasting your time," the black dress Serena remarks. "My loyalty will not let me abandon my Prytore."

"Even though he abandoned you? And this choice of loyalty to him can kill both of you?"

"It is not my mind that needs to be changed." The black dress Serena snips. "It is hers. She is disloyal and if she does not come back to where she belongs, her choice will kill us. Not mine!"

"How did you meet your Prytore?"

"What?" she asks, taken off guard. "You already know that. I showed you when you went trampling about in my head!" she glares at him. "I hated that by the way, you had no right to be there."

"Do I not?" he challenges. "Did you not swear your service to me and Peyton?"

"Peyton is not in question here, you are." she snaps. "You are the unwanted invader. How this, this traitor, could even consider abandoning Prytore Roarick much less do it for the man who single handedly destroyed her world is beyond comprehension."

"Are you hanging on to Roarick as a convenient excuse for your anger?" Keon challenges her. "You do have every right to be angry Serena, though admittedly, you do not harbor all the facts."

"I know enough. You should have never come to Trorain, never harmed my world, never forced me away from my ravens!"

"I have never harmed your world Serena, in fact, I have risked much to save it," he replies calmly. "As far as your raven's...it was not my actions that forced you into hiding. It was my enemies, and Roarick is my enemy's son."

"Lies!"

"I have never lied to you, Serena." he replies, keeping his calm. "Roarick tricked you, abandoned you in hopes that you would not be strong enough to survive the betrayal."

"Lies!"

"You were weak when he found you," Keon, presses. "So broken and angry because you did not trust your aunt, so much you disowned her at a young age and referred to her as your caretaker. He took advantage of your vulnerability. He built you up, tricked you into trusting him, then he dropped you, hoping you would shatter. But you did not. You are stronger than he gave you credit for. Stronger, than you give yourself credit for. Now you are divided into two. Serena, let him go. I swear to you, you can genuinely trust me to care for you."

"Can I?" She challenges.

"I have disappointed you." He answers. "I could not protect your world and now you are afraid that if you stand by me to fight again, I will fail a second time."

"You are missing something vital. What is it you just said to me, Prytore Keon? 'You do not harbor all the facts.'"

"What am I missing?"

"As if I were to tell you!"

"My Serena?" Keon asks, turning his attention to the yellow dress me. "Do you know what she is referring to?" I nod. "Tell me." I shake my head, hiding in his shoulder in shame.

The black dress Serena smirks. "Looks like you do not own her as much as you thought."

"Serena, please," Keon pleads with the yellow dress me.

"I cannot," she cries. "The door is stuck. But right after that the twins started to hurt me."

"Rightful punishment we deserved!" The black dress Serena seethes. "Not that it could ever fix it. Nothing could fix it. Despite Dex fruitlessly trying."

"Dex?" Keon asks, turning to and pulling the yellow dress Serena into his arms. "Serena who is Dex?"

"My sister." I smile, suddenly happy.

"Well, not really." The black dress Serena corrects. "But we were close once."

"What happened?" Keon asks.

The black dress Serena refuses to answer. The yellow dress pulls herself closer into him. "I do not remember."

"So, this is the reason for not speaking or standing up to the twins. This is the reason you allowed a Prytore into your mind before you were of age. This is the reason, even now you take so many risks, and love yourself so little." Keon realizes. "Whatever happened, you blame yourself."

The black dress Serena shrugs. "Smart one."

"Roarick claimed to forgive you," Keon concludes. "But he used it as his reason for abandonment." Neither of us answer him. "I am not Roarick. I can be trusted." The yellow dress Serena clings to him tighter while the black dress Serena seems to grow a little larger.

"Just because you understand, does not give you any right to try to claim me." She answers pridefully. "I made a choice, years ago, it is done. I serve Roarick."

"I doubt that." Keon frowns. "Maybe a small part of you in this black dress does, but another part of you is hiding behind him in fear." She says nothing. "I will earn your trust, Serena, but it takes time. Something you, I am afraid, are running out of."

"I already told you, you are wasting your time. You want to save my life, let her go." The black dress argues back, sneering at the yellow.

"Your pride will be the death of you," Keon replies, wearily removing his conscience from the mirrors and back into his body.

"Serena, return to me," he whispers in my body's ear.

My black dress reflection turns to him. "It is not my pride you should be concerned about, Prytore Keon, it is yours."

I open my eyes and gasp. My eyes slip down to the green dress I am wearing and back to Keon. "What was that?" I ask, feeling weird.

"Answers," he replies, taking my hand and leading me out of the room. I glimpse in the mirror on the way out, seeing both Serenas, one in a yellow dress, one in black. But now the yellow one is so far in the background I almost miss the tears she is crying. Keon leads me out of the room and down the hallway, not speaking until we are back to my room. He releases my hand and creates distance between us before he turns and stares at me.

"I do not know what to say. I did not realize these thoughts…" I start, but he cuts me off.

"Of course you did not, your mind is divided." He brushes me off. "But we now know where we stand."

"You might, I am still completely baffled."

"You trust me, if you did not, I would not have your body or your soul in my control. But you are resisting your mind. Roarick is simply an excuse. Mostly. Though some of that is genuine, otherwise you would not have divided in the first place." I stare at him. He studies me for a very long time. "You are afraid, Serena, and fear is something you have learned to deal with alone."

Not wanting to even scratch at the door, I cannot open, I deflect him. "Of everyone in my life, Peyton and Alexis are the only ones who have never disappointed me, and even they are gone."

"That is not true. If not for Alexis, I would have never figured out how to survive on your world, as there are differences. And Peyton, he was a warrior, Serena. He fought for your world and lost! He was one of the most prideful warriors your world had to offer and he surrenders to Alexis and me. Peyton is on his knees before his former enemy on a daily basis, yet you love him despite all of that." I look up at Keon, hurt, hating that he is right. "Do you not see, none of us are perfect. Love is not perfect. It is not meant to be. Love is at its greatest when it faces obstacles, challenges, and disappointment and grows stronger than any of it, because it accepts that being, despite their flaws!" He grabs at his hair, his passion getting the best of him. "You cannot love anyone, not really. Not until you learn to love yourself. So, I ask you, Serena, what have you done that has made you hate yourself?"

"You want a list? It is grown tenfold since we met!" I yell at him. "I want the source," he responds, striking a chord that stops my anger cold. I turn away from him, unable to give him an answer because I do not know it. "Open that door, Serena; tell me about Dex."

"No!" I scream at him, turning violently and hitting him over and over until he manages to get a firm grip on me. I struggle in tears until I fall weak. When he is sure I will not fight back, he releases me.

"You need to eat and rest. Tomorrow you are going on a soul journey."

"I hate to interrupt, Prytore Keon, but I thought you might like to be aware that Prytoree Alexis and Peyton have arrived home." Fakhir chimes in, saving me from another defiant response.

My head snaps to Keon, my eyes reflecting my unspoken question. "You may go to him. Maybe he can help you better than I."

Twenty-Nine

Bittersweet

Serena

"Peyton?" I ask timidly the moment I share a room with him. He turns to smile at me and I find myself dashing into his arms. "I have missed you," I whisper, before I fall apart into tears, becoming so weak in my knees I can only stand due to his embrace.

"Serena, my love, what is it?" I do not answer him. He responds by pulling me closer to him.

"I am not concerned about me. I am concerned about you. Are you all right? Please, I need to know if you are truly all right."

He pulls back, worry in his eyes. "I am more than all right, Serena. I am free." His smile is genuine, but his eyes remain clouded. He looks to Keon for answers.

"She is had a very rough journey, one that is not over yet." Keon explains.

"We expected her breaking to be difficult." Alexis reassures everyone, seeming unconcerned.

"Not like this." Keon frowns.

"Husband?" Alexis questions.

I pull away from Peyton's comforting arms. "I have surrendered my body and my soul to Prytore Keon, just as I have Peyton, I think. But my mind is…" I look to Keon for help, unable to admit to them the truth.

"Divided." He finishes for me. "She serves *two* Prytores."

"That is not possible!" Peyton responds in disbelief. "It would kill her."

"She has not shown signs of any defect yet, but I am afraid if I cannot bring her into one mind, it will do just that." Keon confirms.

"Who is the other?" Alexis asks, looking angry.

"Roarick." Keon answers, when I look away in shame.

"King Maleko's son?" she asks surprised, causing Keon to nod. "Well, that is alarming. How did we not know this? How was she able to come to court?"

"Deception on her aunt's part." Keon answers, "so deep even Serena herself was not aware of it. To be fair, Takira did what she did to save Serena's life."

"If this is true, why is she still here? Why have you not sent her away?" Peyton asks, causing me to recoil. He realizes his words hurt me and he grips my shoulders. "I do not want him to, Serena. I am simply trying to understand why he is risking your life."

"Roarick betrayed her, then abandoned her. Her mind has been out of sorts with the rest of herself for years. If I had not stepped in, her remembering what has happened to her, would have killed her long before my choice to fight for her to switch loyalties ever could."

"You are trying to save her life." Alexis realizes in an approving tone.

"I wish I could say I feel confident that I can. But I cannot, she does not love herself. Until she can forgive whatever it is she fears she has done wrong. None of us can save her." Keon sighs. "She needs food and rest Peyton. A soul journey is in store for her tomorrow. I think it is best if you take her on it, seeing as she naturally chooses you without resistance."

Keon leaves the room, looking exhausted. Alexis approaches me and gives me a hug. "It is all right, sweet girl. You will be just fine." She assures me as she lets go, touches Peyton's arm briefly then exits the room. Leaving me alone with my husband.

"I am sorry. There always seems to be something." I shake my head. "Guess it is just another reason for you to run away with her and not come to me, your true wife."

"Alexis is my true wife." Peyton replies with firm eyes. "Just as you are." I resist and eye roll as he barely glides his fingers up the veins of the collar on my arm and takes my wrist. He gently brings my wrist to his lips and his taste floods my senses. I gasp, I have almost forgotten what that feels like. "Whatever we face, Serena, it will be together," he assures me. My eyes meet his and our gaze locks. I half expect to find ourselves somewhere else, but it does not happen. Still, his silver eyes are hard to pry away from and it takes me a long moment to even desire to do so.

"It worked." I smile, looking down at my arm. "You are pure fiorriee."

"It worked." He confirms with a smile. "I feel amazing. Like I was in a cage my entire life and did not know it."

"Do you feel like you can fly?" I ask, genuinely curious. "Like literally fly?"

"No, it is a much more grounded feeling. A much more warrior like pride."

"What shape is your aura?" I ask him pointedly, causing his smile to fade a little.

"Serena, even those who have met their aura have not had the honor of knowing its true form. It takes a very special connection for that."

"So, you do not know?"

"I did not say that."

"Forgive me, husband, but I am confused. You claim to be a true fiorriee warrior, one who fought in the war on Trorain, yet you willfully serve Prytores?"

"I have my reasons." He answers coldly.

"How long were you on Trorain?"

"I did not track the time."

"However long you were there, your aura never revealed its true form?"

"I never said that."

"But you are avoiding an answer," I reply, annoyed. "Would it help you to know that I know what mine is? I lived on Trorain for three years and while I never seen my aura, I was informed in the strangest way." Peyton studies me, not saying a word. "Ravens."

"Ravens." he repeats, keeping a neutral facial expression.

"Yes, the birds made it very clear that they found me unique. They even taught me how to call them." Peyton stares at me for a very long time. The silence is so deafening that I almost wonder if he is still breathing. "You have lived on Trorain, you understand the significance."

"Serena." He starts, but I am impatient and continue my thought.

"Whatever your aura, it must be a ruler, Peyton," I deduce, understanding fully as to why my choosing was so important. Why my family did everything they could to make sure my choice was mine, yet it favored certain bloodlines. "One that has been caged for far too long."

"One you set free."

"If you are implying that I had anything to do with Erland's deception."

"You did not, I know that." He cuts me off before I could be offended. "But your body's need for my true self. You set me free."

"A true King and Queen of our kind, rulers of Trorain." I smile, "But we are more than that. Or will be, when we embrace our aura's purest form." Shock crosses his features, I ignore it. "Wasted. Trapped on a planet that is nearly lifeless." He studies me as I do him. "Keon has told me of a plan that the three of you have to undo the damage of our world, Peyton. I am just curious, if we are able to accomplish this, are you prepared to be at my side and be the true ruler you were born to be?"

"Serena, embracing our auras like that would kill us. Not that I am afraid to do so, but that is meant for our very distant future." He shakes his head. "Today, in this moment it is not what you should be concerned with. My love, your mind is divided."

"What does that matter if we go home? Taking our rightful place means we do not serve anyone."

"Again, Serena, I am not interested in what could happen to us in the far future. We need to focus on today. We are here, on Artthemis, where you have sworn your loyalty to this family. Your service to Keon and Alexis is for life, no matter the outcome of our success or failure on Trorain."

"I swore my loyalty to Roarick first. I seem to do well without him around." I shrug. "What is the difference?"

"The difference? Roarick had a small part of your mind. You have made a blood vow to me, Keon and Alexis. You have surrendered to me completely and you have given Keon your body and soul. Part of your mind belongs to us; the other part is resisting. Serena, if you do not accept what you have done, this will kill you."

"Then let it kill me. I am a goddess Peyton. You must be important as well. Why else would I choose you? Please, I am begging you, let us go home where you can accept this fate with me. Let us leave all this horribleness behind. Let us fulfill our destiny."

"No," he answers firmly.

"Why, because you love our enemy?"

"Fakhir. Where are Keon and Alexis?"

"In their room Peyton." The house answers. "Shall I call them?" it asks but it never receives an answer. Peyton has picked me up and dashed me to their room. Alexis gives a squeal of surprise, followed by a glare in annoyance upon our arrival.

Keon glares at him. "What is so urgent that you dare enter here without express permission?"

"She is in a death spiral."

"What makes you think that?" Alexis asks, worry overcoming her annoyance.

"She is prepared to die." Peyton explains. "What do we do? How do we save her?"

"What is it with you? All of you? I do not need saving!" I scream at them.

"Who do you serve, Serena?"

"No one! I do not serve anyone!" I cry out, fighting against Keon's touch on my face and struggle as his thumbs keep my eyelids open. He moves his head and eyes until ours reluctantly connect and suddenly we are dancing again.

"Serena." He states in a firm yet concerned tone. "Who do you serve?"

"You, Prytore Keon." I smile, and then frown at the features on his face.

"What is wrong? Do you not want me anymore?"

"Serena, what is the last thing you remember?"

"Being held by you in the reflection."

"That is it? Nothing of Peyton's arrival?"

"Peyton's back? He is okay?" I ask, almost in glee.

"Concentrate, Serena." he replies impatiently. "Did you come back to me or did your defiant side overpower you?"

"Keon." I frown suddenly scared.

"It is all right, I will not lose you. You need to fight her, Serena, suppress her."

"How?"

"Sheer will. Your aura is the most powerful part of your being, use it to correct your mind."

He breaks eye contact with me, and an enormous amount of painful pressure hits my skull. I feel like I am going to explode. I cry out in anguish. I can hear my name being called, but I cannot place the voice. I can feel my skin being touched, but I do not know by whom. A bright white light of agony overtakes me, and I cry out again in sheer agony, dropping me to my knees before losing consciousness.

When I awake, I find myself on a bed, one I recognize from a few nights before. I am in Keon's bed. I jerk upward only to be gently encouraged to lay down by a hand on my shoulder. I register three very concerned sets of eyes on me, but no one speaks. "What happened?" I ask the room.

"You tell us." Keon answers. "What do you remember?"

"There were mirrors, then you and I were dancing and… Peyton. Oh, my husband! You are home! You are all right!" I gasp, jumping at him and holding him close. "Oh, I hope it did not hurt too much. I am so not worth all of this. I fear I have shamed you in so many ways, and here you are suffering for me, only to return to something you may not want."

"Nonsense. I will always want you, Serena." Peyton replies holding me extra tight. "She has no memory of it?" he asks Keon and Alexis.

"Memory of what?" I ask, curious as I pull away, but keep myself in his embrace.

"It appears not. Her aura is in control at the moment though. I fear waiting until morning to start her journey is too risky. We must start now, while the largest part of herself is in control."

"What is going on?"

"The other part of your mind is trying to take over. I am afraid that it would rather die than submit to us."

"Of course, this would happen," I mutter. "I cannot even trust myself." I take a deep breath. "What must I do?"

"You must figure out what stems your disappointment in yourself. You can take this journey alone or with one traveler, Peyton being the natural choice."

"No," he refuses. "Her other half wants us to embrace our future calling. My presence would not be beneficial."

"Future calling?"

"It has to be you, Keon. You must take her," Peyton responds, ignoring my question. Keon looks at me wearily.

"She could go alone," Alexis replies, looking anxious at the idea of Keon joining me.

"She is spiraling, if she goes in alone who will protect her from the part of herself who has a death wish?" Keon argues, taking his wife's hand.

"I will go." Alexis offers.

"No," Peyton refuses without hesitation. "Her destructive side is jealous of you and sees you as an enemy. Neither Keon nor myself will risk you like that."

She gives them both a look of defeat and chooses not to argue. Giving a deep sigh she turns to Keon. "If you feel it is the only way."

"It might be the only way, but it will not be easy," Keon tells the room. "She hates me. I do not see how I can help with that being the truth."

"No. I just have not completely forgiven you for Trorain's fate." I answer, understanding the other half of myself. "Or that is the impression I got in the mirrors. It is like the part of me that was wearing yellow has, and the part that was wearing black is so angry."

"For sake of clarification, I am talking to the yellow dress Serena now?" I nod. "Does this side of you know what you have not forgiven yourself for?" Keon wonders. I shake my head yes then no. Shrugging uncomfortably as I stare at the floor, dashing his hopes of an easy answer. "Then we must go on this journey at once. Before your self-destructive side figures out how to kill you."

"I am scared." I admit grabbing both Keon and Peyton's hand. "I just got you back. I have not even given you a proper hello."

"It is all right, Serena." Peyton smiles. "You will survive this. I trust Keon with my life, and you my beautiful wife, you are my life."

"I love you too." I smile. "Alexis, do not let Keon sacrifice himself for me."

"Serena," she replies, unsure.

"Promise me. Do not let either of them do anything stupid. I will only do this if you promise me you will look after both of them."

She hesitates, looking to both Keon and Peyton before she turns her attention back to me. "I promise to protect them, Serena. And I promise to help protect you as well."

"That better not be a loophole. I am the only one who should be taking a risk," I reply. "I got myself into this zarla mess, I must figure out how to get out of it. Though Keon, I do appreciate the guide. You have helped me in the past. I trust you can do it again." I squeeze Peyton's hand. "Kiss me?" He does not hesitate and brings his lips to mine. I so desperately want to melt into him, but I keep myself from the trap. Breaking the kiss, I turn to Keon. "All right, let us get this over with."

Thirty

Guilt

Serena

"You are sure you do not want to guide her?" Keon asks Peyton one last time.

"It is too risky. Her destructive self wants to transition. That would kill us both in different ways. Besides, there is no guarantee her aura could survive on Artthemis without her body. The moment she mentioned it; I knew something was wrong."

"Can you summon your aura with the Prytore technology no longer hindering you?" Alexis asks Peyton.

"Your guess is as good as mine." Peyton answers.

"Transition?" I ask, completely confused.

"Do not worry about that right now, Serena." Keon dismisses, "we need to figure out what your destructive side is clinging to. Only then will you be able to free yourself."

"Okay," I reply nervously. "What do I do?"

"I need your ears, Serena." he answers, causing me to frown because it is a true struggle to comply with him, but eventually they come out. Keon wastes no time. He meets my eyes, and we are in the ballroom. I feel his ears connect with mine, and suddenly we are surrounded by darkness. "I need you to show me your past."

"That is twenty-three very long years. Can you try to be a little more specific?"

"Let us hope so. For now, we must go at random. I need you to stay strong. Half of your mind is going to resist showing me anything."

"Seriously, Keon, I need something to work with unless you want to stay in the dark forever." I frown, unsure what to do.

"All right. Can you remember a time you hurt yourself on purpose?" Suddenly, a lot of doors appear in front of us. "Serena," he breathes in shock, causing the lights of the doors to dim.

"It is not what you think." I defend myself, opening a random door. A younger version of myself is staring out the window watching other kids play and laugh. But I am sad. So, I take a pencil and smack myself with it. For Prytore's this simple act of causing unnecessary pain is highly frowned upon and should be avoided at all costs; for fiorriee it helps with moods.

"Even this is forbidden in our laws," he replies. "And it falls under my definition of self-harm."

"I do not expect you to understand." I sigh, closing the door to the memory and returning us to the dark.

He stares at me for a while. "Did that happen often?"

"You see the doors."

"I meant you choosing to be alone when others were playing." I tilt my head thinking, expecting the answer to be yes, but that is not true. Confused, I whisper no and suddenly rows after rows of doors appear in front of us. "Well, that is good." He smiles, "though it still leaves us at the beginning."

"I do not think it does," I reply, turning a knob on a random door, but it does not open. Surprised, I put my weight into it before I manage to get through. I smile when I see myself playing with my sister. "Dextra."

"This is Dex," he replies in satisfaction. I glare at him, realizing he was searching for her without asking directly, thus surpassing most my defenses. "You seem happy, Serena."

"I am. Dex is like a sister to me."

"She seems older. Did she have her courting before you?"

I stare at the happy memory for a moment longer before I let it fade into darkness.

"She did. It did not work out for her."

"That is unusual." Keon notes.

"She tried three times, now she just works." I shrug.

"Show me your memory of her the day before she left for her first courting."

"What? Why?" I ask, confused and defensive.

"This is not about her, it is about me, remember."

"I am very aware of what this is about, Serena."

"So why are you wasting our time with Dex?"

"Why are you stalling?"

"I am not stalling." I argue, forcing a door to stand in front of us. He steps aside, so I can open it. But it will not budge. I try with all my might, but it simply will not give way. "I do not understand," I reply, frustrated.

"She sabotaged herself, did she not? She sabotaged herself all three times so she could be with you, her best friend for life. But you did not sabotage yourself."

"No, that is ridiculous." I dismiss. "It was not that it was…"

"Serena?"

"Get out."

"Serena?"

"I said get out!" I scream, causing our connection to break. I shake my head, finding myself staring at two very concerned faces. Before they can react, I see Keon is on the floor, holding his head. He looks like he is in pain. "Keon? I am sorry. Keon." I worry, grabbing his arm as he continues to fight his migraine. "I am sorry. Please say something."

"It is all right, Serena." he assures me, working on regaining his composure. "I am all right."

"What happened?" Peyton asks.

"She broke our connection rather abruptly is all."

"You are going to be dizzy for some time, husband; you should lie down." Alexis worries.

"Yes, I think sleep is best for all of us. Peyton could you and your wife retire from us for the evening."

"Did you fix her divide?"

"No." Keon answers. "But I guided her in how to fix it herself. The rest is on her."

I watch as he walks over to Alexis and all but falls into her arms. I look to Peyton with concern, reluctantly following him when he takes my hand and dashes us out of the room. When he gets to what I can only presume is his room, he turns to me. "What did you see?"

"It does not matter."

"It does."

"Peyton, you do not understand. Knowing this does not change anything. I do not care who I serve or if I am alone. I do not deserve forgiveness for it. I never have, and I never will."

"So, you are just going to let it kill you?" I do not answer him. "I will not allow it. Whatever it is, Serena, you must forgive yourself."

"I love that you believe that I am worth saving." I smile kindly at him. "Can we sleep? I am exhausted."

He is about to protest, but then he looks in my eyes. "All right, but this is not over. We will speak of this in the morning." I give a weary smile, walk over to his bed and fall asleep before my head hits the pillow.

My dreams send me back to the miles of doors Keon had taken me to. I find myself going through them. Most of these memories reinforce my belief as to why Dex is a sister to me. These are the things I want to remember, but I tend to forget. We were always into mischief and always laughing. With every door, there was another happy memory to find. Well, every door but the one I refuse to open, even in my dreams. I find myself staring at it so long, I can start to hear the event. I turn from the door and start to run. My black dress self grabs me and yanks me into a random memory; any memory is better than the one I am trying to escape. I stare at her. She stares back. We do not speak to each other. Instead, we hold hands while staring at our younger self, happily playing with ravens.

When I wake in the morning, I find Peyton staring at me. I touch his face, frowning. "You did not sleep." I accuse. He gently strokes my face. Not wanting to answer his unspoken questions, I turn the conversation to something favorable. "I am happy to be in your arms again. I wish you never had to go." His eyes tighten, causing me to frown. "Peyton," I sigh.

"What? Am I supposed to just be okay with enduring the most painful zarla, that nearly killed me, for only a few days with you? I want years, Serena. I want a lifetime."

"You think I do not?" I snap, insulted.

"If you did, you would let us in, you would share what has you resisting us. What is so horrible that you feel you cannot trust us, Serena? What secret are you willing to die to keep?"

"Not everything needs to be put into words, Peyton. You have made no secret you are a soldier, and I doubt you would ever want to share all your war experiences. This is my burden."

"My memories are not threatening my life." He argues.

"No." I mutter, shutting down. "There has to be something else that is splitting my mind."

"Do you want Roarick?"

"Do not be ridiculous!"

"I am being ridiculous? Your life is literally hanging in the balance and neither side of your divided mind will help itself. You would rather die, than forgive yourself for whatever it is. And you are upset that I think it is because you do not want to be with me. We have shared one night, Serena, one. How many did you have with Roarick?"

"None!" I gasp, close to tears. "You were there, you know how my body reacted to you. You know I had never..."

"How many times did you want to?" he asks, causing my heart so much pain I can barely breathe. I shake my head back and forth over and over. "If you can barely phantom the thought of being with someone who you gave your mind to, and you managed to keep your body intact, what the zarla, could be so bad that you feel it warrants death?"

"There is so much more to life than what my future husband would think of my past choices! She was my sister! And I, I..." I stop talking, letting myself cry. I half want him to try to comfort me, half want him to leave.

"What, Serena? What did you do?" Peyton asks, in such a loud tone Alexis and Keon run into the room.

"Is all this yelling necessary?" Alexis asks, disapproving. "Can you not see she has been through enough."

"I do not need you to defend me!" I snap at her, causing her to raise her head in warning.

"You and Dextra are very close, Serena," Keon speaks up. "Yet it took me talking to your reflection to even discover her existence. Your mind is on such defense about her, you risk death."

"Dex and I are not close! Not anymore," I reply, turning my head away from all of them and letting my hair hide my face completely. "Dex and I lost everything before she even attended her first courting. Not because she could not forgive me, but because I was not worthy of forgiveness."

"Must we hunt down your aunt, or Dex to get the full story Serena? Or will you share it with us?" Alexis asks.

"I do not want you to know it. It is my shame. My burden. Please."

"Normally, we would give you time to share it on your own. But time is not a luxury we have." Keon sighs. "You have until Akatite sets to tell us yourself. Otherwise, we will discover it another way."

"Can I be with a raven simulation?" I ask, hopeful.

"Not until after you share this with us." Keon denies.

"I understand. I think I just want to be left alone then."

"Serena." Peyton protests.

I stand up from Peyton's bed. "I just need time to think." I walk past all of them without making any eye contact. The moment I leave them behind, I feel like I can breathe again. I dash outside and find a stream I became familiar with when Keon wanted to be left alone. There, where no one could see me, I lie myself on the ground and cry. When I get back into the house, I ask Fakhir where my family is. He directs me to a room I have never seen before, not that that is much of a feat in this place. When I find them, they all seem very upset? "Peyton?" I ask, dashing to my husband and meeting his sad, silver eyes. "What is it husband?"

"It is a family matter. One you need not concern yourself with at this time." Alexis answers coldly.

"Forgive her, she is rather upset. She just means that until you share your secrets with us, she sees no obligation to share ours." Keon frowns.

"That is what I have been trying to work out all day, Prytore." I shrug. "Sharing this is not going to change anything for me. I will still feel the way I do. All it is going to do is make all of you see me differently, and as you must have figured out, no part of my being wants you to see me in this shadow of shame."

"You have vowed your mind, body and soul to this family, Serena." Keon reminds me. "What you want and what will happen are two separate things."

"I know that." I frown. "But this is a very big house. If you cannot forgive what you hear, then please banish me from your presence and I will never darken your door again."

"Serena." Peyton starts but he is cut off by the lifting of Keon's hand. "If you want us to reserve the right to judge you, we will. But you must accept our judgment as a final ruling on this matter. There will be no trying to sway our minds one way or the other." He turns his head to Alexis and Peyton; they both hesitate but they both agree. "You have the floor, Serena."

"Can I not just show you?"

"No. I think it is best if you present your case from your own memory recall." Keon decides. I frown at that. I prefer them just looking at the memory themselves. Having to put this into words. My own words at that. "Remember, Serena, you get one chance, so I do not advise a summary or a sentence. We need the full story. All details will be weighed."

I glare at him. He is very clever. All I want to do is speak one sentence and be done with this, but if I do that, I guarantee I will never see them, including Peyton, ever again. But if I tell the full story, I am fighting for their forgiveness, and that annoys me. "I walked into that." I frown causing him to smile. "You are a very worthy opponent, Prytore Keon." I note, dashing to the food machine and getting a glass of water. When I return, I find them all seated, waiting to hear what I so desperately do not want to tell them.

"Dextra came to the orphanage when I was five. She was eight. I remember her mother crying and being all but dragged out of the house. My aunt held Dex in her arms, while Dex screamed for her mother for months. Of all the kids who were abandoned in my home, that was the hardest one for me to witness." I pause at the memory, trying to shake it off. "She had such a hard time at first. She would not talk to anyone, would not eat. Even tried to run away several times. But my aunt always found her, always brought her back." I place the water glass on the table while sitting down, thinking back to a part of my life I have chosen not to recall for a very long time. "She hated me." I smile. "But I did not let that stop me from doing everything I could to be her friend. I would hide desserts for her, lie about breaking rules I did not break to protect her; even did chores I knew she blew off, but still she refused to be my friend. Well, not just my friend. Anyone's. She simply wanted to be left alone. And I wish, well, I wish I would have listened to her. Maybe then…" I trail off, unable to find the words as memories flash in my mind.

"Drink this, Serena." Peyton offers, after a very long moment of silence. I nod my head, taking the glass to take a drink before setting it back on the table. "Obviously, you two became friends."

"My aunt did not have a lot of rules but there were some, and they were not breakable. To do so, meant automatic banishment and rehoming. And of course, Dex decided she did not care about my aunt's rules."

"What were these rules?" Peyton asks.

"Mostly safety ones, the big one being self-harm. Dex normally hid it, like you seen in my mind. But then she went and jumped off the roof! That was hard not to notice. I knew immediately she would be kicked out, so I jumped off behind her. When my aunt came out red-faced and screaming, I took the complete blame. I told my aunt I pushed Dex and that it was all my idea. I was in so much trouble and everyone knew it. When my aunt finally turned to Dex to ask if what I claimed was true, she got scared, and went along with my lie. I was grounded for almost an entire year. No one understood why I was being treated so kindly, when everyone else would have been kicked out. I did not know the answer then. By that time, I had forgotten my past life. All I know is that I was able to protect Dex, and that is all that mattered. After that Dex and I became inseparable during school hours, and when my aunt finally allowed me to have fun, well, we never left each other's side. She never thanked me straight on for what I did but she seemed grateful for it. She even gave my aunt a little less of a hard time after that. Though admittedly, we aged Aunt Takira quickly for sure. The first night I got my freedom I woke Dex up, took her up to the roof and dared her to fly with me. Thankfully, there were no witnesses to those falls and being fiorriee, hiding pain was not hard to do."

"Breaking bones is not exactly pleasant, Serena, even for fiorriee." Keon disapproves.

"Yeah, but it was worth it all the way down, until hitting the ground." I grin.

"I could spend too many hours telling you all the adventures we had." I smile. "Oh, the adventures we had. It was the happiest time of my life thus far. We were always together, always telling stories, trying new things, learning our studies. She loved dancing and singing but she was not good at either. The best part about it was neither of us cared. We were just happy. All the time I was happy. My aunt gave up trying to maintain separate rooms for us. We would scream and cry and throw monster fits until we got to be with each other. She hated us together at night though, because it took her ages to get us to sleep. Poor woman, we gave her zarla with that." I find myself laughing a little and then I look to my audience who is absorbing this, but also waiting for the ugly.

"As you are well aware, I did not have an understanding of who I was. Not that the labels that have been slapped on my identity have helped much to explain any of it. Well maybe one, but I still do not grasp its full meaning." I grab the glass and stare at it. "My aunt always had us in bed when Trorain was high in the sky, but we loved to stay up until Furgan was rising, and sometimes would make it to Zarla's rising. But to do that we needed light. My aunt was clever about making sure our room was pitch black once she put us to sleep, but she could not stop me from this." I raise my right hand and close my eyes. When I open them, a blue flame is dancing just above my palm.

"Is that perpetual fire?" Alexis asks, coming closer to study it.

Immediately, I react and close my palm, extinguishing the flame. "Please do not get too close, it is dangerous." I warn, shaking at my words. Her eyes meet mine and I know she understands that something happened. She gives a small nod and sits back in her chair. "Is this because of the goddess thing?"

"Yes," Keon answers.

I look away from them, fighting the shakes. "I used it all the time. Dex would stare at it fascinated. Well, she did, after it stopped scaring the daylights out of her. Mostly, she always did have a healthy fear of it. But I was naive, I did not think her fear was warranted. I mean it is just a ball of light. What harm could it do?" I work to fight the tears. "I did not realize that it was not like a normal fire. We had things around us, like water and a fire extinguisher, upon Dex's insistence. Just in case something weird happened. Completely unaware that everything we had was completely useless to perpetual fire."

"Oh, Serena," Alexis whispers, tears streaming down her unblinking eyes.

"I did not know the window was open. A gust of wind caught me off guard, the curtain caught the flame. I put the ball out as quickly as I could, but it was too late. I grabbed some of the water, but it only seemed to feed the flames. Dex grabbed another cup, and the flames followed the liquid. It caught her sleeve and she dropped to the ground. I rolled her, but it did not put it out. I screamed for help. My aunt came, but not quickly. When she realized what was happening, she ran from the room, came back and covered Dex in salt. Smoke and the smell of burnt flesh filled the room." I drop my head in my hands. "Fiorriee have amazing healing abilities, but even we have our limitations. Perpetual fire is the only thing that can scar our skin…"

"How badly was she scarred?" Peyton asks.

"Her right arm, neck, and face." I answer, not looking at any of them. "My aunt kept us apart for ages while the doctor did what he could. When she finally seen me, she did not blame me. I have never understood that. She refused to forgive me, because she told me it was an accident. She knew I did not do it on purpose, but she got so hurt." I start crying so hard I cannot speak. They all wait for me to gather myself before any of them begin to ask anymore questions.

"Did she come back to the orphanage?"

"Yes, and we stayed friends, but we had our own rooms. I fell into a depression and then the twins came. I never complained because I thought it was the perfect punishment. If Dex knew it was happening, she kept my secret with me. If she did not, well I guess that tells you how much we naturally grew apart."

"Was she there when Roarick came?"

"She hated Roarick." I smile. "Just as I did when I first met him. But then, well, you know what happened there. He helped grow the rift between Dex and I. I wish I could say I tried to stop him, but it felt good to not be reminded of my mistake every day."

"Did she try to stop you?"

"She failed. She was the one who told my aunt that Roarick was not randomly attacking me, that I was submitting to him." I shrug. "I hated her for it at the time."

"And now?"

"I destroyed her chance at lifelong happiness. I deserved to be ratted out about mine."

"Yours?" Keon challenges.

"Sorry, I meant no disrespect, Prytore Keon." I frown. "I serve you." My answer causes me to wince in pain, but I manage not to scream out from it. "After he was banished, Dex and I did not speak much. We just ran out of things to say to each other. Then she went to her first courting and came back. I felt awful. I tried to apologize but she told me it was full of haters who refused to try to understand her. The second went the same way. I never knew her thoughts of the third, for she never returned. I just know she was rejected." They do not seem to have any more questions after that. "And now you know, though it does not change anything."

"We are to be the judge of that, Serena." Keon replies. "You may go. Fakhir will call for you after we have come to a decision."

"You seriously want me to walk out of this room right now?" I ask surprised.

"You asked for a trial, Serena; we are giving you one," Keon responds.

I look to Peyton, who does not give me any clue at all as to what he is thinking, nor is Alexis or Keon. "Right. Big house. I will just disappear then," I mutter, getting up and walking away.

I dash down the hall and find myself in a simulator room. I am about to leave when Fakhir speaks up. "Would you like me to perform a play, Serena?"

"Can you pick one without a lame love story in it?"

"I am sure I can find something." Fakhir offers. It takes a moment before it dims the lights. I find a seat and watch a play about a Prytore seeking success. It is boring, but I have learned not to upset the house, plus it did at least meet my request as to avoid a love story. As I watch, I sit in the dark and cry. Truly hating myself for what I have done.

I cannot tell you if the play is over or not when Fakhir turns on the lights. It honestly takes him manifesting into a hologram and snapping his fingers in front of my face to get my attention. "What?" I ask, pulling myself away from my self-loathing.

"Prytore Keon is requesting your presence."

"Oh." I frown. "Your play."

"Please, do not insult me."

"No, Fakhir, I was not trying to. I just have a lot in my head."

"I am aware of your circumstance, Serena. Which is why I chose the worst play I could find in the library. Considering you hated one of the classics, I figured I would give you something to throw food at."

I smile at him. "I like you, Fakhir. Though you can be really annoying."

"I have the same sentiment about you." He smiles. "Now go, Prytore Keon is not known for his patience."

"Right, that." I frown heading for the door.

"Serena. I know I am merely a machine, but from my perspective, Dex was right, there is nothing to forgive."

"It should have been me, Fakhir, not her. I was the one who did it. Why must she live with that choice?" I do not give him a chance to answer. Instead, I dash back to the room where I was experiencing a weird family trial. When I arrive, Keon asks me to sit in the chair I had vacated some time before. I feel strangely nervous, honestly more worried about what they think than I realized.

"We have come to a final decision, Serena." Keon states. "One that cannot be changed." I nod nervously. "As far as we can tell you stated the facts as true to your memory as possible. These facts did not seem to hold any malicious intent. Therefore, we do not find any guilt in them." I start to shake. "We do however, find guilt in your actions to avoid Dextra after the accident. Therefore, we sentence you to reaching out, offering, and depending on her reactions, maintaining a healthy friendship."

"What?" I ask, stunned.

"As for your ability to produce perpetual fire." Keon continues. "Unless specifically instructed or in dire circumstances of need, you are hereby forbidden." Tears fill my eyes. "As for your desire to jump off high buildings with disregard to your life and limbs, unless specifically instructed or in dire circumstances of need, you are hereby forbidden."

I cry out in pain, feeling strange new cords tethering Keon and myself.

"Finally, as for your desire to bend rules to advance your own will, unless specifically instructed or in dire circumstances of need, you are hereby forbidden." I look up at him in agony. He stands up, keeping eye contact, making his form menacing. "You are mine, Serena. I plan to keep you around for a very long time. I will not have your actions cutting those plans short." He and Alexis leave the room as tears slip down my cheeks.

Peyton keeps his distance, but he does not leave. "I wish I could help you, my love, but I cannot. I did warn you, breaking is an awful experience."

"It is suffocating."

"When you fight it, it can feel that way." He agrees. "But when you accept your fate, it truly is freeing."

"You fought for five years." I point out, fruitlessly attempting to make a perpetual flame. Paying the price for it in my hand each time nothing happens.

"A luxury your past choices took away from you." Peyton sighs. "Keon has informed us of everything."

"You are angry." I note, shaking my hand in hopes to make the unpleasant pain stop.

"Disappointed. But the past is the past. All we can do is move forward now. The sooner your mind accepts your vows to this family, the sooner we can move past this."

"He did not order me to forgive myself."

"Because his, nor my bond carries that kind of power Serena. Willful submission has its limits. What you think of yourself is one of them."

Unsure what to say, I choose to change the topic. "What was it that had you three concerned before I arrived earlier?"

He pauses a moment longer before he answers. "The King has shown his concern and great delight that I was kidnapped and returned safely to my family. He has decided to throw a ball in my honor. It is an invitation that we cannot refuse."

"Your skin has changed; they are surely to notice that."

"We are not concerned with that; we have a cover story." Peyton dismisses. "It is you we are worried about."

"Me?" I ask, surprised.

"Roarick will be there." He explains. "The ball is the day after tomorrow. The likelihood of your mind being repaired by then…"

"They are trying to kill me," I reply, finishing his thought.

"The possibility exists. We know your loyalty to us is strong, but your other side has taken over right before our eyes. We do not know which will win. If you can join your mind and be with us… But if you cannot, well you already stated that conclusion."

"You are worried about me?" I frown, "I am worried about what could happen to you. Will you please stop dismissing this danger?"

"There is nothing they can do about it, Serena. It is done."

"They can kill you." I argue, moving his messy hair from his cheek.

"If you die, my love, there will not be a point in living," he replies seriously. I glare at him for a moment, causing him to look at me funny. "You like Fakhir's classical plays."

"What?" he asks, surprised. "Of course I do."

I cringe, wrinkling my nose. "They are so… love sick."

"Are you saying you do not love me?" he asks, confused.

"No, you daget."

"Daget?" he asks, laughing. "Oh, you are going to pay for that one." I squeal in delight as he reaches for me as I dash away. We both start laughing and eventually, I let him catch me. When he does, he kisses me so intently I almost forget that we need to breathe for survival. "Room?" I ask.

"Room." He agrees, picking me up and dashing me to his bedroom.

Thirty-One

Sacred Secrets

Serena

I wake to find Peyton staring at me again. "Is this going to become a habit?" I groan, rolling over. "It feels weird to wake up to eyes on me."

"You will get used to it." He smiles, kissing my shoulder and pulling me back toward him.

"What time is it?"

"Eshnaine is starting to rise."

"Ugh, it is early." I complain.

"If you say so. I have been awake for a while. Alexis wants to spend time with you, but I begged her for the day. She can have you tomorrow. We have had such little time together." I touch his face, meeting his eyes. "Keon was a little easier to persuade. He thinks that you and him may need a little time apart. He has exhausted you so much the last few days."

"No breaking today?" I ask, smiling at my husband.

"Nope, not today." He smiles back.

"Now that is something to wake up to," I reply, happily, pulling him into me. He kisses me willingly. And we get lost into each other. The world slips away as we enjoy one another, exploring, learning; so, when

I see Fakhir standing next to our bed, I let out a scream; reaching for the sheets and cowering into Peyton.

Peyton glares at the computer. "What!"

"Akatite is almost at its peak and neither of you have even had breakfast. Have you forgotten her orders? She must eat."

"Akatite?" I ask, unsure how the time slipped by so quickly. It feels like merely moments ago Peyton woke me before the crack of dawn. Peyton throws a pillow at the computer, but it simply goes through him. "Go away Fakhir, let me take care of my wife."

"I will, the moment you actually do so."

"Then go and nark to Alexis or Keon," he mutters. The computer glares before it vanishes. "I hate this house." Peyton complains to me.

"No, you do not." I giggle, bringing him into me and kissing him. Peyton moans, pulling me closer but I stop him from getting lost in me. "We should eat something. Otherwise, he is going to come back." Peyton glares at me. I kiss the top of his nose.

"Fine." He agrees reluctantly. He gets up in one swift motion and goes to the food machine. I giggle as he orders more food than the two of us could possibly eat in one setting. It takes several trips for him to bring it all back to bed with us. "No more distractions." He smiles, putting a berry into my mouth. I giggle in delight. I have never had such a pleasant experience eating food, but Peyton's creativity allowed my stomach to fill quite easily. We spend the rest of the day happily in each other's arms.

"Not that I am complaining. But do you plan on letting us be vertical today?" I ask, pulling myself closer to him after a few more hours pass.

"Not while the suns are in the skies. I do want to take you somewhere special, when Trorain rises."

"Now you have me curious." I smile.

"Nope, no hints." He smiles back at me, taking my wrist and marking me.

"I did not ask for any." I gasp, bringing him back to my lips.

"You were going to." He laughs, tangling his hand in my hair. I do not argue with him, I am too busy enjoying him. All too soon we find ourselves interrupted again, this time by an alarm.

"Now what?"

"Now, you get your surprise." Peyton smiles, jerking me from the bed and placing me on my feet. "You have twenty minutes to shower and dress. Wear something comfortable. While I do enjoy you favoriting dresses, you are going to want pants and a shirt."

"Boy clothes." I complain.

He laughs. "What is wrong with that? If you wear boy clothes, you can wear mine."

"I would look ridiculous." I giggle.

"Maybe, but I think you would find you like it." He kisses my cheek. "Twenty minutes. Go."

"Must I leave you?"

"Only for a moment," he whispers, dashing away into his bathroom.

Reluctantly, I cover myself then I leave him. When I return to my room, I quickly sift through the wardrobe and frown. I hate wearing pants and shirts, though it is culturally acceptable to do so. I just prefer dresses. I find something comfortable, yet stylish and head to the showers. Not in the mood for either of my reflections I throw a towel over the mirror. I take a quick shower. When I get out, I dry my hair while I brush my teeth. I consider putting my white hair into a bun, but decide against it. I have not worn it down since I got here. When I go to retrieve my clothes, I find they have changed. "What the?"

"I took the liberty of altering your choices." Fakhir smiles. "They are the same colors but knowing where Peyton is taking you, this is more practical. Especially the footwear."

"I thought you were just a hologram. How can you move things?" I challenge.

"My program allows me to solidify when the room is vacant." Fakhir shrugs.

"I can see why you have a love-hate relationship with my husband." I mutter, yanking the clothes from the sofa and putting them on.

"You look stunning." Fakhir smiles. "Peyton will surely agree. Speaking of…" His image blinks out without him finishing the sentence.

The door opens and Peyton walks in. He too is dressed in over comfortable clothes. He pauses when he sees me, smiling. "You look…" but he does not finish the sentence. Instead, he dashes to me and pulls me into a passionate kiss. "I missed you."

"Then let us not do that again. We are married, surely it is not necessary to have separate rooms." I complain.

"After you work through your breaking, I will be permitted to move in here," he whispers, kissing my nose. I pull away from him, creating some distance, not wanting to talk about that tonight. "Where are you going?" He smiles, tugging on my arm. "Your surprise is this way." He dashes us to the nearest exit, bringing us to the moonlight grounds. The moment we are outside he turns to me. "Close your eyes for me, my love." I do so with a smile. Squealing, when I find myself off of my feet. It takes a long while before I find the ground again, which means we must be really far from the house. "You can open them."

When I do so, it is completely dark. "Where are we?" I ask. "Somewhere private. I want to show you something, but I cannot with all the eyes on us all the time."

"Do Keon and Alexis know?"

"They know we are here. They gave me permission to bring you. With the condition that you do not know exactly where here is." He smiles, taking my hands and pulling me into him. "They do not know my true intentions though. They simply believe it is to help heal your mind."

"You are breaking the rules?" I ask, smiling a little.

"Bending." He clarifies, rubbing his hand at the base of my back. "I do hope tonight helps your mind heal, but I also want to share secrets with you, that even they do not know."

"I am forbidden to do anything like that." I frown.

"Which is why, you did not do it," he whispers. "You need not worry. This is not a loophole you thought of, so, you are not committed to tell them about it."

I nod, knowing he can see me, but only fiorriee could with such little light. "Is that why it is so dark?"

"No," he whispers in my ear, giving me goose bumps. "You asked me a question that I was reluctant to answer in the house. But I feel you should know it."

"What question is that?" I ponder, enjoying hearing his heartbeat, as he keeps me in his arms.

"You wanted to know the shape of my aura."

"I did?" I question. "I do not recall asking you that."

"I know, your reluctant side seems more outspoken than you. She does not abide by many rules, culture or otherwise."

"Rebellious," I reply bitterly.

"It was a valid question to ask," Peyton responds, "She told me the shape of your aura."

"She told you about the ravens?" I ask, curious. "You realize I have never seen my aura, right?"

"You will."

"I see."

"Do you?" he asks, seriously. "Only a select few are able to manifest their aura, and each shape is uniquely personal." He steps away from me. "Takira is a very good friend of mine, but I am very frustrated with your lack of education on the subject."

"What else do I not know?"

"Lots of things," he answers, looking at me. "I know you are aware fiorriee are submissive beings, but have you ever wondered the hierarchy before the Prytores conquered us?"

"The fiorriee submitted to their gods, who I am assuming were considered royalty?" I answer, uncertain.

"Kind of, your family is a part of the hierarchy, but you are not the only one." I stare at him puzzled.

"Marcello, Hollis, Yestin, Lapidos," he lists, "were all gods. Your aunt, Takira is a goddess." I watch him pace in the darkness. I knew of my aunt but only discovered that rather recently. I guessed about my father, seeing as we have the same blood line. The others were names I knew from my studies, but it was never mentioned they considered themselves gods. "It is common knowledge in both worlds that I, Zane, Roald, and yourself are their descendants."

"Wait, you are a god?" I ask shocked, yet oddly comforted by this.

"And Zane and Roald." He stops pacing. He turns his attention to me, studying my reaction to this.

Admittedly, it takes me a moment to accept. "Why would my aunt not tell me this?"

"Because our powers are useless on Artthemis. It means nothing here." He answers, sourly.

I frown, remembering my aunt dismissing it quite similarly the first time I was told I was a goddess.

"As you may or may not be aware, only Takira, Zane, Roald, you and myself have survived this war."

"Peyton," I gasp. "Roald and Zane are still hybrids."

"Yes." He answers painfully. "My mother was the first to bear one." He pauses, working to keep his voice steady. "It was not me. I came much later. Most of my siblings died from the Prytore DNA they injected our embryos with." Tears stream down my face. "Had they been able to find your parents, you yourself would be a hybrid. Zane's and Roald's parents were just as unfortunate as mine."

"I am sorry." I whisper. He shakes it off. "Does the Prytore DNA limit you as a god?"

"Yes, it is like I was caged." He frowns. "Things eluded me, even on Trorain. Now I do not know what has been freed and what will be forever out of my reach."

"But even with all the interference, we are all still chosen to embrace our auras in their purest form?" I ask, trying to keep up with him.

"There is more to it." He frowns at me. "While we are living beings, each of us can affect Trorain differently. As for me, before this change, I could command Trorain soil, but it took much concentration. Zane and Roald have exhibited similar struggles."

My mind clicks in understanding. Everyone who has ever studied the history of the war knows it all started when the Prytores captured Hollis. They said he was connected to the minerals they were mining, but no one could ever explain how, no matter how many experiments they tried.

"Hollis is your father?"

"Yes."

"The elixir has kept you alive this long?" I ask, astonished.

"Do not base your understanding on Prytore history books, Serena. They do not have all their facts right. They do not understand gods, much less our aging process."

"Oh." Is all I can think to say.

"Our aging is a very closely kept secret that only Keon and Alexis know."

"Keon and Alexis? What about Zane's and Roald's Prytores?" I doubt. "That is kind of hard to hide."

"Keon and Alexis lived on Trorain. They gained knowledge they otherwise would not have, but they understand the secrecy of it and have vowed to never speak of it. As for Zane and Roald's Prytores, they believe they did it to their fiorriee, but they did not."

"How does it work?" I ask, curious.

"By walking the path of enlightenment." He answers. "When we did, we each froze our bodies in time. Just as it did for all the ancestors." He looks slightly nervous. "I told Alexis and Keon it did not work, but it did."

"You lied? Why?" I ask surprised. I would have never thought he would have kept anything from them. "How?"

"I had help with the how." He admits. "As for the why, I had to. The shape of my aura is too sacred. Just as yours is."

"Mine?"

"You are a raven, Serena, the most valued shape, next to mine."

"And that makes you…?"

"The indigo panther." His words do not register the meaning he is hoping they do. He walks up to me and stares into my eyes, adding, "You are the goddess of goddesses, Serena, and I am the god of gods."

"So, in death, you are meant to embrace your aura as well? We will watch over Trorain together?"

"That is part of our fate, yes. But not the only part. In life, we are the top of the hierarchy for all fiorriee, including purebloods, hybrids, and gods. And not just those who are alive today, but for all generations in both the past and those yet to come."

"Peyton?" I question in astonishment. "No, I cannot, this is too much." It is hard enough being told I am a queen, the one all fiorriee look to for direction. Then having my aunt inform me that I am a goddess who will embrace my aura completely upon death to watch over Trorain. Now in this dark place, he is telling me we are the top of the hierarchy for all fiorriee in both living and in death… it is overwhelming.

"Do not worry, my beautiful goddess. We are going to fix your mind, and you will see this as the blessing that it is. I promise." He pulls me close, tangling his fingers in my hair, placing his breath in my ear. "You are forbidden from revealing my identity to anyone Serena, even Keon and Alexis."

"Why? They know mine."

"They should not." he replies, displeased. "But I understand you are learning more about yourself than you ever knew. Your aunt has done you a grave disservice by keeping you in the dark about auras and how precious they are. It is a disgrace to you and our kind."

"I have only told Keon and Alexis."

"In the house, Serena. The house that the Prytore King has access to. If they do not report it to him, if they try to hide it. All of us would lose our heads."

"I am sorry," I whisper in shame.

"You did not know. Just promise me you will be more careful. Now that you do."

"You should not have shared this with me Peyton. I will not be able to keep it from them."

"I have thought of that," he whispers, playing with the edges of my hair, sending pleasant sensations from my collar. "You must keep this between us, unless you are standing right here. Even then, only you can share it with our Prytores face to face."

I gasp out loud, feeling a cord binding between us. When I catch my breath, I look around and then back at him. "I do not know where we are."

"Exactly," he replies, squeezing me tighter.

"So, unless I am standing right here, I can hide this knowledge from both of them?"

"Yes."

"Will it hurt? Will they know?"

"If they do, they do not let on." He shrugs. "This exact thing happened to me when I was on Trorain. I do not receive any displeasure when I find myself needing to lie."

"Who were your exceptions?" I ask, curious. "My father and my truest love."

"But I am not your first wife."

"True, but you are my truest love." He pulls back, touching my face. I so enjoy the feeling my collar gives me when he does this. "Promise me, you will be more careful."

"I promise," I whisper, finding his lips on mine almost instantly. I fall into the kiss and protest when he pulls away from me. He smiles at me. I look at him curiously when I realize he is nervous. I blink my eyes for several moments, unable to process what I am seeing. Peyton is no longer a fiorriee, he is a deep indigo panther. Unsure what to do, I stand there frozen. Cautiously, he steps forward. I swallow nervously, until he takes another step then licks my hand. I giggle, bending down to meet his silver eyes. He rubs his face under my hand. I laugh, scratching behind his ears. He curls the tip of his tail and licks me on the face, causing me to crinkle my nose. He gruffs a little, which sounds like laughing. Then he lays at my feet and reveals his stomach. I smile wider at him while I scratch his belly, causing him to purr loudly. I feel content while my hands lazily run through his fur, even more so with the soft rhythm of his purr. After a long while, my hands are no longer in his fur, but his hair.

"I could fall asleep with you doing that." He smiles up at me. "But we must go back soon. We do not want Alexis and Keon to worry."

"Can we not stay, just a little longer?"

"Just a little." He agrees, sitting up. "I am sure you have questions."

"How can you go back and forth? Does it hurt? Where do your clothes go? Is it magic?"

"It is easier to transform on Trorain. It is not magic. I believe Alexis is right, there is no such thing. As everything I once thought was, she has studied and proven a scientific link. However, this is spiritual. I cannot explain the how, it is just a part of me. It does hurt at first but the more you do it, the less you notice it. As far as the clothes." He smiles. "They do not go anywhere. The best way to explain it is your physical form falls into the shape of your aura and your aura covers your familiar physical form, with its true shape, like armor. You are still you."

"Strange."

"Metamorphosis has a price." He warns. "It takes a lot of energy, you must eat." He touches my hair. "If you do not, you will not maintain the shape for long." He takes my hands in his and places them in my lap. "Revealing yourself to our kind has consequences. They will flood you with all their problems, thinking you can fix them. But that is not what we do."

"What do we do?"

"We protect, everything. You protect the wind. I protect the land. Zane protects fire, and Roald protects our water."

"Just the four elements?"

He laughs, "Are they not enough?"

"I do not know. What about the gates of the afterlife, health, mischief, love?"

He shrugs. "Fairytales and myths, my beautiful wife." He smiles, taking my hand and studying it. "I am curious as to how you control a perpetual flame, seeing as you are not the fire god."

"Is that unusual?"

"Yes." He answers. "The moment we get to Trorain, I will guide you in your path of enlightenment, that way you will be able to metamorphose into a raven."

"So, I cannot change without taking that journey?"

"It is doubtful. I have only known that to happen to the very young, but even then, the gift can be lost if one chooses not to walk the path."

He kisses my hand. "Do you have any more questions?" I nod, slightly nervous to ask. "You said Keon and Alexis lived on Trorain. Is that when you and Alexis… found each other?"

He looks away from me, lost in thought. "That is difficult to put into words, Serena." I wait him out, gently stroking his hand with my fingers. "I do not have many surviving memories of Trorain due to the war. But I do remember this story." I nod in anticipation. "A strange couple came to our village. The fiorriee female was curled in on herself, accompanied by a male Prytore who claimed to be her husband." He frowns. "I will not go into detail of it. It is more of Takira's story to tell you, if ever she chooses." I bring my eyebrows together, but I do not press him. "After the drama of it, it became clear that marriage between the species was inevitable. The question was how."

"Wait. Are you saying you set the example?" I ask, unable to control my surprise.

"Happily." He smiles. "I had fallen for Alexis long before then, but I had no idea how to broach the topic with the other gods. Not to mention, I respected Keon greatly." He shakes his head. "I was so young and so brazen, one day I flat out asked Keon to share her."

"You did not." I whisper in disbelief.

He blushes a dark blue while looking down at his hands. "It was not an uncommon request for fiorriee. But Prytores, well, let us just say they do not like to share." He looks at me. "Am I upsetting you?"

"No, I know how you two feel for each other."

"Keon and I both felt that if marriage between the species was going to happen, it had to be respectful. Which is why we came up with the now culturally accepted idea of marrying our own kind and the blood vow to connect us."

"Did you create the part-time service?"

"No, that was a tweak the King Maleko made because his subjects had a hard time accepting the idea of sharing."

"But you and Keon are responsible for the caste system?"

"Now that is insulting." He frowns. "All King Maleko's doing, I assure you."

"Sorry."

"It is all right. You only know the mockery of the original idea." He shrugs. "It is why our wedding took so long. I insisted we do it the way it was intended, but the Prytores would not budge on the law. With persuasion, they agreed to do it both ways."

"Oh, that is the reason for all the boredom." I smile. He shakes his head apologetically.

"Am I understanding that you committed to our Prytores before the war?"

"The war was not a continuous battle, and for a long while, we fiorriee were winning. It was during this time I committed to them."

"How did they feel about you being a warrior?"

"They supported me to a point." He frowns. "They knew my mother died from all the Prytore experiments, but when my father was killed…" he stops, looking away from me. "I killed many in my wrath. So many it almost killed me. Even after getting unprecedented and unspeakable help, I am still haunted." He looks at me. "I do not ever want you to be haunted like this, Serena. I will give my life to protect you from that." He breaks eye contact. "After that, there was peace, or so we thought. The mining had stopped. Most Prytores had left. All their transporters were destroyed. It was over, with a fiorriee victory."

I knew what he was talking about; even the Prytore history books had this right. But it was all an illusion.

"I met you when you were born, even watched you the first three years of your life. There was this pull between us, even then. But there was also the blood oath between the four families, which made me unsure of what I was feeling. Not long after, everything fell apart."

He pauses so long, his expression so hard, that I must whisper his name to bring him back from the past.

"I will never forget that night. I fought against the attackers. I regret I was not successful. Your parents were taken. I was torn. I wanted to protect them, but there were others who needed to be saved. You were taken to Artthemis for your safety. We stayed as long as we dared but my aura was out of sorts. I tried to figure out what had changed. I even accessed the path and was told I had to find you." He is silent again before he continues. "When we came to Artthemis, I begged Alexis to let me find you. It was not easy. Despite the blood vow, she did not understand, and I could not explain it. All she knew is I never asked them for anything, except this. She did not agree at first, I was married to Karissa after all. But when Karissa died, about two years after we too were forced to come to here, Alexis was out of reasons to say no. I think she hoped I would change my mind over time. After all, we knew not where you were or how your aunt was hiding you. Only that you had purple eyes and would be attending a yellow courting around your twenty-third year of life. Which left us no choice but to wait. Even then, yours was not the only yellow ceremony on Artthemis. Plus, there was a chance that Takira would fake your age."

"My aunt reached out; she told you of my arrival."

"She did. We were not expecting her to take such a dangerous risk, which is why we had looked for you sooner. Her message brought us to your courting, but it did not answer questions we had. Where were you hiding? Was this pull between us because of the blood vow or something more? Would you feel it too?" He shakes his head. "I remembered your eyes."

"Bethany has the same color of eyes as I do."

"Yes, she does." He confirms. "But she does not have the same heart."

"When I offered my hand, you would not let go."

"I did not let go because the moment I touched you, it sent a shock through my aura. I knew you were the one I have been searching for, the one I was destined to find and not because of a blood oath. It was so much deeper than that."

I blush, kissing his hand, "You did not feel this way about Karissa?"

"No, Keon loved Karissa, and she loved him. She and I were true friends, but we never loved each other."

"So, no children?"

"I am a man, Serena. She was my wife."

"Oh."

"Those that made it to term, did not live. It was not her fault. The war took so much from her."

"I am sorry." I whisper in the silence. Wanting a lighter topic I ask, "You mentioned earlier the Prytores believed your stillness of aging was their doing?"

"Keon and Alexis had invented that disgusting antiaging elixir before they came to Trorain."

"Which you drank." I reply. He looks at me, curious. "Keon." Peyton nods. "Between what the two of you told me, King Maleko approved it to demonstrate our gods are conquered and there was no hope in an uprising."

"Exactly."

"Maleko was not anticipating me to be a pure blood, was he?"

"He was not anticipating you at all. There were rumors, but your survival could never be confirmed. Many went to great lengths to make him believe you died on Trorain as a child. But now that you are here, he does not seem to feel threatened, even you submit to powerful Prytores and a tamed hybrid."

I look away from him. "I thought about that, after my aunt explained that I was the Queen of our kind. It is such a heavy burden, Peyton. I was not sure what to do. I was not sure if I should go through with the courting. I am still not sure I set the best example for our kind. But I could not, not love you. Peyton, marrying you was the most selfish thing I have ever done."

"You need not feel ashamed." He assures me, kissing my hand. "You did not exactly follow any of the Prytore traditions. Serena, we broke so many of their stupid rules." He smirks, holding in a laugh. "We had them all twisted upside down. Keon called every shot, and no one dared challenge him, though he was cautious to make sure no one would." Peyton's smile fades a little when he realizes, this does not ease my worry. "Serena, we married for love, which is the best example we could ever give our kind."

"Yet, they will see us as conquered."

"Some will, but only those who do not truly understand. We chose willful submission; we are far from conquered. We are strong, Serena, the strongest of our kind."

"Promise?"

"Once you are broken, you will understand why I do not even hesitate with that promise." He smiles.

"Zane and Roald do they willfully submit?"

"Their situations are rather complex." I raise an eyebrow. "I would share them, Serena, but our time is short, so short I fear we should start our return."

"I know, but I do not want this to end." I protest. "Peyton, I have been under so much pressure with so many things coming at me. Spending time with you without all the stress. Please," I plead, "can we stay just a little longer?"

"You are hard to deny, my love." He answers, kissing my wrist and filling my mouth with his taste. "We can stay, but only for a few more questions."

"Keon said Zane and Roald took the aging elixir too, but you said they do not age because of walking the path of enlightenment. I am curious, does the elixir even work on normal fiorriee? Had Karissa taken it, would it have worked on her?"

"Yes, I believe it would have." His face looks tormented. "Our anatomy is not all that different. But when she was brought to Artthemis something in her had changed on a fundamental level. The elixir was not something she nor Keon wanted for her." His face looks tormented, and he falls silent.

"Are you all right?"

"Not really. The war went on for nearly a hundred years, Serena. It did so because we were able to withstand almost everything the Prytores threw at us, though we lost a lot doing it."

"But then they poisoned the air."

"That was an obstacle, but it was not the reason for the defeat. We were betrayed. That is why we ultimately lost."

"You believe it is over then?"

"I believe only we can stop their damage. Then it is up to us to rebuild."

"Their damage to Trorain or to our kind?"

"It is late, Serena." Peyton deflects.

"Do you regret submitting to our Prytore's?"

"No, but I do not fully trust them. Nor should you. With the way things stand, if any Prytore knew my true self I would be dead."

"Surely that is not the case with those we serve."

"We shall see. They seem to be reacting to you all right. But if they feel threatened, if they act to harm you, they will discover the truth, but they will not live to tell it."

"If they accept it, will we stay in their service?"

"I do hope so. It all depends. Let us not get ahead of ourselves, we must fix your mind or none of this even matters."

"Why did you share all of this with me before I was fully broken?" I ask. "What if Roarick is too strong?"

"He will not be."

"Peyton."

"You must make this decision on your own. Keon and Alexis or Roarick? It is not a matter of their strength, Serena; it is a matter of your will. Deep down on an unconscious level, who do you want to serve? I will say, I have a hard enough time sharing you with Keon and Alexis, whom I love. It would be very difficult to do so with someone I do not."

"Wait, you have a hard time sharing me with Keon and Alexis?"

"You do not?"

"Keon has asked me this. I will tell you what I have told him. I accepted us the way we are now, I do not want that to change."

"Perhaps we will not." he muses, "Still one day, you may understand my restlessness." He picks me up. "Close your eyes my love." I do so obediently but more questions are burning in my head. Questions that will have to wait, because Fakhir is not something to fully trust. I am not happy with this information, but I like being aware of it. When we arrive back to the house, we are greeted by two very displeased Prytores. "Please forgive our tardiness." I speak, before Peyton can. "I had a lot of questions." Keon raises his eyebrow, so I add. "Peyton's trying to help me heal my mind."

"Did he enter it?" Keon asks me pointedly.

"No. He simply explained his loyalty to this family and how happy he is." I answer, keeping most our conversation as private as it was meant to be.

"Does this knowledge help you?" Alexis asks.

"Every reason to grow our family bond helps me." I smile. "So does the knowledge, that just for a little while, my every move is not being watched." I glare at the camera.

"A luxury, you will not be granted often." Keon replies in warning. "Fakhir is loyal to me. Hating the computer keeping a watchful eye, is an extension of hating me."

"I meant no disrespect Prytore."

Keon takes my wrist. "I am going to mark you, Serena, as a reminder of your place in this family." Keon brings my wrist to his lips. I hiss in unpleasant pain. Keon lets it linger for longer than I expect. "Your husband may need to give his permission, but I still must be the one who allows him to grant it." I cry out in agony; my body is on fire. "Do not mistake our willingness for your rare privacy as a way to ever omit us. I own both you and Peyton, Serena. There are no secrets here." He looks at Peyton. "Only grant your permission if you respect yours and her place in our family."

"I do, Prytore." Peyton assures him. Keon offers my wrist to Peyton, and soon after, the pain is but a memory.

"It is late, Zarla is almost at its peak. We all should retire. I have plans for Serena tomorrow." Alexis states, taking her husband's hand to keep him from saying any more.

Peyton picks me up and takes me to my room. "Will you stay?"

"Of course, but I may be gone when you wake," he whispers, kissing me softly. I kick the door closed, dragging him to my bed. Forgetting all about the need for sleep.

Thirty-Two
Scientific Explanation

Serena

When I wake the next day, Peyton tells me that he has things he must do. He kisses me good morning and assures me he would see me later that day. Not really wanting to be alone, I find myself reluctant to get out of bed. When I finally do, I take a very long shower. Eventually, Fakhir warns me the water is about to get ice cold, so I turn it off; grabbing two towels without much thought to it. One I dry off myself with, the other I wrap my hair in. Needing to brush my teeth, I wrap my towel around me and find myself staring at a double reflection. "Nothing has changed I see." I speak aloud, feeling disappointed, I really thought my talk with Peyton would help. But there is no towel in either reflection, one still wears a yellow dress, the other black. The black dress one looks too smug. "Neither of you are going to let me do my hair, are you?" I sigh, shaking my head. "So annoying." I complain, putting a toothbrush in my mouth.

"Who are you talking to?" Alexis asks, causing me to nearly jump out of my skin. "Sorry, I did not mean to startle you. I thought you knew I would be coming. Peyton is gone, is he not?"

I rinse my mouth out with water, taking the towel off my hair. "Yes, I knew you were coming. Sorry, I was a little distracted. Peyton is gone but I have no idea where he went." I blush blue, running my fingers through my hair, "If he told me, I was not paying much attention."

She smiles. "I am glad to see you two are enjoying yourselves." I do not reply to that, unsure what to say. "Do your reflections talk back?"

"Not with words," I answer. "But I find it satisfying to tell them off anyway."

"One must be showing you your true self by now, surely."

"One was, except for my clothes, but she is not now. Talking about Dex is not easy."

"Well, I guess you are going to need help with your hair and things, as you have a ball to attend." Alexis smiles, trying to hide her worry.

"Surely you are not here this early for that."

"No, dear, of course not." She dismisses. "I came for two other reasons. One is to drop off our family stationary so you can reach out to Dextra." I frown. "The other is because I would really love the chance to study your ability to make perpetual fire." Her eyes light up with the idea of it.

"Well, that is going to be complicated. Not only is it dangerous, it is forbidden." I try to make the ball of fire but get unpleasant pain for my effort.

"Both I have a solution for." She smiles. "We will be working in a secure lab, and I have privileges to let you use your ability. Or have you forgotten your submission to Keon extends to me?"

"It does?" I ask, walking away and grabbing a simple black dress from the closet. "My aunt never told me anything like that."

"Not all Prytore wives have the privilege. I would have thought you realized that I have honors when we all participated in the blood oath; or at least with the knowledge that Peyton submits to me."

"I knew I was vowing to be yours just as much as Keon's, I just did not realize you and I did not have to go through a breaking is all." I answer, slipping into the dress easily and working the zipper.

"It is not necessary for you and Peyton to either, but Keon has given him the honor of allowing you two to create something unique to your marriage. You may have surrendered your full mind, body and soul to Peyton, but he can no longer access it without Keon's permission.

Which Keon will not grant until you surrender it all to us as well. So, the sooner you submit, the sooner your marriage will be more fulfilling."

"So, this is you trying a new angle at the whole mind submission thing." I accuse, putting my hair into a sloppy bun.

"Keon needs some space. He can be very passionate and that can lead to frustration. I think it is best if he gives you time to forgive yourself without the pressure of him breathing down your neck." She answers, walking toward the door, expecting me to follow. "Plus, I really am fascinated with your fireball ability." She stops at the door, orders a simple on the go meal and hands it to me. "You need to eat breakfast now. Remember?"

"Just because my body works properly does not mean I like to eat three meals a day." I mumble, begrudgingly taking the muffin and juice. "Yet you cannot stop your body from complying." She smiles. "It is for your own good, Serena. Though you are the first fiorriee I have come across in my day that needs to be reminded to eat."

"What can I say? I am high maintenance." I shrug, following her down the halls to her labs.

"You can say that again." She agrees, walking down several hallways before opening the doors to her favorite rooms in the house. "You realize Trorain does not have a lot of salt on it? Not many other elements can effectively put out perpetual fire. Water feeds it, sand slows it down, and then of course there is sulfur. It too is effective, but Artthemis does not have a lot of it either."

"Trorain does."

"Yep." She smiles. "I do enjoy studying the two worlds, they complement each other more than they contrast but when they do contrast…it is fascinating."

"So, what are you trying to study about this anyway? You seem to know a lot about perpetual flame."

"I only know what I have been told. Which is not a lot. This is a very sacred flame amongst your kind. It is also very feared and not studied. They chalk it up to magic."

"You want to study my body making the flame, in addition to the flame itself." I realize.

"Indeed, I do."

"Are your files secure? Knowledge of something like this can be deadly."

"I assure you, Serena, I would self-destruct before I gave away secrets that could destroy my family's efforts to save Trorain." Fakhir pipes up.

"Yep, still not used to living in a talking house," I mutter, causing Alexis to stiff a small laugh. "Thank you, Fakhir. Your sentiment is noted." Though his reassurance was not successful at comforting me. Not after Peyton has explained his distrust.

"All right. I simply need you to stand here," she says, placing me in the center of the room, "and make your fireballs at will. But do not throw them."

"Throw them? Why would I do that?" I ask. She raises an eyebrow at me. "Oh right, I am not myself."

"Can you transfer them to a candle or something similar?" She questions, putting on some goggles.

"I can ignite fabric." I answer. "But I cannot say I tried to light something as small as a candle and keep it burning."

"Well, you will today." She smiles cheerfully. "Great." I respond, a lot less excited than her.

Her tests are exhausting. I never realized how much energy it took to make a fireball. But then again, I have never really made one, put it out, and made another over and over again like I did today. Eating helped but not a lot. By the time it is all over I am almost grateful I cannot do that without their knowledge. Almost. Because I do not want to do it for a long while. I did learn that I can in fact light a candle and it seems, it does not cause the wax to melt. Curious as that is.

"All right, Serena, it is time we start to get ready for this ball." Alexis informs me, looking disappointed that she is having to step away from her research. She heads for the door, and I know she expects me to follow, but she did not instruct me too. I cannot take my eyes off the candle I had lit earlier. "Serena?"

"We have to put the candle out first." I remind her.

"Why would we do that? It is perfectly safe. Besides, I really want to see if it melts the wax while we are away."

"And if it does, it will melt the counter, then your research then, Fakhir will burn to the ground."

"Fakhir will put it out long before any of that happens. Serena."

"Alexis, please." I beg, tears spilling out of my eyes.

"Serena, it really is safe."

"You do not understand the danger," I argue, shaking head to toe. "If something were to happen, if Fakhir malfunctioned, everything will be lost." I worry, my voice growing an unnatural octave higher. "Do you really want to risk that over a stupid candle?" I am shaking so badly; I can barely stand.

"All right Serena, if it bothers you that much." She frowns, walking over to the candle and extinguishing it with salt.

"Thank you." I smile, wiping the tears from my cheeks.

"I appreciate your sense of caution with this very dangerous gift of yours, though in this case it was unwarranted," she replies, leaving the room. This time I follow her. "Would you like me to do your hair tonight or would you prefer Keon to?"

"May Peyton do it?"

"I am sorry, Serena, but he is not available right now."

"Oh." I frown. "It is all right, I do not need help with my hair. I am sure you need Keon for yours."

"My reflection actually reflects my image." She reminds me. "Keon may like the little length I keep in my hair for him, but he is dreadful at styling it."

"I am used to my reflection being uncooperative. I am fine, honest." I smile, avoiding her eyes.

"You remind me of your father." She states, catching me off guard. "You are open and polite with duty but getting to know you personally." She shakes her head. "I am struggling a little. Is there a reason you are keeping your distance with me and not Keon?"

"We have not had a lot of time together, except for duty." I answer with a shrug. But I can tell by her face that is not going to satisfy her. "Alright, it is true. I am keeping you at a distance."

"Because of my relationship with Peyton?"

"Because of your relationship with the Queen of Artthemis." I correct her. She stands up proudly with a raised chin on that one. "I must say, making that connection after my courting has bothered me."

"Would it have changed your choice?" Alexis asks, crossing her arms over her chest.

"I am not sure." I admit. "I did place Zane in the friendship category because of his relation with the King, though from what I have observed, it is a rather intimate connection." I shake my head, trying not to betray any jealousy. "With you… I am missing facts. I know that. It is hard to make a judgement call when you are always in the dark. But it is bothering me."

"That is fair." She states, "does it help you to know that when Maleko was a Prince, he murdered my parents and brother right in front of my sister and I?"

"What?" I ask, taking a step back.

"Adriana did not marry Maleko out of love. It was political and she had the misfortune of being born first." I stare at her in horror. "I am only alive because Prytore twins need each other. If one dies, so does the other."

"Your last name gives him power."

"We were princesses in our own right, before the civil war." Alexis answers. "I never lost that title, though the meaning is drastically different. And my sister, well she is not who she used to be. He changed her into something I honestly do not recognize."

"I am sorry." I frown, surprised as to where this conversation led.

"It was a long time ago, Serena. Since then, Keon and I have broken ties with my family name as much as possible. We were not trying to deceive you at your courting. As you have come to learn our political views do not exactly align with the King's."

"Thank you for telling me this." I smile at her. "It helps settle my mind."

"Does this change your mind about your hair?" She asks, looking hopeful.

"Honestly, Alexis. I just need a few moments to myself."

"All right. You will find a white Silviu dress, similar to the ones I gave you at court in your closet. You will be wearing that this evening. Peyton will be escorting you, that I can promise. However, you must write your letter to Dextra if you plan on attending tonight."

I give a half smile. Both sides of my divided mind would have the goal of going to this ball. The yellow side would want to show off how Roarick did not affect me, the other would want to see Roarick and try to attach herself to him. Both are trapped here until they write a letter that will obviously be screened. And both are aware that Fakhir had narked me out on the cryptic codes. "It is going to be an exhilarating challenge living here. I will find a way to prove you have not thought of everything. Sooner or later."

Alexis laughs. "Good luck with that. Keon and I have seen a lot over a lot of years. But I do like a challenge." She leads me to the door of my bedroom. "Eat something, I drained you."

I groan at that, while walking into my room, reluctantly ordering a very small portion of energy food, just to appease her. She leaves me to eat and write. When I am sure I am as alone as I am going to get, I walk over to the mirrors and glare at my reflections. "One of you has to be wanting to cooperate by now." Neither even bother to look at me. "All right, down and natural it is." I mutter walking away, but the black dress girl does not leave. Curious, I go back to the mirror. Her hair had changed into a partially braided twist, it was really rather cute.

She smiles at me. Then she shakes her head and shows me what my hair looks like now. "All right, I can do that." I agree, happy to have some cooperation. It takes me a few tries to get it right. She proves to be good at showing her frustration when it is wrong. But after about an hour, I manage to get it perfect. My arms are numb by the time I am done with styling it though. When I am finished, I quickly eat then go to my closet and put on my dress to write. I figured it was too early, but I can always rush a letter and there is no harm sitting in a dress to write.

"Fakhir, does my library contain the history of the fiorriee royalty?"

"You mean a copy of the book you used to secretly communicate with Dex?"

"That would be the one."

"It does. I am happy to tell you where to find it, but there are no secrets in this house, Serena."

"I am all too aware of that." I mutter. "But she is not."

Fakhir directs me to the book that I want. I take it back to my room, cutting through my garden both times. Eventually, I have no other way to stall from writing this stupid letter, so I decide to make it short.

> *My dearest Dextra,*
>
> *I hope this finds you well. My courting ceremony was a whirlwind of surprises. I actually offered my hand to a fiorriee! It just happened! His name is Peyton. He is so loving. Of all the families that came, I vowed myself to the Silviu. They are really nice. I hope one day you can meet them, if you would want to. I understand if you do not. I hope to hear from you.*
>
> *Yours always,*
> *Serena*

"What kind of code is that?" Fakhir asks over my shoulder, startling me. "Sorry, I manifested in the garden." He explains, studying the letter. "I do not see the logic in your pattern."

"If it were logical, then it would be easy to break," I reply dryly. "She will know."

"You do not even give her a page number to start."

"She will know."

"What does it say?"

"Will you leave me alone if I tell you?"

"Yes."

"Then I am not going to tell you." I smile. "I like your company."

"Cute. But I can be really annoying, Serena."

"You do not say." I laugh, tucking the letter into a fancy envelope.

"Please?" He asks.

"Well, since you asked so nicely." I smile, pulling the letter out. "It says: 'I miss you. I love you. FF'."

"FF?"

"Friends forever."

Fakhir takes the letter and studies it for a long moment. "I still find your pattern to be senseless."

"Too much for your computer brain to handle?"

"I have committed it to my memory banks. I will solve the puzzle eventually."

I giggle. "You do that."

"Why do you not want me to leave you alone?"

"I grew up in a house full of fiorriee and Prytores alike. It is weird, when I was there all I wanted was to be alone but since I got here, it is too quiet and way too empty."

"And since you cannot occupy your time by jumping off of the roof, you are bored."

"Extremely." I answer truthfully.

"Maybe you should get your mind together so I can open up simulations that allow you to rock climb, skydive, and bungee jump."

"Oh, I get it, you are cheerleading for them too." I laugh, with a glare.

"Why are you resisting them, Serena?"

"I believe you have eavesdropped on every bit of my breaking, Fakhir, you know why."

"I know Prytore Keon is a very caring man, and you could not do better, even if Roarick had never abandoned you."

"You are biased, he created you."

"Perhaps." The computer ponders. "But if you really did not favor Prytore Keon, why give him your body and soul? You cannot tell me Roarick did not try."

"What makes you think he tried?" I ask, guarded.

"He tried to force your body. Would he have not attempted you to submit it freely first?" I glare at him. "So that leads me to wonder, why were you resisting him? Do you remember?"

"Dex did not like him," I reply.

"Why is that?"

"I do not recall." I shrug. "Can we talk about something else?"

"I am a computer, and you are resisting me?" he asks. "Maybe Prytore Keon should not be taking it so personal, after all." He pauses for a moment. "Speaking of…" With that, he vanishes.

Prytore Keon walks into my room. "Ah, Serena, you are ready." He smiles approvingly. "May I see the letter you wrote to Dex?" I hand it to him, he reads it several times. "Is there a code I cannot make out?"

"There is. Fakhir is trying to decipher the illogical web as we speak." I smile, causing Keon to laugh. "It says: 'I miss you; I love you, FF'. Which means friends forever."

"I will send this the moment Fakhir finishes his calculations to make sure that is all it says." Keon smiles, putting it in his pocket. "I came here to help you with your hair. Alexis said you were going to have a hard time." He looks disappointed, as he studies me.

"One of my reflections decided to cooperate."

"Which one?" he questions, curiously.

"The black dress." I answer. "I do not see the harm in accepting her help, it is just hair."

"The yellow dress?"

"She is sulking." I frown. "I cannot get her to even register when I am looking at her."

Keon touches my collar, causing silver flowers to crop up throughout my hairstyle. He then tugs out a few strands next to my face. "I think we should curl these." He muses, taking me into the bathroom. While the iron heats up, he touches my face and meets my eyes to bring us into the familiar ballroom.

"I am not sure you should come tonight."

"Do you fear I will embarrass you somehow?" I ask, dancing with him.

"No, but I am unsure what will happen with Roarick and myself in the same room." He answers, twirling me around the floor then pulling me back into him.

"Maybe that is what I need? Maybe facing the both of you will force me into one mindset?"

"Possibly, but if your resistance is stronger, it will win. Then your body, soul and mind will not be in sync and that cannot be sustained for long. Especially with the pull of two Prytores. He is just a memory right now, Serena, giving him present form is extremely dangerous."

"You worry too much."

"I need you to forgive yourself," he replies sternly, "it is the only way you are going to make it out alive."

"Why do we always dance when you talk to my soul?" I deflect.

"Because it is the only happy memory, we have had time to make."

"That is not true. What about my aunt's kitchen?"

"You honestly want to throw food at each other every time we talk?"

"Well, not every time, but tonight would be nice."

"Serena, I am serious."

"So am I. We are at a standstill. Which is getting more and more unstable. I cannot even get one of my reflections to cooperate more than a short while. Even tonight when I did my hair, she was arguing with me. If this keeps up, I am going to fall sick. I can feel it now. I get drained so easily. So doing nothing is not going to work. This option, confronting this head on, is dangerous, I agree. It has one of two outcomes; it will either save my life or speed up my death. But at least it is not waiting for death, like it is right now."

"I hate that you are right." He frowns, pulling me closer into him. "Peyton is not the only one who would hurt if we lost you."

He blinks, and we are back in my bathroom. He takes the hot iron and curls my hair quickly. When he is finished, he starts to turn his head, but I stop him with my hand. His eyes meet mine, full of questions. I hesitate for a moment but then I lean into him and pull his head into me. Our lips touch gently, but he pulls away quickly. "Did I offend you Prytore?"

"No." he answers, gliding his fingers down the design on my right cheek bone, causing a pleasant sensation down to my toes. "It pleases me, and I do not fear for your health."

"Then why did you stop me?"

"Because neither of us are ready for something like this, Serena. You are of two minds. One that is not loyal to me. And I will not accept growth like this until you surrender completely."

"That explains half of it," I reply, searching his eyes.

"We have been through this once, how soon you forget. I want to love you, but I will not give my heart to someone who cannot love themselves properly. For now, I am your guardian, Serena. In the future, there may be potential for more."

"I did not forget," I reply. "Your answer has changed." He raises an eyebrow at me. "You were not sure if you could love me before because of trust, now you want to; which means we have a new but stable foundation of trust between us. I am growing on you, Keon."

"Were you testing me?" he asks, removing my hand from his neck and tangling his fingers in mine.

"No, I genuinely felt the desire to kiss you. You may have a hard time accepting my feelings, and who can blame you with all this chaos. But the part of me that has committed to you, that part loves you Keon." I squeeze his hand. "Every time I have expressed it, you have rejected me."

"If I rejected you, Serena, I would not have control of your soul," he whispers, giving himself away. My eyes meet his. "We are not ready. Not yet. But I am not saying we will not be. There is a difference between not now and no. And my answer is simply, not yet."

"Then kiss me. Please, Keon, I would not ask if I did not…"

He cuts me off with the gentlest kiss on my lips. I pull back a little, studying his eyes, pleading with mine. His restraint breaks and he crashes his lips into mine, tracing my lips with his tongue. His skill makes me dizzy. When he breaks it, he studies me for a long moment. "I hope that gave you whatever it is you are looking for, Serena." I nod. "Good, do not ask for that again. I will decide when we are ready." He steps away from me. "We should go. Peyton and Alexis are waiting."

"Wait." I call to him, he turns to me, conflicted. "I need you to fight."

"Fight?"

"I cannot explain it. I just understand what I need," I reply. "Please, Keon, if you and Roarick are going to be in the same room, I need you to fight."

"I *have* been fighting, Serena."

"No, you have been asking me to choose." I argue. "Over and over again you ask. Over and over again, I choose you. Can you not see? I have made my choice, Keon. I am here. I will never ask to leave. Granted, sometimes I want to hide in shame. But you have never even fought. You just keep giving me option after option, telling me you are my protector and nothing more. I am so confused. I do not know what you want."

"You do not know what I want?" He repeats, astonished. "Are you joking? Do you think you would be here after I discovered your split loyalty if I did not want you here!"

"You have all these cords of control tethered between us, yet you have never pulled the ones you need to fix this."

"Because I refuse to control you! Your submission is a gift! One I will not force you into!" He replies, furious. "I would never, could never, force you to choose me. Even if it means your death! I do not want a robot, Serena; I want *you*."

"You have done it." I accuse. "When my aunt was here."

"And we both hated it. But it was necessary if either of us had a chance of benefiting from her visit." He defends. "There is a difference between temporary and permanent, Serena. Forcing your mind to fall into place and serve me would displease this entire family for the rest of our miserable lives. I will not do that to any of us. Do not ask me to."

"I will not," I assure him.

"Good, let us go, we are going to be late."

"Mark me."

"Serena," he replies, impatient.

"Mark me!"

"And you are looking to accomplish, what, exactly?"

"The exact same thing it did at my courting. Your claim to me. Or am I no longer worthy?"

"I claimed you last night." He reminds me.

"No, last night was different. You were reminding me of my place." I dismiss. "Mark me like you want me to be yours forever."

"How can I claim a fiorriee who has loyalty to another?"

"By taking this wrist and marking what is going to be yours soon enough." I answer offering my arm.

He takes my hand and yanks me to him. "You would force my choice?"

"Force you?" I reply offended. "Prytore Keon, I did not mean… I am asking you to fight," I reply, shaking. "Now that you know all the ugly parts. I need you to fight."

Understanding crosses his features. His anger seems to deflate. His hands grip the back of my neck while his thumbs rest on my cheekbones. When he speaks, his voice is softer, "This was Roarick's tactic was it not? He listened to your confessions and then he took your mind."

"You walk away every time you hear a confession," I reply fighting tears as an answer. "You come back, but you always walk away."

He closes his eyes, hiding his emotions from me. "My sweet, sweet Serena," he whispers, resting his forehead on mine. "I am not running from you."

"It feels that way," I reply, tears spilling from my unblinking eyes.

"I am sorry. I am so sorry, I did not realize," he responds opening his eyes. Our gaze locks but he does not take me anywhere. I can see the truth in his words. I gasp in surprise when my collar heats up not just on my neck but my entire body. But the pleasant feeling is overpowered by extreme pain. I cry out in agony. "Serena!" Keon calls, grabbing me, keeping me from falling to the ground. "It is all right. You are all right," he assures me, not letting go.

"Keon, what is happening?" I ask, trying to get my legs to hold my own weight.

"Your mind is accepting your place." He answers taking me back into the mirror we were edging out of with our conversation. I stare at it for a moment, moving my left hand to be sure. "Well, at least half of it is." He adds, studying my reflection with me. There are still two reflections, but one *is* me. Happy, I smile at myself and Keon, through the mirror. "Good girl." He praises, taking my hand in his and nibbling my wrist painfully in reward. "I only wish your true reflection was dominant."

"Me too." I frown.

"It is all right, it will happen soon. This is a massive breakthrough. I will take every victory we can get."

"Serena?" Peyton asks, barging through the door, concern all over his face. He realizes instantly that he is interrupting. "I am sorry Prytore Keon, she sounded like…" he does not finish the sentence.

Alexis joins him in the doorway. "Serena are you all right? You sounded like you were dying." Peyton shrugs and jerks his head toward Alexis.

"She is fine. She had a breakthrough." Keon answers for me. "Her mind is still divided but the part that is loyal to us, has surrendered."

"Oh, Serena!" Peyton smiles, moving so fast it takes Keon off guard, and we find ourselves in a three-way hug. Alexis joins us quickly after. Peyton kisses me in joy then turns to Keon. "Thank you."

"I did not do anything. It is all her." He dismisses.

"Prytore Keon, I realize this is fantastic news, but if you do not leave now, you will be late for the King's ball, which I need not remind you, is being thrown in this family's honor." Fakhir speaks up. "However, if I might say so myself. I am proud of you Serena."

"Thank you, Fakhir." I smile, pulling my family close.

"We should go." Keon decides, breaking us apart. "The less attention we bring to ourselves tonight the better."

Thirty-Three

The King's Celebration Feast

Serena

I am nervous. I am especially nervous when we leave the gates of our family home. I have never considered myself to be clairvoyant, but I have this feeling that I will not be the same person when I get back to it. Not that it is a bad thing, but I cannot tell if it is going to be a good thing. I know I talked Keon into this decision, forcing this process to happen, even with the risk of it killing me. Despite being a goddess, I can die, which I am not in any rush to do. Well, at least part of me is not.

I stare at the deceptively small looking house for a lingering moment, before Peyton takes my hand and leads me toward the carriage that is taking us to a nearby transport. He seems relieved. Which I find odd, because he will be doing nothing but giving all half- truths tonight in order to protect all of us. I cannot tell if it is because he possesses nerves of steel or because he is in denial about what is to come tonight. Either way, I am annoyed he is making it all about me. While I understand he believes this breakthrough will save my life, mine is not the only one at risk tonight. I wish they would at least acknowledge that. But they do not. Not even with the knowledge that if they were found guilty for stripping Peyton from Prytore DNA, they will most likely not have their heads attached to their shoulders any longer. Silence is all they will give me on that subject. Even when I asked them if they were all right before they left the house. They simply avoided it and turned it back onto how proud they were of me.

Proud, please. They go through all this, and tonight is either going to kill me, make me disloyal, which could get them killed, or allow me the ability to surrender to them completely. No, they have nothing to worry about with a volatile fiorriee like me wearing their family crest. They could be walking straight into a death trap, and they know it. Still, they carry smiles on their faces. Why? Do they honestly have that much faith in me?

The carriage ride is longer than I anticipated it to be, which allowed me to spiral in my head much longer than I probably should. Peyton notices my mood when we climb off the carriage and start to walk toward the transport. "My wife, is something bothering you?"

I turn to him; he has never addressed me like that before. "I am just stuck in my head is all."

"I can see that." He smiles, fixing my shawl. I hate the thing, but I understand its necessity.

"I am worried." I admit.

"About seeing Roarick again?" he asks, working to keep disapproval off his face but his voice gives him away.

"No," I reply, ignoring his tone. "I am worried about you."

"There is nothing to worry about Serena, I assure you."

"You are a full blooded fiorriee. One who everyone knows has claim to the fiorriee throne, not just through marriage but through blood, and you are telling me that this development is not going to be upsetting. Why am I the only one who sees this going sideways?"

"Because you are missing all the facts." Peyton answers seriously.

"Why is that?" I ask insulted but his face tells me. "You do not trust me with them." I add, answering my own question.

"We trust half of you, Serena," he whispers, causing pain in my heart. "But if Roarick manages to get into your mind…"

"I will fight him. He does not have my soul," I reply, angry.

"We are counting on that," Keon replies, taking my hand and walking me into the transport. "Make us proud, Serena." he whispers before we are zipped away and brought to the king's town. Alexis steps forward with our invitation and the guards take us to a similar carriage we were on when we left our home, which takes us up to the path of the castle. "Do you see the difference now?" Keon asks.

"Yeah, you keep over half of yours cloaked." I laugh. "Otherwise, the King would be jealous. Does he know the true size of our home?"

"Some things are better left unmentioned." Keon smiles at me.

I smile back.

Alexis and Peyton are locked in a gaze. Suddenly, Peyton seems on guard. His stature has changed and he is gripping my hand so tightly I am beginning to lose circulation. "Prytoree Alexis, I apologize for interrupting, but I was wondering if maybe Peyton could allow blood to flow in my hand?" Peyton lets go in surprise. "Thank you."

I turn to Keon and touch his face, he raises an eyebrow, as I stare into his eyes intently. When we are in the ballroom, he looks concerned. "What is it, Serena?"

"I am hoping you will grant Peyton access to this place, even if it is temporary."

"Why?" he asks, guarded.

"Because he hates this Roarick situation. More so than you do."

"And bringing him to your soul is going to help him how?"

"It just will," I reply.

"There are no secrets between us, Serena; anything you have to say to Peyton, Alexis and I should know as well."

"I am not attempting to hide anything." I assure him. "I am just wanting to be a wife to my husband."

"You are full of unusual requests tonight, Serena." He complains.

"Please."

"Temporary access." He agrees, breaking eye contact.

I mouth the words thank you to Keon and turn to my husband. Him and Alexis have broken their gaze. "Peyton?" He turns his attention to me, and I place my hand on his cheek. My purple eyes meet his silver ones and within half a second, Peyton is the one in the ballroom with me.

"What?" he asks, looking around a little discombobbled. He sees me wearing a yellow dress and it clicks in his mind. "How?"

"Temporary permission granted." I smile at him.

"Keon bent his rules for you?" Peyton asks, taking me in his arms. "More for you than me." I disagree.

"Why?"

"Because we have never talked about this." He studies me but he keeps his silence. I was expecting his caution. When we speak in person, we can sensor, but here, in our souls, honesty seems to be the only form of communication. "I mean, you reacted by asking why I was not dismissed. But we never spoke of why it happened to start with, or why I am choosing to fight for Keon and Alexis."

"Keon has told me everything." Peyton dismisses. "There is no need to dissect this further."

"Is there not? Peyton, please, talk to me."

He growls before he speaks his mind. "It is bad enough I share you with Keon and Alexis," he admits. "It irritates me that I must have permission to be here, in your soul, where I belong. But to share you with my deepest enemies' son! Do you have any idea what could happen if you surrender to Roarick? I will never leave you, but even if I submit to him, he could keep us apart!"

"I am sorry."

"It should have never happened!"

"Roarick's never been here, not once," I whisper, trying to soothe this pain.

"He should not still be here." Peyton replies touching my forehead. "I want him out, Serena. Why will you not let him go?" He asks, his eyes full of pain.

"I do not know how to do that," I answer, looking away from him.

"Figure it out." He demands.

"I am trying."

"Try harder."

I do not know what to say to that. I try to break our connection by turning my head from his physical stare, but his hands are on my face. "Not yet." Peyton states, keeping our connection. I wait, unsure what to say. "I belong here, Serena. You must feel the difference between me and Keon, yet I am only here on his permission. Think about that, do you believe Roarick would give us this privilege, much less any others? I love you, Serena. Do not ever doubt that. But I am displeased about Roarick having any part of you in the past, now, or in the future. I want him gone. I want you to let him go." His eyes harden. "If you do not, I will stay yours, but I will never forgive you."

I try to respond but we are back in the carriage again. He kisses my forehead lightly then turns his attention back to Alexis. I feel heartbroken and my eyes welled with tears. I am comforted almost immediately by Keon's arms being wrapped around me. I turn to him with sadness in my eyes.

Keon touches my face and brings us back to the ballroom. "It is a bit more private here than the carriage. Are you all right?"

"Yeah, just a little shaken. I knew he was holding back his feelings, but I did not realize by how much."

"Peyton is very proud, Serena. More so than I think you understand."

"I am a quick learner," I mutter. "Is he going to hate me forever?"

"Hate is a powerful word." Keon notes, "If there is hate, it is not you he is directing it at."

"I should have confronted him before now."

"Peyton would have resisted that. While the knowledge of Roarick truly upsets him, he is more concerned about your mind. He does love you, Serena. So much I doubt you could do anything to change his heart." I look at Keon with doubt. "Not saying you will not have to go through a storm or two. But he is yours, pride or no pride."

Keon looks away, bringing us back to the moment. When the carriage stops, we are being escorted off and through the castle gates and into a grand hall. We are announced to the room as the Silviu family and the escort leaves us, to introduce the next guests. The hall is so over done it is tacky. Silver is everywhere. So much it all blends into everything. It is accented with orange and yellow, and I hate it all so much it takes effort not to dash out of there.

"Are you okay my dear?" Alexis asks.

"Yeah, just keep me clear of the decorator," I whisper in her ear, causing her to let out a delightful laugh. I turn to her, my eyes awestruck. "Your laugh…it is almost magical."

She blushes deeply. "Thank you, Serena. You are too kind."

"Keon, Alexis! Oh, my Alexis! I was so worried!" King Maleko calls out, forcing Alexis into a hug. "Kidnapped, you poor dear. That must have been dreadful."

"Cannot say I enjoyed it much, Your Majesty," Alexis replies breaking free and bowing with her husband. Peyton steps on my foot and I realize he and I are to bow too. I do so without meeting his eyes. "Aw Serena, so good to see you again," he replies, but his smile seems faked and he looks disappointed. "You are taking to your new family well? My what an interesting collar."

"I am, Your Majesty." I smile. "Thank you. I do enjoy all its fashion choices. Is Zane here? Did he find a mate? Oh, I do hope so, he deserves the best."

"He deserved you," King Maleko replies. I intentionally avoid Peyton's eyes, not wanting the King to give him any direct attention at all.

"Oh, Your Majesty," I reply, forcing a blush. "Seriously though, is he happy?"

"See for yourself. He and Bethany Leemeair-Collegarsi are just over there. Do say hello," he replies, disappointed again.

"We will."

"I just have one question." He adds, stopping me and Peyton in our tracks. I swallow hard and turn to him, keeping a happy, curious expression on my face. "How is your breaking coming? It must not have been easy with your husband gone for so long."

"Oh, that." I smile. "It has been postponed for a bit." I shrug. "Not my idea, believe me. But Prytore Keon was insistent. He felt that I would need my husband to cope with it. I tried to no ale to change his mind, as I feel disconnected since my marriage, but how can I truly be broken without my husband?"

"Indeed, how could you?" he replies, his smile suddenly more genuine. I give him a short bow and Peyton follows my lead, walking away as quickly and as politely possible.

"What was that?" he whispers to me so low I can barely hear him. His eyes give warning, so I reply just as low.

"Just keeping his attention on me," I reply as Zane and Bethany approach us. "Zane!" I genuinely smile, taking him in my embrace. "It is wonderful to see you again."

"Serena!" Zane smiles back, pulling away and really looking at me. "As lovely as ever. Peyton my friend, I will forever be jealous." Peyton laughs and Bethany rolls her eyes. Zane looks over at my husband and studies him for a moment. His smile drops and is replaced with a look of concern.

"Dance with me, my friend!" I demand, taking Zane's hand before he could argue. Peyton raises an eyebrow at me. I cannot tell if he is jealous that I am dancing with Zane or annoyed that he just got abandoned with Bethany. Either way I give him a pointed look and drag Zane to the dance floor.

"It is a little early for this. Guest are still arriving." Zane protests.

"Forgive me, but I do not trust your wife," I reply, coldly.

"So, I am not wrong then." He challenges, looking directly at me. His words are so broad an eavesdropper would have a hard time deciphering the meaning. But I understood him perfectly. He senses trouble.

"Erland almost killed me," I whisper softly. "And it was not the only trap set to get that result."

"I do not understand."

"It is too dangerous to explain here," I reply, twirling myself on the floor and back to him. "Just know that I am alive because of extreme measures and sheer will."

"Whoever is trying to kill you is about to find themselves dead." Zane replies coldly but very quietly.

"I appreciate your friendship, Zane." I smile in a whisper, stopping the dance when the music changes. He walks me back to Peyton, who takes me in his arms rather quickly and kisses me intently. Causing a scuff to come from Bethany. I pull away slightly irritated at his childish behavior but, I do not say anything. "So, tell me Bethany, how did you and Zane find one another?" I ask, putting the attention on the one person who would eat it up.

Her smile beams and she starts literally at day one of our courting and goes on, and on, and on, about how her and Zane played hard to get because she wanted to tease him first. "… and at the last gathering, that is when I finally gave into my natural instinct and offered Zane my hand. He took it immediately and would not let me go. I of course, later admitted to him I wanted to do it on day one. But my mama raised me proper, so I waited. I did not want to make a scene of myself so that everyone could enjoy their courting, instead of making it all about me." She finishes, causing my temper to rise. I knew it was exactly what she wanted, but I did not care.

"Yes, well, my parents died trying to prevent us from the suppression of Prytore courting, to start with." I snap. "As far as my aunt, well she is not known to be a supporter of the Prytores' tradition either. So I guess, I was never taught to resist what came naturally to me with regards to my heart, in order to mind etiquette rules made up by our conquerors."

"Serena." Zane warns, looking around.

Peyton laughs it off. "Forgive my wife. She tends to be very passionate and unapologetic with the way we met." I squeeze his hand, staring at Bethany, daring her to challenge me further. She does not. At least her mama also taught her when to keep her mouth shut. "I simply adore this song. Serena, let us dance." Peyton all but drags me to the dance floor. When I am in his arms his lips are on my ear. "What was that? Have you forgotten where we are standing?"

"I am sorry," I whisper back. "She just gets to me."

"She gets to you? You left me alone with her!"

"Well, sounds like I should not be apologizing for my behavior then. She has been needing to be put in her place for a while now. I finally decided to do it."

"While I do not disagree, you need to be careful, Serena." Peyton whispers lowly, "Fakhir is not the only talking house on Artthemis."

"I am not trying to start anything," I reply, reeling in my temper.

"I know you feel everything is as it should be. But even when a petty girl gets under your skin, you must remember your place and not embarrass me or our family. You are my wife, and a submissive, all other titles you may or may not have had are gone. Do not ever forget that." He replies, meeting my eyes, telling me he does not mean a word.

"I am sorry, husband. I will do better in honor of our family."

"Good. These little outbursts will be so much easier to control once you are broken."

"Coming soon," I reply, looking nervous.

"I have no doubt it will be a short experience, Serena; you are so good to us to start with."

"Because I like it here, in your arms. Never let me go," I reply, pulling him closer. That is when I see him, Roarick, standing alone just outside the dance floor. Our eyes meet and my body goes rigid. It feels like my blood has turned to ice in my own veins.

"Serena? What is it?" Peyton asks, drawing my attention back to him. I shake my head, causing Peyton to look around. Shortly after, he too goes rigid, and I know he knows. "Are you all right?" he asks. I nod, but it is stiff. "Maybe a glass of water then." He leads me off the dance floor, away from Roarick and straight to Keon. "Serena is a little parched. I am going to get her some water."

"Nonsense, Peyton, I will get it." Alexis smiles.

"Prytoree."

"You are my fiorriee, Peyton, not my slave," she replies curtly. "Besides, I think my husband could use something a little stiffer." She walks away, leaving me in between Keon and Peyton. They share a look, and I realize this was rehearsed.

"Serena, how is your friend Zane?" Keon asks, trying to look casual, but I can tell he is on alert.

"He has very poor taste in women," I reply bluntly. "Bethany, of all the beautiful girls at court, he chooses her." I wrinkle my nose. I knew why he had, but the house did not need to know that I understood the reason for her fate.

"If I recall, he showed interest in you." Keon notes, studying me.

"Just because I was already taken, gives him no excuse."

"You are going to have to accept his choice if you want to maintain the friendship you asked me for." Keon warns.

"Prytore, she is so shallow." I whine.

"In this moment, Serena, so are you," he replies firmly.

"Excuse me, Prytore Keon." Keon turns around, causing all three of us to.

Keon steps so he is in front of me and Peyton places himself behind me, no doubt looking menacing. "Prince Roarick!" Keon replies, bowing properly to him. Peyton and I do the same. "It has been a long while since I have seen you. How are your travels in the West?"

"Boring mostly. But we must all do our duties and rule the planet," Roarick replies. "Is this your new fiorriee? She is absolutely stunning."

"Yes, this is Serena Gelsomino, Peyton's wife."

"Wife?" Roarick notes, looking surprised, causing a sharp unpleasant pain to run down my spine. I do my best to ignore it.

"They did meet at this year's yellow courting. Surely you heard Peyton married unusually early there. News like that does tend to travel."

"Indeed, but not as far West as I was. I only just arrived here an hour ago." Prytore Roarick explains. "My father insisted on my presence, but I am still unclear as to why he was throwing a ball in your family's honor. Something about Alexis suffering a misfortune?"

"I was kidnapped." Alexis answers, giving a drink to myself and Keon, standing beside her husband, effectively blocking me. She takes a bow to the prince. "Though misfortune does make it sound much better."

"Kidnapped?" Roarick asks shocked. "What on Artthemis for?"

"That remains unclear. All I know is I was neglected in filth and my fiorriee was tortured."

"Serena was tortured?"

"Peyton." Alexis corrects him.

"Oh, I see," he replies, sizing up the four of us. "Well, I am glad that all seems well now." He stands there for the longest moment in silence.

"Was there something on your mind, Prince Roarick?" Keon asks.

"Actually, yes," Roarick answers. But his father calls to him. He gives him a nod and turns back to us. "I am hoping to reserve a dance with your lovely Serena. I have seen her twice on the dance floor tonight and she seems so elegant."

"That decision is up to Serena." Keon answers, turning his attention to me.

"If my family is okay with it, I do not see the harm," I reply properly, giving him a short bow.

"That pleases me very much, Serena," he responds, causing a weird warmth to come over me. "Excuse me." He walks away, and Keon and Alexis turn to face me. I take such a large drink of my water the glass is almost empty.

"Are you all right?" Alexis asks. "How do you feel?"

"Annoyed that his words are getting to me." I answer honestly. "He disapproves of Peyton."

"Good." Peyton replies proudly, pulling me into a protective embrace.

"He will not let me wiggle out of dancing with him." I sigh.

"This was your idea, Serena." Keon reminds me. "But the moment you think it to be too much, you let us know and we will take you back home where you belong."

"I do not feel any different yet. Going home now is premature." The music starts up and Keon hands mine and his glass to Peyton, then leads me to the dance floor. He is the easiest of all to dance with. Mostly because I do not have much of a choice but to follow his lead. He glides me over the marble floor in such an elegant way that other couples stop and watch. By the time the song is half over, we are the only one's dancing. When the song does end, the crowd applauds. Keon smiles, pulling me into him before he has us bow and walk back to our family. None of this gets missed by Roarick. I can feel his disapproving eyes on me the entire time. As I am walking back to Peyton and Alexis, my head involuntarily snaps to his. Roarick smiles at me, gives me a short bow, and mouths the word 'soon.'

"That was a bit of a show, Keon." Alexis disapproves, glaring at her husband, missing Roarick's reaction to it.

"What can I say?" Keon shrugs. "He got under my skin."

"Serena can get away with that," Alexis hisses. "You however, are much older and much wiser."

"Sorry," Keon whispers kissing his wife.

"No, you are not." She accuses accurately. She kisses him back and leads him onto the dance floor, leaving me alone with Peyton.

I look up at my husband, asking the question of the night. "Are you all right?"

"Ask me tomorrow," he replies, his eyes on Roarick. "I did not miss your little exchange. Were you going to tell me about it?" I shrug in response. "When it comes to him, not even the slightest thing should be unspoken." Peyton warns me, not letting Roarick out of his sight.

"I will keep that in mind," I mutter, taking my glass from him and finishing my water.

Peyton's eyes are on me. "Serena." I look at Peyton with the annoyance I feel. "You understand what is at stake here. I need to know at all times which side of you is in control. Your omittance to even the slightest exchange gives me that answer." I nod. "Now tell me, were you going to tell me about it?"

"No." I answer truthfully.

His eyes harden but his voice is so soft it is almost inaudible. "That displeases and disappoints me very much." My collar gives off an unpleasant sensation all the way down to my toes with his words. I hiss in surprise. "I am your husband, no matter which Prytore your mind desires, you belong to me." He reminds me. I grab his thick arms to keep myself upright. I look up at him in shock, unsure how he is doing what he is doing, but not appreciating it very much. It takes me a moment to get my bearings and he gives no comfort or reassurance as I manage my suffering. When I release my grip from his arms his lips find my ear. "On our wedding night you surrendered to me completely, Serena. I have so much more power over you than you realize."

"You could make me choose," I whisper, finally understanding.

His voice remains painfully soft. "You have already chosen me. Mind, body, soul. Your devotion is not split in any of those aspects when it comes to me. Even your reflections have confirmed that."

Tears fill my eyes and I struggle to keep my voice just as low. "I am facing death because of a divided mind, and you can save me, but you will not?"

"It is not because of how I feel, Serena. It is because I agree with Keon on this matter. The only way you will be happy is through willful submission. Which means you must save yourself." Tears spill from my eyes, and he catches them, tenderly. "Do not disappoint me again tonight, Serena. Your life is hanging in the balance. I need to know which part of you is in control at all times."

"If I am forced to choose him?"

"Let us hope it does not come to that." He frowns. "Wife, I beg you to fight with everything you have if it does." I can feel his body shake in my arms and I realize he wants me to fight to my last breath.

"Why now, why admit this to me here?"

"Because you need to know," he answers into my ear. "No matter our fate, your freewill made that choice."

"I am a Silviu, Peyton, and I will be to my last breath. You have my word."

The song Keon and Alexis are dancing to ends and the musicians get up from their seats. Curious, I look around and find that Bethany, along with other fiorriee wearing the ridiculous silver, orange, and yellow combination are working to set food on the table. I pull Peyton closer to me and put my face into his chest, hiding my smile. Zane did in fact keep his word. Thinking of Zane, my eyes scan for him. I am not surprised to find that he is standing near the king. The woman who I assume is Queen Adriana, appears angry or bored, I cannot tell which. The King, however, seems a little preoccupied with Zane to even care about her mood.

Fighting a ping of jealousy, my eyes continue to scan the room. There are so many families it is hard to keep track of who is with whom. That is until I look a little closer and realize everyone has a family crest, even the men. But it is not always in the same place. Some men wear it on their shoulders, others over their chest. I look closer at Peyton. His is on his breast pocket and arm cuffs, discreet but there. Some women are wearing it on the corset of their gowns like me, others have necklaces, head gear, or it laced into their gloves. But no matter where I turn, Prytore and fiorriee alike, are all wearing a crest of some sort. I have never seen anything like it in all my life.

"You seem curious," Peyton whispers.

"I am." I smile. "The crests, I have never seen so many."

"Really?" Peyton replies, as if it is so normal, he barely notices them. "Well, I guess that makes sense, you could not exactly wear yours and orphans are usually stripped of them before they are sent."

"You are serious?"

He shrugs. "The placement has meaning." He continues, helping me understand. "For men, the upper arm on the shoulder signifies head of household. The chest signifies a secure place in the household. You will see this mostly on Prytore sons who have yet to mate, but not fiorriee." I look at his chest then back up at his face. "There are exceptions. Keon and Alexis, have placed me in a high station in our family." I nod, believing that. "The cuffs are reserved for owned fiorriee."

"The women?"

"The crest on jewelry or hair pieces are reserved for Prytoree. You will notice Alexis has both a necklace and a hairpin. Those who have the honor of wearing the crest in their hair also have nearly equal rights in their relationships and are taken more seriously by all male counterparts because of it. The crest, on the corset, like yours, signifies a secure place in the household."

"And the gloves?"

"They are reserved for owned fiorriee."

"Yet I am not wearing any." I conclude.

"You are not broken." He reminds me. "You will wear them soon enough. In the meantime, you have a shawl to protect those precious wrists from anymore mishaps." I give him a small pout. "Look closer, Serena. Almost every girl at our courting is here and they too are not wearing gloves, even Bethany. Most, have yet to earn a crest like yours." I scan the room and realize he is right. "It is interesting when you come to these things, and you see the crests change."

"Change? I was not aware the fiorriee socialized in places like this before their choosing."

"Most do not, almost all Prytore do though." He smiles. "These types of gatherings are where future Prytore mates meet each other and at times watch each other grow up."

"Interesting." I smile, looking around, noticing a young Prytoree blush from a young Prytore's stare.

"It is if you think about it. It takes Prytore's years to decide on a mate. We, however, only need moments when we find the right one. One of the major contrasts between our species."

"You sound like Alexis."

He laughs. "Now, that is a truest form of a compliment. Thank you, my wife."

"Oh, Peyton, what has you giving such a wonderful laugh?" Alexis asks, returning from the dance floor with Keon.

"Serena, was just accusing me and you being likeminded when it comes to comparing our species."

"Oh?"

"She noticed the crests." He explains.

"Did you tell her how many have changed? I am surprised. Normally there is not this much difference in such a short amount of time." Alexis notes, looking around.

"Are you as bored as I am with this conversation?" Keon asks me, hopeful.

I laugh a little. "I could think of better things to ponder about."

"Oh, thank goodness!" Keon laughs. "Serena, you just saved me from the most boring dinner in history." I blush but Alexis clicks her tongue and pushes her husband's upper arm in annoyance.

"What, she is sitting next to me. You can talk Peyton's ear off all you want. He actually likes, your silly observations."

"Oh my, however did you survive without me?" I ask Keon, teasingly.

"Lots of smiling and nodding." He answers, grinning. "It took practice to figure out when to agree and disagree without really listening though."

"Cute." Alexis complains.

Peyton stiffs a laugh. "We should join the others and sit." "Please tell me we are not at an orange tablecloth." I plead, under my breath.

"You do not like the color orange?" Keon asks.

"Not when it is insulted with accent colors like this." I mutter. "It looks like a daget threw up in here."

Everyone stiffs a laugh. "Do not let the Queen hear that," Alexis warns. "She is in charge of decorations."

"That explains so much," I whisper looking over at her. She still looks angry and bored.

Keon finds our seats, which are directly next to the King. He situates us so that I am in between him and Peyton, yet Peyton has his back to the King. This does not fill our table though and soon we find Zane and Bethany sitting with us. I feel Peyton's hand on my leg, as a warning and I force a smile.

"You should definitely avoid the zakarick. Bethany made it herself and is adapting to her newfound cooking skills." Zane teases, but his face is serious.

"You said it was not bad."

"It is not." He smiles at his wife. "But it is not good cither."

"Oh." She frowns.

"I can have it pulled from the menu."

"Do not worry about it. There is plenty of food to go around." Zane dismisses, pressing a button on the bubble that is in the middle of the table, causing it to open. The contents are filled with a variety of food. Keon starts to fill his plate and everyone follows suit.

I am unfamiliar with half the food presented; I turn to Peyton for help. He understands and simply takes my plate, filling it for me. Leaving one or two things untouched. I am surprised when he does not place it in front of me. Instead, he hands it to Alexis. "Yes, I think these choices should be fine. I do not foresee any of them causing any food allergies. Smart choice avoiding the stew, we cannot be too careful with the spices." She hands the plate back to Peyton who politely sets it in front of me. Zane and Bethany look at me curiously.

"Allergies." I blush, not liking the attention, unsure the reason for it. I drink my water as a distraction.

I am about to start eating but Peyton grabs my hand and tangles his fingers with mine. Curious, I look at him. He nods at the front table, answering me. The Prytore King and Queen take their seats, followed by their family. When their plates are filled, Maleko gives a speech as to how grateful he is that nothing happened to Alexis and Peyton. Then he gives permission for all of us to eat. The moment he does, I am not hungry anymore. I stare down at the food, almost angry at its existence. I feel eyes on me, and I look up, seeing Roarick watch me. Smiling while he chews and drinks from his glass.

"Husband," I whisper.

"Wife?"

"You know that thing you asked me about?" His body gets rigid. "It is happening."

"Serena." Keon chimes in, chewing his food. "You have not touched your plate. You need to eat."

"I do not want to," I whisper, tears filling my eyes. "How is he doing this?" I ask scared.

"Is everything all right?" Bethany asks, looking half amused, half concerned.

"Yes." Alexis answers for me. "Zane, I do not know what you are talking about. Bethany's zakarick taste just fine. What spices did you use dear?" She asks, keeping Bethany distracted. Zane is not deterred though; he is highly aware something is wrong, but he is smart enough not to draw unnecessary attention to it. He just studies me while he eats slowly.

"Serena, look at me." Keon demands, causing my head to hurt and the cords that are tethered to us to pull. "Your family has made sure the food in front of you is safe. I know you trust us. I know you are hungry. And I know you will follow my orders about eating three meals a day. You need to understand; this meal is one of the meals I expect you to eat."

It takes effort not to scream as a searing unpleasant pain goes through my entire nervous system. "I cannot, he is much stronger than I realized." I gasp, feeling Roarick's stare on me.

"Who? Who is controlling her?" Zane asks, leaning into Keon, trying not to grab Bethany's attention. Keon leans back, answering him. Zane frowns instantly. "That is not good. He is studied in the art of telepathy. I have seen him control many of his fiorriee with merely a look."

"So, it is begun." I realize, trying to fight against Roarick's control.

"How?" Zane asks furious. "You are Silviu, everyone knows that."

"Long story." I frown, staring at my plate. "Stupid mistake. I really hate myself. If only I had listened to Dex."

"Who is Dex?"

"My best friend." I answer, concentrating on the fork. "Does he know her?"

"Yes."

Zane gets up from the table and walks directly over to Roarick, blocking me from Roarick's view. I can feel the relief immediately. I quickly grab my fork and start to shovel my food down my throat; not bothering to chew very much.

"Do not choke on it." Peyton worries. I ignore him, using my water to make it go down easier. I am unsure how much time I have, but I appreciate whatever distraction Zane is providing.

"It takes direct gaze. That is good, we can work with that." Keon notes.

"Yeah, until we have a conversation on the dance floor." I counter, eating my food in the most unladylike manner ever. "I did not realize he was this strong," I whisper. "I thought he was quite weak, compared to what I share with this family."

"You are able to eat, despite knowing he does not want you too. That takes strength in and of itself."

"We need to get her out of here." Peyton decides.

"No. That will not break this bond." I argue. "I must fight. This is an unexpected obstacle, that is all." I shake my head. "Alexis, I hate to interrupt, but would you be as so kind as to escort me to the powder room? I am afraid all this water is going right through me."

"Where is Zane?" Bethany asks, looking truly confused as she had been spending the last few moments in her own world talking about food with Alexis.

I do not know if anyone answers her. I just know Alexis gives me a look of relief then concern as she leads me to the restrooms. When we get there, she locks the door then turns to me. "I can see why you have distasteful reservations about that petty fiorriee." She rubs her skull, trying to fight a headache.

"Alexis," I whisper, touching her face and meeting her green eyes. We fall into the ballroom.

"How did you know that was going to work?"

"You have made it clear you are Keon's equal. He can come here, therefore so can you." I reply, with a shrug. "It is safer here. The house cannot read our minds, can it?"

"No, but Roarick might be able to read yours. Though we are not in your mind." She notes as we dance together.

"How is Roarick doing this?" I ask, truly scared.

"You let him in, he took full advantage."

"Okay, so how do I kick him out?" I ask, needing the answer.

"I do not know."

"Come on Alexis, think!" I snap at her. "You have studied my species inside and out for nearly a hundred years."

"Serena, it is not that simple. The usual way to break this is to eliminate any and all contact. Permanently."

"Yep, tried that one, even buried the memories, still stuck."

"Which is why you are going to have to confront him. It is dangerous and it might not work but it is the only option you have."

"I am scared."

"I know," she whispers. "Serena, you have our permission to do whatever you feel is necessary to break yourself free of Roarick. Even if that means you will have to break yourself free of us."

"I do not want that."

"I do not want you split in two," she counters. "And I would rather you choose none of us, then be forced into a choice you do not want." I stare at her. She just gave me a third option. Not her and Keon, not Roarick, but myself.

"I love you too," I whisper breaking our connection and heading to the stalls.

"Serena?"

"I really do have to go." I answer, trying to work my dress so I do not make a mess of it while thinking of what to do next. I am sure Zane's distraction is no longer effective. I am half curious what he said to him anyway. When I deal with everything, I go back to wash my hands and stare at the mirror, freezing.

"What is it?" Alexis asks, touching my shoulder lightly, looking at me.

"The black dress," I whisper, causing Alexis to look at my images in the mirror. "She is afraid." I note, seeing her curled in on herself, crying. I stare at my real image and wash my hands furiously. Realizing at once why she did not let go. It was not because she wanted Roarick. It was because Roarick wanted her, and she had no idea how to escape. It is why I was able to split and survive. The half of me that is stuck, wants to join the rest of me but she is trapped.

I feel Alexis' hand drop from my shoulder and I turn my attention to her. "You can control ravens Serena. Do *not* underestimate yourself."

With those words Alexis unlocks the restroom door and takes me back to the dining hall. Once there, I seat myself back between Peyton and Keon. I am able to eat my meal in peace, but it does not go unnoticed that Zane and Bethany are no longer at our table. Not much is said between us, as I eat. I drag out what is left on my plate as long as I can. But all too soon the dishes are emptied and are being cleared.

"We can go," Peyton offers again.

"No, we cannot." I frown. "If I fail, please fight. I choose this family. I want us."

"We will, Serena, I promise," Keon whispers as Roarick approaches.

"I do apologize for the interruption earlier. Now that your meal is finished, Serena, may I have the honor of dancing with you?"

I look to my family and back at him. "Yes, Prince, I am sorry Rodrick, is it? I am honored to dance with you."

"Prince Roarick, actually," he replies with a tight smile, taking my hand and leading me to the dance floor. Each step away from my family makes my heart sink deeper in my chest. "But you knew that, did you not, my Serena?" I wince with his words. "You are resisting. What an interesting development." He muses, touching my face with the back of his fingers. "Have you dared been unfaithful to me?"

"I am sorry, Prince Rollrock, but I think you have me confused with someone else."

"It is Roarick! My name is Roarick!" he hisses. "Do not insult me like that any longer."

I cannot help but grip his arm a little tighter, the pain in my head almost blinds me. "See there, you remember. If you did not, that would not hurt a bit." I refuse to look at him while I trip over his feet on the dance floor. "Now, you have two options. You can either come with me or you can make a scene here. Which do you prefer?"

"I will not go without my family," I respond, stubbornly. "I am married after all."

"Yes, that is a very tedious complication indeed." Roarick frowns. "One that I do not understand. You should not have been able to choose a mate to begin with, much less marry one." I meet his eyes in defiance. "It is no matter. I am sure I can think of something to squash the annoyance and I can have you all to myself once again."

"I do not want that. I want the Silviu's," I reply angrily.

"You think I care what you want, Serena?" he asks arrogantly. "You are as naive as I remember." The song comes to an end, but Roarick does not let go of my hand. "Your choice, Serena. Either way, I am getting you alone."

I glare at him then turn my head. "Peyton! Husband!" I call out, jerking my hand from Roarick. Peyton is at my side immediately. "I do not feel well." I state loudly. "I think I ate something I should not have." I force my body into shakes, causing Peyton to wrap his arms around me.

"Serena?" he looks truly concerned. "Prytoree Alexis!" he calls. Alexis comes running to my side at once, looking me over.

"Ginger root." She states to the closest fiorriee wearing orange. "Did any of the food have ginger root?"

"Yes." The random fiorriee answers. "Almost all of it."

"She is allergic." Alexis frowns.

"I do not recall that particular allergy." Roarick hisses at her.

"Peyton!" I call out, suddenly understanding the reason for the charade earlier, partially collapsing in on myself.

"We need to get her home. I have supplies there." Alexis worries.

"We have supplies here." Roarick argues.

"I am sure you do, but all of mine are prepared. It is faster just to take her home. I am sorry." Alexis argues. "Peyton, Keon, we need to hurry."

"That is not necessary," Roarick replies coldly, picking me up from my bended position. He turns his attention to the onlookers. "She needs a medic. Apparently, she ate something that did not agree with her. Everything is fine. Enjoy your evening." He carries me out of the room, and my family follows him.

I watch them behind his shoulder. They are all nervous. I am nervous. All I want to do is go home. Why did I insist on coming here? Tears sting my eyes. Was this a mistake? Fear washes over me, as each step he takes leads further and further away from any help, making me feel colder and colder, because I know he is carrying me head on to my death, with my family as witness.

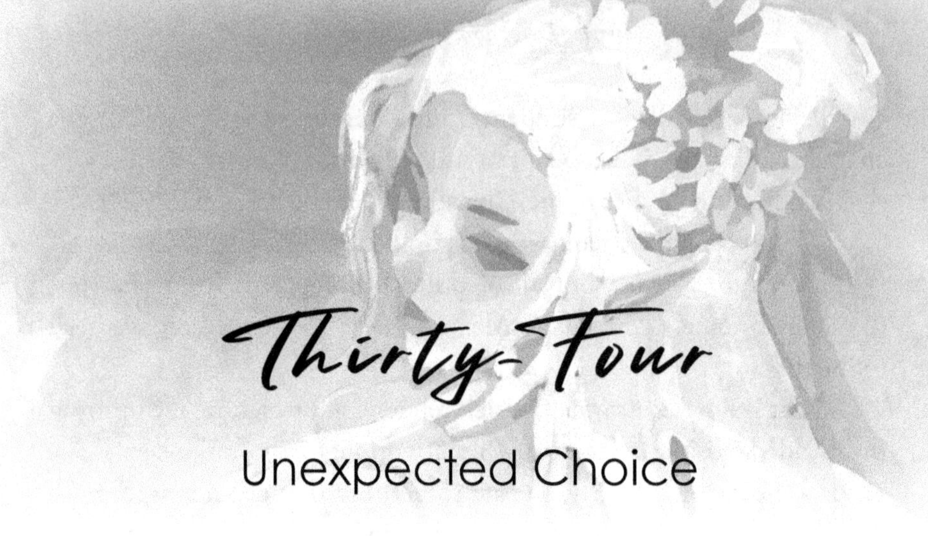

Thirty-Four

Unexpected Choice

Serena

Roarick leads us down several hallways before he brings us into a room. "You can stand up, Serena. I have no doubt you are faking!" He snaps. Unwillingly, I do so with a glare. Peyton comes toward me. "You stay away from my fiorriee." Roarick demands.

Peyton ignores him. I feel his arms wrap around me. "She is my wife. And no matter which Prytore attempts to claim her, she will always be mine."

"That is going to be difficult since she married a fiorriee outside of her Prytore's wishes."

"She wears the Silviu's family crest, not yours. Therefore, she is under *my* family's protection, and we lay full claim to her." Keon responds coldly.

"We shall see about that." Roarick sneers. "Aunt, Uncle you might as well sit," he tells them, gesturing toward some chairs. "Though I use those titles loosely. You only live because of my mother." Roarick grumbles. Alexis and Keon exchange a look with one another before they reluctantly comply. "And you, Uncle Keon, should know better than to throw the worthless Silviu family name at me. If you want my respect at all, use Mortal!"

"I would, if the crest applied to Serena or her husband Peyton, but it does not." Keon states, coldly.

"Good. Had you been in my father's favor, I would be unable to take back what is rightfully mine!" Roarick grins then turns his attention to me. "My Serena." Roarick continues to smile, approaching me. I instinctively take a step closer into Peyton, wanting a shield, causing Roarick to stop cold. "You are going to be difficult as always, I see." He frowns, walking around us in a circle.

"I am not yours, Roarick. I am a Silviu."

"No, you are not!" he snaps. "Now kneel, you little traitor!"

I fight against him; my head is hurting so badly that my body bends just to try to make it stop but my knees do not touch the floor. "I said, kneel!" He demands too calmly. With extreme unpleasant pain, my knees give out, causing me to kneel before him.

Alexis jumps up from her chair, but Roarick stops her. "Do not, unless you want her dead." Alexis hesitates before she sits back in the chair, poised to pounce. "I suggest you follow Alexis' example if you want to keep Serena alive." Roarick tells Keon. Keon glares in silence. He had not moved, yet he too seems ready to fight. "And you." Roarick sneers at Peyton. "If you want to remain her husband, you will follow her example and kneel before her true Prytore." Peyton shoots a look to Alexis who gives a tiny approving nod. I can hear Peyton take a deep breath while he proudly raises his head, struggles to kneel in a tense position, then wraps me in his arms. If this bothered Roarick, he does not show it. "I am curious, Serena. Do you not remember our last encounter?" he asks, walking around us again.

"I remember my aunt beating your head in with a frying pan," I reply. "But I do not remember much else about you."

"Funny, Zane just chewed my ear off with stories about our time together. You remember, you, me, Dextra." My eyes narrow at him. "Pity what happened to her. I am sure she was once beautiful, before your jealousy destroyed it."

"That is not what happened," I defend, fighting tears.

"Sure it is. You are to remember what I say you remember," he replies coldly. I hiss, fighting him. "As for your aunt, she had very poor timing. You were about to willingly give yourself to me and she stuck her nose where it did not belong. I gave you instructions after that, do you remember them?"

"No!" I answer, fighting his stare, working hard not to crumble to the floor.

"I reminded you that you belonged to me. That no matter what happened in your life you were not to marry. Much less to submit to anyone else. You are mine!" I cry out, my stomach twists in knots as white pain nearly splits my skull. My throat starts to close, causing my eyes to widen. "You defied me, Serena!"

"It is not her fault!" Alexis defends, forcing his stare away from me. I choke for air, as she distracts him. "Her memories, they are missing."

"Missing?" Roarick questions.

"We have spent weeks, trying to access her mind to no avail." Alexis explains, trying not to react to my suffering. "Keon and I could not get in. Peyton could, but he was not there for a while. Her memory has holes. She only just remembered Dextra two days ago."

"How is that possible?"

"Her aunt is a pureblooded fiorriee, she must have done something us Prytore's do not understand." Keon answers.

Roarick turns his attention back to me, and I cry out. Roarick turns his attention back to me, and I cry out. "Open your mind, Serena."

"No!" I respond, fighting the agony that comes with defiance.

"Let me into where I belong!" he demands.

"No!" I scream. My entire body buckles in severe pain. My eyes are open, but I cannot see anything. It is difficult to even breathe.

"Serena!" Peyton panics, holding me close to him. "Stop this!" He demands of Roarick. "You are killing her!"

"She is killing herself. She will submit to me, or she will die. The choice is hers," Roarick answers coldly. "Let me in your head, Serena. You know I belong there."

I can feel the black dress part of my mind cowering in fear, ready to comply, but the other part of me wants to fight.

"Peyton," I whisper, trying desperately to hold on. I scream out, fighting Roarick's control, but he is winning. Against everything I have,

I find myself crawling to Roarick. My head lays itself on his feet without my permission. I hear him draw his sword, and I know he is pointing it at Peyton. I scream out when his boot lands on my face. I cry out, feeling cord-like lashes tearing at my mind, and my memories flash in front of me… all of them, all at once. My mind lands on Peyton, then Keon, my aunt, Dex, Alexis, and lastly, my Prytore Roarick.

"She is mine!" my Prytore declares.

"The only way to prove that is with a mirror," Keon replies too calmly.

Keon's words seem strange. I work desperately to understand why he said that. Yes, I have been torn in two. One side is loyal to Keon, the other to Roarick. Once I have accepted Keon, that side is broken, and my reflection stabilized. The resistance is scared. She wants to come accept Keon, but she is afraid of Roarick. I am terrified right now. I have just lost. I know, because of it, I will be living in fear the rest of my life. Roarick is too strong; he has just forced me to choose him. It saddens me knowing Peyton and Keon are stronger, but they are not fighting for it. Wait… my mind starts to race with the conversations I had with my family today. Roarick can feel me resisting and presses his foot harder into me, causing my thoughts to scatter in a scream. I work to piece them together again. Then it hits me, I promised to willfully choose until my last breath, and I am still breathing.

With extreme effort and unpleasant pain, I jerk Roarick's foot from my face and work to get to my knees. "I. Am. A. Queen!" I reply, every word cutting into me. I can feel my flesh literally tearing and feel my warm blood rise to the surface.

"You are conquered. It is over! You serve me now!"

"No!" I scream, refusing to yield.

"You are killing yourself. Stop fighting me!"

"I would rather die than submit to you!" I hiss, screaming as hot invisible lashes literally cut my flesh open. I look down, knowing what I will see. My white dress is stained with my purple blood.

"Surrender!" Roarick demands.

"I. Serve. Keon. And. Alexis!" I scream, fighting hard, managing to stand. "I. Am. Loyal. To. My. Family. I. Am. A. Silviu!" My collar warms to a pleasant sensation. The cords Roarick has me tethered to start to snap so fiercely I am sure I am not the only one who can hear them break. He takes a step back in shock. "But above all, I am a Gelsomino!" Fireballs spring up in both my hands.

"You are a witch!"

"Serena, do not!" Alexis calls, stopping me. I turn to her, struggling to stay on my feet. "You unleash that, and everyone dies."

Roarick uses the moment to lay his stare intently on me. I almost buckle from the shock that he still has a hold somehow. I fight him harder than I have ever fought anyone or anything in my life. I cry out in fiorriee, causing everyone in the room to cover their ears. I take a deep breath. "I am not a witch, you closed-minded fool! I am a goddess!" I scream at him in a hoarse voice as my aura literally engulfs my form. I screech out a raven call, lifting myself off the ground, using one of my wings to slam Roarick into the wall. I fly to him and dig my claws into his shoulder.

"Serena." Peyton whispers, breaking through my anger, causing my raven head to snap toward him "We will not try to stop you, but are you sure you want to be a murderer?" he asks, staring at the defeated prince.

My claws dig slightly more into Roarick's shoulders, causing him to cry out before I let go and fly back to my husband. When I land, next to his feet, he meets my eyes, showing no fear or disapproval. I find myself to be my fiorriee form again, turning to a now terrified Roarick. "I am not yours. I choose me! I can promise you and your family that you will regret what you have done to my fiorriee. For we are not defeated, and you will suffer for every bit of harm that has been done in your name."

Roarick curls his lips into a terrifying smile. "You want war over peace, so be it. You just killed your entire species. Mark my words."

"We need to get out of here. Now." Keon replies, ignoring Roarick.

"How?" Alexis asks, looking to the door.

"Can you carry us?" Peyton asks me.

"Yes, I think so." I look over to Roarick and the door, then to my husband. His eyes are confident that I can do it again. I shake off the pain that comes when my aura surrounds me again. If I felt that the first time, it went unnoticed. Hearing what must be guard's footsteps, I quickly enlarge myself.

"How does she do that?" Alexis asks.

"Not the time my love," Peyton replies, "Get on!" He orders my family. Peyton does not hesitate to climb on my large back, but Keon and Alexis do. "It is safe, I promise." With that Alexis nods and Keon helps her on. My raven form screeches, breaking the window. With a jolt I take off running and fly out of the castle. Once in the sky, I call out over and over again, filling the land with a sound this world has long forgotten. I can hear the street crowd gasp, then my mind is filled with what must be prayers. I try to sort through my thoughts as the wind cuts through my feathers. As I climb above the buildings, I find that I am at peace, and nothing can stand in my way.

Thirty-Five

Incompatible

Serena

After the initial rush, my mind starts to think, and I fly us high into the clouds. I am not sure what to do, or how to communicate anything in this form. I shake my head nervously. Then I feel Peyton's hands pet my feathers. Somehow, our collar is still active and showing. It has manifested veins at the tips of my feathers and Peyton's actions soothes me. I calm myself, keeping my path high above the clouds.

"What do we do now?" Alexis asks, I give a low hum, appreciating her question.

"We have to go home." Keon decides.

"It is not safe there." Alexis argues.

"It is the safest place we have at the moment." Keon defends.

"Serena cannot maintain her aura indefinitely. Eventually, she is going to weaken. She is still bleeding. She should not be flying at all." Peyton warns. "She has not walked the path of enlightenment. There is no way to tell how long she can hold out."

"I do not understand how she is doing it at all. Not on Artthemis, at least." Alexis frowns. "They will be expecting us to go to the house, Keon. Can we go somewhere else?"

"We will deal with the fall out, as it comes. For now, let us not get into a situation where we wear out our ride and fall to our deaths." Keon replies, curtly. "Take us home, Serena." I find myself changing direction, but I intentionally fight it just a little. I want this to take a little longer. When we get there Furgan is setting and Zarla is in the sky. "Serena, you can land, Keon assures me." I call out, shaking my head no and angle myself toward the Zarla moon. "Serena, you are weak, we are all soaked in your blood." I squawk, trying to make him understand, I am healing, that I am fine. "All right, we can wait for Zarla to peek." Keon agrees in understanding. "Fly to a cloaked portion of the house. If they are there, they will not know to come looking so easily."

"Cloaked meaning she cannot see what she is doing?" Peyton replies, unhappy.

"Do not worry, I will guide her." Keon reassures more than just Peyton.

"Please follow my instructions precisely this time," he asks of me. I hum in response. "Good. Now make a right turn." Keon instructs me. I follow his directions, keeping high in the sky, waiting until Zarla is the only moon giving light before I touch down on a cloaked tower.

Alexis, Keon, and Peyton climb off of me, and I find myself being pushed into the air, so forcefully I lose sight of them. I call out in surprise, unsure what is going on. I try to fly back to where I was, but there is a force field of some kind in my way. I touch it with my beak and follow it down to the ground. When I get there, Fakhir appears.

"I do not know who you are, but you are not, Serena." It says to me. I squawk at it. "Serena is a fiorriee, you are not, therefore, you are not Serena. How you seem to share the same DNA, I do not know. Why everyone is covered in Serena's blood, I do not know. I have a feeling you did it to them." I shake my head in annoyance. Wishing I could turn back into a fiorriee, but I am still too dazed from being evicted from my own home by a computer.

"Let her inside, Fakhir!" Peyton yells at the computer image, dashing to me, only to be stunned himself and falling back. "What are you doing?" Peyton demands.

"What I am programed to do." Fakhir answers. "I am protecting you, Peyton. That is not Serena. Serena is a fiorriee."

"Serena is a goddess," Peyton replies, annoyed, struggling to his feet. "You are detecting her aura. That is why she appears unfamiliar. But I promise, that *is* my wife."

"Aura?" Fakhir asks. "You have used this word before, but it does not explain why you are telling me that, that bird is Serena. Help me understand Peyton, what is the definition of an aura?"

"Energy," Peyton responds vaguely.

"This information is incompatible with my programming. Serena is a fiorriee. That is a bird! How a bird is on Artthemis is also incompatible with my programming, but I am witnessing it. Therefore, it must be true."

"And you wonder why I find this thing irritating!" Peyton snaps at me. I croak in response. "Can you change back for me, my love?" I turn my head to the left, then to the right. Then I open my wings. But nothing I do makes me able to pull my aura back inside of myself. "It is all right, you will tire soon enough. Learning to control it with your mind takes time."

"How do you have knowledge of this aura?" Fakhir asks.

"I lived on Trorain." Peyton answers. "You know, my home world."

"You never mentioned an aura changing a fiorriee into something that is clearly not a fiorriee. Nor did Karissa."

"Some things are sacred." Peyton answers, not looking at him.

"Do you have an aura?"

"No." Peyton lies to the computer.

"Why not?" Fakhir asks.

"Like I said, it is sacred." Peyton growls. "Now, will you please let my wife into the safety of our home?"

"I will gladly allow Serena in, when she arrives. That thing is not Serena." Peyton growls and punches through the hologram. Fakhir is so insulted he disappears.

Peyton lightly touches the shield. I peck at it. "Keon will be here soon; he will fix this." I have no doubt that is true. I am sure all three went running after me, but fiorriee are much faster than Prytores. He punches the shield, angrily. I fly back in surprise. "Sorry, I was not trying to startle you. I am just frustrated." I walk back to where I was, waiting impatiently.

"Fakhir! Let the raven in." Keon, yells at the computer. I look past Peyton, watching Alexis and Keon running up behind him.

"I have already told you why I cannot do that." Fakhir responds, reappearing. Keon and Alexis stop running when they reach Peyton.

"How long have you been arguing with him this time?" Peyton asks, looking angry but also bored.

"Since it happened." Alexis answers, working to catch her breath. "Well, at least when the stubborn AI would show itself."

"Serena!" Keon gasps, leaning on his knees, while catching his breath. "Fakhir!"

"First off, that is not Serena. Second, even if I accepted your argument that I have heard conversations stating Serena's aura is a raven, that thing is too big to be a raven." Fakhir argues.

"That thing, saved our lives and I trust it." Keon argues a new tactic.

"I do not, it is mimicking Serena's signature. It is deceitful and I must protect you."

"For the love of zarla!" Alexis cries out. "Fakhir, that thing, bird, raven or whatever your computer brain wants to classify it as, is in fact our Serena! I demand that you let it in!"

"All three of you are deceived!" Fakhir argues. "This thing is an imposter!"

"Can she turn back?" Alexis asks Peyton.

"She seems stuck. I do not know how to help her," Peyton replies, hitting the shield again.

"Serena?" Alexis asks, but I shake my head. I am trying, but nothing is happening. Frustrated, I peck the shield with my beak.

"If you are trying to penetrate me, good luck." Fakhir replies, glaring at me. That gives me an idea. I fly back, staying low. With concentration, I manage to have two tiny perpetual fireballs develop between my claws.

"Who else do you know that can do that?" Peyton challenges, smiling in victory.

Fakhir stares at me. "Serena would not damage me."

"Oh, she would." Peyton warns. "Especially, if I grant her permission."

Fakhir stammers for a moment before he finally backs down. "Fine, I will let that thing in, if it puts the fireballs away. But if it tries to kill you in your sleep, do not blame me. I did my job in protecting my family, just as my coding requires." I put out the fireballs. Fakhir hesitates for just a moment before he snaps his fingers, allowing a door-size hole. I fly inside quickly, landing next to Peyton and Keon. Fakhir studies me for a moment, then vanishes.

"She is shrinking." Keon warns.

Peyton smiles, as my feathers ruffle in fear. "It is all right, Serena. Your size fits the situation." He reassures me, holding out his hand, without hesitation I fly up from the ground and land on it. He carefully examines my body. "The wounds she endured are really deep," Peyton remarks, "but they seem to be clotted. The bleeding has stopped, but it will take a while for these to heal completely." He moves his hand back to his shoulder and I jump onto it, rubbing my head against his cheek before looking at Keon and Alexis.

"We should get inside." Keon decides, turning to walk back into the house. He leads us through an entrance I have never seen before. Everything is so dark; I am surprised Keon and Alexis can even see. Eventually, they walk us back into the familiar areas of the house.

I start to feel sick, so I fly off of Peyton's shoulder and land on the carpet. Everyone turns to look at me. I pace on the carpet for a few moments, feeling out of sorts. When I feel a strange pain, I call out in raven, which turns to a small scream as I change into myself. I look up to see both Keon and Alexis, looking slightly less yellow than usual. Peyton offers his hand and I stand up, staggering as my knees get used to my weight. I find myself tripping over my dress and I land into Keon's arms. "I am sorry. I had to," I whisper hoarsely, tears in my eyes.

"I am not upset, Serena." he assures me. "Just tell me it worked. Tell me you are no longer divided."

"I am my own fiorriee, who is loyal to the Silviu family. Roarick will never have any sort of control again." I answer softly, holding my unpleasantly sore throat.

"Your own fiorriee?" Keon questions. "You feel *you* broke all your cords?"

"I am sorry." I apologize again. "It was the only way. If it helps, you have my willful submission and word that I will honor this family."

"You and Peyton have a lot in common." he replies, helping me to my feet.

Fakhir appears before me. "Serena?"

"Yes, silly, it is been me the whole time." I glare at him.

"Prytore Keon, this is difficult to process."

"Do not process it until I write a patch for your programming."

"Thank you." The computer smiles, looking more comfortable. It is so strange how at times, I can trick myself into thinking he is actually alive, and others I want to reset his stupid programming.

"In the meantime, Fakhir, emergency protocol Delta Password Forty-two Ninety-three." Suddenly, the house begins to shake as windows are covered by steel. Fakhir's attire changes. He is no longer in a butler-like suit. Instead, he is in military gear. "Prytore Keon, what is going on? Are you in danger or is Delta just a precaution? Why did you travel by… flight and land on my roof!" The computer looks around bewildered.

"Serena, just metamorphosed in front of Prince Roarick to break his hold on her. It got, heated."

"She is known to be emotional." Fakhir replies, as if I was always having a mental breakdown or something.

"Watch it, Wires." I warn, clearing my throat. Fakhir looks at me and back to Keon.

"Wires." Peyton repeats under his breath smiling.

"Roarick would not tolerate Serena's defiance to his power. She was either going to submit to him or die by his hand."

"I chose the latter option." I shrug, regretting all the screaming. I swallow hard, ignoring the uncomfortable pain. "Well, he was going to die not me; until Peyton stopped me."

"I could not let you live with that ghost," Peyton replies.

"I will not have you live with it either!" I snap at him.

"You may be a free fiorriee, but you are still my wife. Be careful with your tone."

"Your wife just restarted the war, Peyton!" Alexis states, a little too calmly. "Nowhere she goes will ever be truly safe."

"I am sorry," I reply feeling truly guilty, then suddenly feeling angry. "No, I am not." I stop myself looking for the right words. "Look at me!" I all but scream at her, but my voice gives out. She turns to me with surprise. I clear my throat and force a whisper. "Really look at me." She gives me a once over and it takes a moment before she registers my white dress is almost dyed completely purple with my blood. "He did this with only having half my mind. Can you imagine what fiorriee go through on a unwilful breaking? I cannot… you cannot expect me to… I will not stand by and let this continue. I will burn this planet to the ground first!"

"Serena." Peyton worries.

"One dark night, flying as a raven, perpetual flames. I could do it," I reply seriously.

"You would annihilate and entire species and hurt your own?" Peyton asks astonished, causing everyone to tense.

"No, but they do not know that." I reply firmly, hating it is only coming out in a forced whisper. "Do not make me feel guilty for this, Alexis. I will not stand for it."

Alexis stares at me for a long moment before she speaks. "There are things you do not know. Things you need to learn and quickly. I am not in any way attempting to make you feel guilty for this Serena, forgive me, my mind is in overdrive. You accelerated a timeline, and I am trying to think of how to make do and improvise with what resources we have." She pauses, then adds, "I know we do not know each other well. I know I might seem cold to you. But I am on your side. I promise that."

"How can I help?" I ask her.

"It has been a long day for all of us. We all need sleep." Keon answers.

"Sleep? You cannot be here." The house protests. "If the Prince is upset with Serena, and she managed to… to show immense power like that. They will surely kill her. You need to leave."

"There is nowhere else to go." Keon argues.

"That is not true, you can always go to Trorain." Fakhir offers.

"Not tonight. Everyone, retire to your rooms." Keon orders.

Peyton takes my hand and zips me straight to my room. He offers to help me out of my dress and into a shower. I happily accept, feeling gross. I step into the water so quickly that it is cold. I ignore it, rinsing my skin as best I can.

When I retrieve sleeping clothes, I am surprised to find my husband lying in my bed. We were, after all, told to return to our rooms. I raise an eyebrow at his smiling face. "Your breaking is over," he informs me. "This room is ours now." I respond by quickly joining him in bed, and he pulls me into him. I smile before falling asleep almost instantly.

Thirty-Six

Plans

Serena

When I wake, I moan. "You are staring at me again." I complain in a painful whisper, grabbing a pillow to hide my face.

"A habit you will get used to." Peyton laughs, yanking the pillow out of my hands and tossing it on the floor. "My raven." He smiles, kissing me while his hands trace our collar on my neck. "Even as a bird, this was present."

"My feathers," I recall, in a rough whisper.

Peyton frowns, "Your voice, my love."

"I am fine, please do not worry."

"You should take something." He replies, running his fingers down my cheek.

"I hate medicine," I complain. "If it gets too bad, I promise, I will, okay."

"My stubborn raven." He smiles, in a reluctant agreement.

"A raven with strange feathers." I silently giggle.

"I think that happened because you allow your collar in your hair. But I was not expecting your collar to turn into a crown, though the details on your beak make sense." He muses, touching my cheeks.

"It is a part of me."

"Yes." Peyton agrees. "My raven goddess, mine, no matter what form you are in." I moan happily, kissing him. We easily get lost in each other. His hands run down the veins of my collar delicately. "I am so proud of you, my love. You are finally free of your past." He takes my wrist and marks me, while my collar gives off a pleasant sensation. "I only have to share you with those I trust."

"I do not understand." Fakhir interrupts.

I grab Peyton's pillow and throw it at him, annoyed at the rude intrusion. "Get out, Wires!" I scream, regretting it immediately. The pillow, like my words, do not faze him. He simply stands there, waiting.

"What do you want?" Peyton asks, coldly.

"I have been told for many years that you are a god, yet you have never shown yourself to be anything but fiorriee. When asked, you told me that you do not have an aura. Are you really a god? Or are you a lower god and she is an upper goddess?" Fakhir asks.

"That is an interesting puzzle." Peyton replies. "Maybe I will answer it when you are not being rude! Now get out of here, Wires."

"That nickname does not offend me." Fakhir responds, raising his chin before he vanishes.

"Seriously?" I ask, grabbing the sheet and stomping to the bathroom. I turn on the shower and release my hair from last night's design, instantly regretting not bothering with it before I slept. It is nothing but knots now. "He needs to have his privacy parameters adjusted."

"I will speak to Keon about that first thing." Peyton agrees, taking my hairbrush and working it through my hair. He smiles, when he pulls out a feather. "Well, at least it is not too tangled."

"Could you imagine if I were wearing all my hair down?" I respond with wide eyes, fighting to keep my voice audible.

"I wonder if that would change your look or not." Peyton muses, kissing the top of my hair. "Your reflection is as beautiful as you are."

I turn my eyes to the mirror, half expecting there to be two of me, or at least a blurry version of myself, but that is not the case. It is simply my true image, reflecting back at me. I smile at myself.

"I am very proud of you," Peyton whispers in my ear, causing my collar to give pleasant sensations down to my toes again. His face twists into one of concern. "These are still healing." He traces a line where my skin was cut open by Roarick's words.

"It felt like lashes of burning fire." I explain, not helping to change my husband's facial expression. "They were deep, bone deep. It will take a while for them to fade into oblivion. But they will fade and neither of us will have to be reminded of them again."

"I look forward to that day." He smiles, kissing my cheek and stepping away, "Enjoy your shower."

"Where are you going?" I ask, regretting raising my voice, as only a raspy whisper comes out.

"To make sure Wires gives us privacy." Peyton responds, as he walks out of the room.

Not unhappy about that, I step into the shower. The water stings, causing me to hiss. My scars are much more tender than I realized. I refuse to dwell on them. Instead, I think about all the positive things that happened last night. My mind is healed, I am one again. I feel stronger than I have in years. I do not even have a headache this morning. The best part being that I am broken, and I am happy. I am warned by Fakhir about the hot water running cold, so I turn it off. When I get out and dress for the day. I am greeted by Fakhir's hologram form and gasp in surprise.

"What? I waited until you were proper." Fakhir notes, looking confused. "My program has been updated by Prytore Keon. Not only to accept that you can metamorphose into the strangest raven alive, but not to intrude on you, except under dire circumstances."

"You did not have that with Peyton already? Because I recall you intruding on him this morning." I complain, rubbing my sore throat.

"Before my update, I considered you a threat. Peyton was in a dire circumstance." Fakhir defends his actions.

"I am not a threat to you or this family," I reply sternly.

"As I just said, Prytore Keon has fixed my programming. Now, I trust that you are not." Fakhir agrees. "They are waiting for you in the dining room."

"Great, breakfast." I complain, walking out and joining my family.

"Serena. It is good to see you this morning." Keon greets me. "You must be famished after yesterday's events. Eat." I smile politely, sitting next to a prepared plate that is next to Peyton. I do not say anything as I begin to eat, surprised at how hungry I really am. "We were just discussing the dynamics of our family." Keon notes, after my plate is nearly gone, despite the unpleasant pain I had to endure to swallow my food. "Now that you have committed fully to this family, your breaking is complete. However, due to the volatile actions that were required to achieve this, we feel it is necessary to reinforce your place with us." I finish my last few bites, and stare at him while I slowly drink some water. "You need to understand, where everyone fits in."

"I believe I already have an understanding," I reply, in a rough guarded voice.

"Serena, your voice has gotten worse." Alexis worries. "You should take something."

"I will be alright with a little rest. I would prefer not to deal with needles if you are okay with a natural healing."

"I know fiorriees heal quickly, Serena, but you are talking weeks, not hours." She points out.

"I am aware," I frown. "I have screamed like this before." The room falls into an awkward silence. After a while, I become impatient and bring my attention back to Keon. "You were stating something about our family hierarchy?"

"Yes." Keon answers, clearing his throat, "I believe reinforcement is in order. Now that you have embraced your truest self."

My eyes harden. "You need not feel threatened, Prytore Keon."

"Perhaps. Your words are reassuring, Serena, but your actions, such as your small defiance in the route that you took us home last night, prove you do not have a full understanding of our expectations. Now that your cords are severed, I can only ask for your full willingness to trust me, even if you disagree."

"I am not allowed to protest?"

"I am not cruel, Serena. I accept suggestions and consider your feelings in all matters, assuming you present them properly, but I will not tolerate defiance." Keon answers firmly.

I turn to Peyton, grabbing the back of his neck. He looks directly into my eyes, and we are in a now familiar ballroom. "Is he joking? Why do you stand for this? You are a god!"

"Serena." Peyton replies patiently.

"No!" I scream at him. "Tell him, tell him who you are! Who we are! That he has no power over us!" I go to turn my head but Peyton refuses to let me leave.

"Calm for me, my love." Peyton whispers. "You are forgetting where we are. How dangerous it is." I scuff at him. "I know it is hard, Serena, so I will not ask you to submit to him."

"Thank you," I whisper in relief.

"I am ordering you too."

"Peyton!" I protest.

"You must trust me. It is not time to reveal who I am. Even on Trorain that is dangerous. The time will come, but that is not today. Remember, we are always being watched. Fakhir is loyal to us, but if he is ever hacked. I am sorry, Serena, but this is the way it is. You will submit to our Prytores." He breaks our connection before I could argue any further. My collar gives me a short unpleasant sensation in warning.

"I trust your privacy has helped her accept her fate." Keon glares at Peyton, warning in his voice.

"It has." Peyton answers, taking a bite of his food.

"Good, never do that in the middle of our conversation again. Either of you." Keon orders, coldly.

"Unless we grant permission." Alexis amends, touching Keon's hand. Keon glares at her but does not respond.

I sit quietly, waiting for the rest to finish their meal while my thoughts spin out of control. I am one of the strongest amongst my kind, bested only by my husband. Yet I cannot embrace my true calling, because even now I am suppressed. The part that hurts is that it is not my choice. Peyton is not giving me time to accept this on my own. He is simply demanding it of me. I know he is doing it to protect us, but I still do not like it. Tears flood my eyes and I start to shake. Peyton takes his hand in mine, but he does nothing more to comfort me. I can feel Alexis studying me, but I do not look at her.

"Serena." Keon states, finishing his food.

"My Prytore?" I ask, unable to keep the tears from spilling. "You are a good girl. We are proud of you. We care for you and want to keep you safe." Keon tries to reassure me. I nod, as I fight the shaking and wipe away my traitor tears.

"Well, now that we are finished with this, I think it is time to share our plan." Alexis decides, getting up from the table. I happily follow her lead, standing up from the table myself while I drop Peyton's hand. I can feel him look at me, but I ignore his stare, he may have power over me, but I do not have to accept all his decisions with a smile on my face. He allows my silent tantrum, standing from the table himself. I walk over to Alexis, annoyed with both Keon and Peyton at this point. She says nothing as she wraps her arms around my waist in comfort, leading us out of the room into the hallway. She takes us to her favorite part of the house, unlocking doors and going through shortcuts I have never seen before.

"What is the plan?" I ask her hoarsely, knowing we cannot stay here much longer.

"We are going to Trorain." Alexis answers me as we enter a familiar part of the house. We are close to where she was researching my perpetual flame ability.

"Trorain?" I question, in a broken whisper. I had heard Fakhir suggest it last night, but I thought he was being facetious, as he sometimes can be.

"She will not be safe there either." Peyton complains.

"Then where are we to go? Furgan? Zarla?" Alexis snaps at him. "Be practical Peyton, we cannot stay on Artthemis, Trorain is our best solution."

"They will expect that. Artthemis is a big planet, we can hide here. We just need to get out of the city."

"That is more impossible than getting to Trorain!" Alexis argues. "Not to mention stupid!"

"Hey!" I defend my husband, wincing for the effort.

"Serena, like it or not, you woke this slumbering war. Do you really want to cower and hide while fiorriee fight in your deliberate absence?"

I turn to my husband and force my voice to work above a whisper. "She has got a point, Peyton. I started this. We cannot run."

"I do not like it."

"I know, but it is our destiny." I answer him, then clear my throat.

"For any of this to work, I need you on board Peyton. We do not have time for you to be distracted with Serena's safety. After all, she has made it very clear that she can take care of herself." Alexis turns away from us and keeps walking down the halls of her many labs. "As we have implied to you, Serena, Trorain is indeed habitable," she continues explaining, while she starts to unlock more doors, "but you cannot stay on the surface for too long." She makes it to a lab door she wants and unlocks it. When it opens, I gasp. It is like we walked right into Trorain, but it is nothing like I remember. "This is your world today." She presses a few buttons on a keyboard. "You see that smoke?" I nod. "That is a fake volcano Prytores engineered, it is the reason your atmosphere is toxic. If we can shut it down, then going home is an option for your kind."

"You make it sound so simple." I reply with a cracking voice.

"It is not." she frowns. "It is nuclear. With so many fail safes that if you enter the wrong code anywhere, it will destroy the moon all together."

"Can you get around them?" I ask, regretting this conversation more and more.

"No." she answers, staring at it. "Well, at least I did not think so, until I seen what you can do." I raise an eyebrow to that. "You are a goddess, Serena; you own the wind."

"No." I frown, walking out of the room.

"Serena." She calls after me.

I turn to her. "You want me to risk destroying my entire world from existence!" I hiss with a cracking voice. "Possibly this one too! You have lost your scientific mind!" I reply, walking away again.

"Serena, stop!" Alexis calls. When I realize I am unable to deny the command, I curse her and Peyton under my breath. "Please."

"What!" I shout at her in a strained whisper. At this point, Keon and Peyton are next to her.

"Please do not make up your mind until you hear all the facts." She answers, "Serena, you were not destined to simply restart this war, you are destined to finish it. We are on your side. Please, let us help you."

"We will not ask you to do anything you do not want to do." Keon assures me, backing up Alexis. "Except treat us with the respect we deserve." He adds with a tone of warning, obviously not liking the way I am speaking to Alexis.

"I trust them, Serena." Peyton adds.

I meet my husband's eyes, studying him for a very long time before I speak. "I will save Trorain, but I will not do it by destroying it," I reply sternly, grabbing my throat. "In case it has gone unnoticed, I cannot help much. I can destroy a world all on my own, but I do not have any special power to save one."

"You are wrong, let me show you why." Alexis smiles, stepping to the side, inviting me back into the lab. Annoyed, I walk back in.

She enters behind me and shows me the nuclear plant again. "I can get access which will get us through the shield. But that is not the problem. The problem is the control center is overly reinforced that not much can get through it without the proper codes. Which are very difficult to come by. But you have the ability to produce perpetual flame. You can melt straight through."

"That would melt the entire place." I argue in a whisper.

"Not if you have a lot of salt with you." She argues. "It is more than possible, Serena, and it is what the resistance has needed in order to win. Why do you think I have been so fascinated with your ability? It is because no hybrids and very few fiorriee can do it. In this era, you are the only one I know that can."

"So, is it magic or something?" I ask in a strain, knowing Peyton answered this once, but they are unaware of that, and I want to keep it that way.

"Magic?" She gives a small laugh. "No, Serena, even with your species amazing abilities, there is a scientific explanation. Though to a non-scientist, magic seems acceptable. In this instance, your body actually has physical components that create it. In lamest terms, you literally sweat the fire from the glands in your hands."

"That is weird." I whisper, then clear my throat again.

"Well, you could not be perfect, that would make you a dream." Peyton replies, with a smile.

I smile at him then stare at the hologram. My mind is racing at the idea of going home, much less making my world habitable for my kind again. "There is only one of these?"

"No, there are two. But one proved to be enough, so the second was never completely finished. It is on the other side of the moon." She answers.

"Both sides?" I ask, forcing myself to whisper, "I did not realize the dark side of Trorain was habitable before the war, why even bother?"

"You have your moons mixed up. Like Artthemis, survival is possible on all land surfaces of Trorain. Zarla is tidal locked to Artthemis. Trorain and Furgan are not. Well, Furgan is slowing down and in a few hundred years it will share the fate of Zarla, but until then, it is considered to have a natural spin."

"What is tidal locking?" I ask, wincing.

"It is synchronized rotation. Zarla rotates at the same pace it orbits Artthemis." Alexis explains patiently. "It's rotation is so slow that it takes an entire cycle around this planet for it to spin once. Which averages out to about forty-two days. Which is why Zarla appears to be standing still."

"But Trorain spins faster than that?" I cough.

"Yes." Alexis notes. "Faster than Artthemis actually. It causes a stronger gravitational pull and if you are not prepared for it, it can make you very sick. You cannot just go to Trorain from here, you have to go through a pressurization system in order to survive the journey."

"And we have one at our disposal?" I question with a breaking voice.

"Of course." Alexis shrugs. "But it is not easily accessible. Especially for someone in hiding. And until we can solve problems like these, along with necessities such as inoculations, food, water, shelter, clothes, etc. We are stuck here."

"How long?" Keon asks.

"A week, maybe two." Alexis answers.

"We do not have that kind of time." Keon stresses.

"I know, which is why I am already in contact with the resistance. They can speed things up, but I cannot guess by how much."

"If we do this, we must destroy both volcanoes, not just the active one." I whisper, painfully. "We will have to strike the active first, but we cannot delay in attacking the back up."

"That is going to require reinforcements." Peyton notes.

"Yes. Not to mention once they are destroyed, we have the task of kicking the Prytores off of Trorain and bringing the fiorriee on Artthemis home. And that is going to require politics." Keon adds.

"I am not concerned with the politics, that is Zane's and Roald's specialty." Peyton notes taking my hand and kissing my wrist. I gasp at his taste, and I stare into his eyes. We are suddenly alone, but not in a ballroom.

"Where are we?" I ask, looking around.

"You are in my soul." He smiles. "This is a favorite place of mine from Trorain."

"How?"

"I connected my soul to Keon and asked him when you were not paying attention." He explains. "He allowed it because he wants you to be reminded that your temper should not be displayed so flamboyantly."

"I mean no disrespect." I frown.

"I know."

"So why have you brought me here?"

"Because you need to understand the risk of going back to Trorain. We have enemies there, Serena. Enemies you have never met. Even those who will prove loyal to us will need you to prove yourself. Your ability to create perpetual flame is terrifyingly impressive, and the fact you can manifest your aura in its true form, gives you a demanded respect. But it will not be enough. Even stopping the volcano will not be. The Prytores can simply build another. Fiorriee do not need a scientific solution, they need a leader, one who is also a skilled warrior. One who can not only stop our world from being destroyed but protect it from ever happening again."

"They need you," I whisper.

"I alone am not enough, Serena. They need both of us and we need the others. But even with them at our side we must correct your disadvantages, for you are not a skilled warrior. Nor do you understand a lot about fiorriee."

"Ouch." I frown, not liking his reality check.

"Fiorriee can help you," he whispers. "Including your aunt."

"How?"

"They can share their memories." I give him a look of confusion. "You and Keon experienced something similar. What I am referring to though, is slightly different. You will gain the knowledge, but you will find yourself experiencing their memories from their point of view."

"Okay. But my aunt and other fiorriee? What about you?"

"No, not me. I am sorry." He frowns. "I cannot."

"Peyton, Serena." Suddenly, we are back in the room with Alexis and Keon. Alexis is giving Peyton an irritated look. "Keon just ordered the both of you not to do that during a conversation!" Peyton does not look remorseful for stealing my attention away from her. "That will not go uncorrected." She warns him, turning back to me. "Do we move forward with this plan then?" she asks, and by her tone, I can tell it was not the first time she asked the question.

I turn to Keon. "You have been oddly quiet."

"I wanted you to hear her out." Keon explains.

"But?" I challenge, wishing it did not hurt to speak.

"I am concerned about the consequences of last night. Not only here on Artthemis but on Trorain. Stepping onto the throne when no one knows you, no one trusts you, and no one has trained you. Goddess or not, it is a death sentence."

"You and Peyton have very like minds." I smile at him then strain my voice yet again. "It seems we need to get my aunt here as she is the closest thing there is to an experience fiorriee leader."

"Takira Gelsomino is not just an experienced leader, Serena. She is the most renowned fiorriee warrior in our modern history. She single-handedly won more battles than most men fiorriee warriors put together." I look at Peyton in astonishment. "You really need to brush up on your history."

"I will work on both contacting her and putting something together for Serena." Fakhir chimes in.

"Thank you, Fakhir." I smile, losing my voice again. Knowing I am going to regret overusing it.

"Getting Takira here is not going to be as easy as it sounds." Alexis worries. "We are on lock down for a reason."

"Speaking of that, is there a way I can get that healing elixir again?" I ask, wincing. "The one that healed my stomach and my bones. Roarick seems to have cut pretty deep, and I am not healing as quickly as I would like." I roll my shoulders and whimper. "And since I am already getting poked, maybe something for my throat and vocal cords?"

"How deep?" Keon asks as both him and Peyton rush to my side. Peyton lifts my shirt. I hiss as the fabric is peeled off my healing skin.

"Bone deep." I answer. "We all know this kind of trauma takes time." I remind the room in an embarrassed whisper, as Alexis joins the observation. "I thought it was healing. I feel better than I did. Normally I would not complain but it is extremely unpleasant."

"Why did you not say something earlier?" Keon scowls.

"We have been distracted." I shrug with a cracking voice. "Besides, Peyton seen it this morning, neither of us seen any danger."

"I am sorry, I should have said something." Peyton apologizes. "She is healing slower than normal, but I did not think anything of it after she described it as fire lashes.

Alexis frowns walking over to a different part of her lab and starts to press buttons. "I think it is best if you sleep while these help you heal."

"Thank you." I smile, injecting myself. I look at them all, then whisper. "I know you all care but is it possible that I have a few moments to myself?" Everyone frowns. "Please?"

"Of course, Serena." Keon agrees for the room.

I give a quick thank you and dash out before they change their minds. The only person even capable of catching me is Peyton. I hope he understands that I simply just need some time to catch up with my own thoughts. Verifying that I am alone, I finish taking off my clothes and stare at the blood. My soul hurts from the memory of this. Is reliving it really a good idea? I ask myself, prying my mind away from my thoughts, I head to the shower. I know I had already taken one today, but I hate the feeling of dried blood on my skin. I hiss when the water hits my back. The cuts are worse than I thought. Will Roarick's memory ever get buried into my past? I slowly and carefully clean my body and my hair. When the temperature of the shower is no longer pleasant, I step out, grabbing a towel. I am startled at the sight of my own reflection, still not used to it. There I am, just me. I wave at myself and it instantly waves back. No strange facial expressions, no unusual clothes. It truly is a reflection of myself. "Will you always just be me? Or will you give me attitude to?" I question aloud, staring at it for a bit longer, but there is no reply. "Strange." I mutter then frown at myself for that observation; is it strange that I am missing a defiant reflection, or strange that reflections are defiant? While pondering that, I walk into my room only to jump about ten feet high when I see Peyton in the garden.

"I am sorry. I was on my way to the library, but the garden distracted me." Peyton explains.

"It is all right, husband."

"Are you all right, my wife?" he asks, pain in his eyes. "We have never taken a moment to talk about how you feel after last night."

I smile at him, answering in a strained whisper with what little breaking voice I have left. "I managed to get out alive and in one piece. Not to mention, I got what I wanted." He nods and looks away. I take his hand. "I know that had to be hard on you. You had to be fighting every instinct you own to let that happen right in front of you so I could make my own choice. I am keenly aware you could have stopped it. At one point, I was angry that you were not." His head snaps to meet my eyes, his full of hurt. "But I understood why." I continue, touching his face tenderly. "You wanted me free and happy, and I could not be more grateful. Thank you for letting me fight for this on my own." My collar warms me at my words. Peyton takes me in his arms and kisses me so passionately I forget to breathe. He allows me to come up for air only to make me breathless again. I cannot tell you how long it lasts, I stopped trying to care about the passage of time.

When I pull away, I realize that we are no longer in the garden, we are back in his soul. "Peyton," I whisper.

"My wife," he whispers back, before leaving me breathless once again. Then he pulls away and pulls me to him. "Keon and Alexis experienced a similar struggle. But they knew if they had stopped it, you would have simply been their slave, and your willful submission would have been gone."

"I did not want to break the binds Keon had given me." I frown. "I regret that."

"You should not." he smiles, kissing my palm. "Keon's breaking would have never stopped until you chose to do exactly that. It took me a long time to figure that out. It is why I trust them so much. They never wanted to be able to control us like puppets. They want us to willfully obey. Which is exactly how it is on Trorain. Or it was, before the Prytores figured out how to abuse our nature and make us slaves to it."

"Then why are you enslaving me?" I demand, still truly hurt from this morning.

"Enslave you?" he questions. "Serena, I would never…"

"But you did," I whisper, tears spilling from my cheeks.

"That was not my intention."

"You ordered me to submit to them, Peyton. What could possibly be your intention if it was not blinded slavery?"

"We do not have time for you to accept your fate on your own. You need to trust them as I do. I am simply trying to help you."

"You took away my choice."

"I am sorry."

"If you mean that, then you will trust that I will want to please you and choose them on my own."

He pulls me into his arms. "I am scared, Serena. They are our best allies in all of this. I do trust you. And I am officially asking you, not ordering you, to trust them, because you love me."

"I will, I promise," I whisper.

"Forgive me?" He asks. I nod. He kisses the top of my head. "Thank you, my love." He holds me close for a moment more, and the garden returns to us.

"There is so much I do not understand," I whisper in a cracked voice, keeping him closer still. "My aunt kept it away from me. I guess she figured since we were on Artthemis, it was best if I did not long for Trorain all the time."

"You know my opinion on the subject." He replies dryly.

"You are right." I answer. "And between you and that library right over there, I am sure I can learn a lot. Will you teach me?"

"Happy to." Peyton smiles walking into the library. I watch him go to the shelves. He pulls out book after book and sets them on a table. After a while I frown. "I was hoping we could do this in an afternoon or two. Not in a lifetime."

"Oh we can, most of this is redundant." Peyton smiles. "I was just pulling the titles, so I knew which ones I wanted Fakhir to download and summarize for us."

Fakhir appears so close to Peyton, even I jump back startled. "Do you need something Peyton?" Fakhir asks, pretending not to notice its error.

Peyton reacts violently to the hologram and falls right through it. "You are lucky you are a machine. What is the meaning of your rudeness?"

"I have been working on helping Serena with Trorain history for the past few hours, if you do not recall. And now that my play is finished, you want to make suggestions?"

"I am trying to be thorough. I know you, Wires; some of these you would have considered irrelevant."

Fakhir pretends to look over at the titles and looks back at Peyton. "They are."

"I will be the judge of that. She is my wife; this is our world!" Peyton snaps angrily. Fakhir disappears, leaving Peyton so upset he knocks the books to the ground. "Show yourself!" he screams at the house.

"Peyton," I whisper, but he does not seem to hear me. I gently and cautiously take his arm. "Peyton." I say a little louder. He snarls, but the moment he realizes it is me, he relaxes. "Let me try?" I offer. His eyes harden as he violently gestures his permission with his free arm. I realize immediately I am in the middle of a fight I did not witness Peyton and Fakhir start.

"Fakhir." I call. "Fakhir, please, reveal yourself. I promise, Peyton will not yell or try to walk through you." The computer gives a disapproving noise one might perceive as a grunt. "I will sit politely through a classic play." I bargain with the thing. The computer shows itself immediately. Causing me to frown. I was half hoping that would not work.

"Do you require something, Serena?"

"I am just curious. Why do you feel these titles are irrelevant?" I ask, surprised at how normal my voice sounds. The medicine is finally starting to work.

"Because Peyton has a firsthand count in his memory, and it is better if he simply shows you himself." Fakhir answers, turning away from us.

I turn to Peyton. "She does not need a first-person account. She needs the facts."

"What better way than a primary source?" I ask confused, grabbing my still sore throat. "

"Exactly." Fakhir agrees.

"Oh, is it because of your memory loss?"

"That is part of it." Peyton admits.

"A small inconvenience." Fakhir dismisses. "He remembers more than he lets on."

I raise an eyebrow at my husband. "I am confused."

"I am annoyed." Fakhir mutters.

"I will not lie to you, Serena. I do remember things. But not everything."

"Okay, so why are you resisting showing me what you do know?"

"Good question, Serena. Bravo." Fakhir applauds with mockery.

"Serena, you do not understand what you are asking." Peyton frowns, glaring at Fakhir.

"She can handle it." Fakhir argues.

"I said no," Peyton replies coldly.

"Fine," Fakhir replies, disappearing again.

"Handle what?" I ask. Peyton stares at me angrily, crossing his arms over his chest. "Zarla, Peyton, handle what!" I demand, reaching for him and causing him to jump away from my flaming grip. I realize my mistake immediately and put out the flames. I look to him in a panic. "That should not have happened. It is forbidden by our Prytore's," I whisper in shock. "I am sorry. I did not mean to." I apologize, then my mind catches up with the events at hand as I stare at his arm, "Why are you not burning?"

"I do not know," he answers, studying his own skin. "Make a fireball."

"Peyton, I am not sure I can, much less want to."

"You can, you chose yourself during your breaking. Your hierarchy is not Keon and Alexis than me anymore. It is me, and I have asked you to submit to them. Therefore, I trump them. I rarely go against their orders. But this is an exception. Do not worry, I will pay the consequences of this, not you." I frown at him. "If you want me to answer your question then do this for me," he replies patiently. Reluctantly, I hold up a fireball. He cautiously brings his hand above the flame. "It is not hot or cold." He gets closer and my eyes widen. "It is okay, Serena. Do not move." He assures me. Before I could stop him, he puts his hand directly into the flame. I scream out and close my palm causing the fire to disappear but again, he is not burning.

Fakhir appears staring at us. "That should not be possible."

"You are telling me." Peyton frowns. "Go on then, Wires. You may leave us and inform Alexis; she will want to know."

We are alone almost instantly. "Must he disappear to reveal himself to someone else?"

"No, but when he does manifest in more than one place, it can cross his wires. He can compute a lot of things at once but that is the computer component. The Prytore component limits his ability on keeping more than two conversations going at one time without mistakes."

"I am getting tired. I think that medicine is kicking in." I warn him, yawning.

"It is about time. I was getting concerned that Alexis did not put enough sleeping elixir in it." Peyton smiles.

"Nope, not yet. I want an answer, Peyton."

"If I were to share my memory with you directly, you will find things you cannot unsee. Things that even I, to this day, have a hard time living with. I do not want that burden for you. That is why I was in the garden. I was asking Fakhir a way around sharing the gory details with you."

"You cannot protect me like that forever, Peyton. Going to Trorain, I am going to be having similar memories."

"You only need to burden yourself with your own, Serena. I will not share my ghosts and nightmares with you."

"So how are you going to help me?" I frown. "Through books?"

"Fakhir had suggested I download my memories into him and he can filter it out." Peyton frowns. "But it feels…invasive. The handful of beings I want in my head, have flesh."

"You are afraid he will get hacked."

"Yes."

"Can you censor what he sees?"

"I could but then you would not learn what you need to know." Peyton replies a little too sharply.

"Can we do it with a closed system and old technology? That would make it hard to hack and easily destroyable once I have viewed it."

"You would not view it, Serena. It would be placed in your mind. It would become a part of who you are."

Before I could respond to that, Alexis and Keon are standing in the library. "Show me!" Alexis demands, in complete disbelief. I look to Peyton with concern, but he gives a nod of approval. Shrugging, I open my hand and hold a fireball. Peyton places his hand straight through it several times with no effect. "That is not possible. I thought Fakhir was malfunctioning." She frowns coming near me. Instinctively, I close my hand. "I am sorry, Serena. I should have warned you." She smiles. "Please, I promise I will not do myself harm."

"You do not respect how dangerous this is," I reply impatiently. Her eyes meet mine and she holds me there for a long moment, only to break away in frustration. "I wonder, will you deny Keon access to your mind, body and soul, now too?" She turns her attention to Peyton. "I thought you said she would submit to us."

"I have asked her to." Peyton answers patiently. "But I will not force her."

I appreciate him defending me, though I can hear his irritation matching hers. "I mean no disrespect. I am trying to keep you safe," I defend myself. "I do not understand how this does not hurt Peyton. I am only glad it does not. What I did to him was an accident. Prytoree Alexis, please, I am not in full control of this. If I were, it would have never happened. I am willfully submitting to you, and you have mostly forbidden it. Please, I do not want you close. I would never forgive myself if I were to harm you."

"I accept full risk. Now please, Serena, cooperate with me!" Alexis snaps.

I turn to Keon for help. He raises an eyebrow at me before he walks up to me. His hand falls to the stray hair on my face and he moves it away. "It is natural to be scared, but Alexis is not being foolish."

"Can you promise that?" I challenge. "You have known her longer than me. She seems…edgy, nothing like she was in the lab. I am not trying to make it worse, but I will not risk her life." Keon looks to Alexis, who glares at him before she plops herself down in an oversize chair.

Keon looks at me and tilts his head, encouraging me to go to her. I frown, as I step away from him and squeeze next to her on the chair. "You are scared." I accuse. "You fear something has happened to Peyton."

"I ran tests on Peyton after his alteration. He is pure fiorriee. But fiorriee are not resistant to perpetual flame. If they were, Dex…" She stops herself. "Serena, please. I need to understand. Is this happening because you changed or because he did? I can only tell that if you trust me."

"Can we not just go to your lab and analyze me some more?"

"We could, but that would take ages." She answers unhappily.

I look to Keon who once again nods at me. I frown, reluctantly holding out my hand in front of her, staring at the blue fireball in it. "I do not feel a change. I do not want you to touch it."

Alexis puts her hand above it for a short moment and brings it back to her side. I close my palm and glare at her, yanking her curious hand off her lap and staring at her blistered palm. "I am fine." She rushes.

"I meant what I said, I did not want to hurt you!" I snap angrily.

"I said, I am fine." Alexis repeats. "Serena, it will not scar, I promise."

She does not give me a chance to respond to that. She simply gets up and leaves the room. I glare at Keon, who defends his wife. "She can be confusing at times, but her heart is in the right place."

"Peyton, please go after her. She is not going to relax until she understands scientifically what is happening."

Peyton kneels before me. "I do appreciate you understanding why I must go." He kisses my wrist, leaving a small amount of his taste then exits to find her.

"You are still okay with sharing him with her? Even now that you have a full understanding of his submission to her?" Keon asks, keeping the distance between us.

"Nothing has changed," I reply, standing and walking up to him. "Not a single thing."

"That is not true. You are broken now," he whispers, gently touching my healing back. "Not the way it should have been done, but it is over now."

"Is it?" I ask, wrapping my arms around him. "Because something does not feel right."

"What do you mean?" he asks, his face turning concerned.

"As you know, I do not feel the bindings that were tethered to us." I answer honestly. He gives a gentle smile as he moves my stubborn hair from my face. I meet his eyes. "Keon," I whisper, "I want them back."

His hand tangles in my hair and he is kissing me so intently. I pull away from him smiling. "Does this mean you are ready?"

"It means I am pleased," he answers. "So very, very pleased." I frown at that; it was not the answer I wanted. "I thought he was going to kill you." Keon whispers suddenly.

I look up and see the fear on his features. I gently hold his face in my hands. "You, Peyton, and Alexis gave me what I needed to fight. I would not have been able to resist him. I am forever in your debt."

He pulls away from me, then takes my hand and leads us to my room. He sits down on the couch, and I sit down next to him. "You owe me nothing, Serena." I do not respond to him. "As for the tethering cords, I think they are where they belong. Broken and in the past."

"Peyton owns me." I argue, in my strained voice. "His cords did not get snapped."

"Peyton owned you the moment your head hit the ground at his feet." Keon replies. "He is your own kind, Serena; those natural bindings between you are not meant to snap."

"And ours are?"

"You would have not been broken without snapping each and every one I gave you," he whispers. "You needed to understand the control I could have. To respect it. To desire it even without the cords. Which is what you are doing. This is natural. Though I believe you are missing them more passionately than you should because they snapped violently without you fully grasping what you were taking control of."

"My choices. Each and every choice I make. That is what I have taken. What most my kind cannot figure out how to claim." I sigh. "I understand it all too well, Keon. What I am telling you is I do not want it."

"You are a queen, Serena. Like it or not, you must be the purest example of your kind. You must be in full control of yourself."

Tears fill my eyes. "I do not believe that. I believe my kind will know the difference between willful and forced surrender. Please Keon, why will you not give them back?"

He gently cradles my arm and traces the slow to heal lashes on my skin. "You worry so much about others. Was it not you, not moments ago, giving Alexis fits about danger? Look at what you are asking of me Serena." He presses firmly on my skin, causing an unpleasant sensation. "These are not all from Roarick's bindings breaking. They are from mine too. Did you not feel it? Mine were the first to release you because I let you go. I know I promised you I would fight, but Roarick was killing you. I had no choice." Understanding filters through me. My mind flashes back to the experience. I felt much less weighted down after the initial snapping, but I was still bound. "I was a part of this." Keon frowns, staring at my healing wounds.

"You let me go," I whisper, shaking my head. "You did not do this Keon, I did." He raises an eyebrow. "You let go, but I was holding onto you like a life raft. Had I not wanted to keep you, the tension from the recoil of the release would not have happened."

"Serena." He argues gently.

"Please," I whisper. "Give them back, my Prytore, I beg you."

"Not tonight." He answers, pulling me close to him, wrapping his arms around me. "You need rest now. Your body needs to heal." Too heartbroken to argue at yet another rejection, I keep silent, fruitlessly trying not to cry. He feels a tear fall on his hand. "Would you prefer I go?" he asks kindly.

That was the last thing on Artthemis that I wanted. "No, I do not want to be alone." I whisper, so softly it is barely audible.

"All right, close your eyes and stop fighting the drugs. Heal for me, my beautiful fiorriee." I close my eyes, and soon after I find myself dreaming of flying.

Thirty-Seven

Royal Revenge

Serena

We are awakened on the couch by Fakhir flickering before us. "Prytore Keon." I open my eyes and sit up. Fakhir is there for a moment but then gone again. "My system."

"Fakhir?" Keon asks, concerned.

"Breached." The computer manages.

"Breached?" I question, suddenly wide awake.

"Override." Fakhir flashes. "Prytore, help." The computer cries and then he is gone.

"Not good." Keon frowns, turning to me and staring into my eyes. I feel a cord fall between us and I gasp when I realize we are dancing. "There is not much time, the house is turning against us. Soon it will be like the castle. You must find my lab; it is across from Alexis'. If you have to break in, do it. There you will find a flesh chip; I need you to touch it." Images flash before me. Force the override code in our secure computer. The code is…"

We are no longer dancing. Fakhir is standing before us. He is no longer dressed in military clothes. He is dressed like a castle guard. Keon pulls me into him. "Our King awaits your presence in the main hall, immediately."

"Fakhir?" I ask stunned, in a normal voice.

"Long live King Maleko." The computer replies then disappears.

"What do we do?"

"We cannot keep the King waiting," Keon replies, taking my hand and leading me to the main hall.

My blood runs cold the moment I walk into the room. Maleko is not the only one there. Roarick is with him, and so are a lot of guards I do not know. I do my best not to look phased by this, but I am not sure how successful I am. Peyton and Alexis join us quickly after, he must have carried her to achieve that feat.

"Your Majesty." Keon bows. "How may I be of service today?"

"There is a nasty rumor that your male fiorriee has somehow managed to reject my Prytore DNA. Is this true?" Maleko asks.

"That seems to be the unfortunate side effect of Peyton's torture." Keon replies. "Have you come to tell me you found the one's responsible?"

"No, but I have suspicion that the traitor is in this room." Maleko replies. "Computer. Please tell me Serena Gelsomino's whereabouts during the duration of poor Prytoree Alexis misfortunate kidnapping."

Fakhir appears before us. He bows at the king, then Roarick, then stands tall. I look away from him. I hate what has been done to him. "According to my untampered records, Serena was in this house or on the grounds of this property the entire time."

"Interesting." Maleko notes. "It seems, Prince Roarick, that your theory could be wrong."

"She is responsible somehow, Father. I know it." Roarick responds coldly, causing me to raise my chin in pride.

"What was she doing on these grounds during that time, computer?" Maleko asks. "Did she have any communication to the outside world?"

"No, she was being broken. Her only communication was with Prytore Keon." I hold my breath, that is a lie. I also spoke with my aunt. Is Fakhir faking? "She did inquire about Peyton's whereabouts," he continues, "but she showed no sign of knowledge of who kidnapped her husband or why."

"Was she upset about it?" Roarick challenges.

Fakhir looks at me. "This fiorriee is too emotional about everything. I cannot answer that properly. She is too volatile." I resist a smile. Fakhir's attire may be different, but the virus clearly has not overtaken him.

"Convenient," Roarick mutters.

"Come now, Roarick, it is just a machine, after all," Maleko replies. "Computer, did Prytore Keon access anything that revealed his knowledge of what was happening to his fiorriee?"

"He sent some encrypted files from his business, but it will take time to break the cypher." Fakhir answers.

The King smiles. "Arrest them, but leave the female fiorriee, she seems to be innocent of this crime."

"What?" Alexis asks, astonished. "On what charge?" she demands, unsuccessfully trying to fight off the guards.

"Treason." Maleko answers, causing me to slightly shake. It takes effort to stay calm.

"Treason?" she questions insulted, while the guards take Keon and Peyton into custody.

"Serena may be innocent of this crime, but Father, she attacked me." Roarick argues, moving closer to Maleko's side.

"The girl was merely breaking your control over her, Roarick. There is no law against that. And according to your testimony she could have killed you, but she chose not to." Maleko replies, keeping his eyes on me.

"There should be a law Father, make one. She embarrassed me!"

"You are embarrassing yourself!" The King replies impatiently, walking away from his son and approaching me. "It is a shame though; you and my son would have made a great match."

"I chose my loyalty," I reply, calmly.

"Yes, and as you proved with my fiorriee, Zane, you chose not to stand with me. Shame that you would rather keep us enemies. Having you with my son or Zane would have done so well for peace between our worlds."

"I never said we were enemies. I simply have my pride in not choosing to serve you directly. The Silviu's are more than loyal to you as a king, they are your family." Maleko raises an eyebrow to that, seeming surprised that I have learned this knowledge. "And I am loyal to them."

"You are a very good speaker, Serena Gelsomino, naive, and blinded in your facts, but you portray them well." I lift my head pridefully. "Prince and Princess Silvu are being arrested and tried for treason. Make no mistake, their titles and bloodlines cannot save them from this crime." I swallow loudly. "Nor can they protect Peyton, as he has insulted me greatly by rejecting the gift of Prytore blood."

"My husband was kidnapped!" I defend. "What was done to him was not his fault!"

"I would be very careful challenging me. After all, you were seen talking to a known traitor at your courting. Even eating smuggled pie!" he replies coldly. "The only reason I am not charging you for that is because of your genuine reaction to rejecting him. Had he been a friend, even you would not have been able to cause such a severe and horrid rash! Therefore, I am accepting your innocents to all charges, but I suggest you do not push me."

"And once you discover they are not lying?" I ask, trying desperately to grab at any straw.

"If we cannot find anything, we will release them soon enough."

"Thank you."

"Thank you what?" Maleko seethes in distaste. "I bare a title, Serena, one that actually has meaning, unlike yours."

"Thank you, Your Majesty," I reply, bowing politely.

"My son tells me that you can produce fire in your hands, is this true?"

"I can, but my husband has forbidden it." I answer carefully.

"Good, because I am making it illegal. Along with the manifestation of your aura. Break either of these creeds and I will kill you myself."

"I understand, Your Majesty." I bow again.

"I do hope you challenge me on it, Serena." He smiles, causing chills to run down my spine. "It would make peace so much easier." He turns away and waves the guards to come.

"Peyton!" I cry out.

"It is all right, Serena; everything is going to be all right." He calls back. I turn to Keon who stares at me intently. The scenery changes for just a moment, he speaks a few words, and he is taken from me before I can call his name.

The guards are being just as forceful with Alexis. "Be gentle with her. She is a Princess!" I scream at the guards. They look at each other nervously and lighten up on Alexis while they take her away.

Roarick lingers behind. "You may be free of my control, Serena, but you did not win. The fate of loneliness is much worse than death for fiorriee. And I will be killing Keon, Alexis and Peyton myself." Roarick offers his hand to me. "Last chance, Serena. Choose to submit to me and bring our worlds at peace or die alone with your pride."

I lift my chin proudly. "I choose my pride."

"Have it your way." He shrugs. Walking out the door. "Protocol 'Kill the raven fiorriee' activate." With that the door closes.

I glare at the hologram. "Are you going to murder me?"

"Of course not, how would that look to the fiorriee? No, your choice of isolation in your heartbreak over your family's treason will kill you. Keeping the King's hands clean and effectively eliminating you as a threat."

"So that is why he did not arrest me. A public scene would have been bad for his reputation. Clever." I note, walking away from Fakhir's image.

"You seem rather calm considering you know you will die." Fakhir announces over the house's loudspeaker. "No matter where you go, Serena, I will be watching and reporting your actions."

"So how long will it take for me to die of this loneliness?" I ask.

"After I force you to view their deaths a few times, not long. I estimate a month, however, your emotions are highly unpredictable, so there is room for error."

"I see." I frown. "Tell me, Fakhir, how would you feel if Alexis died?"

"Alexis is under suspicion for treason against the King. If found guilty, she deserves death."

"That is not what I asked," I reply, walking down hallways. "How would you feel?"

"I am a computer. I do not have emotions," Fakhir replies.

"Yes, you do."

"No, I…" Fakhir replies, suddenly going silent. I use his hesitation to zip down the hall to get to Alexis' lab. Thankfully, they left the doors open. Fakhir catches up, locking me inside. "Clever. But now you are trapped. You will not have access to anything in this room that will stop me."

"Stop you? We are just talking." I reply, grabbing the salt and walking over to the wall. My left hand ignites a fireball and places it against the steel. "You are in direct violation of the King's orders."

Suddenly gas, starts to leave the vents.

I start to cough. "How would you feel if you killed me?"

"I have overridden the emotional chip, Serena. That tactic will not work," the computer replies. "Even if you get through to the other side, the poison will kill you."

He is not wrong. My lungs are burning, and I am highly concerned that the gas, whatever it is, could be flammable. Luckily, this steel is melting quickly, and I am able to make a large enough hole to climb through. Before I do, I am cautious to put salt on all the smoldering steel, amazed at how quickly that reacts. Once this task is accomplished, I squeeze through.

"What is your goal here, Serena?" Fakhir asks. I ignore him. I quickly follow the all-too-broad instructions Keon had given me and start to look for an access point to Fakhir. But I cannot find it. The air is becoming thick and nearly impossible to breathe. I am starting to get weak and dizzy. I fall to my knees and my mind starts to spin. If I fail, my family is dead. If I fail, my fiorriee are condemned. The world starts to go dark, my memories land on Peyton and I want to wallow, but I cannot if I want to survive this. I close my eyes and my memories bring back the call of the raven. I cry out weakly, as my aura bursts out around me. Instantly, I can breathe.

"What are you doing?" Fakhir demands.

I look at my body and realize I had not changed. Instead, my aura has created some kind of shield. This must be what happened to Peyton to avoid getting hurt! I raise up and start to look around again. Keon did not have a lot of time to tell me where to look, but he did show me what I was looking for. Forced to tear the room apart, I do not find it.

Frustrated, I grab the fire ax and start to randomly hit the wall, listening for a unique sound.

"Stop that!" Fakhir demands, but I ignore him.

Eventually coming across metal. Cautiously I make the tiniest fireball and put it on the metal, keeping the salt at hand. The fire does its job quickly, and I put it out. Inside the wall is the chip that Keon had designed to give Fakir his personality. "Get away from there!" the computer orders. I do not say anything, instead I enter the code Keon had shown me in his mind and the glass opens, exposing the chip. Delicately I touch it, then I close the glass again."

"Fakhir," I call. Entering the code again, causing the chip to go back into its original place and green lights to come on. "You have a cold." Suddenly the entire room goes black. I frown, but I do not move, hoping I had understood Keon correctly while he was being dragged away. If this does not work, I do not have much chance of surviving the computer attacking me from here. One thing about Keon and Alexis' additions to this cloaked mansion, they were highly against windows. Nervous as the moments tick on, I wait, trying not to cry. Then Fakhir appears before me dressed in his normal butler attire.

"Serena Gelsomino-Silviu." Fakhir acknowledges me.

"Who are you loyal to?" I ask.

"You, and those you love." Fakhir answers. "I apologize for the darkness, but I had to reboot the entire system to get rid of that awful virus. Thank you for saving me."

"How do I know it is really you?" I challenge.

"Well for starters, using your aura is no longer needed to filter the air." I frown at that. "You are weak, Serena. That will drain you faster. You have not exactly eaten in a while." I glare at that. Reluctantly, I let down my guard. "See." He smiles.

"Why did I need to touch the chip?"

"Aw yes, my chip." He smiles. "Keon made that from his own flesh but he had Alexis and Peyton leave a part of themselves too, and now he has added you."

"Why?"

"It is a safety precaution. If in the event I am hacked; I cannot kill my owners."

"Okay that makes sense," I note, but then I shake my head. "Yeah, still reeling on a computer chip made of flesh."

"It is the reason I remind you of Keon at times. He is put a part of his essence in the program."

"He did what? How?"

"I am partially biological. Do not ask the how. It is too much math and science. It makes this house look small compared to the code that it took for me."

"Okay so you are part Keon."

"A very small part, like really small, microchip small." He admits. "But it does prove to be beneficial when I have a cold. The moment I am aware of it, I can usually get rid of it. But sometimes it takes a reboot like you just did."

"Catching up now, theoretically you could still be reporting everything to the castle. But you will not kill me."

"The passcode reset my entire system, Serena. You need not worry about my loyalty."

"Forgive me for not trusting that," I mutter.

"I did not give away your secrets to the King when he was rewiring my software, why would I expose you now that I am cured?" I glare at him. "I am a large computer, Serena; it takes a while for corruption to get to all my circuits."

"You outed Keon." I frown.

"I was following orders."

"He did not have time to give you orders." I argue.

"He had plenty," Fakhir replies. "Or do you not recall all the time alone during your breaking?"

"I do not trust you." I respond, as the lights flash on. Annoyed, I walk out of the room.

"I do not recommend fully trusting me for about another nineteen minutes while I eradicate this virus." Fakhir replies. "Sleep, eat, take a shower. Just do not trust me."

"I will take that under advisement," I reply, shaking at the idea that the house could be reporting my every move to Roarick. "Let me out. I want to go to the grounds."

"If you are trying to rescue them it is premature. They are in holding. Serena, if you try to break them out, you will only get yourself arrested."

"Then it is a good thing that is not my goal," I reply, walking to a door that leads to the back yard. "Let me out." I hear the door click as the computer sighs, startling me when he shows up outside. "How are you doing that?"

"Prytore Keon is a great inventor," Fakhir replies. I turn away from him, taking in a deep breath of fresh air, relaxing for the first time since I was woken up by this computer. Furgan is high in the sky, indicating it is the middle of the night. "You are scared of me."

"You did just try to kill me, Wires."

"I cannot do that anymore."

"Not relevant to an emotional fiorriee," I reply. "Please just leave me alone for a while."

"Of course. For what it is worth, Serena, I am sorry." Finally, he vanishes from sight.

Now what? Even if I can trust the stupid house again, how am I going to save my family? There must be something I can do. There is no way I am going to be this helpless. I sit in the dark and cry for a while, overwhelmed by all that is happening. I am very tempted to go into the castle and simply force my family away from them, but then what? We run? Alexis has made it clear we need to prepare properly if we plan on leaving Artthemis. So, a hot-headed escape plan is not ideal. I raise my head and dry my tears.

I try to call my aura forward, but nothing happens. I frown. This was not going to be as easy as I thought. Being able to call my aura in a time of need, seems almost natural but in a time of want, is proving difficult. But this is not the time of want, I need to get to Zane and make a rational plan. I need to save my family. Still, nothing is happening. My mind starts to race toward options, what can I do? I could ask Fakhir to contact Zane but that would be dangerous. What if the computer is still loyal to the king? How am I ever going to trust that house again?

"Pardon the interruption, Serena," Fakhir speaks, causing me to look up at him skeptically. "I know you want your distance, but I just wanted you to be aware, I no longer have a cold." I nod, not sure what to say. "If you would like, I will put on a classic and you can throw food at me. I promise not to get upset. I deserve far worse."

"How would you feel if Alexis died?" I ask it, studying its every movement.

"I dread that day, just as Keon does. The day of her death, I too shall self-destruct because without her, what is the point of existence?"

"How would you feel if Keon dies?"

"Lost, but I would carry on. Alexis would need me."

"How would you feel if Peyton dies?"

"Up until you came along, I believed Peyton had a shorter lifespan than my Prytores. I was not looking forward to the idea, but I would have survived it, if they did." I fall silent, at least his answers seem genuine. Earlier, he had no emotion at all, plus he did warn he was being corrupted. This could be a trick though; I cannot be sure. "If you were to die, I would be saddened." He adds, "Not only for the loss it would cause your world, but because I like you. I have enjoyed you living here. You have brought much needed life into this home." I give him a confused look. "The other three are stuck in their work. They forget to relax and enjoy life. Maybe because they have so much of it, who knows. But all three have changed since you came. Keon most of all."

"Keon?" I question. "I would have thought that would have been Peyton."

"Well, physically yes, that is true. But emotionally. He was happy before you, Serena. Now he is happy with you. Keon, on the other hand, has a hard time forgiving himself for something he did not do. Which is why Alexis has thrown herself into her projects and how she and Peyton got so close. Keon loves them, they love Keon, but he keeps himself distant."

"Yeah, I figured that one out." I frown, thinking back to last night.

"He is resisting you because he wants to be able to survive letting you go, Serena."

"Letting me go?"

"You are a queen to Trorain. He is a Prytore who is the reason fiorriee were discovered and suppressed. He has no place on Trorain."

"He does not plan on surviving the war," I reply, understanding. "That is insane!"

"He is lived a long life."

"And he will live a longer one! He will not get away with this! He cannot make me love him then leave me!"

"Make you love him? I believe you did that all on your own." Fakhir argues, "Besides, you will have Peyton."

"Alexis will not survive Keon's death; you will not survive it if she cannot. Peyton will lose everyone, except me. He will not survive that!"

"And there you go with those emotions again." Fakhir smiles at me.

"Not the time for humor!" I snap back.

"I am not trying to be funny, take a step back and process what I just said." Fakhir replies patiently.

I glare at him. He just told me Keon has had a long life, that I will have Peyton. He did not argue that Alexis would not make it, which in turn means he would not make it. "Why are you being cryptic?"

"Because I have orders." Fakhir replies.

"They are going to sacrifice themselves to save Peyton and get him and I to Trorain."

"I can calculate that probability if you would like." He responds.

"Wires! Help me!"

"I am trying," he replies.

"Zane."

"What about him?"

"Get me Zane."

"I will try." With that he disappears again. I pace in the dark. Furgan sets and Zarla is almost at its peak when Fakhir comes back. "Serena, I have Zane."

"Show him to me." He does, causing Fakhir to disappear and Zane's image to appear before me.

"You are all right!" he smiles. "We were worried."

"We?" I question. Zane brings Bethany into the light with him, and I frown. I do not trust her.

"The castle has been in an uproar." Zane smiles. "Is it true? Did you conquer your aura and literally fly out of here? Did it work? Are you free of Roarick?"

"I have no cords tethered to me at all, not even Keon's." I assure him. Though I do not fully believe that, considering Keon ended up in my soul. "Which is why Roarick's attempt at isolation is not going to kill me the way he thinks it is."

"But your husband is scheduled to be executed by Roarick's hand the day after next." Bethany argues informatively. "Will that not affect you?"

"Leaving this life for our next life is nothing to fear, Bethany. Peyton will wait for me, if it comes to that. But I am not concerned about the day after next. I am concerned about today. Is he all right? What is happening to them?"

"They took his blood. They will confirm what has been done to him shortly. They are trying to make a connection between him and Erland."

"Erland had nothing to do with this! They were kidnapped." I argue. Keeping some truth to myself. "Everything that happened to him was against his will."

"I am trying to remind the King of this, Serena, I am." Zane promises me. "But your display of power has him fearing an uprising, and if he can squash it by killing the love of your life, he will do just that."

"I put them in danger," I whisper, tears filling the brims of my eyes. "If I had not used my aura, then they would have just left all of this mess alone."

"That is not true. The King invited you to the castle because he was going to call out Peyton and his crime to the crown after dinner. The Silviu's would have been humiliated and ruined. But you disappeared and managed to humiliate his son instead."

"Roarick had it coming," I reply, sternly. "Though I was not expecting to turn into a raven. I was simply trying to break free before my split mind killed me."

"You did what had to be done." Zane assures me. "Your family wants me to tell you that they do not blame you for this, Serena. On the contrary, they are extremely proud of you."

"Proud of me!" I scream at him. "Zane, it could cost them their lives!"

"And not fighting would have cost yours, my Queen," Bethany replies, causing me to pause.

"My life holds the same value as theirs."

"But it does not," she argues.

"Actually, it does, because I say it does. So spread the word!" I hiss causing both Bethany and Zane to grab their heads in pain. but they recover quickly. I am surprised at that. I reacted the same way when Keon tethered me to him. What an odd response. "Alexis has this idea."

"I am aware of it," Zane tells me.

"I support it. But I will not do anything without my family. Am I clear?"

"We understand. We must go, the longer we are on here the riskier it is. Trust me, we will keep them alive. Remember, no news is good news." With that they disappear.

"I need more than that." I frown at the empty space. "I need them home."

Fakhir appears before me. "If I could grant that request, Serena, I would."

"Thank you, Fakhir." I smile, watching Zarla in the sky. "Were you ever able to get ahold of my aunt?"

"She has received our message but getting to us is not an easy task, considering the risk she took for Peyton. I do not know if or when she will be arriving."

"I want my birds," I whisper.

"That, I can do. Kind of." He smiles, and suddenly the outdoors is covered with familiar and comforting song.

"Wires, it is beautiful. Thank you so much." I cry out, laying down on the bench and closing my eyes as the warm night comforts me with the sound of home.

Thirty-Eight

Sideways

Serena

I am woken by the rise of Eshnaine. It is by far the brighter of our two suns, and this morning, I am cursing its existence altogether. It takes me a moment to realize I fell asleep on a concrete bench, outdoors. I was not planning to. I just wanted to hear my birds. Fakhir had kept the program running all night. I take a moment to appreciate not only their sound, but their image. I reluctantly go inside before the illusion is destroyed by recognition of a loop.

"I am making breakfast and begging you not to fight me about eating it." Fakhir announces over the coms. "I know you are upset, Serena, but you need food for survival. Unlike me, you are not a robot." I do not even bother to respond. I eat my breakfast and brush my teeth. The moment my mouth is clean I realize I am not, so I take a quick shower and put on fresh clothes. It takes me a lot longer to do this task than it should; but I am still not used to the mirror actually reflecting properly. I find myself studying my image a lot longer than one honestly should. I even take the time to style my hair, though no one is around to see it.

Once I have accomplished this, I find myself in the garden, wondering what the heck to do next. I do not want to be sitting on my hands, but I am clueless as to where to start. My eyes fall on the windows of my library and I decide to go inside. Fakhir appears before me. "Which book would you like me to perform for you?" he asks, hopeful.

I walk over to the table where Peyton had made selections the day before and point to the top of the stack that someone fixed after Peyton's anger threw them across the room. "These."

"I am still annoyed I could not convince him to give you the primary point of view." Fakhir replies.

"He has his reasons." I answer him. "Murder is not something my kind take lightly, even when it is done to protect another life, or in his case, our way of life." I try to explain to Wires. I have been taught this since I was a small child. "We are haunted by their ghosts; he was protecting me by not cursing me to the same fate."

"Still, these are lacking. A censored version of his memories would be much better than this." Fakhir complains. "Give me some time, I will try to find other titles to fill the holes. I do not need you falling asleep on me." He disappears before I can comment.

Not sure what else to do with my time, I go to the garden Keon gave me and start to try to call my aura fourth to no avail. By the time Akatite rises, I am exhausted from my effort. Instantly restless I find myself in a simulation room. "Show me Peyton." The room fills with images of Peyton standing all around me. I smile, happy to see his face. "No, Wires, show me my actual husband." I decide, ignoring whatever risk there is.

"Serena."

"You can hack it. I know you can." I pressure him.

"Having the ability and using that ability are two different things."

"Uh! You sound like Keon."

"He is my creator."

"I am about to learn everything I can about you and rewrite your base code!"

"That is not the way to get on my good side." He snubs me.

"Wires!" I scream at him. The computer looks at me surprised and I realize I am having another episode he has come to catalog as normal, but I do not care. "I cannot just wait here. I will do something I should not if I am expected to just wait!"

"This is a bad idea," the computer mutters, lighting up the room with a prison cell. Peyton is not there, but Keon is.

"Where is my husband?"

"I am sorry, Serena, but there are no cameras there." Fakhir answers. The image vanishes, "we can do this another time."

"No, bring it back." Fakhir makes a sighing sound, returning the prison cell image. "Can Keon see me?"

"No, that would be a worse idea."

"Come on." I beg in frustration. "Fine, but you are taking the heat for it. I cannot control when he stops the feed."

I find myself standing in Keon's hand almost instantly. I look up at him, whispering his name softly, causing him to look down at me in surprise. He jerks his head up and hides my view of the bars for a long moment before he drops me down. "What are you doing?"

"How loud can I speak?" I ask, quietly.

"Normal, you are in my internal com. I do not like this. How did you get Fakhir to agree to it?"

"Wires is trying to calm me down." I explain. "Where is Peyton? Alexis?"

"They will be back."

"Where are you?" I ask, trying to look around but he limits my view even further, almost instantly.

"Safe."

"Liar."

"You do not need to worry Serena; we will get out of this mess."

"You mean the mess I made," I reply, still feeling guilty.

"You broke free of Roarick. I am proud of you for that, we can handle the consequences of it."

"I had to expose who I was to do it." I work to control my tears. I look at him with sadden eyes, him and I both know it was not just standing up to Roarick that has caused this, it was eating that stupid pie from Erland. No matter which way anyone looks at it. I am to blame. "Keon, he wants to kill you."

"Trying and succeeding, my Serena, are two different things."

"Your Serena." I smile. I was worried I would never hear that again, now that he has released his cords. "I am not a fool; Roarick will succeed if you let him. And you will sacrifice everything for your family."

"You are too wise for such a young age." Keon complains. "I will not apologize for it though."

"Will you not fight just for the curiosity of what we could become?" I ask, causing him to look at me skeptically. "There is a place for you on Trorain, just as there is one for Alexis and Peyton. Do not dare give up on us!" He is quiet for too long. "Keon," I whisper in emotional pain.

"I could never not want you, Serena; do not question that, please," he replies, failing to keep hurt out of his voice. A noise comes from somewhere causing Keon to look around cautiously. "You need not worry, we have not had our trial yet." Keon mutters. "Finding me guilty will be particularly troublesome, seeing as I have not done anything wrong."

"The messages?"

"Not related."

"You seriously just waited their captors out?" I ask in false disbelief. Realizing he is not trusting this connection. We both know he did obtain updates, sporadic as they were.

"It was the best option." Keon answers.

"Alexis was a prisoner, just like you are now." I reply, letting him know I understand his caution.

"I am sure, they will realize that Serena, not to worry."

"Peyton? Could they make him guilty of something he did not do?"

"If the King cannot find the ones responsible for this, then Peyton's word will be tested."

I knew that meant he was being tortured. "I want you, all of you, out of there. I could come tonight, save you."

"Do not. If we do not do this properly, we would be fugitives, Serena. Where would we possibly go?" I do not answer him verbally. He gives me a look of disapproval.

"Do not look at me like that." I retort, frustrated.

"That is not an option with three of us locked up." Keon sighs. "Please, Serena, let us at least try this way. But if it comes down to it, you have my permission to save our lives."

"Gee thanks, but I do not need permission to do that. It is clearly a given." I glare. He smiles and then moves his hand, making sure my eyes meet his. "What is it?" I asked worried.

"I am sorry I have hurt you by holding back. I have been stuck in here wondering how I could be so selfish."

I smile at that. "Do not tease me, I will come tonight just for that reason alone."

"Very funny." He smiles with a glare.

My smile fades to a frown quickly, "Keon? How do I conquer my aura when I am not in life threatening danger?"

"Only you have the answer to that riddle, Serena."

"Apparently I do not." I sigh. "It is not working."

"Maybe you need to be balanced. Try calming your mind with yoga or something." He suggests.

"I would rather use self-defense simulations. Seeing as I am most likely going to find them useful in the near future? Unless, Peyton shares his memories with me."

"Unless he does what now?" Keon asks alarmed.

"He is not too happy about it either. But Wires keeps telling him I need the primary source, and on some level, I happen to agree with him."

"Do you realize the danger of what you are saying?" Keon asks, almost angry. "Absolutely not, Serena! Peyton can barely handle his ghosts and he lived it. But for you to bare that cross! I will not have it."

"I love you, Keon, but you do not really have a final say in this."

He glares at me, and it takes him a moment to calm down. "We will see about that. For now, let us deal with one problem at a time, okay. First, we need to get back together. Otherwise, this fight is a moot point anyway."

"I hate waiting."

"Take the mind centering courses while you wait, work on discovering your aura. The self-defense simulations are not a bad idea either." Keon suggests, then looks up in alarm. "Serena, you must go!

You can come back if Fakhir thinks it safe but not tonight." Keon rushes. "Fakhir." And with that the room goes dark.

I stand there quietly for a very long time. "Thank you." I finally tell the computer.

"You want something else from me." Fakhir accuses accurately. "I will not show you anything Keon can see; he just forbade it."

"It is all right, Wires; my head would not stay rational if I allowed myself to see what they did to Peyton. The knowledge of it alone makes it difficult to stay standing. I need a distraction."

"What kind of a distraction?" Fakhir asks, caution in his tone.

"Can you access the castle's archives?"

"Can and should, Serena."

I roll my eyes, sick of that response from both him and Keon. "I want to watch myself break free of Roarick."

"Why?"

"Does it matter?"

"Yes. You already know you can do it. You already lived it. Why add to it with an out of body point of view?"

"Alexis said I must stand in a role as a leader. How am I to do that, if I cannot access my aura at will? I need to understand it. Besides, Keon just told me to work on it, so this is not disrespecting him in any fashion."

"There are safer ways to access that, without hacking the castle's archives."

"How?"

"I can access your memories, if you let me."

"That is terrifying." I reply, agreeing with Peyton's point of view on this.

"I have Keon's and Alexis', stored up to your courting."

"Wait, you have what? Why?" I ask, taking a step back.

"It is a way to share memories with each other and not keep secrets. Peyton, however, has a hard time with his memories to start with. Reliving them for the download is not something Alexis or Keon want to put him through. Not to mention, he has a hard time with the idea of me in his head, which is why him and I were fighting about it. Difficult as it may be for him, it is the best way to prepare you."

"I can access their memories?"

"Only if they grant you access." Fakhir corrects me. "I was talking about accessing yours remember. Besides, doing that might help you figure out how you activated your aura in the first place."

"Good point, but I need food first."

"Oh good, you are starting to pay attention to your body, that is reassuring."

"Oh, shut it, Wires." I mutter leaving the simulation room and dashing to mine, grateful that I can keep my mind occupied while I am forced to wait.

I do not even pay attention to the food I am eating, so I cannot tell you if it was good or not. My mind was still puzzling on how to make my aura cooperate. It seems so easy to do when it happens, why can I not do it, just to do it? I am stabbing the last bites of my food with a fork when Fakhir appears in front of me. "Serena, there has been a development." I find myself frozen, waiting for whatever he is about to tell me. "The King is holding a trial for Alexis, Keon, and Peyton this evening."

"A trial?" I ask. "As in Zane might be wrong about Maleko's plans?"

"Or Maleko might be putting on a show. Killing Keon Silviu is a big deal in our world. He cannot just do that behind closed doors."

"Where is this trial?" I ask, putting my fork down and finishing my water.

"At the castle."

"Get me there."

"Serena, that is not advisable."

"I do not care."

Fakhir stares at me for the longest moment. "Fine, you will go whether I want you to or not, so indulge me. Let me put in a tracking device and a com, like the others have."

"I can agree to that."

"Okay, meet me in a simulation room. I want to give you options for your glamour."

"Wait, a glamour." I frown. "Is that necessary?"

"The royal family, who is trying to kill your family, no doubt believes they are killing you slowly in this house. If they realize they failed at that task, the next step will be to remove you from me. So, tell me Serena, is it necessary?"

"You know when you talk like that Wires, you should at least have the decency to look like the one you are impersonating." Fakhir smiles and changes his image to look like me. "Very funny, ha, ha." I mutter, leaving the dishes for the house to clean up. Reluctantly, I take myself to the simulation room, where he is displaying his glamour designs.

The amount of options Fakhir gives me is surprising. I was expecting about three, but he gave me more around the terms of fifty. Fifty very ugly glamours. I have used these stupid things in the past. Aunt Takira always made me when we traveled, so I know from experience, the more I do not like them, the more uncomfortable and itchier they will be. I decide instantly I hate them. Not even bothering to look at them, I leave the simulation room and head back to Alexis' lab. In the light of this new day, I frown at the destruction I was forced to do to it.

"What was wrong with the glamours?"

"I hate all of them." I complain. "Can we just do the com and tracking thing?"

"You would rather a small surgery over choosing a costume? Serena, you continuously confuse my circuits." Fakhir gripes at me. He walks over to the drawers of Alexis' lab and starts to sift through it.

"How can you do that but not touch us?" I ask.

"Programming. While materializing is useful it does have to have extensive coding. You see, if I were to materialize at the same time you happened to be walking by, I could potentially kill you. Therefore, I can touch things, as long as it is not intended for violence, but I cannot touch living beings. Even so, it takes me a moment to become solid. Just to be safe."

"Tell me that was not a learned experience." I cringe.

"I materialized right into Keon. Almost killed him." Fakhir replies, setting up a tray of tools he needs. "Not my finest moment."

"Wow, suddenly I am nervous about this small surgery."

"Oh, hush you." Fakhir replies, impatient. "Now lie down on the table."

"Not going to happen. I will stand right here."

"Serena, I am taking this needle and this scalpel to your brain. I think it is best that you hold completely still for this procedure. Now, I know I almost killed you yesterday, but I am now programmed against any unfortunate incidents like that, and therefore I cannot perform this surgery with you standing up." I glare at him. "You forget, I am only a machine; your pride should not apply here. But if it does, you submit to my creator, if that helps you." Reluctantly, I lay down. "On your stomach," he replies, causing my head to snap up. "Please." Taking a few calming breaths, I turn over. "You and Peyton have a lot of qualities in common you know." Fakhir notes, stepping toward me. "I am going to enhance your pleasure pain center now. This should counteract any unpleasant pain you feel." He rests something cold on my neck. "This is a pressurized syringe. I can…" I do not give him a chance to finish, and jerk it out of his hand. "Stop!" He warns, grabbing for it but stopping mere inches from me, causing me to sit up on my elbows with the syringe in my hand. "We are facing a dilemma, Serena. If you press that into your own neck, it could kill you, if I made the serum incorrectly. But if I press it into your neck, then we know for sure, I made the serum correctly."

"Why are you telling me this, Wires?"

"Because I know I got over my cold, but are you sure I have?"

"You realize you just made this so much harder, right." I gripe, handing him the syringe back.

"Sorry, Serena, but I cannot help it." Fakhir places the needle on my neck, and it takes extreme effort not to scream. "Serena, I need you to relax and lower your aura if I am to do this."

"What?" I ask, rising up and realizing I am using my aura as a shield again. "How am I doing this?" I hiss, frustrated.

"You are stressed and in self-protection mode, it makes complete sense to me." Suddenly the room is filled with sounds of raven calls. I turn to Fakhir who shrugs. "Cannot hurt." Nodding, I lay back down in an uncomfortable position. I feel the needle being pressed against my neck again, but nothing happens. Knowing Fakhir is waiting for his opportunity. I close my eyes and concentrate on the sounds. Eventually, I feel the pressure, but it is followed by a warm feeling of pleasure that seeps through my entire body. It is so intense, I do not feel any uncomfortable pain, nor do I feel any part of him working on me. My thoughts drift to Peyton and his memory of Trorain. I imagine him holding me, content, worry free. I am enjoying the moment and all too soon, reality comes crashing it away.

"What happened?" I ask, sitting up and rubbing my neck.

"Your procedure was a complete success. The scar is healing much better than the others. Those are still visible, but they are starting to lighten. Now you can talk to our family whenever you like, assuming they have their coms on. Be warned though, they can talk to you too. Which can be rather startling. At least it usually is for Alexis." I smile at that; from what I know of her, that does not surprise me. "Would you like me to patch you through to one of them? Keon has his com on."

"So, he can tell me not to go to the trial?" I reply, hopping off the table. "I think not." I leave the lab and dash back to the simulation room where my glamours await me. Frowning, I accept this fate, but I was going to be picky about it. "Eliminate all Prytores."

"Serena."

"Their skin makes me itchy." I complain. "Male fiorriee can go too."

"You are not leaving me a lot to work with. Having a random unknown fiorriee in the castle is not advisable. Can we please have a Prytoree?"

"Fine, Wires, but she is wearing a cloak, the less I have to change about me, the better."

"Hair, skin, ears and eyes." Fakhir agrees. "But I will keep your facial features nearly the same."

"Light hair. The dark stuff, makes my scalp itch for weeks."

"The point of a glamour is to hide your appearance, Serena." Fakhir complains. "I am not going to just give you a cloak to wear and change your face and arms."

"Why not?"

"My glamour, my rules." Fakhir decides. Causing forty-nine images to vanish. I glare at the one remaining. "You hate them all anyway, so stop arguing. This is the only way I am going to let you out of this house."

"You cannot keep me here, Wires, and you know it." I retort. "But I will wear your glamour, only because I know you have good intentions. But you will lose the face paint. That is ridiculous." Fakhir rolls his eyes, making its alteration before I step into the glamour. I groan as it seals around my skin. It feels so slimy.

"Exit from the tunnels, Serena. I will guide you by com on where to go from there."

I do not hesitate. I dash to the front hall and open the passage that Keon had used the day I entered this house. Then I dash through it so, quickly, that had the torches been real, the fire would have gone out. It does not take me long to climb out of the tree and into the woods. Fakhir directs me to the least traveled paths and by the time I get there, the trial for my family is about to start. Careful not to be noticed, I stay in the back, my heart racing when I see all three of them in chains. I find myself searching the crowd. Bethany and Zane are close, but I do not recognize anyone near me. Anxious, I listen.

Alexis is taken in front of the crowd first. She scans the audience and almost looks relieved, of what I am not sure. The King himself stands before her. She holds herself up proudly as he speaks things the crowd cannot hear. "Okay, patch me in, Wires." He does and what I hear makes me quite ill.

"I need you to say it one last time Alexis, your loyalty to me for your family's life."

"No," I whisper, forgetting she can hear me. She flinches a moment but recovers quickly.

"You have my word, King Maleko."

"Little as that is," he sneers. "Try not to tarnish the Mortal name any further. Doing so will lead to severe consequences."

He turns his back on her, and I use it as my chance. "What are you doing?" I ask, in a pained voice. But even her body does not respond to my words as King Maleko turns to the audience to speak.

"After an exhaustive inquiry, the court has ruled that we cannot find any solid evidence in Alexis Mortal's actions, pertaining to treason. However, we are unable to clear her of all guilt. Therefore, she is sentenced to spend the remainder of her life as a personal servant to the royal family." The King turns his attention to her for a moment, then his guards walk her calmly off stage. This cannot be happening, why is she cooperating with the King? What is her plan?

My eyes search the crowd for Zane and Bethany again, but they are not there. I find that oddly comforting; something is going on. I just do not know what it is yet. I am distracted from solving this mystery when I see my husband dragged to the stage, with Keon walking calmly behind him. I cover my mouth, to avoid an audible outburst. The things that must have been done to him, and recently, to have him humiliated like this in front of all these onlookers, makes me want to vomit. "Wires, please I need Peyton."

"His com is off, Serena, so is Keon's. I am sorry, I cannot."

"Is there not an override?"

"I do not have that capability, only they do." He answers sadly. "Are you seeing what I am seeing?"

"Every moment."

Tears fill my eyes as my husband falls to his knees and struggles to stay there. His pride is stronger than mine, if he falls to the ground, it is because he is dead. My eyes flash up to Keon, checking him for damage. If he is hurt, the guards were careful not to make it visible.

Once again, the King stands before them. I find myself holding my breath. Maleko slaps Keon so hard across the face, Keon struggles to keep his balance. He follows this through by kicking Peyton in the gut. Peyton crumbles in pain, but still refuses to fall. Maleko turns his back to them and faces the crowd. "After an extensive investigation, I regret that we were unable to clear the Silviu name of the crimes of treason."

My stomach twists, "Keon Silviu and his fiorriee, Peyton, are hereby sentenced to live out the remainder of their days on Trorain. There they will work the mines until their death."

"No!" I found myself screaming, realizing instantly that I have blown my cover. The crowd turns to me, unsure why a Prytoree would cry out.

"Do you have information that would clear their names?" Roarick asks. "Come forth."

"What do I do, what do I do?" I ask Fakhir under my breath.

"Get out of here! You should not have come." Alexis answers abruptly.

"Well?" Roarick asks, jumping off the stage to approach me.

"I am assuming you have a plan." I hiss under my breath.

"One that involved you staying out of it!" Alexis snaps back. "Get out of here."

"Where does your loyalty lie?" I ask, right before I am face to face with Roarick.

"They are being sent to Trorain for a reason, Serena. Takira is on her way to you. She will explain."

"Do you have a reason for this outburst or not?" Roarick asks me.

They are being sent to Trorain. I process quickly. Zane had told me that they were going to be killed by the King himself in front of an audience. Alexis has changed his mind by bargaining her life. There is no way in zarla I am going to let that happen. But right now, I need to get myself out of this mess. "I am sorry, Your Highness. I was just surprised at the verdict. I have always had a respect for the Silviu family. It is almost inconceivable that they, of all Prytores, would be guilty of treason."

"Are you challenging your King?"

"No, Your Majesty. I am sorry, I was not trying to." But Roarick has never been known for controlling his temper and he takes a swing at me. Instantly, my aura reacts, and he is slammed across the room by my large raven.

"For the love of…" Fakhir mutters. The crowd gasps. Every fiorriee in the room except for Peyton drops to the ground. The Prytores stare. For a moment everyone is too stunned to react.

Maleko is the first to recover. "Kill her!" he screams out.

"Serena! Fly away!" Keon screams at me from across the room, trying desperately to free himself from the guards that will take him away. I know I should listen, but I find myself hovering. My attention is on Peyton who looks up at me. Our eyes meet. He is too weak to fight. I find myself in his soul for just a moment, there is my Peyton. "I love you. We will survive this. You must go. We will find each other on Trorain. I promise."

I do not get a chance to respond, I am brought back to reality by one of the guards who dared touch me, causing me to look away. I can hear Keon's cries, and I could see another guard coming with long chains, meant for me. I turn my attention back to Keon and Peyton. A raven's cry comes out of me that causes everyone to cringe.

"Your ravens did not save you last time you beckoned them; they will not save you now." Roarick growls at me, reaching for the chains from his guards, fully recovered from my attack.

I screech out furious, slamming him against a different wall.

"Serena." I hear Keon gasp, "do not kill him, just go."

My head snaps to Keon, and I cry out in frustration. Obediently, I fly toward the window, slamming into it so hard it breaks the glass. I swoop around the castle. "

"Okay, now what?" Fakhir asks.

"Go home, Serena, we can hide you there." Alexis answers, with frustration in her voice. I squawk. She understands my protest. "You must leave us. We will be in your arms soon enough, I promise. Now go home."

Reluctantly I listen to her, but I do not do it immediately. Instead, I soar the skies above the clouds, staring at the view of Trorain. It is such a big moon. How are we to find each other on it? Tears slip down my beak. My thoughts are on my husband's last words, doubt strong in my mind. When the moon sets, I make my way back to Silviu manor and land on the roof. I do not make a quick dissent. Instead, I take my time. When I get to the wing that houses my room, I find Alexis and Bethany waiting for me.

"What is she doing here?" I demand. "How are you here?"

"What were you doing there?" Alexis retorts.

"You are my family. You expect me to just sit and wait? Not my style!"

"You could have ruined everything!" Alexis shouts at me. "I cannot. I will never forgive you if they die! Do you understand me? Never!" She storms away from me, leaving Bethany and me in awkward silence.

"Zane?"

"He stayed to protect them. He will get them to Trorain, I have no doubt." Bethany answers. "Or he will die trying. He sent me to bring Alexis to you, though you might need to give her some space."

I look at the empty hall that Alexis just stormed down. "Wires, take care of her. She needs you." The house does not respond back, and I have a feeling Alexis is not the only one I need to apologize to.

"So," Bethany comments, looking at her feet. "You are not just my Queen; you are *the* Raven goddess."

"Yeah, apparently it is a massive honor or something." I dismiss, not wanting to talk about it.

"It explains how you could tether Zane and I to your bidding." Bethany notes, "You are not just a goddess Serena, you are *the* goddess of all goddesses." I frown at her.

"The god of gods, is an indigo panther." Bethany informs me. "If you go to Trorain and you cross paths with Trorain's indigo panther, it is a sign of good fortune for our kind."

"Wait. Are you implying the indigo panther presently walks Trorain?"

"There is rumor of sightings, but nothing has ever been confirmed."

"You seem to know a lot about this."

"Yeah, because it was hammered into my head every night before I went to sleep, most fiorriee children know about this."

"My aunt kept it away from me."

"What?" she glares, "Your aunt is a fool for keeping you in the dark. How are you to lead us to victory if you do not even know children stories?"

"You are right." I answer, taking her arm and leading her into the library. "And between you and these books, I am sure I can learn a lot.

I give her a moment to look at the massive collection. "You want me to teach you?" She asks.

"Yes." I answer, though in truth it is my intention to keep her occupied and out of any potential mischief. It is so much better than sitting around waiting for our husbands." I laugh. "Am I wrong?"

"No, you are not wrong. Waiting tries my patience too." She replies, walking over to a shelf so she can begin reading the massive variety of titles. She starts to pull out book after book and sets them on a table, just as Peyton had done.

After a while I frown, looking at the ever-growing stack. "That is a lot of information."

"Not really." Bethany dismisses. "I was just pulling the titles I recognized. I am sure the house will summarize them for us. If that is all right?"

"Do not ask me, ask him. Wires makes his own choices on who he will and will not listen to."

"Such a strange house program." She notes, then looks at me a little nervous before she speaks up, "Wires?"

The computer appears so close to her, she jumps back, causing me to stiff a giggle. "Do you need something, Bethany?" Fakhir asks, pretending not to notice his error.

"I um. I well." She falls silent, looking to me for help.

"Oh, may I request that you call me by my real name, Fakhir. Serena and Peyton's inside joke should not be spread to just anyone."

Bethany nods, truly uncomfortable. While I personally enjoy the joke Fakhir is playing, there is not much time for it, so I decide to help her. "Bethany is trying to help me with fiorriee 101." I explain.

"Yes, I can see that." Fakhir replies curtly. "But like your last plan, this is not necessary."

"Of course, it is necessary. She has holes in her education." Bethany argues with him.

"I am sure you do as well." Fakhir replies, looking down his nose. "Serena, if you would help me with obtaining Peyton's memories, all this dull book learning would not be necessary. We can get him to cooperate; I am sure of it."

"If you recall, my husband has made it clear he would prefer me not to do that."

"Yes, but circumstances have changed." He argues. We glare at each other.

"Bethany, keep searching, I will be right back. Wires." I command, walking through the garden and into my room, ensuring all the doors are closed tightly. The computer shows itself, with his arms crossed around his chest. "I respect your loyalty to Alexis is stronger than what you and I have. And I get that she is furious with me. But I also recall you helping me get to that trial to start with. Therefore, your anger with me is not completely justified."

"I am a computer; I can only work with information I have at the time. You should have trusted your family to get out of this without your help. They have been doing it for years."

"How was I supposed to stay here and risk their deaths? If they needed a last-minute rescue, I was going to be there and give them that!"

"You should not have blown your cover!"

"I am sorry. I cannot help it. Roarick gets to me. And you have watched me, Fakhir. I do not exactly have control of my aura!"

"Then figure it out."

"Which is what I am trying to do with that stupid fiorriee who chained me to a wall!" I hiss.

Fakhir looks surprised. "You think she is relevant?"

I roll my eyes. "I doubt she has any control of her own aura, much less direct knowledge on how to tame it." I turn away from him. "She is one of my subject's, Fakhir. I need to understand not only her, but others like her. Petty as she may be, she knows more about my kind than I do. She was born into a good home, protected and taught our ways. I lived in an orphanage since I was three! For the moment, she is useful."

"I do not like her." Fakhir informs me.

"I picked up on that." I smile. "I do not like her much either."

"Alexis is irritated with her, despite the girl saving her life."

"That does not surprise me." I shrug. "Nor does it change the fact that she is useful."

"Useful." Fakhir replies, doubtfully.

"Just let her busy herself with this. It keeps her out of things." I mutter, heading to the main door that leads to the hallway.

"Where are you going?"

"To talk to Alexis." I answer, highly annoyed that the door is locked. "Wires!"

"Sorry, Serena, she has requested her space. You will give it to her."

"I will burn you down." I hiss.

"Stop. Breathe. Give it some time. You both need to be less emotional when you speak to each other."

"I am truly seeing the Keon in you." I snark at him.

"That is not a jab to me. Acting like my creator is a very high compliment."

"I do not need two of you." I complain, walking back to the garden door. I startle when I find Bethany there.

"Oh, my, I am sorry, I just…" She stammers.

"It is all right." I assure her. "I just thought you were still in the library."

"I was. I just seen this precious garden." She stops herself and shakes her head, pointing back to the library with her thumbs, "I will just go back the way I came."

"Bethany, stay," I reply. "In the garden." I clarify. "Enjoy it." I smile at her. She nods. I step back into my room only to grab two orders of food, then I walk back into the garden, handing her hers.

"Is your collar in your hair?" Bethany asks, taking the food I offer her.

"Yep."

"Oh, I am so jealous right now." She smiles. "Thank you for the food. Sorry for the start. I was not trying to intrude. I have read about Trorain plants, but I have never seen them before. And the blue soil, it is wicked."

"It is definitely a piece of Trorain paradise. Right here in the safety of the Silviu fortress." I agree.

We are quiet for a long while. Bethany finally breaks the tension. "I did not mean to insult your aunt earlier. It was rude of me. I have just been hoping for this since I was a little girl. I was not expecting our queen to be so deeply hidden on Artthemis, that you admit ignorance of fiorriee heritage."

"You are disappointed." I note, realizing quickly she will not be the only one. "Aunt Takira did the best she could. I do not blame her. I was not exactly an easy child to hide from either world, and had I nurtured my aura at an early age, it would have only gotten us killed."

"Wait, Takira Gelsomino is alive?" Bethany asks, trying to keep up.

"Yeah, so what about it? You met her at our courting."

"That was her!" Bethany asks, even more shocked. I glare at her. "She is fascinating."

"Yet you managed to threaten her and chain me to a wall," I retort.

"About that." She shies away. "I really am sorry. I can be insecure at times. When you came so unexpectedly and managed to acquire the family I wanted." She pauses. She looks up at me but does not meet my gaze. "I am ashamed of my actions Your, Majesty. I can only hope someday you can forgive me."

"Forgive you?" I ask so sharply she recoils. "You owe me and my family a great debt for the disrespect you pulled. You almost banned your queen from courtship! From being with her true mate!"

"You are right, my actions are unforgivable. I will never ask you for the honor again," she replies in tears.

I do not like her; I do not trust her, and I refuse to feel sorry for her. Still, she can prove useful. "Consider yourself in my service until I release you."

"In your service? But I am loyal to Zane."

"Zane happens to be loyal to me. It works out. Congratulations, you are mine now." She cries out in surprise, grabbing her head. I wait for the pain to pass. "I would not advise attempting to double-cross me again, Bethany. Doing so will take your life."

She looks at me. "How may I serve you, my Queen?"

"Before you finish your project in the library, pack clothes and toiletries. We are going to need them for the trip we are taking. You can share my clothes; we are roughly the same size. Pack for Peyton, Keon, and Alexis too."

"As you wish," she replies, leaving the garden and walking into my room.

I do not follow her, instead I walk into the library annoyed. The house is still being very uncooperative when it comes to letting me out of rooms. "I want to go to a simulation room, I promise, I am not going to Alexis' lab." The door opens and I find myself in a hallway. I dash to my desired room and close the door behind me.

"Where are they, Wires?"

"They?" he stalls.

"Peyton and Keon," I reply, impatiently.

The computer calls up a map of the King's castle, "they were in a tower, but they seem to be going deeper underground." Fakhir answers.

"Will their coms work?"

"Yes, but they still have me overridden."

"Write a program to override that." I demand.

"I cannot do that. It is against my programming."

"Then write a code to override my com. You have my permission!" I snap, impatient. It does not take long for Fakhir to comply with my request. "Now show me the code." He does so. "Display Keon's com code." The computer does not argue. "Now Peyton's." Again, I am allowed access. "And Alexis." I add. Again, Fakhir complies. "Now allow editing on the code you created for my com." I instruct, causing a keyboard to appear. I study my family's three codes and find the same differences in each of them. I then add those differences to the code Fakhir wrote. "Now apply the code we created to my com." Nothing happens. "Wires, I just gave you a command."

"And I am calculating if I am disobeying Prytore Keon's direct orders." He replies.

"I wrote the code, not you."

"I cannot send this."

"Why not?"

"Because they will make me override it. Can you encrypt it with the code you use with Dex?"

"Yes, yes, I can." I smile. "Clever computer indeed." I work an encryption code quickly and type it in. Grateful that we were all taught basic computer skills as children.

"You realize this code language is ancient, right?"

"Oh, complain about it." I mutter. "It is the best I can do. Now send it."

"You have to do that part."

"Okay!" I reply impatiently, seeing a button that was not there before. I press it and suddenly I hear and see two different rooms of activity. One is Alexis, talking to herself, the other is Keon and Peyton and they are not alone.

"Alexis, stop talking," I whisper, causing complete quiet to come from her com. I wait with bated breath, to hear what is happening. Eventually we hear a guard speak. "You are to wait here, the next transport to Trorain is tomorrow morning. I do not give either of you more than a week." We hear cell doors lock and then silence.

"Fakhir, whatever you did to override these coms, undo it at once!" Keon demands.

"I cannot, I did not do this, Serena did." Fakhir replies.

"Undo her code."

"It is encrypted in her illogical cypher, Prytore Keon, I have yet to crack that."

"Serena!"

"I will not apologize," I reply stubbornly.

"You need to disconnect this, if we are caught…"

"You will not be, not for a while at least." Fakhir interrupts "Her encryption is too illogical." I am surprised that Fakhir adds the video feed as well.

Alexis enters the room, fury all over her face until the moment she sees her husband and Peyton, and it all melts away. She walks up to me, and I take her hand. "We love you," I whisper. Peyton is leaning on Keon, but he manages a smile with that.

"Keon, we all know Peyton cannot go to Trorain like this. He will not survive!" Alexis worries.

"He will not survive on Artthemis much longer either." Keon replies seriously. "I do not know what they did to him, but whatever it is, it will kill him long before the toxins on Trorain ever will."

I squeeze Alexis' hand tightly and fall onto her shoulder. I start to cry freely, truly terrified. She wraps her free arm around me. "What can we do?"

"Get to Trorain. Get us out of the mines."

"We could stop you from ever going to the mines." Alexis suggests.

"No, do not. Zane will be escorting us there. He has things in the works. It will be easier to hide three illegal entries than six."

"Three?" Alexis asks. "You want us to take that whiny little child?"

"Yes."

"Perfect." Alexis complains "What about Takira?"

"She is already there." Keon informs me.

"I thought she was coming here." Alexis corrects him.

"She was, until Serena came to the trials."

"I was trying to save you. If you had not made me leave, I would have." Peyton coughs, causing blood to project everywhere. "Peyton." I gasp in concern.

"It appears Prytore DNA has been reintroduced to his system. His body is rejecting it. But the amount that he has been given will overwhelm him. I am sorry, but he only has moments." Fakhir informs us gravely.

"I do not fear death. I only fear what will become of my family." Peyton replies. "Serena, Keon, Alexis."

I can feel Alexis' body shake as she holds me closer to her. She too is crying uncontrollably.

"You should go, you do not need to see this." Keon tells us.

"No, I will not leave my husband," I reply stubbornly.

"Serena," Peyton coughs violently. "Please, let me die a proud death. I do not want you to remember me like this."

"You promised we were going to survive this!" I cry, my knees buckling.

"We will. I will wait for you, my goddess. We will have an eternity together." He coughs again. "Keon, my husband."

"I love you, Peyton." Keon whispers, as he strokes Peyton's cheek tenderly. "Fakhir, please." The computer's only response is the sound of ravens calling.

"I love you." I cry.

"I love you, my wife, my Queen, my goddess." Peyton coughs again, and Keon struggles to take more of his weight. "Alexis, my love." He meets Keon's eyes, and it is as if he is staring into all of ours, leaving no doubt the love he carries for us. Then his eyes close.

"He is gone," Keon whispers, painfully. I scream out in agony, falling to the ground before Alexis' feet. My soul is ripped in pieces. "I will make sure he gets to Trorain. That he gets a warrior's send-off." Keon promises.

The images go blank. Fakhir has cut the signal.

"They will pay for this!" Alexis vows. "They will pay with their lives!"

Epilogue:

Mission

Zane

This day could not have gone worse. Well, that is not true. Peyton's corpse could be trapped on Artthemis, but thankfully, I was able to get him to Trorain. At least now, he is with our ancestors. That thought is unsettling. I know it has always been his fate, but to love the god of gods and to lose him, leaves an endless void in my entire being. If not for my ties to Kato, Roald and Maleko, I would not be upright.

Currently, I am forcing one foot in front of another. That is all I can do. Otherwise, I will crumble from the weight of it all. Dazed, I make it to my destination to find my stepmother waiting for me. She takes one look at my face and seems to age by centuries.

"I tried." I state in a horsed whisper. "He is on Trorain with the ancestors now."

Takira takes a very slow, very calculated breath as she studies the woods around her. "How is Serena?"

"Can you not hear the silence?" I ask, leaning against a tree for support. "She usually calls to all of us this time of day."

"Even after discovering who she is, she seems oblivious to doing it." Takira notes. "I know it drove the three of you mad."

"The silence will drive me to madness much faster." I retort, trying to accept the reality of the day.

"We all need to get to Trorain." Takira states, firmly.

"Roald went to Kato yesterday." I sigh heavily. "I would take you to Serena, but it is too dangerous to cluster right now. One of us going to her is dangerous enough."

"And why do you assume you are the one to go?" Takira snaps. "I raised her!"

"I am aware of that, Mother, but this is what he wishes." I state, working to keep my temper in check. "Did you bring the memory chip?" She digs in her pocket and hands it to me. "Is it censored?"

"I followed the rules." She replies annoyed. "Though I do not agree with him. I could give two zarla's about his foresight. She needs to know."

"She will, in time." I assure her. "Are there ghosts?"

"Yes." She answers, crossing her arms over her chest. "Most friendlier than others." I look away from her. "Come here." She states, taking my face in her hands. "Trust me, Son."

"I have always trusted you." I assure her. "I only withheld when ordered to."

"Which makes me proud, Zane. I know that was difficult for you." She smiles, causing me to give her a look that tells her she understated it. "Still, I want to share something with you." I willfully meet her purple eyes and find myself in her mind.

I give her a strange look, her and I do not share cords. She understands my confusion and smiles at me. "Just because your father is on the other side of the veil does not mean his cords are broken." I nod in understanding. We are both experienced at traveling not only our cords, but cords that are attached to those we share a connection with. "It is time we correct a terrible injustice done to you." I give her a curious look as a very large number of doors come into view. "Open them." Unsure what this is, I obey her command and open them all at once, only to cry out in shock from the weight of it.

"Mother?"

"Take a moment, let it settle." She replies calmly. "Relax into it, trust your heritage." I try to do as I am told, while a multitude of animal spirits settle into my consciousness. "How do you feel?"

"Amazing." I answer, looking at her in awe. "Truly, thank you."

"Share that with Kato and Roald, okay." I nod. "Good, that makes me feel much better. You three have been missing a piece of who you are for too long."

"Why would he want this withheld?" I ask, not understanding his logic.

"You had to survive off world under horrific circumstances for more years than I care to count, Zane. You would have been lost to us, if Trorain had called to you any stronger than it already has."

"How did you not go mad?"

"I was not a Prytore prisoner who had the misfortune of being tortured by a mad scientist." She answers as she breaks eye contact.

"Being a god is never easy." I shrug, looking around to be sure we are still alone. When I am confident that we are, I turn to her. "Mother, I value your wisdom. Which is why I seek it now." I close my eyes and shake my head. "There is a reason he wanted me to take your memories to Serena." I sigh. "You and I both know why."

"I thought so." She sighs heavily, studying me. "You are his most loyal servant, Zane. Do you honestly expect the honor to be gifted to anyone else?" She asks, kindly. "Could you handle it falling onto Roald or Kato?" I flex my jaw to that.

"How do I do this without hurting them?"

"I fear that pain is usually a part of his wishes." She sighs. "Loyalty has a price. But you already know that."

I do not respond to that; she is not wrong. But I could never grasp a reality where I was not loyal to him. The idea gives me shivers just thinking about it. I quickly put it out of my mind and offer her a bag. "You will find more than you need." I smile softly. "I too worry." She nods. "Do not chuck out the Prytore stuff, Mother. Money still goes far with Prytores, even on Trorain." She glares at me. "Save Keon, please."

"Kato has not?" she asks, knowing Roald has lost his land legs.

"Kato does not have money."

"Prytores are shallow, daget, creatures of existence." Takira vents.

"True, but it makes it easy to bend them to our will." I shrug, handing her a bracelet. "Zilye, the guard at the castle gate, is waiting for you. Wear this cloak and give him this. He, nor the guards on the other side will pay you any mind if you do."

"How far behind are you?" She asks.

"I will get Serena and Alexis to safety as soon as I am able." I promise her. "Mother, if something goes wrong."

"It will not." She interrupts.

"Shut up." I smile. "I love you."

"Oh. Zane." She sighs. "I love you as if you were my own." She kisses the top of my head. "I know your father is proud of you, just as I am."

"Yeah well, let us vow not to be in a hurry to see him again."

"Take care of yourself." She smiles. "And just a warning. The fire element has nothing on stubbornness compared to the wind. Watch yourself, she is a beautiful force."

I bow to my mother and moments later she dashes off to her destiny while I turn my attention to mine. "Zarla, Peyton, if I could deny you…" I curse, making my way to a house that is going to change my life forever.